FALLEN

INTO

Austen

FALLEN

INTO

Austen

Amy Foster Myer

For Sarah, Jane, and Evalyn

CONTENTS

CHAPTER 1

The crowd for the parade filled Bennet Street, little fingers of participants spreading into Russell Street and Circus Place. Emma Woods slipped among the gathered assembly, listening as people greeted one another with murmurs of "pardon me" or "by your leave."

No, Emma thought, this was not a raucous or rowdy affair. Here, no festooned floats rolled by, attached to golf carts. No confetti sprayers nor t-shirt cannons prepared to boom cheap merch into crowds of bystanders. Though some might call it a parade, the festival named it correctly – a *promenade*, a slow and stately procession.

The day would be the penultimate in neatness, propriety, delicacy, and refinement. Ahead, banners attached to streetlamps outside the Assembly Rooms advertised the Jane Austen Festival, complete with her portrait gazing bemusedly upon them. The bright hangings snapped in the breeze, adding to the chorus of greetings, rustling satin gowns, and the occasional slap of a tennis shoe or rubber-soled sandal hidden below the hem.

Emma wove through the little conglomerations of costumed attendees, beginning her search for her festival family in earnest once she reached the small park at The Circus, their go-to meeting spot. She scanned the crowd, eyes keen for Harold's flamboyant scarlet overcoat and impeccably arranged cravat. Finally, she saw them there, standing under the shade of the plane trees. Deb was tucking a stray grey curl under her bonnet while Lorna broke a thread dangling from the hem of Deb's dress. Harold slid a tiny brush along the sleeve of his coat, enhancing its sheen, before readjusting the angle of his top hat. Emma slipped up behind Harold and Deb.

"Oi, this the Jane Austen knees up then, innit?" she said in her best Cockney, which settled rather pathetically between an Irish brogue and a Bostonian Brahmin.

Harold and Deb turned to her, their startled faces transforming into happiness, arms opening to enfold her. Lorna was not far behind, her plump hands reaching round to clasp Emma's shoulders.

"We thought you were going to miss it," Lorna said.

"Should we blame it on jetlag or is this just your usual American tardiness?" Deb queried.

"Both," Emma had to admit.

Harold took Emma by her hands and stood back to appraise her. "My dear," he said in his best Sir Walter Elliot, "you look absolutely ravishing. I believe Gowlands has completely carried away your freckles." Then he tipped his head, gazed at her over his half – moon spectacles, and dissolved from Austen's geriatric dandy to the man she had come to consider a second – and better – father. "Oh wait, your perfect American skin never had freckles. Well, bollocks."

From far ahead, bagpipes shrilled through the morning air. Harold organized them into two sets of two, with Emma at his side and Lorna and Deb behind. Ever an eye for detail, he made sure Emma gripped her parasol just so, that Lorna and Deb walked arm-in-arm and never, god forbid, fingers entwined. Emma turned to shoot them a grin both simpering and sympathizing.

"I saw that, you," he said, tugging at his waistcoat. "I'll not have our little group embarrass itself." He spit on his handkerchief and worked at a scuff on the side of his shoe. "We'll do that well enough at the open bar later this – what the? Gum! I've got gum on the bottom of my shoe."

From the reticule at her wrist, Emma retrieved a travel flosser, something she'd learned never to do without when steak and mash were a regular part of her diet.

Harold thanked her and dug out the gooey pink clump. "Bloody kids."

As the procession began to move forward, Harold tipped his head toward Emma's gown. "Went full fancy, I see."

Emma smoothed the pleats of her pink satin ballgown and shook her head. "Spilled coffee on my muslin at the airport. You wouldn't believe what a crapshoot it is trying to find period piece drycleaners in Bath." She shrugged.

She had been in such a rush at the airport, late there too, when she suddenly had the terrifying thought she'd left her lecture notes at home on her desk. She dropped her carry-on, fell to her knees – nearly tripping a mother and her three leashed toddlers in the process – and jerked the zipper around. There the pages were, right where Emma had packed them the night before, but as she re-zipped her bag and tried to answer Quinn's incoming call, her latte tipped forward and the last of her milky brown revival dumped all over her new muslin day-dress, the one she planned to wear for the promenade. "Had to Uber all the way to Bristol yesterday evening, but they should have it back by morning."

"I can imagine that cost a pretty penny," Harold said.

Emma shrugged again. She'd put it on Quinn's card actually, the one he'd pressed on her saying they were building a life together now, that what was his was hers. At dinner the night before she'd left, he'd given her a Platinum Visa in a velveteen watch-case, watching with bright eyes and a goofy grin as she opened it. Was he being ironical or not? As much as she'd have preferred the former, it seemed to be the latter. Over the past 24 hours, he'd sent her two links to dress shops in Bath where she could purchase another muslin dress, but the conversion from pounds to dollars made her eyelids race for her brows, and so she shook her head and told herself a ballgown would do. Fortunately, no one here was as much of a stickler as Jane Austen herself might have been, or she would have been at risk of being laughed out of Bath all together for wearing evening dress at eleven in the morning.

She pushed Quinn out of mind. She had ten days here, ten days with her beloved festival family, ten days before she had to give Quinn her final answer. The less she used the shared card, the less she felt her answer was sealed.

Further on, a round curate's hat bobbed a head above the crowd, and Emma found her breakfast starting to climb up her throat. Then the man took off his hat and ran a hand over a bald scalp. Just another of those wildly tall, goofy-looking Englishmen. "Oh, not Mark," escaped before she realized she was speaking.

"What's that, dear?" asked Lorna from behind.

"Oh, I just . . . thought I saw Mark ahead."

"You didn't get his email?" Deb jumped in as Emma began to sweat – did they know? "Mark's been held up with a book shipment." Against Harold's glower, she pulled her phone from her reticule, tapping and swiping until she found it. "Yes, here it is. Says he'll arrive after lunch."

"Oh, right," Emma said. "I'm sure we'll catch him later, and if not, oh well." She focused her attention on the curtains of a window in a building to their right, hoping her cavalier tone disguised just how oppositely she felt.

The crowd paused. Harold bobbed side to side, trying to see what the holdup was, then flipped open his program.

Taking advantage of this slowdown, Emma bent to pull the heel of her ballet slipper back on, cursing her haste in buying flats on Amazon. In the process, her poorly-pinned bun spilled from her bonnet. "Son of a bitch," she proclaimed, then followed up with a "sorry, sorry" to the stares around her as she bent to gather it up again. Returning upright, she found her friends gazing back open-mouthed. Her hand went to her nose. "Is there something on my face?"

It took only half a second to realize: she had forgotten to lace her ring onto the long chain she'd brought just for that purpose.

"What. Is. That. On. Your. Finger," Deb said.

"Engaged?" from Lorna and Harold in stereo.

Emma tucked the diamond toward her palm. Quinn insisted she wear it to get the "full effect," perhaps without realizing his full effect was just as likely to have the opposite outcome than the one he intended.

"Sort of?" Emma said around a mouthful of bobby pins. "It's a, uh, trial engagement."

"A trial what?" Deb put on the guise of shock, but her tone was amused, a perfect Mrs. Jennings if Emma had ever met one.

"Oh my dear," said Lorna, taking her hand to gaze at the ring. "If you need a trial, then there probably shouldn't be an engagement. If you listen, the heart already knows what it wants." She patted Emma's hand and gave her a meaningful, if a bit dramatically doleful, look.

But for all her sensitivity, she was met with a sharp elbow in her side from Deb. "Don't listen to that one, love. Engaged twice before she let me cart her down the aisle."

At this, Lorna squared her shoulders, returning Deb's elbow with one of her own. With her tendency toward romantic moralizing and a splash of good sense for balance, Lorna was a perfectly matched Mrs. Dashwood to Deb's Mrs. Jennings. Since meeting them, Emma could hardly keep from giggling when she read *Sense & Sensibility*, her beloved friends' faces taking up residence on Austen's pages.

"Well, the heart doesn't always get it right the first time round, does it?" Lorna said, pulling Deb's hand to her lips for a kiss.

"Who can think of hearts when there's a rock like that blinding our eyes," Harold said, forcing the diamond back around to look at it. "Did you say his middle name was Darcy, per chance?" He held Emma's hand out, pulling his spectacles down to get a better look.

"Well," said Deb, "a ring like that tells us less about his heart than his pocketbook. Which, we can safely venture, is rather . . . how shall we say, well-endowed?"

Lorna cuffed Deb, as Harold used his pocket handkerchief to wipe his eyes. Emma pretended to glance at the watch she was not wearing. "And that makes it less than 10 minutes before the first raunchy joke. A new record!"

Lorna raised her own hand and waved it around, pretending to admire the ring that was not on her finger. "One might wonder whether well-endowed is the right term for our little romance considering our ceremony consisted of a backyard picnic, a wedding cake I made myself, and a collection of East-Enders on Blu-ray instead of a ring. Oh yes, my dear, romance abounded that day."

Deb planted a wet smooch on Lorna's cheek. "The wedding that lives in infamy."

"Speaking of which," Emma said, getting very busy picking at the lint on her cap sleeves. "Your own wedding plans coming along, Harold?"

Harold gave one of his great exasperated sighs. "Well, would do, except Carl's being a bloody beast. He says short and simple. I say lavish and grand. So far, short and simple is winning out."

"Not a Regency wedding?" Emma said. "Harold, I'm disappointed in you."

"Believe me, honey, I tried. Carl's not having it. But at least I found the man a set of tails he'll wear."

Emma laughed. "And top hats. Please God tell me there will be dove-gray top hats."

It was Deb's turn to laugh. "Act of Parliament, Em. If there's no top hats, we're revoking their citizenship and sending them to your side of the pond."

Emma groaned and threw an arm Isabella Thorpishly over her eyes. "God, I was born in the wrong country!"

"Oh, love," Lorna said. "If Austen teaches anything, it's that one cannot help the accident of one's birth."

Finally, the procession began to move forward again and Emma hoped she had escaped any further investigations into this yes/no, do-I-love-him/do-I-not?? space into which she'd fallen. Who knew that an afternoon sitting on a blanket drinking sparkling water on their favorite hill, with the city lying before them like so much possibility, and Quinn's stubbled face offering her all the promises she'd been asking for – that all of that could result in so much back-scrabbling, shame-faced excuse-making, and awkward changing of subjects?

As they turned the corner, Deb caught sight of a group of women waving from the steps of a townhouse. "Oh, that'll be our LLFA group. We'll just pop over to see when our luncheon shall be," and Deb pulled Lorna behind her to meet with a group of women, half of whom were garbed as Regency gentlemen and soldiers, the other half in muslin day dresses and brocade ballgowns. Emma scanned for the face of Chrissie, the spot-on Elizabeth Bennet she'd met at last year's Lesbian Ladies for Austen luncheon, which Deb and Lorna had dragged her to, mother-henning her out of eating alone as she otherwise would have. Theirs had been an unexpected flirtation, made even more perplexing when Mark met up with them for the afternoon lectures, and she found herself being flirted with on each side in a game that seemed to amuse the other two much more than it did herself.

"Your little change of subject might have thrown them off," Harold said once they were out of earshot, "but it won't work on me." He gave her one of his over-the-rim-of-the-spectacles looks. "What about Mark."

"What about him?" Emma summoned as much nonchalance as she could manage while feeling her cheeks burn as crimson as the velvet on Harold's sleeve. "He'll probably show up with Nora again like last year. Wherever Mark is, she's not far behind."

"You tell yourself that, sweetheart, if it makes you feel better about that bit of Pemberley perched on your finger, but come come." Once more, Harold shot The Look. "Let's have no secrets between friends," he said in his own mock-Mrs. Jennings voice.

"What?" Emma said, this time truly baffled.

"Did you really think Mark could have written that email all by himself? He asked me to proof it for him, and I – let us say – 'helped' him express his true intentions." He tucked Emma's hand through his arm and patted it in that fatherly manner he had which, at that moment, drew from Emma a desire to curl into him and weep. "And last I heard, you still hadn't replied?"

Emma slumped against him. Truth was, part of the reason she had been late that morning was having realized her own reply was still sitting in her drafts folder, a thing too light and airy and flip. A slap in the face to the sweet earnestness of Mark's – and Harold's too, apparently – hopes that she would come unattached to the festival. Because he had finally exorcised Nora well and good from his life, he wrote. Because he was hoping...

Dot. Dot. Dot.

So much possibility hopped the distance between those three black circles at the end of his message, possibilities Emma had lost hours falling into.

And she never even replied.

Harold put his arm around her. "Sometimes the dream of something is all there is. Just smoke – poof." His hand rose into the air, the tips of his fingers dancing like the twinkling of long-dead stars. "But no real substance. That's what makes it so fun." Harold pulled her close and kissed the top of her head. "Socks balled on the floor and someone who turns the lights off when you forget, that's where true love happens, eh, my dear?"

Emma nodded, and slid the diamond into her palm.

CHAPTER 2

The cathedral square sparkled gold and white as the sun dried the last of the puddles dotting the stone slabs between the Pump Room and Bath Abbey. Emma stopped under the portico, watching an opera singer in tight jeans and flowing emerald tunic belt Italian arias to passing tourists, half wearing Austen regalia and half in normal summer attire. The non-Austen tourists seemed as interested in staring at the be-garbed dreamers as the sites themselves.

She leant against the arm of a bench and gazed at the Jacob's Ladder adorning the abbey's facade. She understood its meaning and the story of Jacob, who woke one night to find a great ladder stretching into the heavens, angels ascending and descending, each engaged in diverse divine affairs. But as she stared up at the faces of angels climbing down the ladder, seeming always on the verge of tipping off and falling inert to the earth below, it seemed to her chaos lurked in the shadows. The edge of insanity seemed to loom over her, drawing her toward the uncertain fate of those who slip into liminal spaces.

She pulled her phone from her jeans pocket and checked the time. She had arrived early and passed time browsing the shops facing the Pump

Room, picking up a Union Jack mug to replace the one she'd left half full of curdling milky coffee on her desk back home. As she perused the window displays, she kept an eye out for Harold's scarlet coat.

After the promenade, Emma had sped back to her room at Adelaide Garden and peeled off her gown, sniffing the armpits and cringing, hoping it would freshen up before the ball at the festival's end. She was back in regular clothes now, her bra strap making a nuisance of itself. A pair of women strolled by, apologizing as a parasol snagged her hair. Though polite enough, there was something smug to them. How much of an outsider she appeared to her comrades. She had a perverse desire to scream "I'm one of you!" at their backs. As much as she wanted to avoid using it, perhaps a small purchase with Quinn's card might have left her feeling more in than out.

Then again, had she ever really felt "in" anywhere? She had always been an outcast, an introvert. An only child, she had been left to fall into the rabbit hole of book after book after book, and it was there she found camaraderie and friendship, with the characters of Lewis and Alcott and Bronte and Austen. Even through high school, college, and grad school, friendships had been superficial and brief, lasting only as long as she shared classes and professor gripe sessions and finals cram-a-thons. She thought of herself like Pluto, a far distant body in orbit with all the others, but apart, formless, neither part of the system nor out of it.

As her phone chirped the two o'clock reminder, Emma entered the Pump Room, standing at the end of a long line of those waiting to add their names to the list. She closed her eyes and tried to shut out the sounds of the busy café and the giggles of tourists pointing out this and that from their guidebooks. She tried to imagine it in Jane's day, an entirely open space with windows facing out to the square, opposite windows looking down into the murky green water and the bathers in their brown linen and bonnets below. Classical music would have wafted from the half-circular raised gallery at the far end, the only other sound the murmurs of polite conversation, the shuttle of gowns, the click of canes and umbrellas.

But it was no use.

Cameras flashed, preceded by calls to "say cheese!" A Japanese tour group wandered past, the guide speaking into a megaphone. And to top it all, a passing waiter dropped a tray, glass goblets shattering on the parquet floor. With a shake of her head, she opened her eyes and caught the host in earnest, if annoyed, contemplation with another waiter over the reservation system, one of them checking his watch while the other shrugged. Emma slipped past the line to the host's podium.

"Yes," the host demanded. If he was this annoyed on the first day of the festival, Emma couldn't imagine the state he'd be in by its close.

"I've a reservation? Under Harold Leadbetter?"

"And you're Harold, then?" He gathered menus and waved a hand. "Whatever. Follow me." He led Emma to a table and deposited the menus on the swan napkins, crushing them flat, as flat as the soul of a man who hawks over-priced smoked salmon-and-cucumber sandwiches in tourist trap hell.

Emma scanned for Harold, catching sight of him making his way to the entrance. A few paces behind, a woman drifted past the windows, her orange hair teased into a beehive, a pale cloud of powder rising as she mis-stepped at the threshold and nearly toppled into Harold. She had to take the door sideways as her hoop skirts added almost a foot to either side. The neckline of her dress was low and squared, ample freckled cleavage spilling over while the bodice itself travelled down the length of her body, ending at a sharp point below her waist. If X marked the spot, Emma could only guess what that V was marking. Emma shook her head and returned to her menu. It wasn't the first time the Samuel Pepys-era wires got crossed with the Austen ones.

Harold bypassed the host's stand. In all the bustle of a busy tea service and the hordes of Austen Festival attendees gawking about, he did not see her waving. Finally, she stuck two fingers in her mouth and blasted out a whistle that caused those at the tables nearest to jump and glare.

He raised a hand in what might have been salutation or shut the hell up. Incomprehensibly, he turned to the orange-haired woman and beckoned her to follow.

"Where'd you get a bloody whistle like that?" Harold said, sighing as he sat.

"I'm American," Emma returned. "We're born with it."

"A simple 'Oi' will do next time."

As the other woman approached, all three of them realized the size of her hoops and petticoats meant she would have to occupy an entire side of a table meant for only two. Harold and Emma squeezed in opposite.

"If I could detach this shit, I'd do it." She gave the bodice a tug and opened her legs so the plunging V could sit more comfortably between her thighs. "Wanda," she said, extending her hand and giving Emma's one firm pump. "These weren't made for sitting. Bloody sadists, you ask me, the men who designed women's clothes."

"Yes," Emma said, drawing out the word as she took in Wanda's pale make-up, rouged cheeks and lips and even – was it possible? – the tiny moleskin patch on her chin. "It's a bit . . ."

"Out of date?" Wanda snapped her fingers and shook her head. "There's where you're wrong, luv." She grabbed a cucumber sandwich before the server had even placed the tea tier on the table, took a massive bite, and went on speaking as she chewed. "Think about it. The old biddies of Austen's time would have been holding on to the fashions of their youth. In fact, Austen's early letters include a few jokes about out-dated hair and clothing. The Georgian era was itself this mash-up of conflicting styles. When Jane was born," she finished, gesturing at her dress, "this was how people would have been dressing."

Emma shot Harold a look as he poured tea and pretended the Bath Trio was the most riveting thing he'd heard or seen all day. He glanced back and gave the tiniest of apologetic shrugs. Harold was known for gathering little festival orphans to foster. But this one? That muzzy takes the cake and no mistake, came Lorna's Yorkshire burr.

Wanda pointed to the window, at a gaggle of young women in flowing muslin skirts. "More comfortable, I'll grant you." A breeze picked up and the gowns stretched taut against their skin, showing the full outlines of their legs, waist, and . . . crotch. Wanda smirked. "Then again. Three Graces, eh?" She put fingertips to her puckered lips like she'd just witnessed something risqué.

Harold laughed along. "Too right. How glad I am I wasn't a Janeite back in my drag days. I don't think I could have resisted giving it a go! But lord, can you tuck enough for muslin? One has to wonder."

Wanda slapped his arm and guffawed. "I said no thank you to that. Anyway, this is my first time at the festival, so I went 1770s, the decade of Jane's birth. Next year, the 1780s, and so on." Wanda glanced over at Emma. "And I see you've gone a bit different. What you call this then? Time travel Jane? Central Park after Sunday brunch Jane?"

Emma glanced at her black shirt, pulling it once more over her bra strap. The sunglasses perched on top of her head toppled off and landed in her water glass. "Had a bit of an issue with my day muslin."

Harold chuckled. "Issue? Spilled coffee on white muslin is a bit more than an issue." He patted her hand and gave a paternal tsk. "Em here's our little crew's bampot. Give her a drink, she'll spill it. Give her a curb, she'll trip over it. But you made it back to Adelaide Garden then? Mrs. Pickering pickle you about a mid-day entry?" He turned to Wanda to explain who Mrs. Pickering was, the owner of the B&B their little group called home during the festival and who was known to demand extended explanations through the intercom when someone rang to be let in at what she determined to be odd hours.

Emma smiled through Harold's story and Wanda's rude comments about their beloved-if-annoying hostess. She was determined to be pleasant. It was one meal with an abrasive woman. Her mother had given her enough practice, after all. "And how did you and Harold meet?" she asked Wanda.

"Staying at his 'otel," Wanda said. "Weren't no rooms available when I bought my tickets. Can design and sew a dress what takes six months, but can't remember to make a bloody reservation in time."

"Wanda rode in with me on the bus this morning." He pulled out a little pamphlet with bus times and routes between Radstock and Bath, passing it to Wanda. "You'll want to keep an eye on the times. The buses don't run as late here as they do in London."

Wanda took the timesheet and tapped it on his sleeve. "Thanks. But don't worry about me. I don't have trouble finding a bed to sleep in."

Wanda's elbow jiggled Harold's arm and an impudent expression unfolded across her face.

Harold laughed right along, leaning in to say, "I bet you don't, you saucy fox." He clapped his hands suddenly and let out a bark of laughter. "You know there's a rugby tournament this weekend. Our hotel is just chocka-block with burly bashers."

"Oh yes, pleeeeease," was Wanda's rejoinder. "Make you a deal. I take half, you and Carl the other."

While the bawdy banter continued, Emma tucked in to her tea and cakes, indulging in her own reminiscences of Radstock. The first time she'd been was with Mark and Harold some years before.

Harold had forgotten something back home and Mark was the only one with a car. Desperate to get away from the crowds and see something other than the white glare of Bath, Emma had begged a seat in the back. While Harold searched for his missing breeches, Emma and Mark took in the sights of the small mining town. Mark's only connection to Radstock had been to recognize its name from a sign, which had puzzled Emma, who'd assumed everyone on this tiny island knew every city, town, village, or hamlet. Pretending astonishment over her American ignorance, he chucked her chin and told her she was cute. As he'd exclaimed over the inn with its dark wood-paneling and low ceilings, the narrow canal, and the squat rock wall separating the old-world feel of the dirt path from the shopping plaza on the other side, Emma stared not at these things, but at Mark's delighted, toothy grin, himself the most quirky, quaint, and enchantingly English thing she could imagine.

They had talked about the past year, about Emma's hope to make tenure and finally be freed from the drudgery of 100-level composition and intro lit courses. Mark chatted about the graduate program he'd entered, in publishing and small presses, as well as the decision looming before him as to whether to take the Master's and run or continue to a PhD. Neither spoke of Quinn or Nora, presences that lived on the periphery of their ten days together. Once, their hands had bumped when the path narrowed, and Mark slipped his fingers around her own, swinging their arms like schoolchildren, a gesture she convinced herself was just platonic jest, just two mates strolling along. But when they touched, words floated out of her head, and there was simply Mark standing beside her, the feel of his hand cradling her own, a warmth spreading through her until she made an excuse of tucking back her hair to escape from the unexpected intimacy that both enticed and frightened her.

She had actually stopped by Radstock the day before, slipping past the hotel and hoping neither Harold nor Carl would see her from the windows. She wanted a moment in silence, there on that bench by the squat stone arch where she had sat with Mark. As she fiddled with it, her ring fell off and rolled away in the grass, and for a very long time, Emma considered just leaving it there, walking back to her car and completing the drive to Bath a few ounces of platinum and a lifetime of commitment lighter.

"Em!" Harold said, obviously for the third or fourth time. "Are you bloody well done?"

Emma nodded, only half sure of the question she was being asked, as the waiter slipped her cup and saucer from the table.

"Anyway," Wanda said, dabbing the tears their uproarious laughter had brought on, "just love your inn. Beautiful place. And historically accurate. You've done well in keeping it to time. Oldest coaching inn in the region, innit?"

"You seem better informed than the general festival attendee," Emma said, finally rejoining the discussion.

"Well, I should bloody well hope so." Wanda pulled a flier from a backpack she'd slung over her chair. "I didn't get a PhD in 17th, 18th, and 19th century history and fashion for nothing." She slid the flier across the table. "I'm holding an off-site event later this week, a lecture on everything from clothes to recipes. But there may be a last-minute change in topic if I can get this letter I discovered last month verified. I'm not allowed to say anything yet, but let me just hint that we may have discovered a very real and specific source of Jane's inspiration."

At this, Harold laughed. "Her muse was everyone around her! The people and society! Everyone knows Austen drew from all her friends and family, compiling characteristics, amalgamating experiences."

"No, no, no! I'm telling you. She had a muse and I'm about to find out exactly who she was!"

As their discussion devolved in an argument about who and what inspired Austen, Emma glanced over the list of topics on Wanda's flier.

The evolution of the corset.

What *did* they wear under *there?*

I'm afraid it will fray – Mr. Tilney's guide to caring for muslin. (She could have used that one!)

For the span of three hours, said the flier, attendees would learn the ins and outs of fashion at all social strata, as well as a few housekeeping tips and tricks still relevant to our modern lives.

She had to admit, they *did* sound interesting. Her stomach turned over with the wobbly excitement that brewed whenever she was onto a new set of essay or story ideas. Wanda's lecture might be the very thing to unblock the dam currently in the way of her most recent project – essays on family, love, and home, comparing Austen's era to her own. Oh yes, she could tolerate Wanda if she could get those juices flowing again. And she didn't mind relegating Wanda to the realm of a creative laxative.

Emma returned to the conversation to hear Harold declare, "then you two are, essentially, festival sisters. Em here is giving her very own lecture later this week. On love." He drew this last word out long and undulating, ending with a little air kiss.

"Oh, well, it's not exactly love," Emma began but Wanda was quick to interrupt.

"And I hope a healthy dose of materialism as well. Can't have one without the other. Not in Austen. I mean, Lizzy Bennet? Gold digger." She sang the phrase in a sing-song voice that made Emma want to shove half a scone in each ear.

"You know, that's not really a fair reading," Emma began. "If we look at the sub-texts, we find that . . ." but just as she was about to defend the honor of Jane's motifs, the host came over and made it clear it was time for them to relinquish their table. "Oh well, nevermind," Emma said, grateful to be saved from the effort of changing a mind which clearly had no intention of changing.

"Shall we see what festivities are unfolding at the Guildhall?" Harold asked.

Emma found herself nodding even as she wondered just exactly what it was she had agreed to. It was not an unfamiliar position. It seemed she was always nodding obliquely along, only ever half aware of what it was she was going along with.

The rest of the afternoon, Emma, Harold, and Wanda made a not-quite-friendly threesome. Wanda was a domineering conversationalist, leaving no room for actual discussion, unless of course the rejoinder was ribald and raucous.

So she left Wanda and Harold to it and tried to enjoy walking the ballroom of the Guildhall and Festival Fayre. Out of her formal gown, Emma felt a bit awkward walking alongside the other two still in their era garb, but then she watched Harold tugging at his stockings and rubbing his sore heel, and noticed Wanda repeatedly jerking up the neckline of her dress, constantly in a two-step as she maneuvered her wide skirts through the crowds.

Besides, what she loved about this festival was the come-as-you-are mentality of most attendees. What you wore wasn't nearly as important as who and what you loved, and right now, that was Jane Austen and Georgian England. Sure, there were plenty in the other camp – the hardcore Janeites with their rigid adherence to authenticity, their quickness to correct any inaccuracies when someone dared quote Austen in their presence. And while Emma was certain she could hold her ground amongst them, she simply didn't want to. She'd rather be here, walking arm in arm with her pal Harold, following a woman in a muslin dress with a baby on her hip wearing a onesie that said, "In my previous life, I was Jane Austen."

Emma often wondered which camp Jane herself might have fallen into – unyielding adherent or ironic accomplice. And when she explored that line of thinking, she found equal arguments for both sides. Rigid and strict, Jane could be. But deprecating and self-ironic at the same time, as if she knew the truth other people fought off for most of their young adulthoods: the best source of laughter is one's self! Oh yes, there was something sneakily wry in Austen's letters and portraits. Something that said Jane would have gotten a very big laugh out of the idea of anyone taking themselves, and especially her, so seriously. A stab of regret went through Emma, as it always did when the paths of her mind led her to ruminating about the real Jane – not the version fabricated through movies and fan fiction and redacted letters – a pang in her gut that for all this worship and imitation, the part of Austen who was a daughter, a sister, a homemaker, and a friend – all those things remained gauzy unknowns, the real Jane a shadow behind the spotlight's glare.

As they left the Guildhall and turned toward the Jane Austen Centre, the cacophony of conversation and hawkers was broken by a quartet of musicians busking in Queen Square, two rows of dancers forming up nearby. Emma returned to the moment, returned to the crowd surrounding her, and the happy reminder that she was here again, in her favorite place in the world, her favorite time of the year.

The phone in her pocket chirped with a new message. Emma checked her screen and sighed. Just Quinn. He'd texted a photo of himself at some surgical convention, his face sloppy, the table arrayed with an armada of half-drunk cocktails. His note said one of the residents had shared this and he hoped it'd make her laugh. To a lifetime of laughs, he ended it. She considered sending him off a quick text in return, but before she could even open her phone – or spend any time reflecting on how happy she was here in this moment, a moment that did not include him – a hand reached round Emma's waist.

She turned, expecting to find Harold dragging her toward the reel but instead, her eyes rose to the twinkling green of Mark's.

"Have this dance?" he said and pulled her into the set. There he was, decked out in his black clergyman's costume, heads taller than anyone else, his skinny legs comical in their tight black breeches and white stockings. He looked a bit of a dufus, really, a fact he wore proudly as he led Emma forward, tossing his round curate's hat back to Harold like a frisbee. She caught Wanda turning to Harold, eyes cut one direction, mouth the other, the universal female posture for "and just who might that be?"

But what did she care for Wanda's prying? What did she care for anything when one of Mark's hands was there just above the waistline of her jeans, the other squeezing her fingers, his thumb grazing over the back of her hand, electricity rocketing up her arms.

Emma blushed, as she was the only dancer in their little group in jeans and chacos, but her self-consciousness gave way to the pure joy of bouncing along to the fast pace of the reel: tripping forward, hands meeting, spinning in a circle, and skipping back. If there had been a specific dance called, no one seemed to hear it. She and Mark joined a collage of the many types of reels amongst the others willing to jump off the curb and into a random Regency street dance.

And Emma was glad for the lack of form because she couldn't have concentrated if she'd tried. Mark's eyes were upon her, his face in a wide grin, that little snaggletooth in front announcing his joy. She could feel him drinking her in, feel herself pulled into his gravitational orbit. Their hands joined for the frenzied last measures of the reel, where the couples spun and spun, arms laced round their partner's waist, as the musicians cranked the tempo and around they went, Emma falling deeper into him, both continuing to spin long after the music had ended, destroyed by its own momentum, and stopping only when the crowd erupted into cheers.

Emma put a hand to her heaving chest, breathing heavily, laughing, slumping into Mark, who put his arm round her shoulders and held her tight.

A festival organizer came up, clipboard in hand. "Mr. Landen," she said, pausing to place a hand to the earset and speak into her radio. "The festival director is ready. We really must . . ." and before she finished, she wove away through the crowd. Mark grabbed hold of Emma's hand, thankfully the *un*trial-engaged one, and squeezed. He took out the little tin he kept in his breast pocket and waggled it at Emma, reminding her of his own festival business.

"Dinner, right?"

She nodded as he slipped through the crowd and away from her.

Just then, a feather appeared, white and barred with brown, tipping over the heads of the street dancers as the musicians began another song, this one a slower-paced cotillion. The feather danced along the breeze, spiraling up, and Emma pushed off Harold's shoulder to leap for it, catching it with the tips of her fingers. She smoothed the barbs until the vane was soft and flat, then tucked it behind her ear, a gift she would offer to Mark when they met later for their annual recap-the-year dinner.

CHAPTER 3

Late afternoon sun streamed through the frosted glass windows surrounding the door of Adelaide Garden. Beyond the small vestibule that served as Mrs. Pickering's front-desk citadel, a pair of darkwood French doors stood open to a small parlor long since converted to a cozy bar. Here, Emma waited, pondering the unexpected appearance of Mark, his disappearance with the festival coordinators, and the reminder that he would be back for her, his eyes as full of expectation and hope as they'd been out on the sunny street a few scant hours before.

Emma attempted to concentrate on the festival's program, readying herself for the dinner conversation of who had gone to Waterstones for the reading, who had attended the series of 10-min Austen-inspired plays at Mission Theatre, and who had taken a turn through the Upper Rooms at the pre-ball workshop. The lecture on accents in Austen's age might have been intriguing. If Emma could have attended to it. But all she could remember was sitting numbly through a round of lectures and panels held in the Theatre Royale, her lower back still atingle with the afterglow of Mark's hand, feet often waggling out of nervousness – still in time to the reel's frantic pace – and her breath just as thready as if she'd spent the whole afternoon dancing. Her one clear memory from that afternoon was the lecture on bonnet-making she'd attended where an older gentleman in a black wool clergyman's costume fell asleep on her shoulder and drooled on her sleeve.

She finished her drink in one chest-scorching swallow and spun to face the door. The light coming in from the lobby cast a halo about Mark, rendering him in silhouette, but there was no mistaking him – the tousle of untidy hair, his tall lankiness and the way he stooped a bit when he walked, as though nervous of his own size. With the light streaming in behind, Emma could not see his face, but his features were etched in her mind – his kind green eyes, a little droopy at the corners, and his lopsided smile, slow to come but warm as a summer sun when it did.

He paused, seeing her, but only for a beat, and then he was standing before her. She stood and let him kiss her on each cheek, self-conscious of her awkward Americanness. A button of his shirt was different than the rest, a dark brown where the others were pale cream. She touched it with a finger, thinking how Quinn would never allow himself to be so charmingly, so unabashedly mis-matched. Mark's hand rose to take her own, but Emma slid back onto her stool, swiveling toward the cold brass railing, her hands two coals against the icy metal.

"Emma." Mark took the stool beside her and rotated between examining the bar taps and gazing at her face.

"Mark," she returned, her voice coming nearly as a whisper, a tone that took her by surprise, and so she said his name a second time, with firmness, with friendliness. "Mark. Hello."

"The stout," he told the bartender, "and another of whatever she's having."

"Oh, I probably shouldn't," Emma began, but Mark waved her off. Another whiskey mule on an empty stomach was the last thing she needed, but she accepted anyway and sipped slowly.

"Emma," Mark began. In his voice, in his gaze, there was the note of what she knew must be coming. Sweat broke out along her spine. A blend of fear and hopefulness swirled within, but all was overshadowed by guilt, by the knowledge that as soon as the words rose from his lips, she would bring them down like doves shot from a pale blue sky. His eyes locked onto hers, his gaze saying nothing in the world could be more important than this moment. She picked up her glass to take a swig. The diamond turned in to her palm grazed the glass, scratching it, etching the possibilities of what waited for her in a life with Quinn.

"I'd hoped that we . . . That finally – "

Emma jumped in, speaking over him. "So, how did your meeting go? Did you have that farthing authenticated after all?" Her voice sounded almost frivolous with her haste to delay his earnest speech.

Mark's face contracted, cloudy and confused, but Emma was saved by Harold's booming from the foyer. "Oi! Our reservation's in ten minutes and we've got to get half cross town. If I don't get this risotto, so help me, I'll . . ."

Emma was first on her feet. Mark sighed, then smiled. He shrugged in that beautifully flippant way he had of taking all in his stride. Emma maneuvered herself on Mark's left, taking his offered arm with her right hand and tucking the other safely in her pocket.

Outside, Harold stood at the curb, checking his watch and tugging at the cuffs of his button-down. Deb and Lorna stood further along, poking a finger into one another's plastic swag bags to compare their loot. Seeing Emma and Mark, Harold took off at a strident pace toward Lansdown Road.

Just as they stepped beyond the gates of Adelaide Garden's blooming front lawn, Mark's phone dinged.

"Text from my dean," he said, returning it to his pocket.

"That's right," Emma said. "Congrats. And how are you enjoying teaching? Still working on that dissertation?"

He grinned. "Always." Then a shrug. "Our Dean took a liking to my approach and asked me to teach while I finish the Ph.D. It's a lot to manage between the bookstore and the classes. But . . ." He shook his head, then smiled once more. "Just needed to be doing . . . something." He nudged her with a shoulder, making her trip off the curb and let loose a few choice expletives. He went on speaking as if nothing had interrupted them while a couple walking by pushed their toddler quickly past and glowered in their direction. "I'm teaching a mix of grad and undergrad classes, though most of the time I have no clue what I'm doing there. I'd never appreciated just how much teaching is really all about learning." He plucked a dahlia from a bush, sniffed it, and handed it to her. "I think *you* said that once, actually."

Emma trimmed the stem and tucked the flower behind her ear, realizing the feather she'd been saving had blown away to some other adventure. "Well, undergrad comp courses can hardly compare to teaching at the graduate level. Do we get to call you Dr. Landen, yet?"

"Just Mark," he said, "to you." He smoothed a strand of hair back from the flower, and an electric charge erupted at the base of her spine, making her trip again.

"But that reminds me!" Mark said. "I told my dean about your article, and she was quite excited. In fact, she wondered – ," but before he could finish, a clattering of high heels came running up behind them as a cab veered away from the curb and roared back toward downtown. It was the voice that reached Emma first.

"Bloody well wait up for me!"

Wanda. Just her luck. Apparently, whether in costume or out, Wanda bowed at the altar of the power-clash gods and this evening, her ensemble constituted red heels, fishnet stockings, a flower-print skirt, and a polka-dot halter top. She did her best to run but the tightness of her skirt – could that possibly be pleather? – cut short her stride, making her gait more of a waddle than a swagger.

She immediately, as Emma had known she would, swooped up beside Emma and Mark, who were walking slightly back from Harold's purposeful stride and Lorna and Deb's tidy gait.

Mark leaned down. "Tell you later." He let go of her hand, which she hadn't even realized he'd been holding, the warmth of his touch leaving a chill in its absence.

Wanda laced her hand through Mark's other arm. "What a gentleman," she crowed. "Wanda. Friend of Harold's." And this seemed to be all the introduction necessary to embark on a fresh round of raillery. She leaned into Mark but whispered in a voice loud enough for everyone to hear. "People will think we're your harem!" She cackled shrilly. "Eh, Em, dear?"

Emma nodded, then reddened and shook her head. Harem? And even worse – Em? After half a day's acquaintance? The woman had nerve, she had to give her that. Mark gave Emma another of his loopy grins. He waggled his eyebrows as if to say, who is this joker? She returned a commiserating grin of her own, but there was a twisting-round in her conscience. Because Mark had confirmed that for all her big voice and minuscule skirts, her creepy sexual jokes and blatant passes, Wanda was nothing beside Emma. And what could Emma offer in return? Perhaps it would be a kindness to lope up to the group ahead and put as much distance between them as she could.

But she simply couldn't. She had these ten days with Mark, and though it would all only pass in the same friendly, flirtatious banter as years' past, she also realized these would be the last days. Next year, she might be married. Perhaps the duties of a wife – a mother? – would prevent her coming at all. How sad she suddenly felt.

They passed through the Abbey square again. Wanda chatted away, leaving no room for Emma to contribute. The few times Wanda threw a question her way, she plowed ahead before Emma had time to answer. The few times Emma managed to get a word in, Wanda found something to correct.

As the haze of the second whiskey mule unfurled, Emma's mind swept back to her first festival. She'd been sitting on that bench just outside the Pump Room when she caught sight of Mark, wearing his black clergyman's costume and trailing a woman walking at a determined pace in front of him. No matter how hard he tried to catch up, she always remained three steps ahead.

Nora.

In the years since, Mark had told Emma all about Nora. How they'd met post-university, just after he'd taken over the lease on a little bookstore in Glastonbury. How she was a wedding planner and specialized in Regency-remake weddings. How she'd drug Mark to his first festival and how he'd fallen in love with all the sophistication and satin, the pleasure of stepping out of the realm of their own anything-goes modern reality into the paradoxically freeing rigidity of antiquated social conventions. The whole shebang, he liked to say, affecting a decent Jimmy Stewart. He'd gotten ordained online through the Church of the Divine Forest and memorized the Anglican prayer book so he could perform the period weddings Nora planned. It was a tidy life; his words.

Emma and Quinn were not together that first year, having orbited away from one another again. Nora'd had to leave halfway through the week to care for a sick parent, and Emma and Mark pal-ed around through the rest of the lectures and panels and teatimes and dinners. He taught her country dances and glided her up and down the polished floors of the Upper Rooms at the penultimate assembly. The next year, Mark and Nora had split, but Emma and Quinn were back together. On their third meeting, they flipped back, and Mark and Nora were giving things one more shot, but Emma and Quinn were off-again. And so it had gone, back and forth. Each year nurtured their flirtation, but also complicated the rules of their friendship.

And then this year. In the spring, Emma had posted an unequivocal message on all her social networks that she had given up on commitment, barely veiling her jabs at Quinn. And the universe, finding perverse humor as it always seemed to do, sat Emma down on that blanket in the park some four months later, Quinn begging her to give it a trial run, just see how it fit, and she nodded dumbly as he slipped the oversized ring onto her trembling finger.

A car honked, drawing Emma out of her reverie. Mark's hand was at her elbow, guiding her across a busy street to the inviting dark wood and burgundy interior of the restaurant. When they made it inside, well after Harold had prodded the first of their group through the doors, Emma found just three seats left. Two on one side, the third at the opposite end of the table.

There was no beating Wanda to it. In as much time as it took Emma to recognize the arrangement, Wanda zoomed to the two empty places, dragging Mark behind her. His eyes apologized, and Emma just shrugged and smiled. She was happy to catch up with Lorna and Deb. To put a little distance between herself and Wanda. And, she had to admit, from Mark as well.

The dinner was magnificent – rich, buttery pasta dishes and a magical basket of sweet, warm bread that never emptied. Emma raised a glass to Harold. "For always finding the very best restaurants in Bath. And never making us eat at the shitty ones a second time."

"To Harold," the table repeated.

Harold rose and thanked them. "But," he continued, "there's an achievement far more important to be celebrated tonight. Though," he qualified, "not much can beat that risotto."

Emma laughed along, but her heart raced as she feared what Harold might be about to say. She had not explicitly said the trial engagement was a secret and she was still – out of habit or an urge to self-destruct, she wasn't sure which – wearing the ring.

"Emma, dear," he continued.

She thought she was going to throw up.

"Your article was simply astounding, my dear, and we're all very proud of you and cannot wait for your presentation tomorrow."

Emma barked out a laugh of relief and surprise. She held up her own glass. "Thank you. Thank you all."

"To Emma!" She gazed at the faces surrounding her and was once again swept away by their tide of friendship, the sense that she was finally – though only momentarily, only for the briefest of painful twinklings – amongst the people who loved her best in the world. The people she loved best. Her eyes landed on Mark's face and he held her gaze.

"Oh right, your presentation," Wanda said, her voice a little slurry from the double scotch she'd had with dinner. The word "presentation" had a note to it Emma could not place, but it settled itself halfway between heart and stomach and began to gnaw away. "I didn't realize you'd had an article to go along with it. In Persuasions? Or Regency World? I've been in both."

"Oh, well, neither," Emma began.

She was quickly interrupted by Deb. "In The New. York. Times." She cast Emma a warm, proud gaze, a complete reversal from her own mother's response. It was amazing how Emma could hear shock and disappointment a thousand miles and one profoundly silent phone line away.

But it seemed to shut Wanda up too, for which Emma was quite grateful.

Emma was saved the explanation of her article because Lorna, Deb, and Harold could not tolerate her own understated version. It had been a simple thing really, something she'd written partly in jest, and had never imagined would go anywhere. When friends and fellow faculty kept pestering her to send it out, she'd emailed it to a colleague's cousin, an under-editor at The Times who had asked to read it. It was about how her own love life could have come from the pages of Austen's novels, and how she seemed to find herself trucking right through each anti-hero in turn. She'd written about her Mr. Wickham, a high school boyfriend who'd eloped from the prom with her best friend. Her Mr. Willoughby and the girl he'd knocked up while he and Emma were together, ultimately leaving them both for a third victim of his amorous attentions. Her Mr. Crawford, the reformed woman-izer, who turned out to be not quite so reformed after all. She'd had a Frank Churchill, a decent man actually, but who had been in love with someone else all along. And there had even been a Mary Crawford, a woman she'd dated in college during a surprising phase of her life, but who had sum-marily dumped Emma when she'd switched from pre-Law to English Lit.

And Emma also wrote about the heroes of Austen's novels, one of whom she hoped to find. They all of them had their winning qualities – Mr. Darcy's dashing looks and steadfast character, Edmund Bertram's kind heart, Captain Wentworth's passionate attachment to memory. But, as Emma had written, her ideal man could be captured by one perfect Austen hero – Henry Tilney – clever but kind, good-looking in a sensible, approachable way, a good brother, a faithful friend. The article culminated with the question of whether any Austen heroes, but particularly a Henry Tilney, could yet exist.

Truth was, Emma had found her Mr. Tilney, a bookseller whose warm-heartedness made him an easy facsimile for a clergyman. And though he sat just a few seats away from her, the choices of her own life had separated her from him, a situation that left her feeling as girlishly ridiculous and short-sighted as any Catherine Morland might on climbing down from the horse cart upon her unexpected homecoming.

From down the table, Wanda's brash laugh broke into the conversation. "And you found him then, didn't you? Your Mr. Tilney?"

Mark sat forward, his eyes once again seeking Emma's, but this time, marked with something else – pride perhaps. Possession.

"Wait," Emma said, wondering if Wanda had really spoken or if it was her own whiskey-addled brain. "What?"

"Although perhaps we ought to call him Dr. Tilney." Wanda laughed and raised her glass. "To Emma and Quinn!"

Harold took Emma's hand. Debra and Lorna raised their glasses as well, their faces showing slight perplexity about whether they should behave like they'd known or not. At a table nearby, the same group of young women from earlier, the Three Graces though now in slinky black dresses, overheard Wanda's exuberance and raised their own glasses. Emma gazed at each of their young faces, beaming at her as strangers do who know nothing about the situation at all. Young as they were, perhaps new to such circumstances, the importance of it appeared unspeakably great. They were too young yet to realize what a hard road it was to arrive at this place, in the tying of one's life indivisibly to another's. They saw only the perfect ending less astute readers thought all Austen's novels culminated in. "To Emma and Quinn," they intoned with the rest of the dining room.

Mark's glass was the last to be raised. "To Emma and . . . Quinn?" He slammed back the dregs of his wine. "Waiter," he called to a passing server. "Double vodka here."

Wanda gave a little cheer. "Oh, me too!" She glanced down the table. "Vodka anyone?" Her gaze seemed to perch on Emma's glazed expression. "No? More for us!"

On the walk back, Emma helped Mark stumble along. Harold was trying to keep pace with Wanda, who had shed her heels and sloppily skipped ahead of the group, never minding where sidewalks ended and streets full of passing traffic began.

Mark stumbled and Emma tried to help him back up.

He wrenched his arm away, as though Emma's touch were painful. "And how'd she find out about it then?" he asked. Ahead, Wanda was spinning round a lamppost in a drunkenly demented version of Singing in the Rain. Except she wasn't so much singing as yodeling and the only rain falling was the spittle Harold kept wiping off his face as he tried to coax her down.

Emma worried the zipper of her purse. "Umm, Facebook?" she answered. Emma had spent the rest of the dinner watching Mark descend into an ever-drunker abyss and wondering how Wanda had figured it out. Emma had been quite upset when Quinn changed his status to Engaged, slamming her wine glass on the quartz counter in his posh apartment, reminding him it was a trial engagement. Trial. But then he showed her how many people had liked it– and how many more had responded with weeping face emojis, all from nurses or doctors who'd been trying to match him up with their random cousins, friends, and even themselves. There had been something deeply satisfying, and perhaps slightly unsettling, when she read the comment "oh nooooo! Hot Doctor swallowed the kool-aid?!"

But, damn if Wanda wasn't a quick mover! She'd sent Emma a friend request shortly after lunch, and as if her thumb and ring finger had teamed up on some self-destructive bent, Emma tapped "Accept" before even realizing what she'd done, and spent the rest of that particular lecture debating the possibilities of unfriending her immediately after. She ultimately decided to let it be. So they were friends. She could surreptitiously unfriend her a few weeks later and then blame it on a glitch in the system. What harm could there be?

Well, apparently, Wanda could – in the same short order – send a friend request to Quinn, who, though not exactly identified as her significant other, still maintained primo status on her friend list for how many of her own posts he was always liking and re-sharing and commenting on. And Wanda was about the wiliest she-beast Emma'd met. Poor Quinn, too affable to ever hit the "Deny" button, probably thought he was finally getting an in with her festival family.

Mark snorted. "Bloody Facebook." He launched forward, propelled by another lead foot on his drunken gas tank.

Emma took off her shoes, the better to run after him. "It's not a real engagement, exactly," she offered. "It's a . . . a trial one?"

As stupid as she'd felt saying it earlier that day, nothing could match the cascade of shame when Mark's withering eyes fell on her. "You should've told me. Should've written back."

"I know." She stopped in front of a shop window. The glare from a streetlamp lit up her reflection, the red dahlia at her ear like a bloodstain at her temple. "I'm sorry. I'm not as . . . as brave as you think I am. He asked and I . . ."

"Forgot to answer?"

They stopped again a block further up, Mark bent over. Trying to catch his breath, perhaps. Perhaps trying not to lose his dinner.

"Let's see it then." He wagged his hand until she placed hers in it. He grasped her fingers too hard. Seeing it now, her hand in Mark's, she realized what a gaudy thing that ring was really. An over-exclamation of all the love she could never be certain Quinn actually felt.

But it had wowed all her girlfriends, and there had been something else satisfying, if also unsettling, over the debate of its price tag, numbers that easily outstripped what she made in a semester, two. But, she had reasoned, Elizabeth started to fall in love with Darcy after seeing his mansion and estate. Wasn't her mother always saying the #1 reason for divorce was money problems? Harold calling it a bit of Pemberley both reaffirmed and indicted her.

"Who needs courage with a ring like that," Mark said and let her hand drop away. He pushed off the mailbox he'd been leaning on and trudged forward. Whenever his pace lagged and Emma was about to catch up, he'd suddenly stride ahead, as though sensing her presence and wanting always to keep it two steps behind him, always just beyond the peripheries of his vision.

Back in the hotel, Emma found Harold trying to convince Wanda to go home, sleep it off. But she was not having it. "I'm not bloody well tired," she said. "Who's drinking with me? Markie? There's a good boy, Markie-poo. Come have a drink and we'll learn the catechism of the Forest."

Emma placed a hand on his arm, but he pushed past her and slumped on the bar stool, spinning away.

"Barkeep," he said, raising two slack fingers. "A round for my lady friend and I."

"Goodnight, then?" Emma called, but Mark refused to acknowledge or respond.

"Come on, love." Harold tugged at her elbow. "Leave them to it. Looks like she'll be needing that cab after all." He took out a card for a cab company with his Radstock hotel address pre-printed on the back and handed it to the bartender.

CHAPTER 4

Emma woke early, though on opening her eyes, she couldn't be sure sleep had come at all. The night had spun around her in a tormented combination of too much whiskey and guilt. She rose, a copy of *Northanger Abbey* falling to the floor; Quinn dubbed it her "sweater," the title she always pulled from the shelf when she needed the comfort of the old and familiar, a place she could escape to when she needed to be any-where other than the spiraling rabbit-hole of her mind. Adelaide Garden kept a full set of Austen on each floor just for this festival and Emma had nabbed it as she trudged to her room.

She opened her door to find her muslin gown hanging from the door-frame. A note from the cleaners said they'd done their best and thanked her for her business. Attached was the bill, charged to Quinn's card. In the husky light of early morning, Emma could not see the stain, but knew the glare of full day would reveal whatever shadow remained.

Emma washed quietly in the shared hall bathroom, first checking Mark's door, looking for that slim beam of light to permit her knock. Back in her room, she began a note. Many notes. Within a few lines, each new attempt joined the previous comrades who had fallen, abandoned, a defeated army of paper wads and shredded fragments of all that her soul just would not allow her to confess. Cowardice – courage's unwelcome doppelganger. Safety. Familiarity. She cringed to see those words unfurl from the tip of her pen, and if she made it past one of them, past two, past three even – her pen skidded to a halt when it came time to write Quinn's name. Or worse, her attempts – two times, three? – to argue a trial engagement should somehow be less hurtful than a real one.

His face broke across her vision from that afternoon last year by the streamside in Radstock. His eyes had brimmed with tears as he relayed the discovery of Nora's infidelity. Not technically cheating, he'd said and swiped a tear from across his cheek, but she'd had dinner with another man, someone she admitted had become more than just a workmate. Emma's mind twisted around the possibility that she was treading those same footsteps, might have hurt Mark the same way, and if not exactly the same, at least too close to escape culpability. But then too, it was this similarity that made her hope for a comparable swath of forgiveness on which she might tread.

She closed her eyes and wrote.

Satisfied with the note – as satisfied as she could ever be – Emma returned to the darkened hall. She intended only to slip it under his doorframe, something for him to consider before joining them all for breakfast. As she began the long walk from her end of the hall to his, she stopped at the groan of an opening door. In the darkness, she had difficulty knowing which door it was, but then yes! – it was Mark's. She quickened her pace, hoping to put the note in his hand, perhaps give him the briefest of hugs before dashing back to the safety of her own small space. And then she stopped.

There was no confusing that corona of frizzy red hair. Nor the fishnet stockings looped over one arm or the heels dangling from the other. Emma tried to flatten herself against the wall, but the sun had begun its climb, casting light on all the reckless misdoings of the night before. At the door, Wanda stumbled a bit as though still drunk and Mark's hand appeared, taking her elbow to steady her. She giggled and pushed a hank of Mark's hair back from his eyes. As she leaned in for a parting kiss, Mark's eyes, red-rimmed and sagging, caught the flash of Emma's arm as she brought it to her throat in jealous disbelief. There was Wanda, leaning in, her lips sloppy and wet, and there was Mark, shirtless, in his boxers. Mark glanced from Emma to Wanda and to himself, taking in what this tableau revealed. And then he slammed the door on Wanda's face, the lock echoing as it slid past the strike plate and barred everything without from coming within.

Wanda reeled back from the door, catching herself on a table set against the wall. "What the bloody," she mumbled. She turned toward the stairs at the end of the hall, planting a kiss on Mark's door with her fingertips before lurching away. As she rounded the landing, Wanda turned back to look at Mark's door. Emma drew in, trying to tuck more tightly against the wall, and the floor squeaked. Wanda instantly saw Emma, made a little gesture with her fingers to her mouth as though embarrassed. The shadows were not deep enough to mask her mien, though. Not a face clouded by chagrin, but rather, one shining in triumph.

Emma slouched against the wall until she heard the creak of Wanda's steps receding down to the lobby. She trudged back to her room and let the note fall from her hands onto the floor. She pulled on her muslin dress, grabbed her lecture and shoved the pages into her day bag, kicked at the pile of dirty clothes still stinking of sweat and liquor, and pulled the door firmly behind her.

She stumbled out the front door of the hotel, tripping over a gap between two cobblestones. Her mind tangled round images of Mark and Wanda. His mouth. Her lipstick. Her fingers fumbling at the buttons of his shirt, at the mis-matched one halfway down.

She hardly knew what she was doing when Quinn's groggy voice broke through the monotonous ringing on her side of the phone. She was on auto-pilot and her fingers had tapped her screen in their most familiar rhythm.

He picked up mid-conversation with someone else. She said his name over and over to an empty space, hearing his muffled voice just beyond the reach of her own.

"Damnit, Quinn!" she said and was about to hang up when he came on the line.

"Hey, hon. Sorry about that. Nightfloat."

"Oh, right."

It must have been slightly after midnight back home, and Quinn would just be starting the long crawl to dawn, wandering the halls of the hospital or passing time with the paramedics in the emergency bay, hoping for a gunshot wound, groaning over an appendectomy.

"Sorry. I'm walking over to the festival and thought I'd call."

Ahead of Emma, a mother walked two children to school, the plaids of their uniforms sending out bleats of stability, primness, propriety.

"Early, isn't it? It's only like, what, eight there?"

"Not quite seven," she corrected, realizing there were no festival events for hours yet. A Caffè Nero sat not far from the Mission Theatre where she could drink coffee and flip through the newspapers and tabloids. It would be a weak distraction from the line streaming across her mind like a marquee at Times Square: MARK SHAGGED WAN – .

She shook her head and tried to focus on the scene around her – a streetsweeper chugging slowly toward her, the brush rotating, churning trash into its belly. A bodega vendor setting out plastic crates of apples, oranges, and bananas. And ahead of her, the two red-headed schoolchildren, bobbing along behind their mother, a blonde with her hair tucked under a baseball cap, her once athletic figure a little rounded and plump. It was like a time machine, following these three, what Emma and her own family might look like in another 10 years.

"Seven! Emma, what the hell are you even doing up? Shouldn't you still be snoozing comfortably at Adelaide Terrace or whatever?"

"Garden. I needed a walk. My room was . . . stuffy."

Anywhere was better than that room, than hearing the creaks of the floorboards and wondering if those were Mark's stockinged feet out there in the hall. The phone vibrated in her hand and Emma checked the screen to see a calendar alert for her mother's birthday. "Son of a bitch," she said.

"What?"

"I forgot Mom's birthday."

"No, you didn't." Quinn returned to the conversation on his side of the ocean, then laughed abruptly before resuming theirs. "I figured it would

be hard to remember with your lecture this afternoon, so I sent her flowers. Calla lilies, I think. With a note. Dutiful daughter stuff that hopefully
passes for you."

"Seriously?" Emma's throat thickened, her temples throbbed, and the
scene around her grew blurry.

"Yeah, seriously. You've been so busy getting ready, I figured you'd forget.
Wait, do calla lilies have some message or meaning? Like how yellow roses
mean 'screw off, let's just be friends'? I never can remember that stuff."

At the corner, the smaller child, a girl, stepped into the street while
the mother was busy checking her phone. A car honked and her brother
yanked her back to safety by the straps of her backpack, making the girl
squeal and earning the boy a swat to the back of his head.

"Was that ok? Should I have gotten tulips or daisies or something?"

Emma sniffled and said, "it's great." She took a deep breath, but it shuddered through her, the staccato rhythm of new guilt. "I just can't believe
you remembered. It's so . . . so . . ." Thoughtful, was what she would have
said if she hadn't started crying in earnest.

Ahead, the little girl turned, startled by the sound of adult weeping.
The brother looked too, but he quickly turned back, nudging his sister
to do the same. The mother shepherded them down a smaller street
where a coven of tiny, uniformed humans massed before the gate of a
churchyard-cum-school.

"Em, babe, what's wrong?"

"Nothing!" she started, but before she knew what she was saying, she
told Quinn all about Mark and Wanda, and how she'd seen Wanda coming
out of his room – though she had to do a fair bit of spontaneous revision
to claim she was merely on her way to the bath – and ended with, "can you
even believe it? With Wanda?"

"Why not?"

Emma stopped mid-stride. She balanced on her foot as a whir of
answers befuddled her brain. It was not until a car honked for the third or
fourth time that she realized she'd stopped mid-intersection. With a wave
and a hop, she moved out of the way. "Why not? Because she's gross! And
loud and garish and . . . and . . . not his type at all."

Quinn chuckled. "Sounds like she was enough his type last night. Besides, you said he and Nora broke up. Good for him. Go get him some."

"You're missing the point entirely!"

"So what is the point?" There was a pause. A breath. "Why do you care anyway?"

Emma blanched. "I don't! I mean, he can sleep with whoever he wants." Words swirled in and out of her grasp as she weighed these two sentences. The first was an outright lie, while the second was literally true, and yet a deceit of a different nature. Staring into a shop window displaying an array of British-themed souvenirs, she caught her reflection in the mirror, her stained dress mosaicked with Union Jack paraphernalia, herself so out of her element in this place, stuck in the muck of these words.

"Oh, hey, Em, gotta go. The guys in the ambulance bay are having a cornhole tournament."

Emma hung up in the middle of Quinn's "love you!" She trudged the rest of the way to the Caffè Nero and waited in line behind a short man clearly also on his way to the festival, dressed in a blue cut-away coat, fawn skin breeches, and black knee-high boots, who ordered enough coffee for a small army and nearly spilled it on Emma when he moved toward the sugar and creamer stand. Behind her, a kid with a mohawk rocked arhythmically to the music blasting in his ears, the scratchy decktape on his skateboard snagging her gown.

She ran into Harold waiting for the walking tour, the first event of the morning, and when his cautious attempts at conversation revealed he too knew – had in fact, allowed that woman the use of his en suite – Emma found herself going off on another rant. But she found as sympathetic an ear with Harold as she had with Quinn. What did you expect, love? Harold had said. Man doth not live by bread alone.

Just as the day before, Emma found it impossible to pay attention to anything other than the pulses of thought and image flashing through her mind. As opposed to the day before, though, her inattention was marred by jealousy and anger, rather than hopeful, if nervous, anticipation. As they turned down the Gravel Walk, she fumed. As they strolled up to 1 Royal Crescent, she nearly turned apoplectic when the museum guide had a shock of red hair sticking out from her bonnet. Finally, Emma excused herself and made her way to St. Swithin's, a hopefully quiet and cavernous space where she could rest and hide until her lecture later that afternoon.

In the bathroom, she held a wet paper towel to the back of her neck, trying to ward off the migraine threatening to bloom. She reviewed her notes, doubted everything she had planned to say, and spent a good twenty minutes in a bathroom stall, waiting to see if she was going to throw up after all or just continue to dry heave.

Image after image pounded her. Mark's hands. Wanda's bra – hot pink or leopard print? Garish and tasteless, whatever it was. Wanda's skirt hiked up. Bouncing from wall to wall to bed. Rocking hips. At that one, Emma lost the multiple pastries she'd horked down earlier and felt both better and worse.

Emma avoided eye contact as she wove through the line of women waiting for the loo, and returned to an empty pew, debating whether she'd be asked to leave if she lay down. Another sweating rage fell upon her. She fanned herself with her schedule and held her arms out, cursing her deodorant for its impotence in the face of this particular crisis. Black dress approved? Sure. Catch your fantasy-world boyfriend in a walk-of-shame even though you have a fiancé back home who remembers to send your mother flowers on her birthday when you forgot? Not so great for that.

Emma clutched her knees to her chest as a chill ran through her. A breeze from a side door swept her skirts round her ankles, bringing with it bright-eyed festival goers attending the panel on Austen adaptations in the café. Even more unwelcome than their happy faces was the question she had been trying to avoid like an annoying mosquito buzzing around her ear – and how do you figure Mark deceived *you*? Hypocritical or not, she simply expected more from Mark than to be bedding someone like Wanda.

Now, her attraction was laced with contempt. Because if Wanda had made it to a finish line Emma herself had only reached in her fantasies, what did that make Emma? She was a silver medalist, glaring up at a woman who should have never even qualified for the games.

Emma pulled out her schedule, seeking any distraction. Glancing at the morning sessions and her map, she realized the Austen adaptation panel was actually being held in a coffee shop near the cathedral square and she would have to book it if she was going to make it in time.

As she neared the Pump Room, she saw Mark, dressed in his costume, the wide brim of his round-crowned hat clutched in his hands. By his furtive darting looks, Emma knew he was looking for her. Well, let him look. Emma abandoned the adaptation panel and turned toward the bridge. Air was what she needed. The breeze. The sound of the river below, the traffic behind her. The crush of other bodies. Of any body except Mark's.

But as she half-ran, half-stumbled, she heard Mark calling her name. How she wished this might actually be 1800. If it were, he would not – could not – chase her through town. The protocols of that era would forbid him even considering such a thing, and he would have to wait for some other opportunity for a private discussion, which she could have avoided in any number of ways. But not in this world, where they were but playactors in this game of imitation, like children romping round the barn at Steventon, putting on productions for the delight of the indulgent Papa Austen, the hypercritical Mama. In this world, it was entirely possible she might lay all the inscrutabilities of her heart out before him like one of these street vendors displaying cheap wares on a woven blanket on the sidewalk. She reached the overlook railing and glanced back to see Mark wading through a sea of tourists in their tightly packed group, a neon flag leading them like pilgrims.

Ahead, the Pulteney Bridge opened before her, the best avenue of escape. Made of the same pale stone as the rest of Bath, it had the distinction of being one of the few bridges in the world that not only spanned a river, but did so with a wall of shops along both sides. If you were only paying attention to shop windows, you could find yourself across the river Avon without even knowing how. The shops on the bridge had dutifully arrayed their Austenalia on the sidewalk, trying to catch the eyes of festival attendees and general tourists alike, most of whom were just trying to get across the river and on to whatever awaited them on the other side.

Emma ran onto the bridge and ducked into the first open door she could find, a café and gift shop halfway down the bridge with its door propped open with a little cement bust of Jane, a promise of safe haven.

The menu board offered Austen-inspired lunch fare: a Mary Bennet Veggie Melt and Henry Crawford's Naughty Meat Pie and Captain Wentworth's Salmon Quiche.

Once inside, Emma realized it was not nearly as large as she had hoped and was but a narrow strip of space, cluttered with tables, and a small corner at the back screened by shelves arrayed with tchotchkes and souvenirs. It was to this corner she escaped, back near the windows overlooking the river. From her position behind a bookmark stand, Emma watched Mark stride past. Here she was, Anne Elliot, observing Captain Wentworth pass, and feeling all the same ambivalence of that moment, willing him to enter, praying he would not. And then Mark was past the shop and beyond Emma's sight.

With a sigh of relief and despair, Emma turned to the river-facing windows and dropped her bag to the floor. Framed by white-painted iron sills, the windows were hinged at the ceiling, opening outward at a dangerously low height. Presumably for safety reasons, they had all been sealed shut. All but the one at the furthest end, whose lock had broken off. She opened this one as surreptitiously as possible, ignoring the note taped to the glass which said, "Caution. Low Sill. Do not open window's." If the sign couldn't punctuate itself properly, she reasoned, she didn't have to abide by it. She leaned out and took a deep breath of the earthy breeze rising from the water.

"Emma," Mark said, as if her name were a question.

Emma's shoulders tightened, then fell loose, the sinews of her body losing the will to hold herself together. They were on dangerous ground, she could feel, which made her mouth twitch into a half-smile since they were not on any ground at all. Below, the river rushed between the arches of the bridge, the water as opaque to her as the yearnings of her heart, reflecting a blue sky and clouds that wavered, rippled apart, and reformed again and again.

"You must be lost, Mark. Wanda's back at the festival."

"I'm sorry," he said. His hand gripped her arm and gave a slight tug to turn her around but then gave up, though his fingers remained, five burning points of contact like embers on her skin. "I should have . . ." His voice trailed away. She did not have to look at him to know he had shrugged. Her body could feel it. She realized what a stupid thing it was for him to be sorry.

"Don't be." She wrenched her arm from his grip. "You don't owe me anything." Her words seethed, but it was her eyes, she knew, that stabbed. He tried to hold her gaze, but withered under its fierceness, under the judgment not only for his actions, but also for whom he'd committed them with.

There was a display of glass flowers made to look like a Regency nosegay, the sort of thing a lady would hold as an accessory at a ball, just one more thing to tie her hands with. He thrust one in her hand. "There. Is this what you want? Take them!" He shook his head. "No," he spat, "flowers from a man like me. Too simple. Well, I can't give you a ring like that, Emma." His voice trailed away, lost to anger. Just lost. "I just thought . . . That maybe finally . . . Because you know that I . . . that if there's anyone I could . . ."

Emma turned back to the window. It was too much. Here it was, this moment she'd thought about so many times, when finally they would put honest words behind their silly infatuation and flirtation. But it was too late. And it was all her fault.

The cathedral bells began to chime the noon cadence.

"No," Emma said, "don't." She took a step back. There was nowhere to go in the close space of this shop, but she felt herself sinking below her own surface. Mark's hand was again trying to pull her back, his voice imploring her to listen. A feeling rose within her – the desperation she'd felt over the past decade, that desire for all the normalcy she thought she wanted: marriage, family, successful career. But also, stability, safety, security. She'd glommed onto it at the first possible chance and sunk her hook into Quinn, only to find he slipped in and out of her grasp like a beautiful fish, constantly in motion, impossible to contain. Whatever expectations she'd had were like the fishing poles her father kept in the shed, the reels just a tangle of hopes that could not be unravelled.

And here was Mark, who had presented her with an alternative that seemed just as impossible, forever out of reach, kept away by the limits of distance and geography, by their ping-ponging in and out of other relationships. It was all too much! How could she hold all this in one space? In one moment of time?

And there was Mark's hand, tight on her arm, and she couldn't stand it anymore. The nearness of him, so terribly painful. The thing she wanted most and least in the world.

She fought the tears about to break forth. Looking beyond Mark, out the windows over the river and to the embankment, Emma saw it. Saw her. That poof of red hair, then Wanda's face swiveling back and forth, and knew that here came Wanda, looking for Mark.

With the veriest dramatic action she could imagine, her most Isabella Thorpish moment, Emma wrenched her arm away. The momentum spun her right over the thin iron sill of the window, out of the café, and into the Avon. And Mark, trying to catch her, tumbled out right alongside.

In the moment between her feet leaving the bridge and her body entering the water – the merest hint of time, what could only have been a second, perhaps two – an infinity stretched before her. Into that span, Emma felt the world disconnect, found herself back in those moments when she had likewise stood on the verge of shifting her existence somehow: the afternoon she followed Jackie Larson and two other It girls into the bathroom after poor Martha Hardwicke. That night in the back of Tyler Hammond's car. And suddenly – unaccountably – the moment Quinn slipped the ring onto her finger. All moments when she had felt the world loosen, had felt her place in it detach, and understood that things would forever look differently to her after, a little darker, a little more dreary, a little more . . . less. As if the walls of possibility, of who she might become in the world, had closed a little more tightly around her.

And then Mark's hand found hers. His fingers interlaced with her own, and a flair of hope burst through as they hit the water.

CHAPTER 5

Emma sputtered and gasped. A strong hand grabbed her arm and drug her onto the grassy slope beside the river. Sitting up, Emma used the hem of her gown to wipe her face. The air around her rang with the final clang of the cathedral bell. It took Emma a minute more of coughing and drawing breath to remember fully what had happened, but when she did, she leapt to her feet.

"Mark? Mark!" She spun around, smack into Mark and both fell back into the muddy streamside.

"Here, Em," he said, rubbing his head.

"Oi," said a man's voice, "you all right?"

Emma found a small crowd gathered round them. The man who'd spoken helped them back to their feet. He was dressed in brown wool pants, a brown jacket over his dirty shirt, and a misshapen hat tilted back on his dusty forehead. Near him sat a handcart full of flowers which were broadcasting a dizzying array of aromas that only minimally competed with the man's own smell. She'd heard the festival directors and city commission were trying to give Bath more of an authentic air for the festival week, but seriously, the odor rising from his body could not possibly be necessary for accuracy's sake. In fact, a wave of new smells hit her, some of which she could place – wood smoke, horse dung – and others which she could not. Regardless, all combined into one general olfactory impression – grossness.

"Give 'em air. Air, I tell's you!" the man shouted to the throng pressing in.

The crowd nearby, also in period clothes, took a few steps back. The women tittered behind handkerchiefs and fans, and looking down, Emma saw that where she'd thought dry muslin was revealing, wet muslin was exponentially worse. She tried, in vain, to cover herself with her hands and only succeeded in drawing more attention to the exact body parts she was attempting to conceal. Another man stepped forward with his young son and offered his coat to Emma, kindly averting his gaze. Again, he was in full kit in a pair of tight black pants, a flair-sleeved shirt, black vest, and a gentleman's top hat.

"Thanks," she said and slid the coat on quickly. "You from the festival?"

"Excuse me, miss, you are mistaken," he said, in a tone that caught Emma as haughtier than necessary. "There may perhaps be a market this day. In another part of town." He kept himself busy with his young son to give his eyes something else to look at. "If you'll allow, it would be my pleasure to escort you back to your lodgings. Or perhaps . . . a doctor's residence?"

"No, I – ," Emma looked to Mark, who was staring open-mouthed at the scene around them.

The crowd began to disperse, trickling up the grassy slope to the streets beyond. Two women, however, remained standing toward the back under the shade of a large tree. There was something about them, something familiar that tugged at Emma, though of course in a place like Bath, during a week like the festival, those women were as likely to have come from South Wales as South Africa for all she knew. But she found her eye drawn to them.

Suddenly, a horse whinnied and Emma let out a yelp, startling the helpful man and his son. The space around them cleared of curious onlookers, Emma took in the sights of horses and carriages, men pushing handcarts, and women in maids' costumes passing by on the streets above. The clamor of the wheels and hooves on cobblestone overwhelmed her.

Mark moved to her side, his hand at her elbow. "Emma, I don't think this is the festival."

"It must be," she replied. "Or some movie? Why the city would grant filming permits during the festival is beyond me. Cheap extras, I'll bet."

"Yes, but Emma, look around." Mark took Emma's shoulders and spun her in a slow rotation. It was horses and carriages everywhere. It was muslin dresses and bonnets, breeches and coats. A faint clatter staccattoed over the top of it all, and Emma's eyes finally found the source – wooden pattens of the kind Emma had only seen in museums strapped to the feet of a pair of women trudging along a muck-filled street. But not a pair of jeans in sight. Nor tank tops, nor sunglasses, nor cellphones.

The man who'd offered his coat stepped forward again. "I beg your pardon, sir. I did not mean to offend yourself or your wife."

"Wife? Hardly." Emma snorted and jerked out of Mark's hands, the ire of the gesture in perfect proportion to just how oppositely she felt about the prospect.

The man stepped back, eyes wide, mouth open.

The two women still stood watching them. The taller one, with fairer hair, waved a fan in front of her face, flashing it closed to gesture in their direction, then opening it again.

She seemed to be imploring her companion to stay. Emma found her feet drawn toward them. Just as she came within hearing range, the mud glopped onto the bottom of her shoes required her to bend down to scrape them clean, but she kept the corner of her eye cut their way. She knew them, she must. She just needed another moment to place them.

"But Jenny, look!" The fairer one nodded expressively in their direction. "Wouldn't this make an excellent story? Or a scene?" She pulled a little square of paper from her pocket and tried to exchange it for the package in the other woman's arms. The brown-haired woman did not resist, but rather than taking the paper and pencil, she plucked a tall flower growing at the base of the tree and batted it against her leg. The other woman tapped the paper on her friend's arm, nearly dropping her package. "Come on. Man and woman dragged from river? There's got to be something there."

"You write it then, Cass." She smacked the flower against the tree, showering the grass with sad little petals, and turned to leave.

"Jen, honestly," the other woman said, looking from her companion's retreating back to Emma and Mark, her tone now bordering on irritation.

Jenny. Cassie. The tug in Emma's brain tightened. She spun again, her feet plodding in a circle, her legs shifting shakily. Bath was Bath, and yet she began to take in the minuscule differences – the lack of streetlights and electricity poles. The clatter of hooves and cart wheels – not a car in sight or hearing. The streets and sidewalks – all cobblestones and dirt paths, not a traffic sign anywhere. And the two women observing them, like two good friends met unexpectedly in a foreign city. She found herself staring into Mark's face, his confused and alarmed expression inviting her to recognize the impossible that surrounded them. Jenny and Cassie. Jane and Cassandra. Once more, the recognition in her brain grabbed hold and pulled, and Emma toppled back onto the grass in a dead faint.

CHAPTER 6

Emma woke in a darkened room. Her hand grazed the rough horse-hair of the sofa on which she lay. Between her temples, the blood pulsed and throbbed, but she sat up despite the protest of pain and took in the room around her. Though at first it seemed to be a small parlor, a desk haphazardly strewn with papers and the wall of books told her it was someone's office. A fire burned low, mostly embers, behind the grate. On the wall opposite were two rather small landscapes, one of a hilly, rural scene, the spire of a church poking up from the crest of a hill. The other a seaside sketch of high cliffs rising from a beach. Testing her legs, Emma rose and moved to gaze at the landscapes more closely. She did not hear the door open and close.

"Not very good, I admit," said a woman's voice. "My sister is considered the artist of the family. Hers are truly worth close examination."

Emma turned to find the sad-looking, darker-haired woman from the grassy riverside standing just inside the door. Again, familiarity rose within her like a smell that harkens back to near-forgotten memory. There was something in the other woman's small, thin mouth, high cheekbones, and keen, observant eyes. Something about her gaze, the way she looked at Emma sidelong, a penetration that drew a sheen of sweat. And something else in the tilt at the corners of her mouth. Despite the veil of melancholy hanging over her features, Emma saw a face alert to the prospect of a good joke.

She touched a corner of the frame. "Sidmouth," she said. "In Devon. I would call it delightful, but . . ." She turned from the sketch and placed a hand at Emma's elbow to lead her back to the sofa, then opened the door to a hall lit brightly with afternoon sun. "Dr. Bowen?" she called. "Miss Woods is awake now." The woman turned and was about to close the door when Emma let out a brief noise and raised a hand. "Of course. How rude of me. A stranger chatting away at you. Miss Austen," she said as she pulled the door closed. "Miss Jane Austen."

Emma sank back onto the sofa, her breath pouring out in a disbelieving torrent.

Good Lord. She'd gone completely crazy.

Emma stood and paced, reflecting on the various diagnoses she might assign herself and came to the only reasonable conclusion – she was having a psychotic break.

It was rather fortunate that she and Quinn had been on-again during his psychiatric rotation. He had a patient who, though otherwise normal, suddenly became convinced she was Cleopatra after learning her husband was divorcing her. Well, if significant emotional or physical traumas could cause such a thing, then Emma fit that bill. If she hadn't seen Mark that morning with Wanda, she wouldn't have been avoiding him at the festival. She wouldn't have run into that café or hidden by the window. And she certainly wouldn't have been the seething wreck she'd been all day – angry, hurt, disappointed, and confused. Fine then – she hoped Mark was happy, shivering and muddy, wherever the real Mark was.

The door opened again and an elderly man entered carrying a large leather bag that gaped at its brass hinges when he set it on the floor. He wore tight black breeches ending inside a pair of white socks and black shoes. With his cut-away coat and round girth, he gave a compelling imitation of an over-dressed bullfrog. The fairer-haired woman followed behind. Emma laughed when she saw her. The woman exchanged a look with the doctor.

She stepped forward and gave a brief curtsey. "Miss Woods? I'm-,"

"Cassandra Austen, right? Of course you are."

A look of affront passed over her face, but then she took a position behind a chair near the fire. The older man sat on the edge of the sofa. He gently pushed Emma's shoulders to guide her into a prone position.

"I've asked Miss Austen to chaperone the exam, Miss Woods." He took her wrist and held it delicately in his fingers, almost as if he preferred not to touch her at all. "Twas a nasty fall you had from the bridge. How are you feeling now?" His fingers palpated her temples. She closed her eyes. He lay a cool, wet towel over them. The weight on the sofa shifted as he rose.

"Well, I've got one hell of a headache," Emma said.

Cassandra let out a shocked breath audible from across the room, followed by a muttered, "good heavens!"

"I'm sure you meant to say that your head aches as though pounded by the devil," came another man's voice. A younger man. "Perhaps a course of leeches to the temples? What say you, Dr. Bowen?"

"Leeches?" Emma leapt to her feet, the rag still across her eyes. Before she could jerk it free, she bumped into someone standing just beside the sofa. Pulling the rag away, she found herself being eased back onto the couch by another man, younger, with a mop of curly red hair.

Quinn?" she said, "how did you get here?" She reached for his face, cupping his jaw in her hand.

"There, there," the young man said, gently removing her hands. He cleared his throat and gave an embarrassed chuckle.

No, it was not Quinn, but he was of the same age, with the same hapless red hair, the same athlete's build. They could have been brothers, he and Quinn, but where Quinn was loud and take-charge, this man was softer, gentler. Her gaze fell on the most innocuous thing about him – his hands, the nails trimmed neatly, not jagged and bitten like Quinn's; these were the hands of a gentleman. Inexplicably, she imagined those hands traipsing along her spine. And with that, an embarrassed bark of laughter once more plunked into the otherwise silent, sedate room.

"Dr. Lethbridge," he said, introducing himself. "Dr. Bowen here has been so kind as to let me practice with him while I establish myself in Bath."

"And a fine doctor he is, too," Dr. Bowen said from his position next to Cassandra. "Now, Miss Woods, let's see if we can't ease the aching of your head." From his bag, he withdrew a little vial. "Without leeches."

Cassandra handed him a small glass full of something dark and red, retrieved from a little cabinet by the window. Into this, he shook out a few drops and gestured for Emma to drink it in one go. Emma put it to her lips and drank the concoction, then coughed against the sickly sweet syrupy-ness of it. Port, she realized, just like she had tasted her first year at the festival. It had been the day after Nora left and, freed, Mark had helped Emma get mightily drunk until they were both giggling so uncontrollably, they'd been escorted out by a young but matronly festival warden, who had lectured them severely and circularly, always returning to the same point: that Jane Austen herself would never have tolerated such impertinent behavior. From that moment, they dubbed her Miss Bates and still broke into giggles when one or the other should mention that name or say, with a shrill, trembling tone, "impudent drunks. The impertinence!"

There was a rap at the door. Jane appeared again, this time followed by Mark. "Mr. Landen was concerned for the patient, Dr. Bowen."

Dr. Lethbridge rose, picking up a cane with an ivory cat's head on the grip. He stood next to Dr. Bowen, who tugged at his coat to settle it over his belly. "Miss Woods may receive visitors. I see no lasting harm done."

"Ms.," Emma said.

"Excuse me?" Dr. Bowen turned, his froggy face furrowing.

"Ms. Woods," she repeated. "I'm a bit old for Miss, don't you think?"

Dr. Bowen looked from Emma to Cassandra to the other doctor. His mouth opened and closed, and any second, she expected his tongue to dart out as if he could catch her meaning like a fly buzzing just out of his grasp.

Emma flapped a hand. "Oh nevermind."

Leaving, he shared a glance with Cassandra which Emma could not mistake. No harm to her body, his raised brow and crumpled forehead indicated, but as to her mind? Hmmmm.

Cassandra followed the doctors into the hall where Jane loitered as well, leaving the door open. Mark drew Emma up from the couch and led her to the fire, trying for as much distance as he could from the open door. He was still wet, hair mussed and face dappled with mud. He held his hands out to the embers, rubbing them together as his sleeves dripped on the carpet.

"How are you?"

Emma laughed. "Oh me? I'm fine. I've gone completely crazy and apparently some version of you is also necessary in this fictitious world my brain has concocted, so that's fun for me. Where's Wanda? We can't carry off this charade without her."

Mark gawked, then ran his hand over his face. "Crazy? Fictitious?" He took her by the shoulders. "Emma, this is . . . real. We're really here. I mean, how else would I be here?"

"The brain is an amazing thing, Mark. Quinn's always saying it can – ." Her words trailed away as she caught sight of Dr. Lethbridge just beyond the door. Mark's face clouded at Quinn's name, a scarlet stain spreading from under his collar and over his cheeks.

He reached out and pinched her. She drew back and stifled a yelp. "What the hell, Mark?"

"I'm telling you: This. Is. Real." He glanced at the door and leaned in. "And what's worse is that you're not the only one who thinks you've gone crazy. Those doctors are out there right now debating whether to put you in the mad house."

"So?"

"So – if they do, how will we fix this? Get back to our real time? Look, you've got to play along. You know, be Emma Woodhouse. Or something like it."

Emma considered this. Frankly, she was disturbed to recognize her own psychosis – that wasn't normal. With that patient of Quinn's, the family all agreed to indulge the delusion until they came home to find the woman cradling a garter snake, the little gold tassels of her headband swinging as she spoke a gibberishy imitation of Coptic Egyptian. When the snake bit, the surprise of it knocked her right out of her delusion, and she stood up, wondering when she'd gotten that atrocious bob and bangs.

As though to contribute its own two cents to their discussion, the dwindling fire popped. An orange ember landed on the top of Emma's foot, right where her ballet flats left a large oval of tender exposed skin. She nearly screamed with the pain, but surprise stole her voice. Mark was quick to bend and flick it back into the grate, but not before a deep red welt appeared, and the throbbing of it buckled Emma's knees. It was no snake, but surely that should have been enough to knock her out of whatever catatonia she believed her real self was locked in. She clasped the sleeves of Mark's jacket, squeezing more drops of grainy river water onto the carpet.

"Oh my god, Mark," she whispered. "What are we going to –?"

A slight "ahem" drew their attention. Mark's hand at her elbow helped Emma remain erect as she fought back tears, as much from the pain of the burn as the realization of what she'd done – where she'd taken them. Cassandra stood just inside the doorway, Jane at her shoulder.

And seeing her idol standing there, Emma's heart soared.

"Mr. Landen," Cassandra said. "The doctors are leaving. They offered to escort you to the parish offices."

Mark nodded, his own face pale with clouds of apprehension. To Emma's questioning gaze, he gave her the firmest look he could make, pulled her clenched hands from his sleeves, and set them gently but firmly at her sides. It reminded her of one morning long ago when her father was leaving for work and Emma dreaded the thought of another long day at home with her mother. He had pulled her hands off his collar and held them at her sides, squeezing her wrists hard enough to prevent her from reaching for him again, ever again.

Emma began to follow Mark. "Surely I should go too. I mean, where will I stay?"

At this, Dr. Lethbridge's face appeared in the doorway once more. "With a trauma to the head, Miss Woods, we are both in agreement that you must be watched over, and" – he cleared his throat – "as no purse or reticule was found about your person . . ."

Emma patted the pockets hidden in the folds of her gown, lifting her hands palms up. While an array of things lay inside, there were none she could bring out to show. What money she had would not be recognizable here. And everything else was in her bag back at the café over the bridge. No money. Nowhere to go. A shiver in anticipation of the night ahead with only thin muslin between herself and the cold swept through her.

Jane stepped forward. "We shall keep her under close observation, Dr. Lethbridge. Have no fears."

Once again, hearing her speak, watching her move, Emma could barely contain the shriek of delight ratcheting through her.

Dr. Lethbridge nodded, and the three gentlemen made their bows, Mark's a beat behind the other two, then all swept out the front door.

Emma took Jane's extended hand and followed her, trying to hide her limp, into the hall, now orange with the waning light of late afternoon. "Miss Woods, we understand from Mr. Landen that you were to meet an uncle here in Bath?"

"My uncle?" Emma said, "my uncle, my uncle." She repeated those words over and over, half statement, half question, until she realized how this must sound. So Mark had concocted the start of a story for her, some sub- terfuge to make her appearance in Bath seem normal. "Yes, he was to meet me at the . . . he was to meet my . . ." Emma's thoughts spun out before her, but the connections between point A and B became a limp trail of nothing that slid out of her hands and into the ether.

It didn't help to be standing in front of a very earnest-looking Jane Austen, her own begrimed hand still cradled in Jane's warm one.

"Your coach?" Jane supplied. "Were you perhaps meant to wait here for your uncle or to change coaches and then travel on to his home?"

"Yes, my coach," Emma said. "His home? Umm, that is to say . . . I don't know where he lives . . . I mean, my uncle resides here." She stopped and pulled at the sleeves of her dress, trying to buy time. If her uncle lived in Bath, then she should be able to go right to his lodgings, and that was obvi- ously not possible. "That is, he's coming here. For the season. But he's still in London."

"Perhaps we ought to send you to London and you may travel back when he is ready?" Cassandra said. She glanced at an upright clock in the hall- way. "I believe the mail coach leaves in a half hour. Surely, the driver will ensure your safety." She moved toward the front door as though ready to shoo this unwanted stray back onto the street. "Or there is the road wagon if you find passage on the coach too dear."

"Well, thanks," said Emma. "But no, because . . . he is coming . . . to Bath. He was supposed to be here, but I received word at the last . . . um, coaching inn, you know the one in Radstock?" Both women nodded. "Yes, well there was a note saying his departure had been delayed."

Jane nodded along helpfully, though her brows furrowed at Emma's pauses. "Because he needs to stay through the Michaelmas sessions?"

Emma shook her head, shrugged, then nodded, as confused by the contradictions of her gestures as the two women watching her must be.

Cassandra, as forbidding as a statue, stood with her arms crossed. "Well, which is it?"

She'd have to cast her story and quick or lose any assistance from these two at all. Finally, an idea materialized out of the mist and she grabbed onto it, threading the words into her mouth before she realized what she was saying. "That is to say, I've been staying the past few weeks, uh, fortnight, with a schoolfellow. I was meant to stay with them until my uncle arrived in Bath and sent for me. But then, last night, her father woke us and sent me to meet the dawn post. I don't . . . I don't know what I did to offend him. But he sent me away, and as I was to come live with my uncle here anyway, I . . ."

Cassandra's eyebrows shot up as each compounding unlikelihood fell from Emma's mouth. She let out a bark of half-laughter, half-snort.

"That's absolutely riveting," Jane said, making Cassandra's jaw drop even further. "And so this father of your acquaintance. He just threw you out? Middle of the night?" She began to lead Emma up the stairs, Cassandra following behind.

Emma nodded obliquely. The truth of what she was saying finally crested the horizon of her confusion. She was feeding Jane the plot of *Northanger Abbey*! But Jane's face appeared vibrant and interested, not suspicious or accusatory.

As they rose, Jane explained which rooms were on the middle floor, but Emma was trying to figure out how much of a blunder she had really made. If Jane and Cassandra were living in Bath, then it was sometime between the years 1801 and 1806. By the looks of the house, the Austen women had not yet descended to renting rooms, so it must be the early part of their years here and *Northanger Abbey* remained, as yet, unrevised in some trunk. She had to hope to God she might be safe.

Jane patted Emma's hand with finality. "You shall remain here with us until your uncle's arrival."

Cassandra drew a breath. Jane turned and smiled down at her sister on the landing below. "Surely sister, we cannot send a respectable young lady onto the streets of Bath at dusk. What would your uncle say if he arrived to find you come upon the town?" Jane winked, the veil of sadness parting for a moment.

"But Jane . . . er, Miss Austen," Emma said, glancing from one sister to the other. "I couldn't possibly impose."

Cassandra, hands on her hips, nodded. "Charles will return soon, Jane. And then we are off to Godmersham. Surely Miss Woods would be more comfortable somewhere else."

"Nonsense," Jane said, rather crossly. Then a smile of triumph lit on her face. "You've found the perfect solution yourself, dear sister. She shall have Charles' room." Jane continued to pull Emma behind her, her pace a little harried as they rose another flight of stairs to a third level. "Our brother Charles Austen, Miss Woods. He is currently discharged from his duties as a lieutenant, but has returned home to visit our eldest brother. He won't arrive here for another fortnight, I am sure." She led Emma to the top of the landing, where they turned down the hall and into a room Jane identified as Charles'.

"If you'll excuse me," Jane said and practically ran back out through the door.

Emma took in the room. It was simple and spare. A fireplace sat black and empty against one wall and opposite that, the bed. Across from the door, a pair of sashed windows looked out on the back of the houses, and though the light was dim, Emma could make out the little walled courtyards of this house and the ones behind. If her guesses were correct, then this was 4 Sydney Place, and if the biography she'd been reading was likewise accurate, then these homes were built for show: beautiful facades facing the street, but no money left to put toward smarting-up the backs. Too true, she saw, as a maid in the house beyond opened the back door and threw a bucket of soupy brown water into the yard. Emma turned away, pulling a set of heavy curtains across the panes. Even with their heft, a draft ruffled the thick fabric.

Having taken in the room, Emma turned to the closed door. When Jane did not reappear after another moment, she got fidgety. Curious, she peeked out to find Jane leaning against the wall in the hallway, frantically scribbling notes on a scrap of paper. Cassandra passed by, acting as if she did not notice her sister, but the furrow in her brow lifted into a more hopeful and happier expression before she turned into the one other door further down the hall. Jane stuffed the pages into her pocket, and Emma eased the door closed and quickly resumed her position by the fireplace.

As Jane entered, a crack of thunder broke through the silence, startling them both. Jane took in Emma's gown, shaking her head. It was nearly dry, though very likely ruined with mud stains. With a finger held up, Jane exited once again, and in the short span of time she was gone, Emma emptied the contents of her pockets and shoved them under a corner of the mattress.

Jane returned with a gown draped over one arm, a petticoat and chemise clutched in the other. "We are about the same size, and these are fresh laundered," she said, handing Emma the underclothes. She shook out the gown and placed it over a screen folded up against the wall. "This will be appropriate for dinner," Jane said. "And I'll ring Sarah to see if anything can be done about this one."

Emma went behind the small screen to change. At her inmost layer, she gazed down at her bra, panties, and satin slip – none of which would make any sense to Jane. When Jane moved to the door and called out into the hallway, Emma hastily shed her undergarments and shoved them behind the curtain, jammed between the heavy drapes and the pane of glass, hoping no one on the outside caught the flash of a frantic, naked woman in an upstairs window.

Moments later, the door opened. Unable to see who had arrived, Emma heard Jane asking the maid if she might wash their guest's clothing. Jane's hand appeared around the side of the screen and Emma placed her dress into it, realizing that the lack of a petticoat might be just as confounding as her own underwear would be. But there was nothing to be done but listen to the maid's exclamation of "Lord have mercy!" and the closing of the door. The maid gone, Jane made a noise that could have been a snort of amusement or a huff of scorn.

"Your sister does not seem to approve of my staying here," Emma said.

"Oh her. Nevermind that. She thinks anyone in unusual situations might be a highway robber in disguise." She let out a huff and Emma tried to hurry but could not figure out which was the front or back of the petticoat. "It's a bit tiresome," Jane said in a grumpy voice.

"It's rather gothic, if you ask me."

Jane let out a chortle. "Don't let her hear you say such a thing. She's the least romantic person I know."

Emma came out from behind the screen and stood in the middle of the room, smoothing her skirts. Jane nodded curtly, then led Emma to the chair. Balancing a basin in her arms, she pushed Emma's hair into the water, using a small pitcher to rinse out as much river water as she could. Then, she began to work, rather brusquely, at the tangles with a wooden comb. She pulled Emma's hair all together and let it flow out of her hands. "Absolutely beautiful," she said. "How do you ever get your hair so full and soft?"

"You mean after the mud soak?" She took a lock from the front and examined the tips. "Well, I usually use a coconut oil conditioner. But the real clencher is the hot oil treatments. They really –," she stopped at Jane's puzzled look. "I mean, the luck of birth?" she finished lamely.

Emma blushed remembering how she'd made the salon appointment mere seconds after accepting Quinn's request to meet her at the park. He just wanted to talk, his text read, and she just wanted to slay him, to watch him flail and stutter and beg, while she tossed her smooth, silky mane, erupted into her best femme fatale cackle, and strode off, alone, into the sunset. And what she ended up with instead was a trial engagement to a trial fiance and a not-really-hers ring which, as a daily reminder of just who had slain who, tended to snag the little hairs on her temple when she pushed loose strands behind her ears.

The ring! Emma grabbed at her hand and found the band still there, the diamond tucked into her palm, all speckled and gritty with mud. It had gone unnoticed so far, and Emma slipped the band off her finger and held it tight in her fist.

Jane continued to comb and stroke her hair.

"So, um, Cassandra . . . I mean, Miss Austen. Maybe she doesn't like me because I'm American?"

Jane let out another chortle that fell between mirthful and grumpy at the same time. "Well, you are from that former colony we're still smarting over," Jane said, her mouth full of hair pins. "I wondered whether the doctor might not slip you a little something in your tonic. A patriotic, poisonous draught." She cackled. "Now that would be delightfully gothic."

Emma flinched as Jane began twisting her hair up on top of her head.

"So you were thrown over by this good friend of yours. And now you're come to Bath to . . .?"

Emma gazed stupidly at her own reflection, willing some story to form itself by the time she opened her mouth. "Well, my parents are . . . dead. And my only relation is this uncle. So I've come to . . . uh, to keep house for him."

"And this uncle, he is a . . . Mr. Woods?"

Emma's mind skipped over the possibilities. London businessman? No, potentially too far below their social sphere. Attorney? Same problem. Baronet? Someone might check the royal lists. Emma's mind stumbled onto a title, the words falling from her mouth before thinking. "Admiral Woods, actually." Her face flushed scarlet. It was ridiculous to worry whether anyone had a Navy list, because of course Jane would, probably one within reach right here in Charles' own room.

But her attention was drawn from the misstep of the moment to the face looking back in the mirror. Emma turned her head one way, then the other, admiring the halo of golden hair surrounding her face, the loose tendrils pulled out here and there by Jane's expert fingers, and the flush upon her cheeks, which in the candlelight made her look bright and intrepid. "He's been in the East Indies," she supplied. Then, remembering Henrietta Musgrove's excited confusion over Captain Wentworth's own status, Emma added, "and he's returned to England . . . or paid off . . . or something." She hoped that would be enough to discourage any curious researchers, though her own academic knowledge could not confirm whether his name would still appear in a Navy list or not.

"Ahh yes, well Bath is just the place for Naval officers. Charles adores Bath and was quite downcast to leave." Jane sighed and her face clouded.

"Rather a busy place, I find," Emma offered, to which Jane nodded. In this young woman's pained mien, she saw the distaste that would be reflected in a future Austen heroine, who would also be removed to Bath with little choice or inclination. For Emma's part, the story she'd woven also required the arrival of a naval man to rescue her, but at least for Anne Elliot, her officer was not the construct of a moment. Whereas Captain Wentworth would make his eventual reappearance to sweep Anne up and away from this place, Emma's uncle was but a mirage keeping the bars of the madhouse at bay.

A crack of thunder sliced the air, and Emma jumped again.

"Odd," remarked Jane, glancing toward the window. "Thunder at this time of year? Strange, indeed."

Jane moved to the door. "I'll leave you to finish your toilette," she said, nodding to a door on the opposite side of the mantle.

Emma nodded as if she knew what Jane could be referring to. Once Jane had pulled the door closed, Emma opened the one beside the fireplace. There sat a little wooden chair, but where a seat cushion should have been, a ceramic bowl rested in an oval hollow. It was her bladder which finally clarified what this odd-looking chair was for, and Emma could not have been more relieved.

CHAPTER 7

Emma followed the murmur of voices to a drawing room on the level below and was admitted by a tall, middle-aged footman. "Thank you," she said, ending on a note of question, desiring to know his name.

The surprise of being addressed gave way to an introduction. "Isaac, mum," he replied and swept a hand into the drawing room, a gesture almost as forceful had he pushed her in by the shoulders.

There, she was introduced to Jane's parents. Emma curtseyed, sending a silent thanks to last year's workshop on etiquette where she had learned as many of the graces of a Regency lady as could be absorbed in a faint two hours.

"So," Mr. Austen boomed, "we've a revolutionary in our midst." He eased himself up and led Emma to the settee, gesturing a place next to Mrs. Austen, whose aquiline nose deserved every bit of pride she was said to have felt for it. However, the boldness of that feature also emphasized the puckered lips over her lost teeth. From her, Emma received a measured once-over and cold nod.

Jane smiled, though, and Emma felt encouraged. "Have no fear, sir. I've always said I was born on the wrong continent." This was the truest thing she'd said all day, and the relief of it felt like stepping through the curtain of a waterfall.

"Do not be alarmed, Papa," Jane said, arranging a pillow behind Mr. Austen's back. "Miss Woods is all for king and country."

Emma nodded, though she wasn't fully sure what Jane had said. Emma was so distracted just watching Jane, she often realized she missed her words.

"A true patriot then," Mr. Austen said. "I imagine it must have been quite difficult for your parents. We hear such chilling tales of how loyal subjects were treated after the war's conclusion."

Cassandra leaned toward Jane. "Oh yes, such as our dear friend Alicia Johnson."

The family bestowed warm smiles on Jane, who flushed slightly, an arch look awakening her downcast demeanor. "Oh yes, poor Mrs. Johnson. But she made a very advantageous marriage and escaped. Or so she thought."

Just as Emma was about to speak, she realized she was supposed to be on the outside of an inside joke. Rather than joining in with a quip from Lady Susan, she pretended to be very interested in the pattern of the upholstery.

Jane flapped her hands. "Let us not bore our guest with talk of people whom she does not know."

The door opened and the footman appeared again. "Mr. Landen," he announced.

Emma rose as Jane leaned toward her. "My father felt you may be more comfortable if a friendly face were at the table."

Emma had little time to compose herself before Mark was through the door. He made a proper bow, and in return Emma bobbed in synchrony with Jane and Cassandra. Jane caught her eye and Emma glimpsed the hint of a twinkle in her gaze, the edge of her lips curling. And Emma also noticed Cassandra perceiving this as well, something like surprise shifting her features momentarily.

Again, Mr. Austen lumbered to his feet to meet the new guest. "Mr. Landen," he exclaimed. "It appears my daughters will be bringing home

every gentleman and lady who find themselves tumbled into the river!"
He stood long enough to make his bow, then sat.

This time, Cassandra was there to adjust her father's pillow. "Now, Papa, you wouldn't want us to leave two poor souls bedraggled on the riverside." For the first time, Cassandra gave Emma what might pass for a friendly glare, and Emma was thankful to Jane who must have either teased or grumped her sister into a speck of cordiality.

Mr. Austen patted his daughter's hand and invited Mark to sit across from him. "Mr. Landen, we understand you are to take over the parish of Walcot for Mr. Sibley."

Mrs. Austen sat forward. "Indeed? We hear our Mr. Sibley is not getting on well at all. But I had understood another clergyman was already coming to St. Swithin's. A Mr. Baynes, I believe."

"Indeed, mum," Mark said. "The nature of Mr. Sibley's illness is, I gather, more urgent than had first been believed and the curate you mention was not able to come so soon. I am myself not, uh, presently attached to any particular, erm, . . ."

"Parish?" Jane supplied.

Mark nodded and swallowed, his face reddening. He turned to Emma, his composure returning as the blush faded from his cheeks. "And how do you do, Miss Woods? You are, I hope, recovered from our encounter with the river?" He turned to the group at large. "This is not my first visit to Bath, but it was my first experience of the river at so close an angle."

Jane and Cassandra laughed, and the conversation veered off into other stories of various mishaps the Austens had endured around town, with Mark as equal a contributor as any with his own revised versions of stories with which he had regaled Emma. The near head-on collision between Mark's compact and a semi-truck seamlessly rewove itself into a narrative about his donkey cart and a mail coach, leaving the Austens thoroughly entertained.

Emma was speechless. Mark played his part nearly without error. His tone remained dulcet and reserved; his facial expressions smooth as a mirrored lake; and his body reflected a calm ease as he perched on the edge of the seat, his posture formal yet relaxed, one leg forward, showing off his

slim, muscular calves in his tight stockings. All his mannerisms and movements were just as they should be, an Austen hero brought to life before
her eyes.

Another massive peal of thunder broke Emma from this reverie. She
found Mr. Austen standing before her, arm held out, and the rest of the
room observing her with concern.

"Miss Woods?" he said, clearly for the third or even fourth time.

"My apologies, sir." Emma rose and took his arm. Behind her, she felt
Mark's presence as he offered Mrs. Austen his arm. Emma caught the whispered breath of Jane speaking to Cassandra from the back of the procession, and realized with a gentle tug at her arm, that she had slowed her pace,
straining to catch any word that might fall from her idol's lips as they made
their way downstairs and into the dining room.

Emma moved to the long side of the table opposite the door, and found
Mark taking the seat beside her, a choice which drew another amused
simper from Jane, who stood at the place on Mark's other side.

Cassandra seemed about to debate the propriety of the seating arrangement, but just as she began to suggest Mark should move next to her
mother, Jane broke into another smirky grin, and Cassandra let it go, taking
that open seat instead. Of course, Emma realized, unmarried men did not
usually sit next to unmarried women. Not, at least, when they could sit
across from them and next to someone who was.

But propriety could be damned. She needed to be next to Mark.

And Mr. Austen merrily held forth at the head of the table, waiting
until all had been seated to lower into his own chair, his wife to his left.
Mrs. Austen managed her husband and the table with a nearly imperceptible method – a touch on the arm here, a slight nod of the head there
– thus ensuring guests were attended to while her husband appeared
master of all.

The first course passed, all eyes turned to Emma, and she realized they
were waiting for her to begin the conversation. She looked to the room
for inspiration. A familiar book title? None. An interesting painting? The
only one in the room was a portrait of a red-haired woman in mid-1700s
style dress – a disgustingly accurate Wanda replica, and she was not going

to bring *that* subject up. In truth, it was a simple room, a room for dining and not much else, with a mahogany table and chairs and a matching sideboard. Finally, the silence became so heavy she had to say something.

"You have a delightful room here, Mrs. Austen," Emma said. "It's very . . . um, delightful?"

Across from Emma, Cassandra's fork hit the rim of her plate with a sharp ting, and a faint puff erupted from Jane. Was it laughter or a sulky sigh? Emma's neck burned with the knowledge that she was either amusing Jane with her insipid conversation or boring her out of her mind.

With welcome charity, Mrs. Austen nodded and gave the appearance, at least, of observing the room anew. "It is rather delightful, isn't it? Not too small, but not too large to be drafty and chill. I've always considered the wall coverings a bit dark for my taste, and only half the windows open, but such is one's lot when one must rely on the industry of others to make improvements." She dipped her spoon into her soup. "Yes, yes, I must agree. We certainly saw much worse when we came a-hunting."

Yes, indeed, Emma thought. Appreciate it now for the time will come when you've just a parlor and two bedrooms to call your own. Aloud, she said, "You know, I always enjoy having visitors. I see my home fresh through the eyes of others. And I come to appreciate what I've got rather than thinking over what I haven't."

This was, in fact, the subject of those troublesome essays Emma had been trying to form into something of a collection, essays that swung between her experience of home – which had always been rather nomadic, hopping from one boyfriend's apartment to the next from the moment she'd escaped her mother's house – and ruminations on what Jane's experience of home must have been like, moving as she had from a large rectory to ever smaller lodgings, landing finally in the little cottage that would be her oasis in the world. Where, Emma wondered, would her own refuge be? Her eyes brushed Mark's face and returned to her plate.

Murmurs of assent came from around the room but the topic was left unpursued. Once again, Emma rifled through her mind's filing cabinets, searching for anything to discuss. She had not yet even placed herself in time, not specifically, and what she needed to discover was just exactly where she might be and how bad of a gaffe her earlier reference to *Northanger Abbey* actually was.

The only idea that arose was to get Jane to talk about the one thing Jane Austen did not talk about.

She waved her fork around, trying to appear as off-handed and cavalier as possible. "I have heard Bath boasts many authors." She popped the bite of roast beef in her mouth and chewed slowly. "Have any of you happened to meet anyone who writes?" She tried to land her gaze equally on all parties.

Beside her, Mark coughed, grasping his goblet of wine and drinking deeply.

At the head of the table, Mr. Austen dabbed his mouth. "I may perhaps know one or two," he said with a twinkle Emma was surely not intended to understand.

Emma looked from Jane to Cassandra. "Neither of you? Ahh well. It must be such a daunting and exciting thing," she said. "To be a writer. To put one's ideas down on paper. To create characters and exciting adventures." Once more, a wave of the fork. "You know, all that jazz."

"All that . . . what?" said Mrs. Austen.

"What an odd question, Miss Woods," Cassandra said, taking a bite and chewing stiffly. "What would ever make you think of such a thing?"

Emma let out an awkward chuckle. "Oh well, you know, it's just that . . . I have . . . uh . . . dabbled a bit myself. But though I may finish a draft, I can never quite see my way toward perfecting it." Once more, she gazed about, seeing how her words might land.

Jane's face was turned to her plate, her fork pushing a slice of onion through the soupy gravy leaking from the beef. The other Austens alternated between nodding along and stealing glances at Jane's face.

"That is, you know," she persisted, still trying to sound as casual as possible, "I've heard many young ladies pen little novels to pass the time. Miss Austen?" She took a bolstering swig from her own wine glass. "Or Miss Jane perhaps? Has the writing bug bit either of you?"

And then Mark's boot came down on her slippered foot. Holding her napkin to her mouth to stifle her yelp, she chuckled. "Well, nevermind. I'm sure writing letters to your brothers is all the creative outlet you need."

Mark eased beside her and Cassandra darted a look at Jane.

"Indeed it is," Cassandra said. "Letters from home are particularly important in times of war." Cassandra leaned forward, her eyes narrowed once again. "Though it sounds as though you have no need for writing to active naval men since your uncle – the admiral, is it? – has retired. Quite unlike our Navy to release a man of such rank when the peace is still in its infancy." She tapped the edge of her spoon on her plate. "Very odd indeed."

The room fell silent. Emma fumbled for an answer, throwing out a string of barely audible and completely nonsensical words.

"There is such an art to letter writing," Mark said, saving her. "Though for men, we are so much taken up in letters of business that we have little time for letters of pleasure."

Emma shot him a grateful smile and snatched at the rescue line dangling before her. "Letters of business. How odious I should think them!"

Mark caught the volley and sent it back across the net. A point for Darcy, a point for Miss Bingley. "It is fortunate, then, that they fall to my lot instead of yours." With a wink to her, Mark directed his conversation to Mr. Austen. "Eh, Mr. Austen? It must be a fortunate thing to be finished with the business of business letters. And how are you enjoying your much-deserved rest?"

The conversation between the two men carried forward as Mr. Austen held forth on the parishes of Steventon and Deane, details Mark probably could have recited as accurately – or more – as the man himself. This left Emma the chance to recline in her chair and take a deep breath. With Mark sitting forward, Emma glanced behind him and caught Jane hunched in her seat, scribbling away with a pencil on a scrap of paper in her lap. Across the table, Cassandra gave the slightest of encouraging smiles. When Cassandra's eyes met her own, Emma darted her glance away. She wished to neither betray her knowledge of Jane's writing, nor bring Cassandra's keen scrutiny upon herself more than absolutely necessary.

Just as she began to pick up the flow of conversation between Mark and the elder Austens, a great clap of thunder shook the panes of the windows and rain swiftly followed, beating upon the glass like a barrage of tiny pebbles.

The storm attempted to make itself as much a member of the conversation as any fire of Mr. Musgrove's might do while Jane and Cassandra debated as to the last time they had heard such a fierce thundershower, quizzing one another as to the chances of flood in the kitchens, and Mr. and Mrs. Austen pondered whether this rain would affect the harvest James had written about. Between the other conversations and the storm beyond the walls, Emma and Mark found a modicum of privacy.

"St. Swithin's?" she asked.

Emma watched his hand trembling as he stabbed a boiled potato.

"Christ, Emma," he whispered. "What am I going to do? They want me to give a sermon on Sunday!"

Emma reached for Mark's hand, but quickly drew back, pretending to be plucking a bit of lint from the table. "Couldn't you just read something? Someone around here has to have a Fordyce's."

Mark dabbed at his hairline with the corner of his handkerchief then scoffed at his utter discomposure. "Suggested that. You'd have thought I had proposed reading from the Kama Sutra, the looks they gave me."

"And the Church of the Forest didn't offer guidance in sermon-making? Tsk, tsk, a serious lapse in curriculum." Emma was rewarded with the hint of a smile and continued. "Well, you've done plenty of weddings with the old prayer book. I mean . . . that is, this one. Whatever."

Mark's face brightened. "Of course! What a dunce." Mark handed his plate to the footman with a steadier hand. "I can put something passable together from that, can't I? A dose of Psalms and collects to intersperse with my 'be good to one another's' here and 'love thy neighbors' there, right?"

Emma nodded, then jumped as another thunder-strike cracked through their conversation. Mark withdrew the hand he was about to place on her arm for reassurance.

As the footman gathered dishes from the table, Mark continued speaking in low tones. "But let's hope Sunday doesn't matter. Have you thought about how to . . . get back?"

"Back?" Emma turned a quizzical look at Mark. "Back where?"

This time, it was Mark who blanched. "Home," he said as if it were the most obvious thing. "Back to our," his voice dropped to a nearly imperceptible level, "time."

"Oh," Emma said. "Home."

Between Cassandra's suspicious questions, Emma's sudden imbecility regarding everything that mattered in this world, and being in such close proximity to Jane herself, Emma had not spent a single second thinking of home.

In fact, now that she did, only one thought came to mind: that she *was* home. And more than that: the question was not, how do we get back but, how do we *stay*?

One look at Mark's face told her that convincing him would be the first order of business.

"Well," she said, "unless you happened to see a De Lorian-shaped carriage on your walk over, I'm not sure there is a way back." She dabbed her napkin to her lips and tried to affect a woe-is-us expression.

Mark gave her the same gape-mouthed stare as when she'd said they were stuck in her psychotic hallucination. "You can't be serious." He looked at her deeply, then gave a chuckle as though to convince himself it was just a joke. "So here's my thought," he plowed on, "we fell into the river and wound up . . . back then. I mean, right now. So maybe, all we have to do is jump in the river to get . . . back to now. That is, back to . . . then." He shrugged weakly.

"But Mark, we were lucky we didn't break our necks." Emma averted her eyes, remembering that if any shoulders ought to bear the weight of broken necks, they were her own. She glanced at Mark. His frown said thoughts of a similar nature were swimming behind his eyes. His face passed from angry reminiscence and quickly into compassion. His hand lifted as though to take her own, but his fingers rounded toward the palm at the last minute and came to rest beside his napkin again.

How she longed for his touch. Just to feel his hand curl around hers was all the forgiveness she needed. And Mark seemed willing to offer it, his eyes having to do all the work of enfolding her as his hands might otherwise have done.

How different this was from Quinn! Quinn who would hold onto any little mis-step, any tiny bump to his emotional chrysalis, and hunch over it, cradle it like a sullen child over a broken toy. Quinn, who would go silent for hours, even days, long after she'd offered her apologies, even when they'd both known the blame should be firmly chalked to his account.

And yet, here was Mark, offering forgiveness simply because he knew her to be sorry.

"Well," Emma said. She could see he didn't consider staying a reasonable option, and in truth, she wasn't sure what she meant by it either, only that going back seemed as fraught with uncertainty as staying right where they were. What she needed was time. Time to compose a plan. Time to work out how to convince him of it. "There's too much to discuss now. Let's meet tomorrow morning. Should I come to your place?"

Emma hadn't noticed the quietness of the table. All the Austens stared at Emma and Mark. Mr. Austen's mouth hung agape, and his wife coughed over mis-swallowed wine. Cassandra's brows were so furrowed, they looked about to cross in the middle. And Jane gazed from Emma to her parents and back again, her own expression alternating between alarm and amusement.

She leant forward and, with a quickness that was quickly becoming a necessity, said, "Miss Woods, we find that attending the Pump Room in the mornings is often the best opportunity to meet new acquaintance. And to, erm, visit with old ones."

"Indeed!" said Cassandra.

"Of course," Emma said. She stared at her plate, wondering if her complexion was going to be anything other than wild crimson.

Mark jumped in. "I shall happily attend both the Miss Austens and Miss Woods at the Pump Room. Tomorrow morning."

Jane nodded and tossed a wink toward Emma.

Emma couldn't decide which to worry about first – Cassandra's ever deepening distrust, or what she herself was intending to do about Mark's question.

A heavily sweating woman entered, heaving a large silver platter onto the table.

At the head of the table, Mr. Austen rose and clasped his hands in anticipation. "Well, well, let us see what delights Baxter has prepared."

Mrs. Austen lifted the lid. On the platter, a mound of little cakes rose like a pyramid. The pale yellow cakes were dotted with darker spots, what looked to be small berries or raisins. The smell that rose from the platter was both savory and sweet, a sugary cloud followed by an undercurrent reminiscent of meat.

"Spotted dick!" Mark looked like a boy who'd found a toy at the bottom of his cereal box.

"Spotted . . . what?" Mrs. Austen asked.

The cook had remained at the open door, her eyes now darting from the elder Austens to Mark and back again.

"Thank you, Baxter," Jane said. "Your puddings are a delight, as ever."

"Puddings," Mark repeated. "Yes, forgive me. Where I am from, we call them . . . Nevermind."

Emma threw Mark as commiserating a glance as she could manage without bursting into guffaws. He may as well have declared it a platter piled with poxy penises for all the indignation Baxter huffed on her way out. Poor man, he'd often exclaimed over the spotted dick desserts his mother had made when he was a child, one of the few indulgences she'd managed to afford on her slim single-parent's budget.

After dinner, Mr. Austen led the procession back up to the drawing room. Jane made tea and Cassandra passed it round. The conversation once more skidded to a halt, and Emma glanced at the various Austen faces, catching hints in their demeanors of some doubt as to the invitation they had made to these two very strange people.

With a gulp, Mark broke into the uncomfortable silence. "Mrs. Austen," he said, "I noticed your pleasure on hearing about my temporary posting to St. Swithin's Church. I hoped you might tell me more about the parishioners. Erm, what kinds of sermons they like? Perhaps quite short ones?"

Mrs. Austen sat forward, her hands coming together in a small clap to punctuate her excitement. "Oh, Mr. Landen! You have struck on a topic that cannot help but give pleasure to the two of us in particular. Mr. Austen and I were wed at St. Swithin's in '64. And do you know, it was April and a fine April we had that year too." She ran a finger over the hook of her nose as she settled into reverie. "You see, it was my uncle who introduced us in the year . . ."

"Yes, yes, I know," Mark said with impatience.

Had there been a table to hide them, Emma would have given a kick to equal his earlier stomp, but as they were, she settled for glaring at him over the rim of her teacup.

"That is to say," he stammered, "I am aware that St. Swithin's has performed many marriages in its day."

"Yes, indeed," Mrs. Austen continued, though deflated. "Perhaps the details of such things bore young persons. Do forgive me."

Mark blushed his shame. "No, it is I to be forgiven. I am happy to hear anything at all you wish to tell me. Stories of happy love matches are truly a favorite." For the briefest of moments, Mark's eyes flicked to Emma's and away again.

With such an invitation as this, Mr. and Mrs. Austen took over the conversation, correcting one another on the finer details as to how they met at Oxford, their introduction by Mrs. Austen's uncle to his favorite pupil, their courtship, and their eventual nuptials at St. Swithin's.

They reminded Emma of Lorna and Deb, playfully duking it out over who had picked up whom at the divey lesbian bar in York. No, Deb would say, laughing and holding up a hand to silence Lorna, I came to you on the dance floor. Don't you remember how I beckoned you over? And she would demonstrate her little "come hither" finger wave that looked like a John Travolta Saturday Night Fever move. Lorna was ever quick to slap those waggling fingers and claim that if it hadn't been for her "come hither" eyes, they'd never have bumped bums on that dancefloor. Emma hid a smile behind her teacup, imagining Mr. and Mrs. Austen "bumping bums" in a ballroom.

Meanwhile, Jane and Cassandra shared the amused, if doleful, looks of daughters who have heard the stories thousands of times. The information was not new to either herself or Mark, but he nodded along, showing surprise at the appropriate moments, while Emma let herself drift off into her own mind. Over and over again, she circled back to what the flick of Mark's eyes might mean, so very like that look he had given her in the restaurant just before Wanda shrilly shattered the crystal glass Emma had poured her secret hopes in. Was Mark thinking of himself and Emma or Emma and Quinn? Could the term "love match" be applied to either since she was so clearly ambivalent about both?

Coming back to the surface, she found Mark making his farewells.

Having pumped the Austens for as much information as he could about the parish – and evidently receiving little to allay his panic as he once more had his handkerchief against his brow – Mark excused himself for the evening. Emma rose and would have walked Mark to the street, but he turned at the drawing room door, kissed her hand, and said, "I will see you tomorrow, Miss Woods," in such a tone that said she should return to the sofa. She resumed her seat, one palm cupped around the back of her other hand, where Mark's lips left a souvenir whose meaning continued to elude her. Then an image raced into her mind, of Mark's lips on Wanda's hand, on her neck, her ear, her . . . Her head shook – her body shook – and she found herself on her feet.

"My apologies," Emma said. "My headache is returning." She made a circuit of the room and came upon a small table set against the wall on which sat a bottle of wine and an array of small glasses. She began to reach for the decanter, then drew back once more as though Cassandra's irritated huffs had become attached to Emma's limbs.

Jane came to her, shooting a little wink. She poured Emma a small glass of sherry and one for everyone else. "For medicinal purposes, of course," Jane said. The others smiled and sipped their sherry, but the glances passed between Mrs. Austen and her husband, the slight shake of Cassandra's head, told Emma she'd once more violated their code.

When the clock struck midnight and Emma struggled to hide her yawns, the maid returned and passed out small candles. The girl was splotchy-eyed as if she'd only just mopped her tears on the other side of the door.

Emma put a hand on her arm. "Are you ok?"

If Emma hadn't still been holding her little goblet of sherry, the shocked look on the maid's face might have made her wonder if she'd slapped the girl instead of spoken.

"Thank you, Sarah," Cassandra said. "That will be all."

And with that, the girl spun on her heel and was out the door, a fresh round of sobs slipping under the jamb as her footsteps receded.

Jane held Emma's candle for her, lighting it from the flame of her own. Speaking as much to Emma as to the others, she said, "it will be a true cultural exchange, having you stay with us, Miss Woods. We see already some very . . . interesting differences."

Interesting indeed. In the course of one evening, Emma had been entirely absentminded, carried her side conversation like a dolt, invited herself alone to a single man's residence, helped herself to a glass of someone else's wine, and conversed with their maid as though she were an equal (which she was, Emma was quick to remind herself, though perhaps it was a point not to be tried just now).

Emma coughed. "Oh yes, well, I suppose we Americans are a bit less refined."

"We have met Americans before, Miss Woods," said Cassandra. "And their manners were not so much different than our own. It did not seem a question of refinement *with them.*"

Emma tried to laugh it off. "Yes, well, too true. The opportunities to learn, I am sure, will all be mine."

At least this was something Cassandra was unlikely to dispute.

At the top of the landing, Emma returned to Charles' room, watching Cassandra and Jane enter their own, flashing with jealousy when Cassandra said something that made Jane laugh.

Closing the door and taking in the small, simple room once more, Emma knew no terrors such as the ones Jane would concoct for Catherine Morland at Northanger Abbey awaited her here, though the storm outside continued to shake the windowpanes and propelled the curtains into a ghostly dance. The bed was simple and small with no heavy drapes to draw closed around a trembling body. No Japan cabinet or mysteriously creaky trunk occupied a shadowy corner. The room's only furnishing other than the screen she'd changed behind a few hours ago was a simple dressing table, which did not even have a single locking drawer.

But there was a shift of footsteps from the hall beyond and the lilt of murmuring voices. Opening her door just enough, Emma peered out to find Cassandra with the maid. She caught a snip of their conversation, of Cassandra saying, "have no fear, Sarah. I'm certain they'll find him." Cassandra gave the girl a hasty hug and returned to her own room.

Closing the door, Emma turned to the little dressing table once again, determined to sit and parse out just what she meant by staying. How she would ever convince Mark to stay too. And what it meant for them both, for them as a "them."

But then a booming peal of thunder shook the windows and sent a little tremor of fright through Emma. She was no Catherine Morland, but she would not feel ashamed of getting into bed as soon as possible. And hiding under the sheets until the storm passed. She could fabricate a plan just as well in bed. At least for the thirty seconds until sleep drew her down deep below its surface and she fell into a heavy, dreamless slumber.

CHAPTER 8

Emma woke early and stepped to the windows. Below, the streets remained damp and puddled, reflecting the bright blue expanse above the city's skyline. In all her trips to Bath, she had only ever stood out on the sidewalk below and stared up at 4 Sydney Place, pondering what thoughts drifted through Jane's mind as she gazed out from the other side of the windowpanes. And now here she was, on the side of the glass she'd dreamt herself into, having no clue how to get out and no desire to even if she did.

It was peaceful this early in the morning, and yet the air hung with the scent of char, even inside this room, little fingers of smoke dragging nails down the back of her throat. Thin tendrils of smoke rose from the chimneys of the surrounding houses, so many wispy columns holding up the sky, casting a grey patina over all. A city of vapour, shadow, and smoke. As for confusion, Emma seemed to be maintaining that one well enough on her own. On the sidewalk below, a maid threw a bucket of soupy brown water into the street, where it gathered in the gutters, along with a range of other refuse Emma did not let her eyes linger upon.

Before she could forget, Emma rechecked the items she had stuffed under the mattress the night before. Just a wad of bills and a tube of lip gloss, but still, what a shock it would be to see the faces of queens and prime ministers who had not yet been born on a currency that had not yet been invented. One bill in particular, the ten pound note with Jane's face, would be particularly incriminating. With a sigh, for she had planned to take this one home, iron it stiff, and laminate it into a bookmark, Emma knelt before the little fireplace, the embers still glowing. She tossed in a few sticks from the rack nearby and blew until the fire crackled back to life. She placed the bill in the grate and watched as Jane's visage browned and curled and turned to ash.

Her engagement ring was the last thing to hide. It seemed so small against the expanse of her palm, and yet the heaviness of the promise it represented belied its size. She found a good-sized chink in the window-sill and pushed it in, diamond first, leaving the silver band protruding just enough for a fingernail to pry it loose. So long as no one took it in mind to give the windows a deep cleaning, it would remain unnoticed.

Pulling on a muslin dress left the previous evening by Jane or the maid perhaps, Emma tiptoed out into the dusky hall. She heard nothing but the deep rasping snores of Mr. Austen, followed by another pitch of snores nearly as loud, though more feminine. The two octaves of snuffles, wheezes, snorts and snores capered on the early morning air, corporeal music composed in the sacred space between two bodies who have built and lived a life together, an unlikely symphony that rooted deep inside Emma, lodging in a place that both called to and unsettled her.

On a table outside the elder Austens' door sat a newspaper. Emma lifted it, carefully unfolding the front page to minimize crackling. In the corner, she found what she sought. The date: 13 September 1802. The Austens had lived in Bath just over a year, and much of Jane's time so far had been spent in visits to friends and relations and away from this place. Emma turned the paper over and saw an advertisement for a hotel in Sidmouth. A chill chased up her spine, erupting at the base of her neck. Finally, the cause of the veil shadowing Jane's features became clear: within the last year, Jane learned of her young clergyman's death, the man who might have altered history, who might have given Jane a life rich in love and children, but who might also have stolen from the world some of the best-loved characters of all time.

Jane was grieving. It was a grief her family would have known of and honored but which, never having achieved an official engagement, the rest of society would not. Emma kept that knowledge at the mental ready. Being star-struck had so far made Emma a mumbly-bumbly, self-conscious fool; as the effect faded, she would have to be on her guard so as not to bely more than she ought to know. And for heaven's sake, wasn't that *everything*?

From further downstairs, the faint strains of piano music tinkled up, interrupting these ruminations and revelations. Returning the paper to its position, she followed the melody to the drawing room and opened the door unnoticed. Jane sat at the piano, her sleeping attire covered by a linen robe, her hair loose, falling in slender curls over her shoulders and around her face. With her left hand, she tapped out a melody Emma recognized from one of the seminars when she first learned to contradanse. With her right hand, Jane held a thin wooden rod, a cup perched at the top and a ball rhythmically swinging up, landing in the cup, and swinging out again. Jane wasn't even looking, but she caught the ball over and over. One hand at the piano, the other playing cup-and-ball. It had all the appearance of a morning passed in the pleasant serenity of solitude – mornings Emma might have cherished had she not been routinely given the 8 am composition courses which tenured faculty managed to escape.

Yet, something about the scene felt wrong, a missed chord squawked into a caesura. Then, Emma saw it: Jane's pen lay on a crumpled sheet of paper atop the piano, the inkwell open beside it, but the page remained empty, the blank expanse an accusation Emma knew all too well. Jane exchanged the toy for her pen, paused to consider something, jotted a few words, then stabbed the page with irritation, and banged out a string of angry minor chords.

Startled, Emma stepped back, right onto a squeaky floorboard in the hall. Jane stuffed the sheet of paper into her pocket and jerked around. There was no creaky door here to alert Jane to approaching footsteps, and the floorboard seemed rather behindhand to operate as any kind of alert system. Wary of violating Jane's fierce privacy – and any additional consequences such a misstep might bring – Emma pretended to be just entering and fiddled with a ribbon at the neckband of her dress.

"Oh!" Emma said, "I hadn't realized anyone else was awake. I've always been an early riser."

Jane's apprehensive expression faded. One hand hovered protectively over the papers hidden in her pocket. "Of course. You are most welcome to share this early morning with me. The rest of the house may not be awake for some time." Moving to the fireplace, Jane poked the embers and pulled a cord nearby, then took a seat on the settee and gestured for Emma to take the place across.

They sat in silence, Jane observing her for a moment before staring blankly toward the window.

With all the missteps of yesterday streaming on repeat in her mind, Emma would have to tread as lightly as possible across the timeline of all she knew of the Austen family, only a fraction of which was relevant right now. Her best approach was to only touch delicately those topics already introduced. "So, your brother Charles is to come soon?"

Jane nodded and smoothed her skirts.

Emma waited but had to press on when no other information appeared forthcoming. "And . . . you are to then take another trip together?"

Again, a nod.

"To . . . ?"

She wasn't sure which was worse: Cassandra's stinging suspicions or Jane's reticent replies.

When it seemed Jane's attention could not be held, Emma rose and made for the door. "I'll leave you," she said.

"What?" Jane blinked hard and her hand rose to her cheek as though testing for a fever, then drifted down to rest on her throat. "My apologies, Miss Woods. My sister tells me I am terrible company these days." She gestured Emma back to her former seat.

"Well, no wonder," Emma began, remembering the clergyman, before realizing it was a topic on which she could not continue. "That is, by which I mean, uh . . ." And then she too drifted into silence.

"Of what were we speaking?"

"Um, your upcoming trip? I mean, travels?"

"Oh right, to Godmersham, the seat of our brother Edward. We shall stay there through October, then return home. Well, not home, really, but here." Her gaze passed over the room, her face downcast, reflecting once again just how far away true home had become. "I am most truly looking forward to another visit to some very dear friends of ours at the close of the year, though."

Emma ran through her timeline. If this was 1802, then the winter visit was to the . . . "The Biggs at Manydown," she breathed.

Jane's eyes narrowed. "How did you know that?"

Emma's eyes darted round the room, as if a clue might leap from behind a curtain or off a bookshelf. "Umm, yesterday, your sister mentioned the trip with Charles. It was said so quickly, I nearly didn't catch their names. Did I get them right? And there is one sister? Or two." She fought down the blush as the false ignorance fell from her mouth.

"You are a very perceptive listener, Miss Woods," Jane said, as the door opened. "Three sisters actually. Althea and Catherine, and Mrs. Heathcote has just returned home after her husband's death. It is their brother's seat, Harris Bigg-Wither."

"Right," Emma said. "And a pleasant man is he, this Mr. Bigg-Wither?" She looked sidelong at Jane, trying not to appear too fascinated with what should be an innocent question.

Jane waved a hand. "Oh pleasant enough. At least according to my mother." She leaned in, the look of a gossipy schoolgirl parting the veil for the briefest moment. "He is quite tall, which is in his favor, but rather awkward and he has a stammer."

With another wave of her hand, she dismissed all thought of him, turning now to the maid, who had been inching further into view until she finally gained Jane's attention. Sarah bobbed a greeting, though her eyes often turned to the door, likely thinking about whatever task she had left to answer the bell.

"A bit of tea, I think, Sarah," Jane said. A twinkle came to her eyes. "And perhaps something sweet?" She looked at Emma and gave a smile. "You are perhaps still too new in Bath to have had the pleasure of our bakeries."

Sarah bobbed and withdrew, but not before Emma observed on her face the same signs of weeping as before, something Emma would have done herself the night before last, if she hadn't been so drunk as to make anything but sleep possible. A wave of anger and shame at herself welled up, but it passed in the merest of moments. How could she possibly be angry when Jane Austen herself sat on the settee just across from her, making jokes about the man who would receive an acceptance and refusal from her in a meagre 24-hour period?

Jane sighed. "Poor Sarah." She readjusted the robe over her sleeping gown and gazed off in the distance, shaking her head a bit. Then she cast a little look at Emma, and Emma realized Jane was throwing a worm to see whether she might get a bite.

If it brought Jane out of that blank-faced staring, Emma could indulge. "Poor?"

"She has a sister. Maid to a friend of ours, the Brooksides. They live nearby." Jane picked up the wood toy and began rhythmically tossing and catching the ball.

Suddenly, Emma's brain blazed with the term she had been trying to find, and she yelled out "bilbocatch!" to which a startled Jane dropped the cup and ball into the folds of her robe.

"Yes, dear," she said, picking it up again. "Just a silly toy we've kept around." She held out the toy. "Would you like a turn?"

Emma blushed at Jane's tone, as though Emma were a ridiculous child, and of course, she was childlike, blurting out the inanities in her mind. Emma shook her head and bit her lip.

After a moment, Jane continued. "Well, it appears this sister of hers got mixed up with a young man of ill repute. That is, she seems to have found herself . . . She is with . . ." Jane paused, sighed, and rolled her eyes. To Emma, it appeared she would have been perfectly happy to say exactly what she meant.

"Pregnant," Emma finished.

Jane laughed. "So American women are just as free-spoken as we'd been warned about. Well, don't let Cassandra hear you."

"And I take it, the man is – ," but her words were cut off as the door opened and Sarah reappeared with a tray. She set it down and bobbed out the door. Jane poured tea, hovering a delicate screen over each cup. Emma took it gratefully. Her head was already beginning to ache and she seriously doubted the possibility of finding a decent caramel machiatto nearby.

A mound of Lunn Bunns sat on the plate, just exactly like those Emma had enjoyed in years past with Harold, Deb, and Lorna, braving the interminable queues and taking their treats down to the parade grounds to lay in the sun and listen to the burbling Avon. It felt like a lifetime ago. Jane offered Emma one, and took another for herself.

"Absconded," Jane finished, through a large bite. "The parish wardens are on the lookout, but it appears he's left Bath. Was a blacksmith's apprentice, I take it, and he must come back for his wages. So on that, all her hopes rest."

"Well, hopefully they'll nab him," Emma said.

Jane took another bite. "Indeed. Scrumptious, huh?"

"What? Gossip?"

Jane laughed, coughing as bread caught in her throat. "I meant the bread, but yes, that too."

"Oh," Emma said, "right." And she was glad to join Jane in taking a second bun, anything to give her mouth something to do other than open for her foot. A moan escaped as she bit into the soft warm center. They were absolutely delicious, even more so than the ones she'd had at the new shop. "Perhaps Bath isn't so bad after all?"

Jane gave a sidelong look and a playful huff. "Well, it has at least one redeeming quality. More than that, I cannot commit to."

CHAPTER 9

By mid-morning, what felt like an eternity to Emma, who had dressed with a fraction of the care of either Austen sister and had simply thrown her hair into the simplest bun she could manage with a ribbon, they were out the door of 4 Sydney Place, strolling toward the bridge and Pump Room.

Emma did her best to keep her head forward, but her eyes were here, there, everywhere. Each street brought a hundred fresh objects to observe. Post-chaises drawn by high-stepping horses, manes and tails bouncing with each step. The barouche box Mrs. Dashwood loved to boast of for her self-important younger brother. And a range of carts and curricles and hired hacks with horses whose xylophone ribs proclaimed their excessive labor and insufficient food. There were gentlemen and ladies, governesses and schoolgirls, nurses with their infant charges. The doorsteps were swept clean all the way to the street, jobs performed by scullery maids before the rest of the houses' slumbering occupants – who themselves had no duties except to look peacefully beautiful all day – had awoken.

As they reached the near side of the bridge, Jane and Cassandra were drawn to where a crowd had gathered, staring over the wrought iron railing.

"Oh lord," Jane said, "not another one." She bumped Emma with her elbow.

As they approached, Emma caught the comments of the surrounding crowd. Never seen it so high, said one. And, 'bout to breach the banks, that is, said another. Emma heard the river before she could see it, but once she did, her heart dropped into the pit of her bowels. The water had risen up the bankside, swirling in angry tide pools and roaring whitecaps.

"Miss Woods," said Cassandra, placing a hand on Emma's arm, "you're white as your gown."

Emma swallowed and took a step back. She felt faint again, felt that tug of something beyond the curtain of her consciousness.

Jane took one arm and Cassandra the other. "Is it any wonder, Cass? Imagine if Miss Woods had had her tumble today? She'd be little more than a note at the bottom of the newspaper: Lady drowns in raging river. Or, wait, something better." Jane tapped a finger to her chin. "Mysterious disappearance of American heiress. Body of woman dragged from seething froth. Yes, yes, that would do."

Cassandra tsked and gave Emma's arm another bolstering squeeze. "Spare us your melodrama."

Emma smiled gratefully, but her legs wobbled long after they had crossed over the bridge. As they passed the abbey and into the square, Emma was nearly run down by a carriage which veered across with no notice. At the doors of the Roman baths, a footman descended from the rails of the careening carriage to assist two elderly occupants, balancing two bath sheets over one arm and keeping the other at the ready for a misstep along the slick stones. Emma watched them enter the door she herself had passed through so many times.

"They're bathing?" Emma asked. She remembered once, how she had knelt down to touch the water and a tiny, old woman had blown a whistle and shook a finger at her. No touching the waters, you, the docent harped.

Jane laughed her surprise, then hurried them on across the street. "Of course! What did you think one did in Bath?"

Emma smiled at her own stupidity. Hadn't Catherine Morland bathed here with Mrs. Allen? And Mrs. Smith with her rheumatic legs, carried into the warm waters by gossipy Nurse Rook? A thrill ran through her at the prospect of dunking into those warm waters as Jane herself must have done – that is, did do. Even more thrilling, to bathe in them with Jane Austen herself. Terrified prickles at memories of the river were quickly replaced by tingles of anticipation.

Jane led them into the Pump Room.

"Oh my god, it's real," Emma said, before pretending to a coughing fit.

The long room was all white floors and columns, tall potted trees sat along the wall, and a few benches had been placed about the room for the infirm. A string quartet played softly in the arched gallery at one end of the room, sending strains of music floating into the air, dancing off the hats and headdresses of the beautifully-attired gentry surrounding them. What a difference from her tea here the day before – where conversation flagged under the cacophony of clattering spoons and tea cups and plates, the click of cameras, the clatter of heels. With all that cleared away and the space open and cavernous, the general buzz of chit-chat created an atmosphere strangely private in this public space where one came to march and preen, to observe and gossip.

Cassandra approached the counter and lay down coins in exchange for three crystal cups of mineral water. She also produced a small glass bottle, which the attendant filled and returned to her, and which Cassandra then slipped into a hidden pocket in her skirts.

Jane pointed out the guestbook to Emma and the two went to glance through the list of names. Catherine Morland had stood just here with Isabella Thorpe, trying to divine whether Henry Tilney had returned to Bath. Anne Elliot had scoured these pages for the name of Frederick Wentworth, balancing equal measures of hope and dread. And now she, Emma Woods, stood before the book and glanced through the names of new arrivals, names radiating refinement – despite the significant repetition of Elizabeth's and Mary's; John's, James's, and Charles's – all written in the sprawling, elongated script that exuded elegance and taste.

"Hmmm," Jane said, "No Admiral Woods, I'm afraid."

"No? Oh dear. Perhaps he is . . . that is, what if? . . ." But before Emma had to fathom any plausible scenario to complete her question, a liveried footman strode through the room, calling, "Miss Woods. Miss Emma Woods!"

Emma noticed others turning to see who would step forward, and she caught a few words – river, fell in – which confirmed that her escapade had not gone unremarked by the town.

Jane prodded her forward and Emma took the envelope from the footman's silver tray. She recognized the handwriting but could not place it. She turned it over to observe the seal, a simple circle of red wax.

"Well," said Jane. "Aren't you going to open it?"

"Duh. My bad." She blushed under the Austen sisters confused looks. "That is . . . what I meant to say was . . . Oh, nevermind." She took the ivory-handled letter opener from the footman and sliced through the wax seal. A bill and some coins were tucked inside.

My dear niece, it began. Forgive my tardiness. Business in London has kept me over longer than expected, but I shall certainly reach you within a fortnight. I have forwarded a note and some coin to Mr. Landen to secure lodgings for you until I am arrived. Here is some pin money. My deepest regrets. Admiral W.

In the signing of the name, the M and L of Admiral were larger than the other letters. Clever Mark. Emma tucked it into the reticule Jane had lent her.

"He is arrived?" Cassandra asked, offering Jane and Emma their cups.

Emma took a sip and shuddered against the hot rotten-egg taste of the Sulphur water believed to be a panacea against all the ills of the humours. She gulped and held a hand to her lips, wondering how she would ever finish this glass without losing her breakfast. "Yes, er, no, I mean. He is still delayed, but he sent a note to Mark – uh, Mr. Landen to assist in securing lodgings." She offered the letter to the other two in hopes of proving the authenticity of this fabricated uncle.

Jane let out a little bark of laughter and turned toward Cassandra to share a shocked look. "Do they let young ladies go off to live by themselves in America, Miss Woods? Because it certainly won't do here in Bath. Are you sure your uncle's a full admiral, for he's showing a surprising tendency toward vice."

Jane laughed at her own pun, then threw back her cup of mineral water as though taking a shot of tequila. Emma had the sudden image of herself and Jane decked out in slinky black dresses, drunkenly stumbling from one bar to the next, a rather surprising, if fitting, daydream for this woman who had always been so ahead of the times that confined her. "You'll continue with us."

Cassandra looked askance, but even she couldn't argue with that reasoning. Emma guessed she was considering it, only to decide the only thing worse than having an American stray in their house was kicking her out to go live by herself. "At least until Charles arrives," she conceded.

Jane directed Emma's eyes across the room. "And there's your Mr. Landen."

"With new acquaintance, it seems," Cassandra added.

Mark stood within a circle of young ladies, two soldiers, and a gentleman noticeably older than the rest. Emma and the Austen sisters approached their group, and on seeing them, Mark opened space in the circle to greet her.

"Miss Emma Woods, please allow me to introduce . . ." And he began the rounds of introductions. The older gentleman was a Mr. Werthing, a frequent visitor of Bath with an estate in Dorset. The taller soldier was a Captain Richards, a young man of about 30, with a tendency to laugh a little too easily and much too loudly. His companion, by comparison, a Lieutenant Listle, was a short man, rather round, who seemed determined to balance his friend's mirth with adamant sobriety. The gentlemen all bowed handsomely at the ladies.

"And this is Miss Meyrick, whose father has taken me in," Mark finished.

Miss Meyrick bobbed quickly, her face young and bright, sweet and enthusiastic.

"And we cannot leave out Miss Brookside," Jane said, directing her words to a woman who stood next to Mr. Werthing, facing resolutely away from them. Jane dipped a curtsey. "A pleasure. And how is your father? We heard Dr. Bowen had been to see you."

Miss Brookside, occupied with trying to appear as little interested in the conversation of her party as possible, turned at the sound of Jane's voice. "Miss Jane. Good morning." She was a tall woman, elegant, but her face remained screwed into an expression of disdain. She appeared to be slightly older than either Jane or Cassandra, but there was something in the way she said "Miss" as though others were to be pitied for the designation, but she herself was not. "Oh, that was nothing. He is off riding with our neighbor. Lord Henry Marchison? You've probably heard of him. Papa is not some gouty septuagenarian after all." She flapped open a fan. "Speaking of which, how is your own dear father?"

Jane stiffened beside Emma. Just as she was about to speak, Emma stepped forward. "The very picture of health," she said.

The conversation lagged momentarily, but Captain Richards needed no help bearing it up. "We hear you are the young lady who took a swim in the Avon yesterday, Miss Woods," he said with a chuckle. "Most come to Bath to swim in the . . . baths!" And he burst into guffaws. He was quite handsome really, and in his smile and winking eyes, landing by turn upon each of the ladies, he seemed very well aware of it himself.

Emma smiled in spite of herself. "No indeed, Captain Richards. I assure you we had no such intention. Mr. Landen and I happened to be gazing over the railing at the same moment and tumbled in simultaneously."

Lieutenant Listle placed a hand to his heart. "In the words of the poet, one must walk 'by the sides of the deep rivers, and the lonely streams.' Not in them." Though his bow was stiff, his eyes, when he smiled, were warm and friendly.

Emma curtseyed in response to this gallantry. Miss Brookside sniffed, and Jane drummed her fingers on her cheek.

"Byron, is it not?"

"Not quite," Emma said. "Wordsworth. We cover him each year in our poetry rotation."

"Indeed," cried Lieutenant Listle. "Good ear, Miss Woods. A poem for every occasion. But what is a 'poetry rotation'?"

"Oh," Emma said. "I teach literature in the fall semester, and after short stories, we move to poetry. My students often groan when we begin but . . ." Mark's stern look put an end to her speech. Miss Brookside looked archly superior while Cassandra appeared confused and Jane rather peeved.

"That is, what I meant was, that I . . . not my students, exactly. But rather . . ." She simply could not conjure a way out of this muddle.

"Oh yes, Miss Woods," Mark said. "I remember you speaking of it in the coach. The literature club you initiated back in America . . .For young ladies? . . . To discuss literature?"

Jane gave a laugh. "Oh, dear me, we have a great appreciation for any such kinds of clubs, do we not, Cassandra. Do not you remember our little play actors' troupe?"

Cassandra gave a self-conscious nod, though the memory drew the edges of her mouth into a smile.

"*Which is the Man* was surely our most shocking foray, was it not?"

"Could have been worse," Mark began.

"Could have been *Lovers' Vows*," Emma finished.

At this, the group laughed heartily, while Cassandra shook her head and Miss Meyrick and her two younger friends looked rather confused.

Jane let out one last chuckle "Yes, yes. I imagine our time might have been better spent had we taken a page from Miss Woods' book and focused instead on the great writing of our age." Once more her finger tapped her chin. "A literature club, eh? Quite the thing for young ladies in a country village. Yes, yes poetry," she rambled. "Or music."

Captain Listle returned to the topic of poetry with alacrity. The group devolved into a discussion of favorite poets, with occasional exclamations as to the worth of one poet over another, and a combined attack upon Miss Meyrick and two other, as yet unintroduced, young ladies who admitted they did not read poetry as a regular practice. Emma said little, though was entreated by both Jane and Captain Listle to state her favorite poet. But Emma could stammer out only a few weak replies. Her cheeks burned with the thought that Jane might even now be brewing an Augusta Elton in the primordial soup of her mind, relegating Emma to the ranks of a supercilious rector's wife and her tedious musical club.

"Ladies," Mark said, "Gentlemen. If you'll excuse us. Miss Woods and I have some business to attend regarding her delayed uncle." With one arm folded behind his back, he extended the other, directing Emma out of the group.

As they began their circle of the room, Emma felt all eyes on them. She especially noted the ladies' eyes on Mark, who seemed oblivious to their stares. He offered his arm, and Emma took it.

"You really saved me back there," she said. "Students? What if they think I'm some governess. Or village school teacher!" She shook her head. "Cassandra is already giving me the side-eye whenever I speak. How long until she decides my station is beneath them and gives me the actual boot!"

"Don't stress it. They seemed to buy the lit club easily enough." He raised a hand as though to clasp the back of her neck and give it a little shake, a pet gesture he'd taken to when she was fretting over some festival faux pas. But as with all his attempts to reach for her, he stopped himself, letting his hand fall and patting the hand laced through his arm instead. "Besides, their father was a teacher. I think you're safe."

"The difference between headmaster of one's own private boarding school and a village schoolmarm is the difference between Sir Lucas and the travelling ragman."

"Good one," Mark said, giving her hand another squeeze.

They walked in silence, both of them taking in the world around them. Mark discreetly swiped at his eyes. Encouraged by Mark's hand squeeze and forgetting all anger or angst, Emma reached up to wipe the trail of a tear from his cheek. When she noticed those standing near them staring, she faked a stretch and yawned loudly, only to realize that in attempting to cover one misstep, she had merely committed another. With a rueful shake of her head, she returned her hand to Mark's arm, her other hand clenching the folds of her dress to keep it from trespassing into the pastures of indecorum again.

No touching, scratching, picking, yawning, or sniffing. Lord give her strength.

"I'm sorry," Mark said, dabbing his cheeks with a handkerchief. "Always been a bit of a blubberer. It's just . . . I can't believe we're here. Look at this, Em. Can you believe it?"

As they reached the top of the room, they stopped again and gazed down the long gallery, past the splendor of the white walls, high ceilings, and beautiful attire of all who milled about. Their gazes settled on Jane, standing demurely at the far end of the room, observing the others with a perceptiveness only Mark and Emma could appreciate as the seeds that would blossom into the best-loved novels on either of their shelves.

Though the conversation did not wilt under the attention of Captain Richards, whose laugh reached them even across this distance, the eyes of the young ladies were frequently drawn toward Mark. The young lady standing next to Miss Meyrick leaned over and whispered something which made Miss Meyrick blush and turn away, then flip her eyes back again.

"Your harem?" Emma said, affecting Wanda's shrill voice. "You certainly don't waste any time."

"Oh for pity's sake, Emma."

Emma's cheeks colored.

The whimsy washed from Mark's face, replaced by an expression heavy with anger and guilt. He looked away and Emma observed his profile, all the things she wanted to say streaming by, coursing past before she could grab hold. Taking the little square of paper from her reticule, she ran a finger over his handwriting. "Your note." She jiggled the coins inside. "And money too?"

Mark's face passed into relief, reflecting his own unwillingness to foray into that murky mirror-world where neither of them would appear to much advantage. "Yes, I thought a note directed here would work. So I've been looking about for rooms for you. It isn't easy, though. No one wants to rent to an unmarried woman. If only we'd thought to start you off as a widow!"

A widow. How often had she looked upon her future as though she were mourning the past?

"But Mark, I can't go spending the wages the parish is giving you. What will you live on?"

"It's not the parish wages," Mark said, waggling the tin from his pocket.

"Not your heirloom pounds! They've been in your family for years." Mark had been preparing for his own event the day they'd fallen into the river, a little table the festival set out for him each year where he talked about how his great-great-great-grandparents had met in a school in Bath and managed, somehow, to put aside this money in a tin. It was found just before their ancestral home was torn down, hidden under a floorboard.

"Generations," he said. "Anyway, we must. I've had to spend some already, so the first sting is past. Besides, you can't live with the Austens indefinitely."

"Well, actually, Jane asked me to stay with them. Insisted, more like. At least until Charles returns and whisks them off to Godmerhsam." She paused, waiting to see if he'd recognize the timeline. "And then in the winter? Manydown?"

Mark's eyebrows rose as understanding broke over him, sharing Emma's expressive nod. He shook his head, forcing himself to stay on task. "That eases things somewhat. Still, you must have some cash." He took her purse and dropped another handful of coins inside.

Emma accepted with a grateful smile, then bobbed a playful curtsey. "No little notebook with which to track my spending? Mrs. Morland would not approve."

Mark looked back and forth as though about to launch into a plot to steal the crown jewels. "Now. About our plan. The river."

"Of course," she said. "The river."

She had in fact put a good portion of time into thinking about how to get Mark to stay. And while it wasn't a perfect plan; it was a start. "It occurred to me that if we fall in that river again, we may go further back in time? I'm sure you've already thought of it, but it's got me worried."

His face went blank and she saw her first arrow had hit its mark. "Go back?" he repeated. "No, I . . . erm . . . that hadn't occurred . . ."

She kept him moving forward. "So I've been wondering about it. What if it's like a one-way passage, or something? What if the current of time travel only goes in reverse." She bobbed a curtsey in response to a woman who had bumped her elbow. "And I don't know about you, but this I can manage. As shittily as I might be doing it now. But 200 years before this? Or 400? Or, Christ, 1000?"

She was getting somewhere. Fear had always been her own greatest motivator; she knew how to wield it well. "We might climb out of a river and into a horde of screaming Gauls."

Mark seemed to tremble under her touch, then shook his head as though to clear it. "Gauls were in France. You're thinking of Celts."

"Fine. Whatever. Celts. Romans. Or maybe just a barren patch of forest and a pack of wolves."

As they neared their group, Emma kept Mark moving with the throng of others taking a turn.

"But Emma, we can't stay here. We have people who care for us. Who must be worried. What about Harold and Lorna and Deb? What about . . . your mother?" Though Emma knew it was not her mother Mark was really thinking of. "Have you thought about them?"

She had. While the initial instinct to stay had broken upon her and been accepted in a flash, reflections of the pain to others lingered. After more deliberation, she arrived at the belief that they had a chance here. Here, where none of the other commitments, the other people, could hold sway. Still, the idea of leaving their friends and family to doubts, fears, and a lifetime of never knowing tore at her.

It reminded her that she was, after all, someone who would cause grief to those she held dearest if only for the sake of easing her own resolutions.

She nodded through it, forced herself to continue on the trajectory she had started. "But if we don't make it home. If we fall further back – shit, if we fall forward – we won't have saved them any pain. Only caused more of our own."

She knew she had to say it. If there was anything that could convince Mark, it was the words she had never yet figured out how to say. "And Mark, if we stayed . . . you and I . . . we . . . we might . . ." It was all she could manage before her own fear took hold and silenced her, but in those halting words, he divined her meaning.

His eyes grew wide. Was that excitement she discerned there? Hope? Then they narrowed.

Just as he opened his mouth to speak, they found themselves finished with their circuit, this time called by name to rejoin their group. Miss Meyrick in particular appeared pleased with their return and lost no time initiating conversation, and Emma was glad to give way, and let the words she'd left like bubbles on Mark's surface sink in.

"Miss Woods," she said, "Miss Jane was telling us about your harrowing experience. How dreadful!"

Emma tilted her head in assent and gave the young woman's outstretched hand a squeeze. "Yes, Miss Meyrick, it was very frightening, but all's well that ends well, right?" She let go of her hand with a kind smile.

Mark piped in next, though his voice still carried a tremble. "Yes, Mr. Meyrick and his daughter have been very kind as to allow me to stay with them this short while as they await the permanent curate, well, which is to say the permanent substitute curate while Mr. Sibley attends to his health. Who, I hope, arrives very, very soon."

He cast a meaningful look at Emma, a look whose meaning remained elusive. Arrive so Mark could jump in the river and flee from here – from her? Or, arrive so Mark and Emma could carry on this charade – together – somewhere else?

"Yes," Cassandra said. "A Mr. Baynes?" Miss Meyrick nodded. "And he has been delayed, is it?"

"No, not quite. He was not meant to arrive for another month, but Mr. Sibley has had an unexpected renewal of his illness. We were quite unsure what we were to do, but as Mr. Landen happened to arrive unattached to any parish at all and Dr. Bowen was impressed with his composure, we find it most convenient to install him as the interim-interim caretaker of the parish. We might have found another hired curate, but you know how those men can be, fractioning their time all over the county so that nothing is ever done right but by half!" As the others laughed, Miss Meyrick blushed, surprising herself as much as the others by her impertinent joke. "At least so my father says."

Emma wanted to be saying something, to distract herself, if not Mark, but she had absolutely no idea what the difference between a rector, a curate, or a hired curate might be, and even less about what their actual duties may entail.

"There are clergymen of many sorts," Jane said, her voice the quietest it had been since they arrived. "They are all of them valuable, are they not?" A cloud passed behind her eyes, as though Jane herself had suddenly travelled away from them, into the mist of memory.

Cassandra moved in front of Jane who had turned away from the group. "Duties of the parish. Yes, we are quite familiar. Pray, what keeps the parish so busy just now, Miss Meyrick?"

Miss Meyrick was on a roll. As she prattled on about meetings with parish wardens and Sunday school, preparing the chancel and more, Mark's face grew paler and paler until he looked like he might throw up in the potted tree behind him.

"There will be Mrs. Smith's funeral this afternoon. Then, we have two christenings tomorrow."

"Oh but surely," Mark said, pulling at his collar, "christenings can wait a little longer. Besides, wouldn't Mr. Baynes prefer to christen the children? You know, as a way to, erm, have a spiritual bond with them?"

As Miss Meyrick set to work reassuring Mark, Jane leaned toward Emma. "Best not put off a christening," she murmured, "lest you find a funeral is required instead." Swiping at her cheek, she tilted her head and smirked. At least until Cassandra's elbow in her rib knocked her into Emma.

"And two couples who will be glad to have the banns read," Miss Meyrick finished. At this, Miss Meyrick looked pointedly away from Mark, two pink spots appearing high on both cheeks.

"Busy parish indeed," Cassandra said. "Now, if we may, I believe my sister, Miss Woods, and I must visit some shops."

They exchanged curtseys and nods of farewell. As they turned, Miss Brookside threw a parting comment that made Emma nearly trip into the tree nearby. "And I expect we shall see your American version of our dances at the Upper Rooms, Miss Woods. We shall await it eagerly."

Emma spun back to look at Mark, who gave the merest shrug possible before patting his own pocket to remind her she had the coin to prepare for such a thing. Then she set her shoulders and smiled. If this was the life she was choosing, let Mark see her embrace it with steadfastness.

It was not a trait she'd been much inclined to practice.

Jane pulled Emma through the Pump Room and out into the bright day. "Eager? Eager to see you trip over your own feet," she said. "That Miss Brookside is hardly eager for anything unless it casts someone else in a bad light and herself in the best."

Cassandra leaned round Emma to give Jane a spikey look worthy of Miss Brookside. "You have the least right to criticize. Funerals indeed." Cassandra strode ahead to a shop across the square, ducking in the door quickly.

Jane leaned in again and chuckled. "No appreciation for jokes about dead babies."

"Killjoy," Emma returned.

"Quick wit!" Jane said. Both laughed and followed Cassandra in.

CHAPTER 10

Inside the shop, Emma stared at walls bursting with every color and pattern of cloth one could imagine. Along one wall, cubicles rose from floor to ceiling, each containing bolts of cotton, a palette of fabric from drab tans and browns near the floor to pale pinks and lavenders at the top. Another long wall held muslins and linens, many of these on long wooden pins allowing the clerks to pull the length of desired cloth and cut it to measure. As the cubicles and rolls of fabric rose, so too did the quality of material. Behind the counter and safe under the watchful gaze of clerks awaiting orders to fill, the lush sheen of satins, organzas, and brocades caught the light. In a corner stood a table loaded with boxes of tiny ribbony roses in every color imaginable. Above the table, ribbons hung from a rack that could be raised and lowered from the ceiling by a rope and pulley, various colors and widths and lacey-edges dancing whenever the door opened and a breeze freshened the room.

"Now, Miss Woods," said Cassandra. "Which color do you need for shoe roses?" She paused. "Oh dear, you haven't got the proper slippers. Nor a gown!"

Emma held up the hem of her skirts, displaying the little white flats she'd been wearing when she fell out of the window. "Oh! Surely these will work."

Jane and Cassandra took one look at her shoes, then at each other. Emma dropped her skirts before either bent for a closer look and might question her as to who or what a Nine West was.

"They're not quite the thing, my dear," Jane said, and drew Emma to a wall where a cascade of tiny boxes teetered to the ceiling. Drawing one forth, she pulled out a delicate little slipper. "These," she said and handed the box to Emma. "French-made."

"And for a gown?" Cassandra asked. "Surely, you must have some luggage somewhere. Where are your trunks, Miss Woods?"

Emma made herself very busy investigating the stitching on the slippers while she worked out a plausible story. Hell, at this point, she doubted she was even working in the realm of the plausible anymore, what with her Naval uncle who would never arrive, nor her friends in the North who would never be found.

"Yes, of course," Emma began. "That is, umm, my trunks were all sent over weeks ago, but have, uh, you know, since been, somewhat, which is to say, we're not really sure where they've, umm . . . Which is all to say that they're . . ."

"Lost?" said both Austen sisters at the same time, one with keen interest and the other acute skepticism.

"Lost," Emma repeated. "My uncle has made inquiries at the port and shipping houses, but alas. And the smaller trunk carrying the gowns I took to my friend's home was lost at one of the coaching stops. That's what Mr. Landen was helping me with when we fell." She thumbed the edge of the slipper. "The stitching looks poor on this one," she said and tucked the box back in the stack with a deep sigh. "Anyway, I had no intention of attending any assemblies while I set up house for my uncle, so I shall stay home and keep your parents company while you enjoy the delights of the season." For all the trepidation she'd felt when Miss Brookside threatened her with a dance, it was pure torment to turn down an invitation to an actual assembly in the actual Upper Rooms in the actual 1800s.

Then again, she reminded herself, if her plan worked, she had a lifetime of assemblies with Mark at her side to look forward to.

"Nonsense," Jane replied. "She'll wear my white muslin with the pink embroidery." She leaned over to Emma. "Pink is no longer my color. Not with these ruddy cheeks, eh, Cass?" Jane's attempts to lighten the mood only managed to uncross one of Cassandra's arms.

"That's so sweet . . . um, kind. But, I don't want to be a nuisance," Emma said. "I'm sure I can find one that fits here." She scanned the shelves and walls, looking for a rack of dresses.

"Ready-made gowns?" Cassandra said, as if Emma'd declared she would prefer to wear breeches and a topcoat – which, frankly, would have also been true.

"Would be nice," Jane said, batting at the tails of ribbons swinging overhead. "But there's no time for the mantua-maker, and we can supply all your needs until your uncle's arrival. That is, in the way of gowns. A little extra washing, but Sarah won't mind the additional wages."

"And yet sister," said Cassandra, "you forget yourself. Miss Woods has no subscription and I doubt one could be purchased now except for very dear."

Emma's hand moved to the borrowed purse, holding the cache of coins Mark had given her. A subscription to the assemblies, paying Sarah extra for her washing, and a dozen other costs she could not even foresee swirled in Emma's mind – how far could these coins last at this rate?

Jane waved a hand. "Nonsense. Charles has one as does my father, which means we have extra tickets. We made Charles endorse his just in case, and see, Cassie, my forethought is making a very nice return."

Pulling another box of shoes from the stack and with a pat of finality on Emma's hand, Jane bent over the boxes of shoe roses. She plucked out a handful and thrust these at Emma. "Now, you'll need ribbons." She eased a cord off a hook on the wall and the ribbon display lowered. Jane tugged down a length of pale pink ribbon and held the end up to Emma's hair. "Perfect," she said, cutting the ribbon and dropping it in a tangle into Emma's open hands. Jane then found a poke bonnet from a display of little cubbyholes near the window, a simple woven thing with cream ribbon which Jane had initially passed over, then returned to. "Not very fine, I'm afraid," she said with a shake of her head, "but it will go with everything and can be dressed with ribbons to match."

Emma placed her wares on the counter and requested an additional pair of shoes, a simple half-boot for daywear which Jane, with another disparaging nod toward Emma's flats, indicated would be required to deal with the general sludge of Bath streets. Emma also requested a package of handkerchiefs and two fichus Cassandra had suggested – all of which were indicated to be necessities. Emma spied a little stack of black journals on a shelf behind the counter.

"And one of those," she said. The clerk added it to the pile along with a long, sharpened pencil.

At this last, Jane gave a little smirk and whispered, "oh yes, you must record all your triumphs and tribulations, Miss Woods. No young lady is permitted to stay in Bath if she is not a faithful diarist."

Emma nodded and pretended to a self-consciousness she did not quite feel. In truth, an idea for an essay had sprung to mind: the modern woman in a Georgian shop. She was curious as to a comparison of items and what a modern woman would and wouldn't be able to find in a shop such as this one. Their costs. The necessities versus the frivolities – all based on modern versus Georgian fashion requirements. Currently, her mind raced between fears and exhilarations over the prospect of the assembly, dread over spending Mark's money, and back to the animation of an essay idea bubbling to the surface. To compound the whole, she sweated under the penetrating glare of Cassandra, whose gaze had not left her from the moment she showed off her incriminating shoes. But if she could get a quiet hour or two, she could return to Milsom Street and its bustling shops for some research.

Then a pang reminded her that if she succeeded in her plan, there would be nowhere for that essay to go.

When the total was tallied, Emma was surprised at just how little of Mark's coins were required, but still, she sighed as she placed them on the counter and watched the clerk slid them into his hand. These were little bits of Mark she was handing over, pieces of his history, of him, placeholders of a life he used to dream himself into those nights he slept on a pull-out sofa in the cramped flat he'd grown up in. Emma remembered a story Mark had shared once, how he'd come home from school at eleven years old to find his mother hunched over the tin can, crying because she'd have to sell the money to an antiques dealer to make rent. Mark took to the streets, wandered all over their dreary village to cut grass, haul junk, clean barns and sheds, and do anything else for a pound or two, jobs he would continue to perform all through his adolescence to ensure his mother never had to sell their heritage. And he had placed those coins in Emma's hands without a second thought. Emma turned away from the counter. She couldn't watch the coins disappear under the palm of a clerk who could not fathom their real value.

"I'll just take these to the back and wrap them, miss," the clerk said, gathering the purchases, but Jane put a hand on his arm.

"Wrap them here, if you please," she said. The clerk, with a roll of his eyes, huffed and left to retrieve shears, twine, and brown paper. "We do not trust Bath shopkeepers to wrap parcels," Jane said.

"Of course. After what happened to your . . ." Emma began but was stopped by Jane's suspicious glance. Emma had stumbled once already into confessing knowledge she should not have had; she certainly could not admit to knowing such a fine detail as the incarceration of Jane's aunt for half a year for shoplifting a card of lace. "I mean, I read something in your papers about shopkeepers tricking customers. Wrapping packages and putting something extra in to blackmail them with later." She cleared her throat. "Oh look! Toothpick cases!" Emma engrossed herself in examining the display of toothpick cases and snuff boxes. "How many there are! In ivory, silver, and gold." She rambled on until she could have rivaled Robert Dashwood with her prattle of cases and designs.

CHAPTER 11

Back on the street, Jane led them past the other shops and then to the Gravel Walk. Each year, Emma and Harold took the Jane Austen In Bath walking tour, and she beamed every time they came to the Gravel Walk, imagining Anne Elliot and Frederick Wentworth strolling here, entering with two hearts and emerging with one. But thoughts of another nature rose like a wave as they entered – the rage she'd felt over Mark and Wanda, Harold's dismissiveness, and her own rising recognition that it was once more her own avoidance and cowardice that had led them all to the decisions of that night.

Between the branches of the hedgerow, Emma caught sight of the Royal Crescent, that wall of cream-colored stone buildings curling like a lover round the park flowing down toward them. On her previous journeys over the pond, this part of Bath was most often filled with students lounging on the green, the aroma of cigarette and pot smoke wafting on the breeze, carried on an undercurrent of fresh-mown grass. Today, the green was relatively empty by comparison. A few blankets were laid out, on which sat nurses in black uniforms, their infant charges rolling back and forth, playing with their toes, a few older babies toddling off and grass-staining their white gowns. A half dozen couples ambled along, enjoying this bit of unchaperoned freedom in the warm air. Beyond the Royal Crescent, rather than the buildings that had sprung up in the centuries spanning this time from Emma's, meadows and forests flowed toward the horizon, here and there dotted with the small white bodies of grazing sheep, like clouds deigning to kiss the grass. It took a beat for Emma to remember that in Jane's day – this day – the Royal Crescent was the edge of Bath, the height of sophistication, the homes here reserved for the most spectacular new arrivals and residents.

On the drive before the curving townhomes, no cars circled, vying for parking. Nothing obscured Emma's view of the buildings and their meticulously scrubbed sidewalks. A carriage drawn by four perfectly white horses pulled up before a large house. An elegantly dressed woman emerged, followed by three younger women, all walking in a line from tallest to shortest, a troupe of ducklings. A footman handed them into the carriage and they pulled away from the curb.

"Old Mrs. Dowager Something-or-other," Jane said, drawing Emma back the way they'd come. "Off to auction three daughters to the highest bidding suitor."

As the din of the carriage wheels faded, the silence was interrupted only by the calls of birds, chirping their approval of this fresh, bright morning. Jane led them back toward Queen's Square and down the familiar narrow street toward Sally Lunn's bakery, which, rather than a replica of the original, with all the modern conveniences necessary to meet health code requirements, was its pure, authentic, soot-stained self.

In the shop, Jane zigzagged between tables to the counter, where she ordered a dozen bunns. To Cassandra's rueful shake of the head, she simply said, "I'm hungry."

Cassandra flapped her fan open to ward off the heat pouring out from the back of the shop. "You'll be as fat as Mrs. Brookside one day," she said from behind its lacey folds.

Jane shuddered. "A serious threat, indeed." She turned to Emma. "What do you think, Miss Woods? Surely, a woman past 25 might be forgiven not caring about such things?" Jane's hands followed the loose drape of her empire-waisted gown. "You see, it does not show," she said with a wink.

"Yet," Cassandra said.

Emma took a bunn offered by Jane, gazing through the small doorway into the kitchen. A pair of profusely sweating young women were hard at work preparing a fresh batch, occasionally swatting flies out of their ingredients. One of the girls kneaded a mound of dough as big as Emma's torso on the floured table. A bit of bunn caught in Emma's throat as she saw the other girl dip a cup into a clay jar marked Lard and plop the shining mound of fat into her mixing bowl and resume stirring with an immense wooden spoon.

When Jane offered her another, Emma demurred, as much from the general nausea over what authentic lard actually was in this time, but also from the momentary thought that she would need to fit into her clothes once she got back to them.

But then, with a sneaky smile, she recanted and enjoyed a second bunn after all.

CHAPTER 12

By nightfall, Emma's face, neck, and chest had been powdered, her hair wrangled into an impossible mound of curls by a hairdresser with a homicidal pick, and her shoes appropriately adorned with tiny ribbony roses. Sweat already puckered her armpits, and she walked downstairs with her arms jutting awkwardly from her sides to vent them before sweat-stains began to appear. What she wouldn't give for a stick of deodorant, even a shitty off-brand! Just as bad: without the slip she relied on for her own dresses, Emma found herself trying to walk with her thighs as close together as possible to avoid the inevitable bunching of the dress in uncomfortable places, which just led to more sweating in uncomfortable places. The petticoat helped some, but could not alleviate her self-conscious knowledge that but a few layers of translucent linen were all that separated her body from the eyes of everyone else.

Waiting for Jane and Cassandra to descend, Emma enjoyed the company of Mr. Austen in the drawing room. Glad for an audience, Mr. Austen reminisced about the boys at his school and told stories of his sons in the navy. He pointed to a couplet of oval portraits hanging beside the fireplace. Emma recognized the faces of Francis and Charles Austen gazing back at her.

"Very distinguished, sir," she offered. "The picture of honor and service."

"Ahh yes, Miss Woods, perhaps you are not aware that our Navy is not quite like our other services. Men rise through distinction and merit! You might purchase a captaincy in our Army, but my boys earned every inch of their promotions." From the pocket of his dressing jacket, he pulled out a medal and passed it to her, tucking it safely away once she had made the proper complimentary murmurs. "Yes, yes," he went on, "we are indeed quite excited to meet this uncle of yours. And you know, neither Charles nor Francis are yet attached. Quite handsome they are reckoned, if I do say so myself. And in need of . . . a helpmate," he ended, though in the pause, Emma rather suspected "connections" had been the word foremost on his lips.

From across the room where Mrs. Austen sat in conference with the cook, her head swiveled around. "Mr. Austen!" she said. Her tone belied he had perhaps trespassed into the repetition of hopes shared in the confidence of their bedchamber.

Emma smiled. "I shall be quite happy to meet any member of the Austen family, Sir," she said, with no need to summon false sincerity. If she weren't so hyper-aware of the strictures of this time, she'd be embracing every Austen she could get her hands on.

Mr. Austen waited for his wife to resume her discussions with the cook, then pointed at the next portrait. "My son Edward Austen is perhaps the most fortunate of all, though. But he is married already, dear. Lovely girl, our Lizzy."

Emma tried to hide her smile behind an appropriately disappointed nod of the head.

"It is a shame he shall have to give up being an Austen, but we may console ourselves that this eventuality will come many years hence." He glanced at his wife and leaned forward, speaking in lower tones. "We are grateful, you know, to the Knights, but that Catherine Knight." He gave a huff and sat back. "She was not so particular about names when she was a mere Kitty Knatchbull, I can tell you." He rolled his eyes, bushy eyebrows dancing like two snow-white hares over his eyes. Then he sighed and waved a hand in submission. "But she is quite a good friend to my girls and sends them bits of fabric for gowns and the odd coin now and again."

Emma gazed at him closely, trying to discern any hint of a pained or betrayed parent. Truly, whatever of pain might have arisen when their middle son was adopted by rich, childless relations had eased with time and now there was only the good of it to be celebrated. It was of this future good Emma found herself thinking. She turned back to the portraits, pretending a close examination when what she needed was a moment to collect herself as the sad knowledge slipped in that in just a few years, the death of this dear, sweet man would require his wife and daughters to rely almost entirely on the charity of these brothers, and especially, the refuge Edward could offer only by leaving his parents' home and becoming the heir of the wealthy Knights.

Taking a sip of port, Mr. Austen pointed to a frame on the mantle. Emma brought it to him, a small miniature of a handsome man with dark hair and Jane's laughing eyes. "And this is Henry. Quite the fine fellow, as you can discern for yourself. The handsomest of our sons, and the most pleasant – or so Jane will try to convince you." He handed back the miniature and Emma returned it to its place. "For my part, I could wish him a little more serious. More like James." Here, he pointed to a portrait on the opposite end of the mantle from Henry's. "The only of my sons to become a clergyman," he said, sighing as Emma rose to observe the portrait.

This one was larger than Henry's, and taken from a more recent age. Emma found it difficult to discern any hint of the satirical humor that had formerly appeared in The Loiterer. He was stern and serious, even taking into account the nature of solemn-faced portraits common to the era. Emma set it back down. "You never know, sir," she said, glancing back at Henry's frame. "There may be another clergyman amongst them yet."

Mr. Austen held out a hand and Emma placed hers in it. He patted it once and let it go. "Kind of you to say, my dear. But I know a lost cause."

The door opened and Isaac admitted Jane and Cassandra. Both were beautiful in their simple gowns, trimmed with matching ribbons. Jane's brown hair had been twisted in rows, all meeting in a mound of lush dark curls. Pearls wove through the twists and fell, dangling and tinkly, to her shoulders. Cassandra's lighter hair was pulled back more simply, but it accentuated the fineness of her cheekbones and the aquiline nose inherited from her mother. Both glowed with the happy anticipation of a ball and the knowledge of their own good looks.

The ladies having assembled in the drawing room, Mr. Austen pushed up from his place by the fire and escorted them to the street, where four sedan chairs waited in the warm glow of evening light. Emma's knowledge of sedan chairs came mostly from Austen's own novels, what were now but mere pebbles of plot points and character ideas bumbling about the brain of the person in the chair just ahead. Once before, Emma had sat in a sedan chair outside the Jane Austen Center for a picture, but she had not imagined what it would have been like to parade through the streets of Bath with one handsomely dressed man before and behind her, their blue coats freshly brushed, their black boots gleaming. Though she couldn't call it the smoothest ride, she thrilled in it nonetheless.

As they approached the Upper Rooms, Emma's mouth dropped, awed by both the magnificence of the facade, as well as the size of it. They halted in front of the portico, where Emma alighted and paid her fare before the men lifted the chair and trotted off into the gathering darkness.

And yet as astounded as she was by the beauty of the building and the falling twilight, she found herself missing Mark, wishing she could have seen this first with him. Together. Still, she told herself, there was time yet. Years of it perhaps. But only if she could get him to come round, and she meant to make it her evening's ambition to do just that.

Jane took her hand, gave it a squeeze, and pulled her toward the door. They entered in a crush of people so thick, Emma felt sure they must be among the first in the Rooms. Passing from the portico and through the columned entranceway, Emma gazed about, admiring the general splendor of the chambers. The walls were a soft, sea-foam green, adorned with bright white trim and molding.

Emma gripped Jane's hand, the silk of her glove catching against the warp and weft of Jane's. All this beauty rucking up against itself produced a discordant rasp, an irritation on the pads of her fingers – but she continued to clasp Jane's hand, her breath going faint and quick like a girl in a dark theater, fingers meeting her amore's for the first time.

They passed the first set of doors leading into the ballroom, and Emma just caught the mosaic of muslin gowns, billowing feathered headdresses, and the pink flushed faces of happy revelers which told her they were not the first in the Rooms at all!

The crowd bottlenecked around that doorway, but Cassandra led them on, down a darkened hall and through the second set of doors. Here, the upper half of the room remained relatively empty and from this perspective, Emma observed the crowd they had just escaped flooding into the room from the first entrance. Couples paired off, glad to be in this public space, where they might be alone in the crowd. Young women followed their chaperones to the chairs set along one wall and glanced wistfully at the young men, grouped together on the opposite side.

For all the ribbons and shoe roses, hair pomade and buffed leather, it resembled nothing so much as the awkwardness of a middle school dance.

Above them, faint tinkling riffs drifted down as the chandelier crystals clanked together, set in motion by the long pole of the candlelighter, who must have just barely finished attending his duty before the doors were flung open. Once again, Emma was reminded how much this world – Jane's world, and hers too if she could manage it – relied on the productivity of the hidden masses. No one else here considered how the candles had come to be lit – they simply were. And when the evening was over, all would return to their chairs and hacks to float serenely home without a second thought for the owners of the feet, hands, and hooves that made their momentum possible. But for her part, Emma saw the beauty and could not ignore the efforts behind it, especially considering that cooks fed their masters without Teflon, maids swept floors without Dysons, and washer women cleaned clothes without Maytags.

Jane snaked a path through the waiting dancers to the opposite wall, where she introduced Emma to Mrs. Brookside, a plump, friendly matron in scarlet brocade, who had managed to secure chairs. The eldest Miss Brookside rose to give Mrs. Austen her place and took up a position near her mother's arm. On her face, she bore that look of supreme indifference, as if standing in the Upper Rooms, the most sophisticated thing anyone in Bath could be doing on this particular evening, was beneath her. Emma was introduced properly to two more Miss Brooksides, girls of 15 or 16, whom she knew by sight as the two giggling acquaintances of Miss Meyrick's in the Pump Room.

"Had to let them come," Emma overheard Mrs. Brookside telling Mrs. Austen. "Can't hold off their coming out another season. If she won't marry, we can't take any chances with the others." And she shot a look at her eldest daughter. Mrs. Austen nodded sympathetically. Mrs. Brookside opened her fan and flapped it peevishly. "I've told her I don't know what's to become of her, for I shall not maintain her when her father . . ." Mrs. Brookside's voice drifted away, words replaced with an angry look. Miss Brookside's neck erupted in an outraged red stain, and she whipped out her own fan.

"There, there," came Mrs. Austen's voice, sunk low, but still just discernible. "At least you have no beautiful interloper. What chance do my girls have now?"

Emma dared one glance at Mrs. Austen whose eyes she could just see above the older woman's flapping fan. Cold, they were. As if she didn't have enough to contend with already. Sighing, Emma followed Jane and Cassandra to form a small circle near the elder Miss Brookside. Conversation was stilted and awkward, with Miss Brookside rebuffing both Jane and Cassandra's attempts. However, Emma did not mind being ignored as it left her the chance to watch the room continue to fill, to watch for Mark's tall frame loping into view. Would he come to her immediately? Would he seek her out or keep his distance?

If he was her Henry Tilney, then she made a very convincing Catherine Morland on the lookout. Their dance on the street flashed across her mind, and she felt the wide span of his hand on her waist as he pulled her to him. But that memory passed as she reflected that while he might be glib and perhaps, dare she even think it, a bit sexist, Henry Tilney would never have bedded some strumpet, no matter how "nice" he thought her, and at this thought Emma spun back into the group, determined to watch for Mark no longer, to give her mind and her heart a rest.

Miss Brookside's younger sisters had quickly gotten over the shyness which left them timid at the Pump Room that morning. They were as full of questions about America as Emma was empty of answers. How unfortunate they weren't asking questions about their own country, as Emma was quickly shamed to realize her knowledge of her country in this era was grossly inadequate in comparison to what she knew of Georgian England.

"What's the fashion for evening," asked Miss Lucy, "long sleeves or short?"

"I've heard ladies wear their hair down during the day," said Miss Margaret.

"Do you have all the same fabrics as we, like satin, damask, and crinoline?"

"Do men wear daggers on their belts when they dance?"

"What kind of shoes do you wear for tea?"

"Are there truly no puddings in America?"

After a few minutes, their questions and a growing awareness of her limited knowledge chipped away at Emma's polite exterior. She looked round for the hope of anyone else who might join their party and distract either herself or the Miss Brooksides. Alas, it became clear the two families would be stuck together the remainder of the evening, as if on an inescapably bad blind date. The room was full of people, and yet it appeared their small circle was complete. What an odd situation, Emma ruminated, to be crushed and pushed and jostled by a hundred other bodies and yet be confined to this one small group. How unpleasant, she concluded, that the rules of society say you spend time with those you know, even if the people you know are not necessarily the people you like.

A wave of excitement swept the ballroom as musicians ascended to the gallery and began tuning their instruments. Gallant gentlemen, some with hair as heavily pomaded as any modern-day pop star, bowed before their partners and led them to the center of the floor. The Miss Brooksides moved a little forward and eagerly looked to and fro, their lips moving as if reciting an invocation that would materialize a dance partner like a ghost from the mist. Jane, Cassandra, and Miss Brookside seemed to have little expectation of dancing the first set, and so too, Emma turned back into their circle hoping the conversation might flow smoother now the younger women were busy obsessing over something other than her reluctant, and probably inaccurate, fashion tips.

But just as the conductor was calling the name of the dance, Emma felt a tap at her shoulder. She turned to find Mark waiting, his hand outstretched, dressed in a simple, flattering suit of dark blue, the white of his shirt and undervest setting off the warm glow of his olive skin. His eyes met hers with a half-wink at the baffling, impossible deliciousness of being in this room, in this moment. Together.

"Miss Woods, I believe you agreed to dance the first with me?"

"Mark," she said. "I mean, Mr. Landen." She took his hand gratefully and blushed under an arch look from Jane. "How good of you to remember." As he led her toward the dance floor, Emma turned back once and was rewarded with a look of consternation from Miss Brookside. As much as she seemed to put herself above the rituals of an assembly, she apparently still expected to be distinguished from the rest.

Mark led Emma to the bottom of the set where they could observe the couples further ahead before beginning themselves. Though Mark was more experienced, she noticed him watching the steps as avidly as she, tapping out the rhythm on his leg. As they parted to take positions on either side, he reminded her which dance this would be and thankfully, it was one she had learned and practiced many times at former festival assemblies – a simple contredance with influences from the minuet. She was not nearly as graceful as the women who had learned these dances from the schoolroom, but she held her own creditably well. She twirled with grace, skipped forward, joined hands, and spun back into the line. When they formed a quartet, she managed to position her hands perfectly, only just touching her gloved fingertips to those of the men and women beside and opposite her.

The hardest part to manage was the requirement for unbroken eye contact. Mark's gaze rested upon her, seeking her out at each turn and spin. When they met and promenaded, his eyes flitted down to the bare skin of her shoulders, drinking her in much the same as he had in the street reel. His hand caressed the small of her back, and heat blossomed beneath his touch. She knew her cheeks could have rivalled the color of

Mrs. Brookside's turban, and she hoped the others would account for it by the exertion of the dance.

She couldn't remember ever having looked into his eyes for so long a time. More often when they were together, their gazes remained averted, batting away the attraction between them as if in a game of tether ball. For their part, Nora and Quinn remained on the sidelines, absently present referees.

But here, in this dance, at each turn, Mark spun back to meet her with his goofy smile, his green eyes the color of a meadow she wished to tumble into. No wonder Elizabeth Bennet recommended dancing as a certain step toward falling in love. As Mark took her hands for the first skip down the line, it did not appear to her as though life could supply any greater felicity.

At the conclusion of the dance, Mark led Emma back to her party, now joined by Miss Meyrick and her father. Emma realized she had been so caught up in the dance, she had made no progress in speaking to Mark about the great question, and as their social circle grew, Emma's chances to speak privately, frankly, diminished by equal degrees.

As they approached, Emma caught Miss Lucy giving Miss Meyrick the slightest of nudges, which produced a deep blush over Miss Meyrick's face. Emma did not have to know what they had been gabbing about – the girlish nudge was enough: Miss Meyrick had set her cap at Mark, or at least her friends had set it for her. And though Mark had come for her hand first, the consolation was lost with the knowledge that Mark had arrived with the Meyricks.

And would go home with them as well.

"Emma, you all right?" Mark asked, his face in earnest, open concern.

"Of course, Mark. Uh, Mr. Landen." She removed her hand from under his, feigning an adjustment to her gown. "Why wouldn't I be?" Emma slipped to the back of their group, taking a deep breath when Mark was detained by the younger Miss Brooksides' compliments on his dancing, hints as to their own hopes of being led to the floor ere long.

Back in their circle, sitting in the second row behind the great mass of Mrs. Brookside, Emma'd hoped for a rest – she'd been lucky to make it through the last dance without falling on her face or bumping into the person next to her. However, her desire was met by the expectant faces of Captain Richards and Lieutenant Listle, both of whom made gallant requests for her hand. She found that when one dance ended, the next gentleman was ready to begin. She frequently caught murmurs of her name as she spun through the set, but just as she turned to find the source, ladies' eyes would snap away, gentlemen nodding amiably before leaning toward their partner to whisper.

Exhausted from three dances with no intermission, Emma returned to their party, where Jane and Cassandra stood alone, Miss Brookside off to dance with Mr. Werthing. The soldiers had been drawn to the cardroom, and Mark had apparently been obliged into dancing with Margaret, the youngest of the Brookside girls.

Emma leaned toward Jane. "How is it possible everyone knows my name?" As she'd made her way toward and back from each set, she had heard her name whispered a dozen times, but when she'd tried to follow the voice to its owner, all she found were averted eyes.

Jane snorted. "Your surprise surprises me," she said, her tone a little more caustic than when Emma had left her. "In 'polite' society, everyone knows everything about everyone." She nodded at a trio of ladies standing at the other side of the room, then again at a group of young gentlemen a little further off. The ladies' faces remained hidden behind their fans, but their eyes darted between Emma and Jane. The gentlemen also observed them, making courtly bows when they found Emma returning their gaze. One of the gentlemen broke away, the faces of his comrades passing from interest to envy. He approached their chairs and bent into a deep bow before them.

"Mr. Carter," Jane said. "You must meet our newest acquaintance – Miss Woods."

Emma exchanged a curtsey for his bow, social currency that would cost her a thigh cramp before the end of the evening, she was sure. Emma prepared herself for a round of pleasant conversation, but was soon solicited for a dance.

As Mr. Carter led her to the floor, Jane tossed her head at the trio of ladies and others watching Emma from around the room. "Be warned, Miss Woods: what they don't know, they'll invent."

Emma was panting when she returned from the dance, a reel she had barely kept up with. Having firmly dispatched Mr. Carter back to his cadre of gentlemen, she picked up the conversation once more. "Invent? How can I be of any interest to them?"

Jane laughed. "You appear ignorant of the capacity of the English imagination." She drew Emma closer, her eyes gesturing round the room. "No doubt someone has put your fortune at close to ten thousand pounds."

Emma let out a little shriek of surprise, clamping her hand over her mouth as another young man from the group nearby made his foray toward their twosome.

"Ahhh, Mr. Morledge," Jane said, dipping into a curtsey. Emma followed shakily. "I see Mr. Carter has regaled you with the delights of Miss Woods' dancing."

Once more, Emma followed the man to the floor. Glancing back, she found Mark at Jane's side. Both seemed to be observing her, leaning together in conversation. Then Jane spoke and Mark laughed, shaking his head. Moments later, he led Jane to the floor, but his eyes often sought out Emma's through the formations, trying to purchase a smile with his little eyebrow waggles and clandestine thumbs ups.

Could it be he was giving a thumbs up to her plan or was that too much to hope for?

Mr. Morledge soon found his partner rather taciturn and gave up his enquiries into her family. For her part, Emma mulled over what Jane had said – ten thousand pounds? That would make her on a level with Miss King, a not insignificant target to any Mr. Wickhams who happened to be in the room. And Emma had the sense that many of the gentlemen present might fall into that category.

The dance concluded, Emma strode back to her group, limping slightly from where another dancer trod on her foot, an accident she wasn't entirely sure was accidental. She wove to the deepest row of chairs and waited for Jane. Mark led Jane back, and Emma caught his eye. Mark sidled into the tiny space between Jane's chair and the wall.

"Well, Emma," Mark began, "I mean, Miss Woods. Shall we have another go?"

At this, Jane opened her fan and fluttered it before her face. "For shame, Mr. Landen. Miss Woods might be forgiven trespassing on the bounds of decorum but you are an Englishman. Would you have Mr. Tyson deliver you a lecture on the protocols of the Upper Rooms?"

Mark's cheeks grew pink under the heat of her reproof. He glanced at Emma and rolled his eyes in Jane's direction, calling forth a chuckle she did her best to hide behind a cough. Even still, a lecture from the master of ceremonies as to how many dances an unmarried man could take with an unmarried woman not of his family would not be necessary.

Emma pulled back the hand she had been about to place in Mark's, and gave him a look she hoped would convey how much she would have liked to accept. With a nod, Mark moved back into the crowd, making a circuit of the room.

"You said people were guessing I have a fortune," Emma said. She dropped her voice. "Of ten thousand pounds." She glanced around to ensure their privacy, but many of the dancers had begun the glacially slow progress to the tea room, foregoing these dances in exchange for sure seats at a table. "I mean, that's not . . . I don't want people to think . . ."

Jane cut her off. "And no doubt someone else has pegged it closer to thirty."

Emma slumped back in her chair. She'd suddenly gone from a Miss King to a Georgiana Darcy. She didn't mind the upgrade, but the more people thought she was worth, the more they would swarm her, little mosquitoey Wickhams and Willoughbys buzzing annoyingly nearby.

Jane began ticking off points on her fingers. "You are the sole heiress to both your parents' fortunes. Educated abroad. Come to live with an uncle who must be daughterless if he needs you to run his house. Thus, you will inherit something from him as well. An Admiral no less, who must have made himself quite rich in the wars."

Emma swallowed and nodded. These were all reasonable surmises based on what she'd said.

"And voila. The conclusion is you are some adventuress come to steal all their beaus. Perhaps infiltrate society with your wicked foreign ways. Who knows what mischief a beautiful stranger such as yourself may get up to?" She patted Emma's hand with her own fan. Whatever mirth she'd derived quickly gave way to a sigh and rolled eyes. "Here comes another," she said and hastily rose to make her own escape.

Emma watched a third unknown gentleman pick his way through the chairs toward them. If Emma thought she was safe from introductions without Jane present to make them, she was mistaken. This young man introduced himself, apparently believing that being an "old friend" of the Austens permitted this impertinence. Glancing at Jane, Emma saw her idol lift her shoulders in a shrug, then turn back to her conversation with Cassandra, the look upon her face darker, and troubling to Emma.

But she had little time to fall into the rabbit hole of guessing what Jane was feeling as all her attention was occupied by the newest dance partner, a Mr. Fraser, who had no lack of questions regarding Emma's dead parents or the health of her uncle, whether Emma knew of – with a note of happy expectation – a festering battle wound. Emma made a concerted effort not to maintain eye contact, sensing if she did, a pair of pound signs would have replaced his pupils.

When the bell rang for tea, Emma was only too glad to follow Jane into the tearoom and sink into the chair beside her. How she longed to flick off those slippers and rub her aching feet. The meager shoes, fashionable though they may be, offered no cushion or support. The ache in her arches was spreading to her knees and would soon bloom across her back. If an actual bathroom was too much to hope for, then so was a creaky medicine cabinet with a bottle of ibuprofen.

"Lord," Emma said, leaning toward Jane, "what an evening. I think my legs may fall off before it's over."

"Indeed. How unfortunate to have been dancing nearly every set," she said and turned to help her mother with her tea things. Jane's tone was cool as frost and she would not meet Emma's gaze. Could it be possible Jane Austen was jealous of *her*? The idea seemed too absurd, and yet Jane was decidedly miffed.

Across the table, Miss Brookside sniffed at Emma's slumped posture. "Perhaps American ladies have not been bred for an evening of entertainment. And your dancing. It was so . . . interesting. Tell me, did you learn some of those dances earlier today?"

Emma's mouth opened, but no words came. All that came to mind were catty comebacks which would be superlatively inappropriate in this era. For all her frostiness, Jane was quick to her defense, her jealousy apparently no equal to a penchant for taking Miss Brookside down a few notches. "I suppose it's easier to observe and criticize the dancing from the bench, eh, Miss Brookside? We had quite a good view of all the fun others were having."

Another sniff. "As it appears your dancing in America is rather limited, tell me, Miss Woods, how else you prefer to pass your time? Perhaps you draw? Play music? Needlework?"

"None of those things," Emma said, wilting under Miss Brookside's superior manner. Thumbing through Twitter or Instagram. Yoga. Meditation (when she managed to make it out of bed at 7 am). Mandolin (which more frequently sat abandoned in the corner). Of all her modern hobbies, only one could pass without bewilderment. "I love to read."

Jane gave Emma's hand a squeeze. "As do I. Nothing like a good book to transport one away."

But a sparkle of malice lit in Miss Brookside's eye. "And tell me what it is you prefer to read, Miss Woods. Histories? Travel? Greek Drama?"

Emma met her opponent's gaze undaunted. She could see where this was going and was not to be shamed out of her love of fiction. She would not decamp to the side of reviewers who abuse novels as effusions of fancy, nor match Miss Brookside's threadbare strains. Not with Jane Austen herself at her side. "I read novels," she said, and might have gone on to argue its merits as the place where the greatest powers of the mind are displayed, the most thorough knowledge of human nature, the happiest delineation ... But her own effusions were cut short by Miss Brookside flapping a hand as though the word were a gnat hovering near her face.

"Oh, novels. How predictable. My two younger sisters seem always in a rage over this novel or that, and yet, when they tell me of them, they all sound exactly the same. A poor young woman in some kind of mysterious and doubtful circumstance. Then she's kidnapped. Then she's rescued. And so on. Hundreds of them, by now, I imagine. And have you a favorite author?"

Emma blanched. Her favorite author was sitting right beside her with not a title as yet to her name. "I enjoy the novels of … of … Mrs. Radclyffe?"

"Of course you do. Novels are bad enough, but women novelists are the worst. How anyone can stomach their drivel is beyond me."

Beside Emma, Jane bristled, drawing up like a cat. "What a limited view of the situation, Miss Brookside," Jane began. She drew breath but before she could continue, Cassandra lay a calming hand on Jane's shoulder.

Now, it was Emma's turn to come to her hero's aid. "It seems to me, Miss Brookside, that one half of the world cannot understand the pleasures of the other. But what a pity. How much kinder we might treat one another if we did."

Cassandra rose, offering Emma a warm nod. She took Jane's hand. "I believe we will take some air."

As they left, Jane gave Emma's hand another squeeze.

"What a . . ." – bitch, Emma was about to say, but caught herself just in time. "Nevermind. If you ask me, the person, be it gentleman or lady, who has not pleasure in a good novel must be intolerably stupid."

Jane stopped short, halting Emma as well as someone behind bumped into them. When Emma looked to see what was the matter, Jane's face was awash in light and inspiration. "My dear Miss Woods, you are a veritable treasure trove. What witticisms abound in you."

Emma laughed. "Well, I read it from . . ." – you. Once more, the word threw out its hands and feet, snagging the sides of her throat, and she tried to hide what had almost been said beneath a coughing fit of consumptive proportions.

A peal of thunder cracked the night. Around the ballroom, women tittered nervously as the intensity of the booms overpowered the musicians in the gallery above. Moments later, rain lashed the windows and thunder shook the panes.

"Cass," Jane said, patting her hips, "have you a slip of paper or something?"

Cassandra searched in her small reticule and pulled out a scrap of paper and a pencil. Jane excused herself, and Cassandra gave Emma a look she was not expecting, as though Cassandra saw something of value she had not considered before. Jane returned moments later, her face flushed, a broad smile at her lips, the warmest Emma had seen yet. Another clash of thunder punctuated her steps as she caught up with them.

"How unseasonable," Jane said, brightly. "Ridiculous weather." She led them back to the general area where they had been sitting, though another group now occupied their former set of chairs. "Uh oh," Jane said, "Looks like your Mr. Landen is engaged."

As Emma said, "He is not *my* Mr. Landen," her gaze fell upon Mark laughing as he spun Miss Meyrick in a fast-paced reel. Their conversation kept as quick a pace as their feet, and more than once Emma saw him laugh at something Miss Meyrick had said. A bubble of jealousy rose, but she popped it before it could disturb the calm waters of her surface. If she were annoyed at all, it was with Jane.

"The threat of Mr. Tyson does not seem to have factored into Miss Meyrick's choice," Emma said.

Emma's gaze moved beyond the dancers, her eyes landing on Dr. Lethbridge standing across the room, flanked on either side by a pair of young women. Dr. Bowen stood nearby, tipping a glass of wine to its last drop. The two women shared their father's wide bullfroggy mouth, often turning their grinning faces toward Dr. Lethbridge's.

If she couldn't dance with Mark, Emma felt Dr. Lethbridge would make a much more pleasant companion than any of the young men she discovered standing near their former chairs. She would have gladly attributed this attention to any of the other ladies, but as they heaved forward to ask for the next dance, she could not deny it was her own presence which emboldened them. Emma's thoughts tumbled and crashed over some pretext for refusing to dance, any excuse other than the tendonitis she felt sure was settling into both feet. But then, remembering Elizabeth's dilemma when Mr. Darcy asked her to dance, Emma thanked the first gentleman who extended his hand and followed him to the floor. Having already danced half the evening away, she, like Elizabeth Bennet, had no excuse not to accept. And they were nice enough gentlemen – if perhaps a bit mercenary – who did not deserve the humiliation of a public rejection.

With that, Emma found herself on her feet the rest of the evening. However, she soon learnt to consider her popularity as a sacrifice to the pleasures of her friends. As Captain Richards and Lieutenant Listle returned, along with other waiting partners, the men passed their time pleasantly enough by dancing with Jane, Cassandra, and Miss Brookside, as well as her younger sisters. By the evening's end, all the women of their party could boast of having danced every set after tea.

Well after midnight, Emma stood shivering in the portico beside Jane and Cassandra as rain poured around them. As gentlemen and ladies passed to their chairs and carriages, they stopped to curtsey and bow to Emma, reminding her of their names, none of which Emma had any chance of remembering. As more and more people said their farewells to Emma – and Emma alone – she began to notice Jane's satisfied smile pulling down once more into a resentful frown.

Mrs. Austen must have been positively stewing, though Emma was too nervous to even risk a glance.

Surrounded by so many chattering people, all waiting for a chair, all crushed together to avoid the torrential shower falling like a sheet between them and the street beyond, Emma leaned toward Jane. "How ridiculous," she said, trying to adopt Jane's ironical tone. "As if I could possibly remember all their names."

"It has often occurred to me," said Jane, "that those who dismiss the attentions of others are often the ones who seek it most." Her face flushed a bit, with what could have been embarrassment or anger, or a combination of the two, and she pushed forward to secure four chairs, stepping into the first one and ordering the men to move on.

Cassandra helped her mother into the next chair and then walked with Emma to the last two. "When the sun shines so brightly on one person," she said, "it casts those standing behind in shadow."

It was not much, but for the moment, it was enough. Perhaps an ally existed here yet. And Lord knew Emma would take any she could find.

There would be no dancing in her chair all the way home for Emma. Instead, she was nearly lulled to sleep as her chair swayed and rain beat a steady tattoo upon the roof. But as they crossed over the Pulteney Bridge,

Emma's ears throbbed with the roar of the river. The evening had been a tumbled, jumbled mess. Worse still, she and Mark hadn't had a moment to talk about what she'd said – what she'd offered – at the Pump Room. Mark's own desires seemed clouded and uncertain, and her newfound friendship with Jane had likewise churned into a stew as murky as the teeming waters below.

CHAPTER 13

Public Bathing at Bath, or Stewing Alive!

The dawn broke clear and bright once again. Emma woke to find Sarah trying to manage a bundle of wood through the door without making a sound.

"You're awake," she said, relieved, dropping the wood with a clatter. "Shall I stoke it up for you, miss?" She tossed in a few smaller logs and gave the embers a good poke to get them going again. Everything was done with a sigh, a swipe of a tear. "Anything else I can do for you, miss?"

Do for *her*? Emma wished there something she could do for Sarah and her sister. She remembered the slick plastic chairs of the women's health center on campus, the mug of coffee burning her hand through the thin waxed paper cup, the pad of her roommate's feet as the nurse led her back to the waiting room, and the feeling that they were both of them too young for any of this. As she'd ruminated on what she could do to help, Emma quickly realized the impossibility of any of her own solutions. There was no pill to prevent or clinic to remedy the situation, to save herself and the poor unwanted child from a life even more limited than that of Jane or her sister.

"Thank you, Sarah. No." Emma yawned and stretched. She had spent the night tumbling in her sheets, woken from dreams of orchestral music by blasts of thunder. The face of Miss Meyrick, the sweet innocence of her mien, and Mark's own oblivious, friendly visage rolled past like a movie reel on repeat. It was all too much like the other night when Mark and Wanda's face had swum through her dreams.

Sarah turned to bob her exit, sniffling as she pulled the door closed.

"Sarah." Emma rose and dug in a drawer for a handkerchief. "I do hope . . . that is . . . I am so very sorry to hear of . . . your family troubles."

Sarah's eyes nearly spilled over, but she merely bobbed again. "Thank you, miss. My sister is poor low about it. Mr. Brookside says he'll keep her 'til Michaelmas, but afterwards, he'll not have her in his house. People will know she's been . . . that she's a . . ."

The sound of approaching footsteps spared her saying what looked to break her heart. Eyes flashing lest she be discovered doing something so indescrete as having a personal conversation, Sarah cast one last appreciative glance over her shoulder and dashed down the hall.

Jane appeared in the door, fully dressed, a bonnet in her hand. "What was that about?" she said, leaning out to watch Sarah's retreat.

"It was my fault." Emma returned the handkerchief to her drawer and gazed at her reflection, tapping the puffs below her eyes. What she wouldn't give for a bottle of concealer. "I encouraged her to speak of her sister's . . . uh, misfortune."

"Indeed." Jane sat at the end of Emma's bed. "A great and increasing one."

"Is there no hope that she may work after the . . .? Or perhaps give the child to another family? An adoption?"

Jane scoffed. "Would be a kinder thing for all, would it not? I'm afraid the only option is to abandon the child to an orphanage and lord knows where it might end up. As to employment, well, her reputation is ruined – at least it will be in another fortnight. Dismissed after so many years of service. And no one will take on a maid with loose morals." Jane cocked a sardonic eyebrow. "Must not tempt the masters of the house, now."

"Loose morals! And so she is to be punished while the man who seduced her goes on to ensnare someone else? Who's to say the father isn't the master of the house himself?"

Jane lay back on the bed, holding her bonnet up to examine its decorations. "You've never seen Mr. Brookside." She gave a mock shudder. "Now, you need to dress. First, we'll bathe. Then, the Pump Room. Then tea at Rickford's. Then ..."

But Emma lost track of all the places that began to take shape like a pirate's map, little black dots connecting one destination to the next, filling her day, exhausting her body. One thought pulsed beyond all the rest – where was Mark and what had he decided? Would he still insist they jump in that raging torrent and if they did, could they possibly survive? And what was happening back home: had time come to a standstill, awaiting their return, or were her friends even now mourning them? Alas, she had little time to fret over any of those concerns as Jane chivvied her into yesterday's dress, which smelled in need of a good dunking itself.

Once more a crowd had gathered at the bridge, gentlemen and ladies both staring into the waters roaring below. As they crossed to the other side, Emma caught sight of a woman begging, two half-naked and more than half-starved children tangling about her legs, as she thrust a metal cup toward passersby. And everyone just moved on as if she were nothing more than a bit of refuse clinging to the bottom of one's shoe.

Emma's eyes were drawn back to her. Jane patted her hand. "That, I'm afraid, is what awaits poor Sarah's sister. Parish help, for what that's worth, but never making ends meet."

"Passed around from man to man," Emma remarked, finding Mrs. Jennings' words at her lips. "Fallen out of all good society."

Jane's brows furrowed. "Yes," she said, "quite possibly. Though of course a maid was never part of good society. But your prophecy is an astute one."

Overhead, the skies darkened. Cassandra broke into a trot and Emma and Jane lifted their skirts to keep pace. They ducked under the colonnade of the bath just as the skies opened and a roll of thunder crescendoed overhead.

"My heavens," Jane said. "This abominable rain!" She shook out her skirts. "Miss Woods, which part of America did you say you were from? Salem, was it?"

Cassandra gave one of her pursed-lip glares bordering on a smile.

"What do you say, Miss Woods? Have I caught you out?"

"Me, a witch? As if!"

Jane's eyes widened at the impertinence of her expression, and it was Emma's turn to laugh. "If I were," she continued, "I'm quite sure I could find better things to do with my powers than inconvenience myself with rain."

Cassandra gave a little ha-rumph. "The weather is remarkably odd. Not a rain cloud in sight for days. And now, it seems to be raining . . ."

"Cats and dogs," Emma said.

"A reader of Swift," Jane remarked. "See, Cassandra? I told you she was worth the trouble."

Emma smiled but was stung by Jane's words. Worth the trouble? Were Jane and Cassandra sitting cozily around the fire in their shared retreat, tallying up the balance between Emma's contributions versus annoyances? Jane's kindness was but one side of a coin she liked to flip, delivering both playful sympathy and hurtful honesty as it flashed and spun.

They entered the door for the women's bathing section and an attendant offered them each a brown gown of coarse linen and a towel. Emma followed Jane down a steep set of stairs into a locker room of sorts. Along one wall sat a row of curtained changing rooms. Across, the wall held cubicles for clothes and shoes, a good number already full.

Behind the heavy curtain, Emma took off her gown and put on the brown one provided by the attendant. She found herself thinking of what Jane had said. A witch? Something tugged at the recesses of her mind. After all, her indignation over Mark and Wanda had been great enough to open the web of time. Perhaps her emotional turmoil – delight at being near Jane, desire to convince Mark to stay with her, fear of societal blunders – was disrupting another facet of the atmospheric equilibrium.

Emma snorted at the idea of herself straddling a broom, a witch's pointy hat tipped rakishly over a brow, swivelling a wand through her fingers.

Finished changing, she placed her things in a cubby, grabbing her bonnet when she realized Jane and Cassandra still had theirs on. Following Jane through a door on the opposite wall, they emerged in a large columned room, dark and husky, with candles burning in sconces. The walls and floor were all stone, large gaping lines where the stones had drifted apart with age, murmurs from thousands of years of bathers rising as whispers from the past.

For all the ancient glory on display, what struck Emma most was the smell. Emma had read descriptions of the baths, and though old accounts were often inflated with bombastic descriptions, the diarists had got one thing right: the place smelled like a gazillion eggs had been boiled in it. Quinn liked to hard-boil a dozen eggs at the beginning of each week for work snacks and Emma often had to flee their apartment, leaving the windows open for hours – whether freezing or broiling outside – to clear the air. She drew a hand to her nose, not caring when Jane laughed nor when Cassandra hmphed another snort of disapproval.

Sinking into the warm waters of the pool, Emma groaned. The water may smell like hell, but it felt like heaven.

"Rather a good cure after a night of dancing, eh?" Jane remarked and handed a copper plate to Emma, demonstrating that one was meant to wrap the leather strap around the neck, then let the platter float before the face. On the plate sat little bottles of oils. Holding them up one by one, Emma recognized the scents of amber and lavender and others she could not place, but heavy and musty and a welcome relief from the vaporous sulfur driving into her brain. Parking her nose millimeters from the plate, she breathed deeply, finally able to quell the gag persistently rising into her throat.

Emma nodded. "Yes, just what I needed."

Cassandra led them to the side of the baths, taking a seat on one of the steps. "Enjoy it now, Miss Woods, for these baths will be ever so full in another month's time."

Jane rolled her eyes. "Oh yes, once the season starts, there's no hope but to be jostled and elbowed by every mister and miss fresh from the countryside."

"You mean men and women bathe together?"

Jane and Cassandra shared a look. "Of course! In the King's Bath anyway." Cassandra pointed to a wall of small windows and arches through which daylight gave slim reprieve from the gloom. Even from their position across the pool, Emma discerned the familiar stone balustrade surrounding the section of the baths which could be seen from the Pump Room windows. Shadows passed by the windows, occasionally stopping to glance down, then moving on to take the waters or promenade.

"Bathers are almost as much worth looking at as those with their clothes on." Jane ducked as Cassandra sent a little splash toward her in payment for her impertinence. A little splash fight between all three ensued, ending only when Cassandra noticed they had drawn the attention of other bathers and more than few "harumphs" reverberating round the room.

Laughing and wiping water from her cheeks, Jane shook her head. "The waters may be warmer over there, but then so too are the eyes seeking to watch us."

They made their way toward this wall and Emma was able to peek in over the crest of a window. Indeed, a group of men and women strolled through the waters, the men bedecked in similar brown linen, though made into long sleeved shirts and breeches. "But I thought that's where the drinking water came from," Emma said, nodding toward the window and the attendant who could be seen handing over crystal goblets in the Pump Room above.

"And so it is," Jane said as Cassandra nodded. Once more Emma fought the gags threatening to erupt, and silently foreswore any further sips of the "healing waters."

Rising from the bath nearly an hour later, Emma once again found herself plucking at the folds of her gown, trying to keep the wet linen from tangling about her legs, growing ever more claustrophobic as it clung and pulled. Dry, her skin still reeked of Sulphur, so Emma took one of the little bottles of lavender and rubbed it into her arms, sighing as she traded the stink of rotten eggs for the grease of oil.

CHAPTER 14

L'Embarras du Choix

Outside, they found the rain shower had passed quickly enough. Jane wandered toward the other side of the square where a shop displayed new wares in the bow window. Cassandra paused by the door to the Pump Room and looked expectantly toward Emma.

"Don't you want to check the book, Miss Woods?"

"The book? What for?"

Cassandra's expression swung quickly from confusion to suspicion. "For your uncle? Perhaps he has left you a note?"

Emma pretended to have something on her shoe that needed her attention. "Oh my heavens, yes. Thank you, Miss Austen, for reminding me. I believe the waters from the bath have relaxed me into confusion."

With that, Emma turned into the Pump Room. She stood at the book for some minutes flipping through the pages, trying not to be unfairly cruel to Cassandra, though Emma wished the woman would just back off! Here she was, trying to enjoy this time with her idol, and Cassandra kept reminding her how happy they'd be when she was gone. Emma lowered the page, then shrugged for good measure, in case Cassandra happened to be watching. Exiting the Pump Room, she found Cassandra in a fierce whispered conversation with Jane, breaking off mid-sentence as Emma joined them.

"Not there?" Jane asked.

Emma shook her head. Jane pulled Emma's hand through her own. "Good, then we shall get to keep you a little longer."

Jane led them up toward Milsom Street, turning at an alley and directing them down a short set of stairs and into a humid, warm shop with a sign hanging above the door illustrating a cup of tea and the name Rickford's. The aromas were delectable. Coffee and tea. Cakes and scones. Along one wall stood a counter where patrons could purchase tea or coffee by the bulk and pastries to take home. Behind this counter and atop its polished wood surface, the finest sweets from Bath's bakeries were displayed in cases and on crystal cake stands. Preserved fruits and jellies in decorative jars lined one end of the counter while a row of pedestal stands offered pyramids of small pastries, tartlets, and sweet rolls. Behind the counter, narrow shelves displayed bottles of liqueur and wine.

Emma followed Jane and Cassandra to a table near the windows, where they were perfectly positioned to gaze at the shoes of passing gentlemen and ladies. A moment later, the bell clanged over the door and the Brookside ladies entered, Miss Meyrick one of their party.

Once again, Miss Meyrick's merry visage and Mark's charmed face flashed behind Emma's closed lids. As would be her luck, Miss Meyrick took a seat next to Emma.

"Heavens," she said, hiding a yawn behind a gloved hand. "How tired I am. Assemblies rarely tire me so, but I find myself unable to keep my eyes open."

Miss Lucy tilted forward. "We all know the symptoms, Miss Meyrick, so you cannot hide them from us. Who here has not spent a morning yawning after dancing with the most delightful man in the room?"

Miss Brookside huffed. "Well, we certainly cannot accuse you of those symptoms, Lucy. The last young man to single you out was . . . oh dear, I don't believe you've had that distinction."

Lucy's eyes flashed. "Well, at least I won't have to marry old Mr. Werthing rather than . . ."

"You hush this instant, or I'll –," Miss Brookside began, but then she remembered herself and hid behind the furious flaps of her fan. The implied threat was enough to subdue her younger sister into a sulky silence.

Miss Meyrick quickly filled the gap, trying to lighten the mood. "Oh, dear me. I do find Mr. Landen an exceedingly pleasant young man." She turned to Emma. "Do you know much of his family, Miss Woods? I understand you arrived in Bath on the same coach. And he is an acquaintance of your uncle's?"

Emma dabbed at the tea she had sputtered on facing another question relating to her mythical uncle. "Indeed. He and my uncle are acquainted though I cannot tell you how. But I do know a bit about his family. That is to say, he hasn't got any. His mother passed when he was at university and his father was never around."

The assembled ladies all looked at her in surprise.

"You can't mean . . ." started Miss Margaret, but she seemed unable to put her words together under the withering gaze of her elder sister and the giggles beginning to erupt from Miss Lucy.

Finally, Emma realized what she'd implied – a bastard. And true enough, Mark was technically that, though no one really cared about such things anymore – that is, not in her "anymore." But here? – she'd relegated Mark to the ranks of the maid's unfortunate condition. "Oh no! I didn't mean – I'm sorry, what I meant was that his father also died when Mark was just a boy. He never really knew him."

"And yet, he managed to get through university and become a clergyman?" Cassandra asked.

Emma nodded and shrugged, then shook her head. Now she had to explain the Church of the Divine Forest? A more constructive use of her time would be find the nearest ditch where she could dig her holes without risk of throwing Mark in too. "The charity of family, I believe. A wealthy uncle or something."

Jane raised her cup, eyes sparkling over the rim. "Know a bit of his story, did you say? You could write his memoirs, I think, with what little bit you know."

"But alas, he has no parish," Miss Meyrick said. "Perhaps my father might know of something."

"A living not already spoken for?" Cassandra asked. "You must not have much experience with such things." Cassandra's incredulity was enough to silence Miss Meyrick's musings.

The waiter arrived to deliver tea as well as a tray of cakes. Emma took a rectangle of layered sponge cake and raspberry jam. Taking a bite, she let out a long, delighted moan, then saw the affronted faces of her companions.

Jane took a cake for herself, biting into it with abandon. "Not, perhaps, so good as Molland's," she said around a full mouth, "but we prefer the quietness of this shop. It is not so popular with visitors."

Emma dabbed a napkin at the corners of her mouth, a weak attempt to hide the flush spreading up from her chest and over her shoulders.

The rest of the table likewise took a sweet from the tray and conversation gave way to chews and soft murmurs of appreciation. Emma took this opportunity to examine Miss Meyrick. She wished she could accuse Miss Meyrick of some sliver of guile. But perversely, Miss Meyrick seemed entirely artless, a simple, sweet-tempered girl just trying to make conversation. And perhaps discover a little more about an interesting man, for which Emma could not blame her.

Nonetheless, a new topic was in order. Just as Emma was about to speak, the shop door opened and the two froggy women from the night before entered, followed quickly after by Dr. Lethbridge.

Emma watched him move with authority down the counter, placing an order for the week's tea and obligingly nodding when the young women at his side implored him for a slice of cake. With his cat's head cane, he directed his two charges toward a table nearby, stopping short when he met Emma's gaze.

"Miss Woods," he said. "A pleasure to see you here. I hope you are feeling better." He doffed his hat and self-consciously patted down his untidy hair. "Or should I say 'Mizzzz Woods.'" His face flushed at his silly joke.

Emma ducked her head and returned his smile. "I am feeling much better, thank you."

"Be careful you don't disorder your digestion with too much cake," he said, "or you shall have to call for my services again."

Emma became aware of how closely the rest of the women of her party observed her. "Oh well, I certainly wouldn't want to do that," she said in as joking a manner as she could imagine under all this scrutiny. And then his expression dropped. "Well, that is, not that I wouldn't want to see you, of course, but just that I wouldn't want to . . . you know, see you . . . under those circumstances. But of course, I hope you're staying busy as a doctor . . . That is, not that I would wish anyone ill, or anything . . . but just that, you know . . . one always hopes one's friends . . . acquaintances! . . . are doing well with their business." She shoved the rest of her cake into her mouth. "Hmmm, delicious."

The server brought three slices of cake and tea to the table where Dr. Lethbridge's companions observed his conversation with Emma through glowering expressions.

"Well," he said, laughing, "It appears I must go and disorder my own digestion." He nodded to the table. "Ladies. Mizz Woods. A pleasant afternoon to you all."

"And to you," said Jane, bringing her teacup to her mouth. "Well, something is disordered, but I sense it isn't Miss Woods' stomach," she said in a voice just loud enough for Emma to hear.

As Miss Meyrick continued with her talk of pleasant parishes and Mark's dancing, Emma fought the urge to lay her head on the table. Or perhaps bang it against the surface once, or maybe twice.

CHAPTER 15

Returning to the Austens's, Emma found this was to be their afternoon at home. She settled herself contentedly in the drawing room as the sisters caught up on correspondence and their mother read aloud the newspaper and Francis' letter from abroad. The correspondence from Steventon came last. Jane paced and huffed as James described all the improvements he'd been making to the building and grounds – so numerous, he said, he could not fathom how she and his father had managed to live in it with any sense of comfort. Cassandra followed close behind when Jane's frets interrupted her mother's reading, drawing her to the window and speaking calm words until Jane's shoulders eased, she nodded, and returned once more to the little round frame of her needlework.

The letter finished, Mrs. Austen sighed in commiseration. "Could be worse," she said.

To this Jane agreed. "He could still be riding with the Kempshott Pack."

Mr. Austen alternated between snoozing in his great chair near the empty fireplace, ambling about the room to check the progress of others' occupations, and standing near the window, remarking on every person, carriage, and street urchin who passed below. Emma was happy to find a well-stocked library, and passed over *Fordyce's Sermons*, which brought a chuckle, before settling on *Sir Charles Grandison*. After all, Mrs. Morland was a sensible woman, and Emma relished the idea of her eyes and fingers traipsing over the very same pages as Jane's must have done, perhaps reading aloud to her family of an evening. Slogging through the dense prose could not help but compare poorly to the light, tripping syntax brewing in the brain nearby. Emma glanced over at Jane, wondering what plot points she was puzzling out at that moment, what witty gems of dialogue were casting their mold in her mind as the needle in her hand slipped in and out of her sampler, perfect yellow daisies appearing in its wake.

As evening approached and the light waned, Emma found reading too difficult. Jane shoved a basket over with a foot. "The poor basket," Jane explained. "Find any old thing to work on, if you like."

Picking through the various garments and fabrics, Emma found a shirt nearly complete, only needing hemmed at the sleeves and neckline. She was no embroiderer like Jane and Cassandra, but she remembered enough from laying under the table during her mother's quilting classes to sufficiently follow the stitching.

However, she found that no matter how she sat or angled her body, the bit she worked on was constantly coming between her eyes and the fire, which she needed for its light. A few lone candles burned atop the mantle and side tables, casting a meagre glow. Finally, the only serviceable position was to perch at the edge of her seat with her back slightly tilted toward the fire and then hold the edge of her stitching right up close to her face. Within a few minutes, her arms and back launched a protest, but a quick glance revealed Jane and Cassandra maintaining the same posture with ease.

How soft she felt herself to be. How unsuited to this life of frills and finery – a life she had previously assumed required little strength or endurance, the only prerequisite being the ability to look passively picturesque all day long.

Did she even have what it took to stay?

"The assembly last evening was rather larger than I'd expected," Cassandra commented. "Though early in the season, I was surprised how many couples formed."

Jane murmured her assent. "Yes, and our friend here was quite a success!" She glanced sidelong at Emma as though still pricked by the sting of envy, but beginning to laugh herself out of it. "I hope you don't mind my remarking such, but some of the dances did seem . . . unfamiliar to you."

"Yes, indeed, I have never once in my life danced so much in one evening. And some of the dances," she stopped to blush and nod, "most of them, actually, I have only danced once or twice before."

This seemed to perplex the sisters. "But surely," Cassandra said, "you have assemblies in America. We cannot think you so behind as all that."

Jane laughed outright. "It is not the wilds of Africa, dear sister. They were after all English themselves. Not so very long ago."

"Yes," Emma said, "we have assemblies. But where my family was situated . . . we had not . . . not so many as the larger towns and cities." Of course, she could not tell them she'd grown up in a farming town in Indiana. Nor that the last thing even resembling an assembly she'd attended had been a nightclub she visited with Quinn's sister, nor how the music pounded in her ears so mightily she'd spent the rest of the weekend in bed with a migraine.

"Not unlike Basingstoke," Jane commented. A match lit in her memory, illuminating her face. "Oh my dear Cass, do you remember that ball? When they'd had nothing but rush lights in the braziers?" She turned to Emma. "The town had run out of candles. Simply, poof! Not a one to be had and not a farmer or gentleman willing to part with his stock. So what did they do? Sent the farmboys around to gather hay and tie it up into bundles. The stack of them must have been higher than our heads! When one bundle expired, a boy would be sent outside to bring in another."

"Sounds positively medieval," Emma joked.

Cassandra chuckled. "The smell certainly was."

"Indeed," Jane continued. "Oh, the assembly was full of Belinda's and Camilla's that night, eh, Cassandra? Do you know, I believe, that was the assembly at which Mr. Lefroy . . ." But her voice trailed away. The mirth drained from her face as she drifted below the surface of memory, into recollections of the great love she was supposed to have lost.

Tom Lefroy. Emma wondered where he was at this point in history. Had he yet become a magistrate in Ireland? Certainly it was too early to be named Chief Justice, but perhaps his daughter had been born, the girl he would name Jane and which some historians alluded was in homage to the woman hunched over her embroidery frame just three feet away.

But Emma suspected the name Lefory had sparked the fuse of another, more recent injury. An image of two sisters sitting in the sand at the beach of Devon flashed in Emma's mind, one sister with an arm wrapped protectively around the other, pages of the letter reporting his death dotted with tears. Perhaps the memory of Tom was not painful for itself, but as a bookmark of the real possibility of love taken from Jane, a pain too deep and too real and too recent to speak of.

Emma understood this proxy substitute only too well. Programs from past festivals, a stack of receipts from when she and Mark went clubbing, even a button from Mark's coat which he had asked her to keep safe in her purse so he could sew it back on later. Little things she kept in the drawer of her desk, little mementos she sometimes felt for, her fingers reaching into the dusty corners to ensure they were still there. She did not have a little Tunbridge-ware box marked Most Precious Treasures, like Harriet Smith. But she had her drawer.

There was a sudden blast from Emma's brain that said, Ask her! Ask her! Ask her!, a throbbing insistence which stole her from any reveries of her own. Right here, in this moment, Emma could discover the truth of the mysterious Devon suitor. Had he, in fact, died, unable to return and cultivate the budding attachment growing between them?

Or was the suitor actually Dr. Blackall, who met Jane the very same season she had danced in Basingstoke with Tom Lefroy? When, at the end of her own long life, Cassandra intimated Jane's only true suitor had died, was this her own revisionist memory, a way to spare her dear sister the ignominy of being passed over so many years after her death, rather than revealing that he had simply gone on to marry another.

It was a question scholars had still not divined.

Once more the drumbeat resounded in Emma's head. How she craved to exist simply in this moment. Three women clustered round a low fire, sharing memories of assemblies long past, not yet themselves past the possibility of attachment and the delicious drift into love and home and family. And yet, how Emma also yearned to feed her store of knowledge. To best Wanda and that supposed discovery she'd made. It was almost enough to make her want to go back, just to see Wanda's face.

But as Emma was about to speak, an idea in that vein pushed through: what's the point of knowing the truth if you've no one to share it with? There was nothing to be gained, nothing but the solitary knowledge it would garner, and Emma began to realize what a lonely prospect it was, staying here, where Jane was just Jane, simply Jane, and all the factoids and trivia Emma had memorized with abandon were only useful in the context of who Jane would be in another 200 years.

As these ruminations passed through Emma, the moment of discovery passed as well, and Jane continued, her tone lighter, her expression trying hard to match. "But yes indeed, the Basingstoke assemblies, pleasant though they were, were at times a paltry affair."

"But one takes what one can get," Emma threw in, trying for a sunnier tone, quelling the frenzied pulse of her heart as the opening where she might have inserted her question narrowed to a perfect pinpoint of light and vanished.

"Indeed, they do," Cassandra said with a kind look for Emma.

"And if you are an Emma Woods at the Upper Rooms, that is plenty!" Jane smiled and whatever green of envy appeared to have been washed away.

Later that evening, the Austens hosted an evening party. Isaac threw open the doors separating the two halves of the drawing room, then began lighting the candelabras and sconces across the mantle and on the walls. Emma helped Jane and Cassandra fluff pillows and move the card table into the middle of the room. It was a clever bit of furniture which tucked neatly against the wall. When the two folded eaves were latched into place, it became an octagonal table around which small chairs could comfortably fit. Cassandra opened the sideboard and set out decanters of port and sherry along with a little armada of empty crystal goblets while Sarah set up a table for food. Once the tablecloth had been shook out and floated down on top, one would never know that beneath the trays of cold meats and other snacks were just a pair of rough-hewn trestle legs, a crossbeam to connect them, and half a dozen planks.

Brushing her hands, Emma thought all the room needed was a big screen TV over the mantle and it would be perfect for an up-market Superbowl party.

As they finished the final plumpings and arrangings, the bell rang below. Minutes later, Isaac opened the door and Miss Meyrick entered followed by Mark, her father, and a second gentleman.

"Mr. Baynes," said Mr. Meyrick, ushering the young man inside.

Standing next to Mark, the poor man could not help but make a shabby comparison. He was short and balding, though he couldn't have been more than mid-20s, and of a rather portly build. It also didn't escape Emma's notice that as the arrivals bowed upon entry, Miss Meyrick managed to be standing next to Mark rather than her father.

The necessary pleasantries followed, with comments from all on the weather, from Mr. Baynes on the state of the roads outside of Bath, and from the young ladies as to whether they had been caught out in it. Mr. Austen and Mr. Meyrick settled by the fire with a glass of port each and carried the topic forward by conjecturing as to whether the riverbanks would rise high enough to cause the Guildhall to flood. Mrs. Austen settled herself on the sofa and offered a quip here and there to spice the conversation.

The young people were left to sort themselves and Cassandra quickly demonstrated her aptitude for the role of hostess by inviting all the guests to the card table for a game of speculation. Emma managed to secure a seat next to Mark, but found that his attention was all for the game.

"My apologies," Emma said, when she played a wrong card and had to return it to her hand in exchange for the correct one. "My family was never much for cards."

"Oh, aye aye," said Mr. Baynes. "I am myself more inclined toward music or reading to pass an evening." He labored over his choice, the tip of his tongue peeking from between his lips as he concentrated. "It has often seemed to me that cards feel slightly beyond the . . . well, scope of a clergyman. It is a slippery slope, you know, from cards to gambling to debt and worse."

Across the table, Jane released a huff and lay a card immediately after Mr. Baynes. "One ought not be too fastidious, surely, sir," she said, making a show about pouring more sherry into all their glasses. "And besides, the same can be said of anything – too much wine and one finds one's self dancing on tables or waking in gutters. Too much food and one becomes as rotund as a bear. Too much reading and one imagines all sorts of horrors that are mere fiction."

At this last, Emma and Mark's faces both lit brightly, their eyes seeking one another's. Emma took a drink to quell the laugh at the obvious reference to the very crux of *Northanger Abbey* while Mark steered his countenance back into seriousness. "Self-control," he offered. "What we all need is to exercise self-control."

"True, true," murmured most members of their group, Miss Meyrick with more alacrity than the rest.

"Everything in moderation," said Emma, "including moderation."

Jane laughed and put the back of her hand to her mouth to catch a dribble of sherry.

Cassandra puckered her lips and lay a card. "A decidedly American perspective, I am sure," she said.

Emma shook her head. "Actually, the man who said it was . . ." she caught a look from Mark, his head giving a firm, if minuscule, shake. "My uncle."

Miss Meyrick looked as though she wished to offer something witty, but after some delay and no contribution, she lay the final card and revealed her trump.

As Cassandra dealt a new hand, Jane turned to Mr. Baynes. "And so you are to take over the interim rector duties from the interim rector, I understand. Mr. Landen here must feel like yesterday's bread to be tossed on the midden so soon after his arrival."

"Oh no," said Miss Meyrick, "we are so glad to have had Mr. Landen and hope he will stay to smooth the transition." She looked at Mark with an expression that couldn't be called anything less than imploring.

He cleared his throat and chuckled. "Well, as to all that, who can say?" He pulled at his collar and ran a hand up and down the buttons of his shirt and vest, a habit he took to when he wasn't sure what to say. "But," he became deeply engrossed in his cards. "I have no current plans to depart." Emma's heart did a triple somersault and if she could, she would have bored two holes through the top of Mark's head with her eyes. "Though, I have duties and concerns elsewhere that I must attend to and which, I presume will take me away from Bath shortly." At this, he met her glance, only momentarily, but enough to squash any further cardiac acrobatics.

Mr. Baynes began to sort his new hand. "I am quite interested to learn more of the parish, if you, Miss Austen, and you, Miss Jane, would be so good to indulge me."

"We shall assist in any way we can, sir," said Cassandra.

"You see, it was the dear wish of my father that I should take orders and in due course, the living of the family estate. Sadly, events of such a nature I referred to earlier necessitated the selling of that living." His pale face flushed as the group politely absorbed revelation. "I do not wish to impugn my dear, departed father. No, my brother was not so . . . skilled, shall we say, either with cards or with economics. So I am now both duty bound to serve out my calling in the church, as well as discern, how shall we say . . . opportunities."

He played his first card and Emma followed after, glancing over the tips of her cards to Jane and Cassandra's faces. Though still a very new acquaintance, she had learned enough to see that Jane had started prickling and Cassandra readying to pacify.

"I understand that St. Swithin's, situated as it is in the parish of Walcot, may offer patrons who have additional endowments to . . . endow." As the round reached him again, he took out a card, debated it, then tucked it away and chose another. "I do not of course intend to imply that these patrons shall have my sole attentions." He shook a finger. "No, no, that is a definite failing indeed of a certain type of clergyman. For all God's creatures deserve the benefit of a watchful shepherd. Only that . . ."

"You'd like to know which sheep are ready to be fleeced?" said Jane as innocently as a Sunday school child. Then, she lay the trump card.

An awkward pause followed as Cassandra gathered the deck. Jane took a sip and gave a little jump which told Emma that Cassandra had very likely turned her role of pacifier to the more effective tack of shin kicker.

Miss Meyrick jumped in. "It is most unfortunate to hear of the loss of your family living, Mr. Baynes, and of course you should like to find a parish where you may commit yourself to your duties." She kept her eyes downcast, her trembling hands belying the courage it took to continue. "And I do not see you as that kind of clergyman. No, you and Mr. Landen are both, I am sure, penultimate representations of your professions."

"Allay your fears," said Jane, rising from the table. "Life is unpredictable. Your usurper may yet meet his employer ere long."

Emma rose with Jane and moved away, but not before hearing Cassandra saying, "she jests, Mr. Baynes. My sister has not always the best manner of showing her wit, but I assure you it was all in jest."

Away from the others, Jane turned to Emma. "Every jest has a kernel at its core."

"True enough," she returned. She glanced back at Mr. Baynes, his face gone scarlet as he swiped a handkerchief across his brow. "But I do think he is harmless enough. It cannot be easy to lose one's entire prospects through the stupidity of a sibling." Emma glanced sidelong as she realized what she'd just said, how true those words would ring in another decade and a half when it would be the beloved, favorite Henry who would bring ruin on his family.

Jane flapped a dismissive hand. "But surely, Miss Woods, whatever livings the sheep of Walcot have to bestow, would you not wish to see them in the hands of Mr. Landen? Is he not the clergyman we ought to champion?"

Emma returned her gaze to the table where Mark sat between Miss Meyrick and Mr. Baynes. He was attempting to amuse them by building a little house out of cards, taking on the air of a grand old gentleman speaking to his architect. With a puff of affected disdain, he blew them all down and slid them with a look of apology to Cassandra, who was waiting to deal the next hand. At the end of the round, he rose and clapped Mr. Baynes' shoulder, a gesture of fraternal familiarity that made the younger man grin up at him with a grateful, if puppyish, gaze. And Miss Meyrick rewarded him with a warm smile that had Emma rubbing at the sore hinge of her clenched jaw.

Emma excused herself and followed Mark to the refreshments table. She had no appetite, but she shadowed his movements, adding the same choices to her plate as he did to his.

"Finally," she said, her eyes on the shaved ham. "A moment alone."

Mark startled as though he hadn't realized she was next to him. "Alone?" he gazed back at the room.

"Well," she admitted, "as good as." She took a breath and stabbed a thick hunk of turkey. "Listen. I don't know what you're thinking . . . you know . . . about what I said. The other day. And I was hoping we could talk about . . . well . . . options."

"Options?" came a voice from behind.

Shoulders sagging, Emma turned to find all the young people of the room lining up with plates.

"Options for what?" Miss Meyrick said again.

"Oh," said Emma, stealing a quick glance at Jane, who was so intently focused on slicing the turkey, Emma knew she was keenly paying attention. "Well, you see, my uncle wrote to ask Mr. Landen his thoughts on . . . on . . . where we might find a place to live. A home," she said pointedly, this time forcing Mark to meet her eyes with the intensity of her stare. "Together. I mean, my uncle and myself of course."

Cassandra plunked a gleaming mound of brown mustard onto her plate. "Really, Miss Woods? I had not observed you receiving a letter earlier today." She turned as though to call out to Isaac.

"These were instructions I was given before I left home," Emma said. Once more, she looked at Mark with a directness that used to make her legs turn to jelly. Now, she found it compelled her to continue. "You see, my uncle was very grieved and shamed to realize he had not responded to an earlier message Mr. Landen sent. Over the summer?" She waited for him to nod. "It is of penultimate importance . . . to my uncle . . . that we sort it out between us now. It is not too late, is it, Mr. Landen? Please allow me to reassure my uncle that the chance for this discussion has not slipped him by."

"A discussion of housing?" said Cassandra. Once more, her tone belied her incredulity. "He is that passionate about discussing where he should live?"

"He is," Emma nodded. "Indeed he is."

Jane held her arms wide, ushering Cassandra, Miss Meyrick, and Mr. Baynes back to the card table, which had been cleared and set with napkins and flatware. "A discussion of this import should not be delayed," she said as they all moved away, though Cassandra again seemed ready to debate its necessity. Or plausibility. "No indeed," she said speaking as Cassandra opened her mouth. "We wouldn't delay you one more minute."

CHAPTER 16

The day appeared bright when Emma opened her eyes, but pulling the curtains aside revealed a thin grey sky, long wispy clouds adding texture as they drifted across. The sun was but a wan white orb hanging just above the rooftops, looking as sickly and uncertain as Emma felt.

Emma quickly changed into her own muslin. Sarah had done wonders with it, even managing to remove the coffee stain the cleaners with all their chemicals and technology couldn't lift. Descending the stairs, she caught the faint strains of the piano, a few notes tinkling out into the new dawn. Emma stopped only briefly to glance through and found Jane seated on the bench, though on this occasion, rather than stabbing at the paper in frustration, she scribbled as fast as her hand could manage, only stopping now and then to tap a melody on the keys before the pen took preeminence once again.

Emma snuck over the creaky floorboard and stole out. She turned in the direction of the bridge, enjoying the view of the church spire reaching up to snag a cloud or two, perhaps drape them over its towered shoulders like a shawl.

This early, the streets were filled with all the invisible people who made this society float along like a boat on calm waters. Scullery maids scrubbed at doorsteps. A horse stood with its head lowered, half sleeping as it clomped down the street, the grocer's delivery boy pulling boxes and passing them along to footmen and kitchen maids before they trotted the goods to the cooks below. The smells of breakfast filled the air and Emma's stomach grumbled. She wished she could have ducked down to the kitchen for an apple or biscuit, something to tide her over, but one's kitchen was not really one's own in this world, and the only option was to eat the prescribed foods at the prescribed times. If she ever did return to her time, she couldn't decide what she'd do first – down two Tylenol, devour a chocolate bar, or order an egg mcmuffin.

She stopped mid-stride, pulling at the folds of her gown until she found the pocket, and within it, her little notebook and pen. She dashed off a few quick lines, her stomach stirring with excitement as another essay idea began to formulate itself, a comparison between the immediate gratification expectations for pain relief, food, and more in our modern world to the realities of this one. Her hand cramped around the tiny pencil, and when she could write no more, she settled the items back in her pocket, rubbing the thick oyster muscle in her palm.

She spotted Mark near the river, his elbows propped on the iron railing extending from the stone rampart. He held the stem of a weed in one hand and was picking it apart, tossing green detritus over the edge and watching it swirl in the waters below.

She sidled up and leaned on the railing as well, bumping him with her shoulders, hoping for one of his friendly grins. "Morning."

"Morning." He looked round them and Emma followed his gaze. The bridge was more active than they had anticipated. The lights in the upper rooms of the houses nearby remained darkened, the curtains pulled. And yet an entire other world, a larger one it appeared, bustled about below so that the days being dreamt of above could pass with the serenity of languor and idleness. Here too, shop boys swept the sidewalks before shuttered stores. Vendors with their carts and baskets milled along, preserving their energies and voices until later, when front doors opened and houses ejected their pretty occupants, pockets full of coin, back into the white glare of society's ever-watchful eye.

Again, Emma's mind erupted with ideas – the chores of the servant class versus the chores of the gentility. Though Jane and Cassandra might whip off a shirt now and then from the poor basket, here were people who not only had to make their own clothes and linens from scratch, but also had to clean and mend those of others. Where did they possibly find the time? Emma slipped the notebook from her pocket once more.

Mark glanced over her shoulder. She could feel his eyes on her pages, and while it made her nervous in a school-girlish way, she did not pause. When Quinn stood behind her at her desk, reading over her shoulder, it rankled and she would turn off her screen until he wandered away to watch the game of whatever sport was in season. But she found she did not mind this time, not with Mark.

"Good ideas, there," he said. "You've listed mainly female servants' duties. Be sure to include the men."

Emma glanced over her list. "Of course." She made a bullet point to hold place for Mark's idea. "Good thought."

"And you know, once they're living in that cottage, they'll have one man-servant. What other chores might spinster clusters have had to do that a husband or son would have done for them?"

"Right," Emma said, breathless as though her hand were drawing every ounce of energy from her. "Good thoughts."

"Just building on yours." His hand reached out to tuck back a strand of loose hair which she was unsuccessfully trying to blow out of her eyes as she scribbled, but just as the back of his cool fingers touched her cheek, he drew away, glancing about as a manure cart rolled past, pushed by a man who looked like he might have slept the night before right on top.

Mark started off toward the parade grounds. "We'll need to get further afield," he said as soon as she caught up. "Away from the crowds."

"Well Mark, perhaps we should just talk." She struggled to get her notebook back in her pocket. "You know, about . . . us?"

Mark stopped under a tree, its branches extending low over the water. Underneath, they could almost pretend they were alone. He helped her find the pocket within her skirts and slip the notebook back inside.

"I figured if you were making notes, then you changed your mind." He looked across the river, put his hands in his pockets and drew the panels of his coat close around himself.

"It's a habit, I guess," she said. "Write down every idea; even the bad ones. It's what I tell my students."

He nodded.

"But I still want to stay." She moved closer to him, slid her hand into the pocket of his coat and the warm nest of his palm.

"It won't be whatever you fantasize. We're not the Austens or the Brooksides."

Across the river, a peddler pushed a cart. Pots of all sizes dangled from its top, rough-made work boots hung by their laces from a series of pegs, and other random bric-a-brac were stacked near to toppling from its sides. Behind the peddler, a woman trudged at some distance, a gaggle of children of various ages from adolescent to toddler strung out behind.

"Life would more likely be like that than what you've been experiencing," he said. "And even if I could pass myself off in some respectable profession, what about the rest of it? You'd be relegated to a life of sewing, knitting, mending, and cooking. You would be a housekeeper in its crudest sense.

"And," he paused, a blush rising on his wan cheeks, "if there were . . . erm . . . children," he swallowed. "You would endure . . . that . . . without medicines. There are no epidurals here and childbed fever is no joke."

"I know it's not a joke," Emma replied. "Do you think I haven't imagined these outcomes myself? Still, the hardships of a life here are known to us. We can survive this world."

It was Emma's turn to swallow. To swallow the truth. To suck back the bitter bile of the forthcoming lie. "It is the hardships of whatever unknown timeframe we may arrive at that scares me most." But the image that sprang to her mind was not of some medieval or ancient past, but Quinn's face, and the decimated look that would surely pass over it when she returned and gave him her answer. It was her own self-knowledge crying out that her courage when faced with his disappointment might just fail her.

She had always chosen the easiest path, the one least likely to upset or incommode. The path that said what she wanted must surely be less important than what anyone else did.

She pulled her hand from his pocket and began twisting up her handkerchief, worrying it into a tight coil gripped in her fist.

She saw the fears of her hypothesis unfold once more upon his face. And it pained her. It pained her that her own desire to stay, her offerings of a life together, the hints of love and commitment – these did not seem to be enough for him. He should want to stay for her and her alone. And he didn't.

And in turn, she had resorted to using schoolyard tactics to frighten him into doing what she wanted.

He had moved to the water's edge and was probing with a stick, checking its depth. He turned as though to speak and stopped. "Emma, what is it?"

She flicked the tear off her cheek. "Nothing." She released the coil of handkerchief from her hand and wiped at her face. "It's just . . . I thought . . . after everything . . . that you'd want to stay . . . with me." Her voice had gone progressively softer so that her final words came out barely more than a whisper.

He stepped forward as though about to ask her to repeat it, then said only, "Oh."

Now it was he who worried the stick in his hands, checking how far the water had come up, testing its pliability. Until it broke.

And he sighed. Worse, he nodded. "Even setting aside the worries of our friends back home, which are not a small consideration . . . well, in truth . . ." He tossed the two halves into the water and watched them float downstream.

Something of a resolve settled on him. She saw it in his face. The way he set his shoulders and strode to her. "I want you to choose me, Emma. To choose *me*. And staying here," he gestured round the streets beyond. "It's just . . . I don't know if you're choosing me or Jane or this era, or maybe just running away from something . . . someone else."

He had held her gaze throughout his halting speech, but now his eyes dropped away, and she saw his shoulders heaving as he drew breath. It had taken all he had to speak to her like this, with an honesty their friendship had never made room for before, and she could see the effort etched plain across his face. A face that would not look at her.

And she too felt the pounding of her heart, her breath running quick and ragged.

Because she did not know how to answer him.

They stood under the tree for many more minutes, silently, gazes cast different directions, until Mark took her hand and gave it a squeeze and suggested they think about their options more and regroup later in the day. Emma nodded and when they parted at the Pulteney Bridge, she realized she had not squeezed his hand back. She felt the emptiness of her palm, closing her fingers tight around an empty fist, clenching until her tendons cried out and she released her hand once more. Still empty.

CHAPTER 17

Back at 4 Sydney Place, Emma managed to sneak to her room and had the sparest of moments to sit at the end of her bed and think. But to think was to be faced with Mark's doubts, his accusations. She wanted to choose him; she thought she *was* choosing him by asking him to stay here with her, form a life with her. But that wasn't how it appeared to him. What would it take to convince him? To convince . . . herself?

Jane's knock calling her down to breakfast was a welcome interruption. At the table, she took a helping of pound cake from Jane and a mug of hot chocolate, but a simple "thanks" was all the contribution she made by way of conversation. She could see her hosts' concern, and worse still, Cassandra's skeptical expression. The best she could manage was a weak claim to a return of her headache and excuse herself.

Shortly after, a knock at her door was followed by Jane's concerned mien. She held a small glass of port, a book tucked under her arm.

"I thought you could use this," she said, handing Emma the glass. "And I could read to you until you dozed off?"

Emma took the offered wine and slammed it. When she remained at the dressing table, Jane set the book at the end of the bed and plucked at some lint on her gown.

"If you would permit me the impertinence, Miss Woods, might I brush your hair?" She smiled shyly. "I've always found it soothing to brush my sister's hair, or my nieces' – at least the ones who don't yelp at the tangles."

Emma held out the brush. Sitting here under the gaze of her idol, having her hair brushed as though she were a little girl was not the panacea she needed, but it was a balm nonetheless.

Jane's expression clouded and she opened her mouth to speak but closed it again. A few moments later, she tilted her head to the side, furrowed her brow, and seemed almost to speak before changing her mind again. After many minutes, she managed one, "Miss Woods, might I ask . . ." before her words trailed off.

"Just spit it out."

Jane's shocked reflection brought the glimmer of a smile to Emma's mouth.

"Now you must forgive my impertinence. It's just a saying that means, I can tell you have something to say, so please proceed."

"I'm of an inquisitive nature," she began. "I've been afflicted since birth, or so Cassandra says." She divided Emma's hair into three sections and began to braid each one. "It's just that seeing Dr. Lethbridge at Rickford's reminded me that when you first arrived, you called Dr. Lethbridge by another name." Jane tapped the comb to her chin, trying to remember.

"Quinn," Emma supplied.

"Yes, that was it. I wondered . . . that is, would I be impertinent to ask who you were referring to?"

Emma shook her head. "It is not an impertinence. He is my . . . that is, he was . . . someone I thought I might marry."

"But you do not think so anymore?"

Emma faltered. What could she say? I might marry him . . . but only if I break through the seal of time and fast-forward 200 years? Where you, Miss Jane, happen to be a veritable god in the little Pantheon of my life? And where I seem to blunder about with all the worst traits of your best characters?

What answer could she give except that she might marry him if Mark wouldn't have her, as shameful as it was to acknowledge. Because she knew it was a truth. She would choose Mark if he would let her. And if he didn't, then she would slip her cart back into the wheel-ruts they were most comfortable in. It shamed her. As she opened her lips to speak, nothing came but a sob.

"Oh, my dear Miss Woods, how cruel of me." Jane put a hand on Emma's shoulder. "Did he . . . die?"

Her face departed from curiosity and moved into the shadows of her own grief. She looked toward the windows, her eyes going dull as memory.

She shook her head once. "My sister has had just such a loss. A fiancé who died many years ago."

Emma nodded. When Jane tilted her head, a puzzled look on her face, Emma jumped in. "That is, while I do not know the . . . uh, particulars of your sister's grief, it . . . uh . . . seems to me that so many young women around us have tread this terrain."

"Yes," Jane said, "the path to the altar is rarely a direct one."

Emma snorted. It was the first real laugh she'd had all day. And it reminded her that despite all the troubles of her life, she was sitting here and listening to Jane Austen query some of the very thematic impulses that drove her creativity.

"I am glad to have amused you." Her tone implied an uncertainty as to whether she should take offense. "What I mean to say, I suppose, is that if my sister and I can both survive such a loss, then surely, you will too."

Emma's mouth opened; she was about to speak when Jane seemed to realize what she'd revealed. "Which is to say, that it was very painful to me to see her in so much grief."

Still, that unspoken truth lay between them. For all her efforts to obfuscate, Jane seemed willing to allow Emma this momentary incursion into her private life. Emma put a hand over Jane's, squeezed it, and said, "the loss of a fiancé, of someone who might have been a fiancé – it is not just the loss of one person, but of a lifetime."

Now it was Jane who swiped the tear spilling onto her cheek. As before, the thought came to mind that this was the time, this the moment. But as soon as it arose, Emma stamped it down. She would not be a voyeur to the pain writ so clear across Jane's face, like paparazzi with their telephoto lenses pursuing bereaved celebrities to the gravesides of their husbands, wives, parents, children. It would be a cruelty, she could see, and though her own academic curiosity beat like a battering ram, she held fast. Whatever he had been, *whomever* he had been, Emma would not forage through that misery to satiate curiosity. Even back in her own time, these proofs would hold no more weight than hypothesis because who would believe she'd gotten the story from Austen herself?

Even now, she could hardly believe it. Even now, she wondered if it wouldn't be easier for this to be a dream, a fantasy, a delusion, after all.

Distraction was needed and thus, Emma returned to herself. "You asked about . . . Mr., uh, Quinn. He's not dead. It's just – now I'm here, I simply don't know what's going to happen. Everything seems entirely . . . uncertain."

How easily these truths seemed to come – some of them anyway. Within the indefinable boundaries that kept her here, separated from Quinn, she could finally speak with a candor made ironic by all the lies built up like walls around it.

"If I'm being totally honest," she said, taking a shallow breath, "I'm not sure I should marry him at all. He's a good man. Kind. Thoughtful – most of the time. But it's not true love. It's safety. And I've gone along because I don't have any better offers."

With those words out of her, suspended between them, she felt release and relief rush through her, and her shoulders loosened, the ache in her jaw eased, and even her heart seemed to take a respite from its furious beating.

"Does that make me a terrible person, Miss Jane? If I just go along with what's easiest and safest and most comfortable."

Jane's laugh was so hearty, it drew a smile from Emma. "Of course not!" she said. "If marrying for ease, comfort, and safety were some crime, you'd have to lock up nearly all the married women you meet with!"

Jane sat at the end of Emma's bed and picked up the book she had brought, flipping through the pages and discarding it with a dissatisfied sigh. "This world is not for us, Miss Woods. For women who think like we do. I have ever thought so. My mother says 'bend to the world, Jane. Bend or be broken.' My sister says, 'it is the world we've been given. Make the most of it and hope for change.' But my brother Henry, he sees something else. 'Remake the world, Jane,' he tells me. 'Shine your light. It is your duty.'" She shook her head. "Easy for him to say, is it not. Men may remake the world any way they choose. But we, we must live in it, mess and all."

She returned to Emma's side and squeezed her shoulders. "Well, those are my own tribulations, you see. But for you," she said, pausing to fasten a tendril that had come loose of the braid. "I rather sense, Miss Woods, that you're not one to let the fates carry you too far off your course. So long as you know what that course is." With a smile and a parting comment that they should see her for luncheon, Jane left.

Emma stared at her reflection. Her hair was braided and wrapped in a loose bun, leaving a corona of gold round her face. She put a hand to her cheek, warm from the crying, but so pale. Her eyes looked both shrunken and swollen, a combination that did her no favors. She did not wear a lot of makeup – just a dab of powder, a little mascara, and tinted lip balm. Now, her face looked every bit of her 34 years, the creases around her eyes more prominent. The laugh lines she admired – symbols of making it this far in life with a smile being her most frequent expression – appeared longer and deeper, startlingly similar to the lines on the face of a ventriloquist's dummy.

If Emma had done anything so far, it was just what Jane had said she'd never tolerate: to allow the fates to push her hither and thither, to follow the whim of one man while secretly pining for another, to give in to a life of passive acceptance. It was how she had always been. She had bent and still been broken. She had hoped but hope was like a bird, weightless and flighty, startled away at the merest disturbance.

And it was not the world that needed remaking but herself.

But what was it Jane had said at the end, about keeping her course once she knew it? Did Emma know her true course? Would she have the courage to follow it once she did? Setting her shoulders, Emma rose from the dressing table. She could sense something just over the edge of the horizon, could feel it the way a story or essay might start brewing somewhere inside her, an idea she couldn't yet see or touch, but which she could feel on the periphery, waiting to make itself known.

At lunch, the Austens commented on the plans for the day. Jane appeared with two letters folded but not sealed. She nodded once at Emma and gave her a bolstering half-wink as she passed behind Cassandra to the sideboard.

She grabbed a leftover breakfast bunn and stuffed it in her mouth, then started opening and rifling through every drawer in the room.

"For Manydown?" Cassandra asked, picking up letters Jane had tossed on the table.

Jane nodded and made a noise round her mouthful of sweetbread. Swallowing her huge bite, she said, "yes, one for Althea and one to Charles as well. I want to confirm the date of our arrival, but I cannot find a single wafer!"

Mr. Austen jumped at the last slammed drawer. "Oh yes, Sarah needed one, and I believe she may have gotten the last."

Jane slumped into her chair, stacking her letters beside her plate. When the thick paper refused to stay folded, Jane clanked her tea cup down on top.

Mrs. Austen, with an eye-roll for Jane's poor table manners, tapped her fork to the table. "There was something I needed as well." She drew a finger down her long aquiline nose in contemplation. "Oh yes, Dr. Lethbridge recommended a tonic for your father. This is the address of his apothecary." She slid a piece of paper to Cassandra. "Perhaps you girls might get a glimpse of him, so do be sure your hair is – "

"Yes, Mama," Jane and Cassandra said in unison.

"And your gowns are – ."

"Yes, Mama!"

Mr. Austen pulled a handful of letters from the pocket of his flannel waistcoat. "And here are mine." He flipped through them. "Yes, one for James. There's Henry's. For Neddie. And Fly." He grinned. "Our son Frances, Miss Woods," though no explanation was needed for Emma, who could have explained the origin of all the pet-names in the Austen household. He passed his stack to Cassandra. "And Charles we shall see in less than a fortnight, so he will have to wait for our news."

"And you Miss Woods," said Mrs. Austen. "I am certain your uncle should wish for news of your stay, how you get on here in Bath, whom you've met. Have you any word from him?"

Emma's tea went down wrong and she had to hide behind her napkin until she could speak once more. "Very kind of you, mum. Indeed, I should get a letter off."

Cassandra watched from a corner of her eye. "We shall be walking to Milsom Street, Miss Woods. You may purchase some stationary then."

"Oh for shame, Cassie," Jane broke in. "Surely, we can spare Miss Woods a sheet of paper. I'm sure her uncle will be more than grateful for all the care we're taking of his charge." She gave an arch look that Emma suspected was meant to convey that her uncle's gratitude might be well applied toward their brothers' progress in the Navy.

It shamed Emma to have to continue this lie when Jane had shown such candor and kindness a few hours ago. She tucked back into her meal and prayed for a change of subject.

"And then we've the ball at the Lower Rooms," Jane said. "Surely you are excited, Miss Woods, to reenact your stunning success of two nights previous."

Emma only sighed. "Balls are pleasant enough," she said, "but it would be much more rational if conversation, rather than dancing, were the order of the day." Oh dear, she *was* low if she was reduced to quoting Caroline Bingley.

"Hear, hear," piped Mr. Austen. "And then I might bother to attend one!"

"Much more rational," Cassandra said, "but rather less like a ball."

Mr. and Mrs. Austen chuckled.

Jane stood abruptly, the legs of her chair juddering over the floorboards. "Excuse me," she said, dashing out with the door ajar behind her, already digging in her pockets for paper and pencil.

Cassandra looked to Emma. "I know that dash," she said. For all her stinginess a moment ago, she squeezed Emma's hand just as lightning flashed beyond the window and a massive crack of thunder shook the panes.

Mr. Austen let out a yelp of surprise, then clutched his chest. Mrs. Austen and Cassandra rushed to his side, while he tried to flap them away, saying, "just a startle. That's all. That's all!" When another thunderclap turned him white as the tablecloth, they badgered and pestered, one to each side, until he allowed them to help him upstairs.

The room at her command, Emma pushed aside the curtain and observed the scene beyond. As rain lashed the pavement, all dashed for shelter – horses and carriages, gentlemen and ladies on foot, hawkers with their wares in carts. She'd learned enough of Bath to realize no one would be out if there were even a sniff of rain, and certainly not with the kind of ominous thunderclouds suddenly commandeering the skies.

There was that tug in her mind again, telling her something was there, something just below the surface, a thought like the fish she used to see as a girl playing in the stream behind her grandmother's house – just a glimmer of scales and then gone, a flash of movement and then nothing.

She tried to remember the past storms. The first had been on the day of their arrival. Jane had been walking her upstairs and she'd . . . Emma paced, tapping her temples. It had to be there! What else had been going on? Oh yes, she'd been making up a story to explain her arrival in Bath, something about staying at a friend's house, being kicked out in the dead of night, taking the coach . . . that plot point from *Northanger Abbey*.

Later that night, Emma and Mark had bandied the conversation about letter writing that occurs between Mr. Darcy and Miss Bingley, and the storm had whipped itself into further fury.

What next? It was . . . it was the assembly. The Upper Rooms. Just after tea, a storm. But what had preceded it? Oh yes, that jerk of a Miss Brookside had been giving her grief over reading novels. And Emma . . . Emma'd said that thing about one half the world not understanding the other half. That was from *Emma*.

It was starting to take shape. The next was the following morning on the bridge. The beggarwoman and her child. Then Emma'd said something about being passed from man to man – poor Eliza Brandon. *Sense and Sensibility*!

How many other lines had she let fall in the meantime, lines that flowed like water from her own mouth, leaving a slippery, wet mess on the floor?

How stupid she'd been. Utterly, completely stupid. She was quoting Austen's own lines back to her, lines that remained, as yet, locked tight in the labyrinth of her genius mind. Emma had to remember that this was 1802, that Jane was still suffering from the move and possibly the death (or betrayal) of the clergyman, stymied in her writing, not yet having even begun the revision on Northanger Abbey that would lead to its acceptance late in 1803.

No, she wasn't rewriting history exactly – how could she? She'd read those lines from Austen – but clearly, she was getting things out of order.

And the Universe was not pleased.

A flashing thought nearly took her legs from under her: what if you're changing it. Changing it all. What if Jane Austen never becomes *the* Jane Austen.

She returned to the table and sank into the nearest chair. The thought made her restless and weak. She wanted to be moving but she couldn't trust herself to stand. Her foot jiggled until the table itself vibrated in time, she gnawed the tips of three fingernails, she dropped her head into her hands until the rhythm of the wobbling table made her seasick.

Simple, she told herself. No more Austen.

Nodding, she stood. The door opened. Expecting Sarah come to clear the breakfast things, Emma tried to tidy the table a bit.

"Oh don't bother about that," came Cassandra's voice.

"Miss Austen! I thought you were Sarah."

Cassandra took a seat and gestured for Emma to join her.

"How is your father?"

"Well enough," Cassandra said. "Though my mother is like as not to come down with some mysterious complaint as soon as he's well." She took out the list her father had given her at lunch and made a mark. "We shall get two of those tonics, I think." She fiddled with a knife for a bit, then smoothed out the tablecloth. On her face, her brows furrowed deeply, her mouth set in a determined line.

Emma rose to give Cassandra privacy to fret over her father. As for herself, she had little thought for anything other than to continue deconstructing these discoveries. She needed the quiet, the safety, of her room.

At the door, Cassandra's voice caught Emma up short. "There is no uncle, is there?"

Emma froze, one foot suspended over the threshold. She drew it back in and closed the door silently, standing for one long and incriminating moment with her face pressed to the wood. Emma took her seat again and stared at her lap. "Miss Austen, I assure you . . ."

Cassandra waved a hand. "I did not like you, Miss Woods. At first. And frankly, I never believed your little tale about the friend and the father. And I have my doubts as to the existence of this uncle, for that matter, though I can't understand why a decent man such as Mr. Landen would draw himself into such a lie."

"Miss Austen," Emma began. "Cassandra, please let me . . ."

"Your uncle," Cassandra broke in. "Which color of flag did he carry?"

Emma rifled through the filing cabinets of her mind. Her studies had focused on Jane's works, the society, the monarchy – and very little on the military. None in fact. She tried to remember what Admiral Croft had been. "Yellow?" she offered. "Or Gold, maybe?"

Cassandra snorted her victory. "But, I find these little lies matter not. You have been a good help to us here, Miss Woods. Kind to my father. And more than that." Cassandra went to the sideboard, rearranging the dried twigs of an old nosegay they had not yet bothered to throw out. "With Jane. She has not been . . . herself. But meeting you has stirred something in her. And I am . . ." Cassandra took a breath. "Grateful."

The silence spread through the room, the fog of accusations and uncertainties thinning, until all that was left was the shining love of one sister for another, grasping onto hope in any form it might take. Emma had herself noticed the change in Jane. She was no longer the morose woman she'd first seen at the riverside. She was light, playful. More than that, she was inspired. Emma could not say thank you, and she certainly could not say you're welcome. For all Emma knew, her "inspirations" had caused more harm than good.

"And so I am resolved, Miss Woods," Cassandra said at last. "To play along with your ruse so long as nothing goes amiss in this household. And so long as your presence seems to do my sister good. But understand me that I will not allow – ."

"I would never – ."

Cassandra waved a hand to stop her words, a gesture Emma found herself grateful for. She would never hurt Jane, and yet she also could not escape the sobering apprehension that she may very well have already injured more than could be atoned for. Realizing her part in the storms, Emma was now clenched by a new fear clawing its way in, made sharp by her uncertainty, and heavier still because she could not even begin to fathom just how much she might have damaged already. If she did not go back, she would never know if she ruined Jane Austen.

Cassandra gave Emma one parting look, what could not be called friendly exactly, but which seemed to solidify whatever truce had just sprung up between them.

And so. She must stop with the Austenisms or risk consequences worse than a few thunderstorms. And if she stopped, she would crumble whatever footing Jane had found, as well as Emma's own.

CHAPTER 18

Once more, the evening found Emma powdered, primped, and be-ribboned, though for this occasion, she had sworn off any assistance by a hairdresser. Happily, it appeared Jane and Cassandra had no thought for his services and only suggested it for her benefit. Instead, the three women crowded into Jane and Cassandra's cozy room and took turns at the dressing table, assisting one another in simpler coiffures. Simple they might be, but Emma watched in amazement as pin after pin disappeared into her hair. For Jane, Emma drew her dark hair back into a chic roll, then laced roses all through.

"A French twist, you say?" Jane used a small hand mirror to look at the delicate single curl. "I've never heard Eliza discuss such a thing."

She looked to Cassandra, who only shrugged, but nodded at the prettiness of the style.

Cupping a hand delicately round it, Jane continued. "Our sister, Miss Woods. Though now but a mere Mrs. Austen, she was once the Comtesse de Feuillide. Now that was a very advantageous marriage. At least until – " Jane drew a finger across her neck and leaned toward Emma. "Monsier le Guillotine."

Emma stifled her laugh at Cassandra's thin-lipped frown.

Cassandra left to find more shoe roses, having been forced to send Sarah to fetch some due to the rainshowers throughout the morning, threatening all with another evening at home. Emma'd had to hold her tongue when Cassandra complained they were not quite right, almost commenting on the risk of shoe roses got by proxy.

Standing, Jane twirled first one way, then the other. She nodded with finality. "Well, are you prepared to conquer the Lower Rooms, Miss Woods?"

Emma shuddered. Prepared to dance until her feet felt like two leaden stubs? Prepared to make asinine conversation – what passed for "pleasant" on the pages of a novel – with all kinds of primping, preening dandies? Prepared to watch Miss Meyrick throw her charmingly naïve self at Mark? Prepared to calculate and weigh every word she was about to say, measuring out doses of Austen like spoonfuls of nauseating medicine? She shook her head. "I should much rather sit upon a bench and admire the room peacefully with a cup of tea in my hand."

Jane tsked. "How disappointing! For I am primed to admire and despise you simultaneously as you captivate the room."

Cassandra appeared in the doorway, unsuccessful in discovering any other colors. "Jane. Miss Woods. We must depart or we shall be late."

Sarah entered to carry their thin summer mantles to the door.

Once more, Mr. Austen accompanied them to the pavement, this time with the aid of a cane and a thick blanket wrapped round his shoulders. Mrs. Austen also stayed behind, though not for the sake of her husband, but because she had come down with a piercing earache and a series of shudderings she feared would result in a faint. She had sent a note to Mrs. Brookside to act as chaperone for them once they arrived.

Setting off toward the Lower Rooms, Cassandra and Jane shared a look. "It was only so long before Mama realized what she was missing out on," Jane said.

Cassandra rolled her eyes. "They shall keep each other fine company."

"Oh certainly," Jane returned. "And argue over who should lie on the sofa and who should have the thinnest bowl of gruel. Poor Baxter. I do not envy her role of dosing laudanum."

Laudanum. Emma's mouth almost watered at the prospect of a few hours' relief from the constant aching of her feet, her knees, her back, her head. But no, the last thing she needed was to muddle her mind with an opium haze. The last time she got shnackered, she'd recited a full half-hour's worth of the newest *Emma* adaptation to Quinn's bored sister – she'd have done the whole thing if Jess hadn't made an escape to the dance floor, after which Emma made the inevitable slide under the table, not so very unlike the ribbon still lying tangled below Jane's dressing table.

Crossing back over the Avon, once more a raging, cascading, thoroughly murkified torrent, Emma followed Jane and Cassandra toward the Lower Rooms. She had never seen them in real life (real life, she smirked, whatever *that* meant anymore). The original building had been pulled down in her Bath, history sacrificed to convenience. But there it was before them, all white columns and candlelit windows. Emma stopped short as she stared.

"Lovely, isn't it?" Jane asked.

"Oh yes," Emma breathed. "So much better than a parking lot." Clearing her throat, she picked up her skirts and strode forward before either Jane or Cassandra could repeat their perplexed, "whaaaat?"

Already, guests teemed around the entrances, the windows showing the faces of young ladies watching for their beaus. As they drew near, Emma felt a tap at her shoulder. She hoped to find Mark standing at her side, giving her a smile, an eyebrow waggle to say their morning at the river was forgiven, forgotten. But it was Miss Meyrick's pretty, artless smile which greeted her.

"How delightful, Miss Woods, to meet here." She slipped her hand through Emma's arm, and gave a polite, though somewhat intimidated, nod to Jane and Cassandra. "To meet one's acquaintance on the doorstep is so much pleasanter than to have to search the rooms, is it not?"

"And Mr. Landen?" Jane asked from behind. "Is he not escorting you this evening?" The tone of Jane's voice had an edge to it, her question as prickly as the sweet gum pods littering the sidewalk in front of Quinn's building, threatening to twist Emma's ankle or spike her soles. Emma turned round to shoot a look and found Jane waggling a satirical brow.

"Oh," said Miss Meyrick. "I believe he will be present. That is to say, he did not say he would not be coming. And so I think that he must. But I cannot say for certain. He has been locked in father's study all morning, and I have not seen him once. Which is not to say that I watch for him, or anything. But I have not had the opportunity to confirm his attendance. Though certainly, I think it most likely that . . ." Emma patted Miss Meyrick's hand and gave her a friendly nod, stopping the girl from whirlpooling further into a verbal spiral of hopes and desires tempered and confused by the polite and appropriate.

"I am sure he will be arriving shortly," Emma supplied, as much for her own sake as anyone else's. She made a quick survey of the crowd beginning to ooze into the building, but not seeing Mark's tall figure, she turned a reassuring smile back toward Miss Meyrick.

Once more, Cassandra led them through the vestibule and into the ballroom. Here, the rooms were not so large as the Upper Rooms, but just as beautiful. The ceiling rose all the way to the roof, tall arched windows lining the long wall opposite the entrance, and chandeliers tinkling high overhead to supplement the waning light as sun gave way to moon.

As the room filled, so too it grew warmer and became permeated with the scents of lavender and rose water. The occasional whiffs of stronger perfumes scraped Emma's sinuses and threatened to bring on a migraine. And below it all, a pungent redolence wafted up from every raised arm, reminding her that for all the gilt chandeliers and be-ribboned slippers, they were all of them just bodies trapped in one place.

Many hours later, Emma sat through tea, the amber liquid sour in her mouth, agitating her stomach. The evening had not gone the way she'd hoped at all. She had tried to reach Mark, to get through to him. But even the process of getting *to* him was almost more than she could accomplish. He had joined their ensemble just before the first dance. He had extended his hand, but when Emma lifted her own to place within it, she found his gaze turned toward Miss Meyrick.

He had slighted her.

She could practically see the sentence itself forming behind Jane's eyes, and the only consolation she drew from that moment was to remember that none of Jane's heroines would be so publicly shamed as she had just been. A slim consolation since they would all feel it at some point, whether it be a dropped comment about altered appearances, a hasty exit from the discovery of a sister's shame, an angry retreat after the confession of ignorant assumptions, or worst of all, watching one's beloved court another. If only she had the fortitude of an Anne, a Lizzy, a Catherine, or a Fanny.

Then again, fortitude was perhaps just another word for how a woman walks in the world when the shell of herself is filled with disappointment, regret, and resentment. For what else could a woman do – not just of this age, but any – except persevere?

"Miss Woods?"

A hand at her arm startled Emma. She gazed down to find the slick silk of Jane's glove upon her own.

"Miss Woods, you seem lost in thought."

"Lost," Emma repeated. "Indeed, I believe I am." She gave a rueful smile. "Lost in thinking how sore I am become."

Every muscle in her body was in revolt over the exertions she was putting them through. Her heart ached for Mark, and oddly, a small corner kept a candle lit for Quinn as well. And her mind throbbed against her inability to figure anything out. Or perhaps, more accurately, for her refusal to embrace a new truth – that an entire demolition of who and what she had been to make way for someone new, someone better was an impending next step. Sore was an understatement.

"Well, you did dance nearly every set," Jane said, this time with none of the envy that marked the same comment a few days before. "But it occurs to me that perhaps this soreness you speak of relates to just one dance." She cocked an astute eyebrow in Emma's direction and took another discreet sip of her tea.

Emma could not help but smile at Jane's playfulness, remembering also that just a few days ago, this was a woman whose face was as dark and troubled as her own must be. It seemed they had traded that cloudy veil over the past few days, which was another bit of respite: to feel she had eased something for Jane, even if it meant wrapping it round her own shoulders instead.

In response to Jane's allusion, Emma shrugged and nodded and shook her head and both of them laughed.

Emma had been dancing nearly every set, once more beset by more suitors than she had hands to offer or the orchestra had songs to play. After Mark's slight, they were ships passing, Emma being dragged back to the dancefloor just as Mark returned from it. It was only at the dance before tea when he had managed to snag her arm and lead her to the floor.

"I came for you after the first set," he said, tetchily. "But you were gone off. If they used dance cards, I'm not sure there'd be room for my name on it."

Emma held her hand as lightly in Mark's as she could, the sting of his snub still tingling. "Well, I thank you for the condescension," she said.

As they strode up the outside of the set and rejoined under the canopy of the top dancers, she fumed. "But as you see, I need not scrabble for part-ners," she said when their hands joined once more.

He huffed. "Oh, I am well aware."

Around them, couples danced gracefully, faces parting in shy smiles or animated displays of pleasure. As the dance wore on, Emma's ire rose until she thought she might scream until every crystal dangling from the chan-deliers above popped and covered them all in sparkling dust. She was once more struck by the ridiculousness of her jealousy and anger, that she had no claims on Mark, that whatever claims she was trying to place now were simply no longer good or deep or meaningful enough, a fact he had made painfully clear that morning on the riverside.

As they made a turn toward the top of the room, Emma glanced over to their group, and saw the giggles Miss Meyrick was sandwiched between and the hastily concealed finger as Miss Lucy pointed at Mark while Miss Margaret jabbed a teasing elbow.

Mark had followed her gaze. "For heaven's sake, but this is all so ridicu-lous. As if I don't have enough to worry about without a schoolgirl crush on top of it."

"Worry?" Emma's eyes rolled and she wouldn't have even noticed she'd done it but for the sharp look that crossed Mark's face.

"Yes, Emma. Worry. I have a sermon to give tomorrow, I'm stuck in a time where every rusty nail reminds me of the tetanus shot I was due for last spring – among a number of other similar worries, I don't have any idea how to get back, and the person who brought me here thinks only of ..." He stopped.

"Only of what, Mark?"

Mark shook his head. "Nothing. It's just. This isn't all about you, you know. Other people are suffering here." He gazed at the room around them. "Forget it. It won't matter once we've returned to our real lives."

Though he hadn't said it, Emma could feel different words skimming beneath – me to mine and you to yours. Whatever he imagined for them on the other side of time, they would be just as separated there as they were now. As they had always been. And now Mark was revealing what he really thought of her, a self Emma couldn't disclaim but which shamed her nonetheless.

The dance concluded and rather than lead Emma into tea as was the custom, Mark had excused himself, saying he needed air. When he came in later, he took a seat at the farthest end of their table.

Emma sipped the dregs from her cup and gazed toward him, the ache in her stomach turning over until she thought she might be sick. Worse still was the ringing of the bell announcing the recommencement of the assembly.

"Miss Jane, could I ask you the greatest of favors?"

"I should be glad to oblige any request you make of me."

"Good. Stomp on my foot." Emma extended her leg, offering her foot like a golden calf. "If I have to dance one more set with one more conceited toff, I may just implode."

Jane sputtered her tea. "What a violent solution, Miss Woods," she said, as she laughed and dabbed the tablecloth. "But if you wish, I shall plead your excuses to your would-be suitors."

Emma nodded gratefully. She had only been half-joking about the foot stomping. She would take any excuse not to jump and spin and promenade. Not another single time. Not even if Mr. Darcy himself with his devastating good-looks and £10,000 a year entered the room. Not even Captain Wentworth in his dashing naval coat. An image of Mark down on bended-knee flashed in her mind. Ok, well maybe then.

A noisy to-do interrupted the entire room, and the sea of tea drinkers parted to reveal the Prodigal Gentlemen, whom the younger Miss Brooksides had spent the entire evening lamenting the absence of: Captain Richards, Lieutenant Listle, Mr. Werthing, and surprisingly Dr. Lethbridge. The gentlemen grouped around the end of their table, apologizing for their lateness and offering excuses of having dined at their club and losing track of time discussing politics. As they spoke, Captain Richards patted his pockets in a manner indicating that "politics" might well be a polite stand-in for the gaming table. Emma could not be sure whether his taps were for the triumphs of winning or lamentations over losses, and doubted whether his indefatigable good nature would be much influenced by either.

"Politics? Bah! Lost in talk about a certain young lady," Captain Richards joked, winking at Emma "When a certain someone heard you were a regular in our set, he insisted on joining us." He nodded toward Dr. Lethbridge who made himself very busy offering to escort Mrs. Brookside back to the ballroom. Captain Richards extended a hand. "We hope you've saved us all a dance, Miss Woods, some of us hoping perhaps a little harder than others."

Jane was quick to intervene, making a big show of helping Emma to her feet. "Oh dear, I'm afraid you will have to be satisfied with conversation. Miss Woods, it seems, twisted her ankle most horrendously on some steps as we came in to tea. She is unable to dance the rest of this evening. However, I have no partner, you see."

With a gallant bow, Captain Richards took Emma on one arm and Jane on the other, guiding Emma to a chair.

Emma's relief was only momentary. She found that sitting down meant either being drawn into the trivial conversations of the younger Miss Brooksides as they waited for partners, enduring the flippant gallantry of Captain Richards, playing "who's the poet" with Lieutenant Listle, or noticing that whenever she should turn her eyes in his direction, Dr. Lethbridge was gazing at her, a situation which only caused her to glance his way more and more often, the result of such glimpses being an admiration for the firm set of his jaw and an appreciation for how the tightness of his breeches showed off his physique.

Miss Brookside's aloof presence was eventually drawn off by Mr. Werthing, whose gentle voice was no match to Captain Richards, rattling away to any female close enough to be flattered. Dancing, Mr. Werthing must have decided, was the only remedy and finally he managed to lead her to the floor, though how he could dance with an ice sculpture without being frostbit was beyond Emma. She found she liked Mr. Werthing best of all; she was completely irrelevant to him. The other gentlemen paired off eventually, but they always circled back to Emma between sets.

Perhaps even worse than dancing, Emma found that Mr. Baynes considered it a professional duty to sit by her side and make little noises of concern every time she moved. Then, he must have decided distraction was the best remedy and quickly launched into a series of topics upon which Emma could not hope to contribute.

"I have been doing some study lately, Miss Woods," said he, "and I wish to get your opinion on the best herbs one might plant in a small kitchen garden. I would like my garden to be both useful to the kitchen as well as the sickbed, and so I wonder, what herbs do you most recommend for common ailments?"

"I really have no idea," she said. "Though mint is good for an upset stomach."

Mr. Baynes colored at her use of such an anatomical term, but he plowed forward. "Yes, yes, mint is commonly known. And an onion boiled in milk quite sets me to rights. Do not you think so?"

To this Emma could only shrug and nod. "Certainly. If you say so." That seemed to bolster him.

He ceded his chair to Miss Meyrick, who returned breathless from another dance with Mark. Not wishing to cede his conversation, though, he stood just beside her, putting Emma in the very unpleasant position of having to either crick her neck to meet his eyes or otherwise stare at his crotch.

"Gardens," he said to Miss Meyrick by way of catching her up. "And should I be so fortunate as to receive a bit of glebe land, I believe it would be incumbent on me to raise some food for my own table. Chickens and perhaps a pig or two each year. What are your thoughts, Miss Woods, as to the best method of keeping chickens?"

"Truly, sir," Emma said, unable to keep the annoyance from her voice any longer. "I have no opinion whatsoever. I've never raised an animal in my life."

He nodded formally, his expression reflecting his horror at having given offense. "My apologies for misunderstanding, madam. The fineness of your upbringing must have precluded any such training."

Emma could not read his expression. He seemed both affronted and intrigued, simultaneously awed by her supposed "fineness" but uncertain how it might suit whatever other plans were brewing in his mind.

"No, no," Emma said. "You have not misunderstood. It's just that . . ."

"Misunderstood what?" Cassandra returned from the dance floor as Mr. Baynes rose from his deep, apologetic bow.

"Oh," said Miss Meyrick, uncertain how to go about it but clearly intending to help. "Miss Woods is . . . a bit . . . inexperienced in the managing of gardens and farm animals. It is perhaps not how American young ladies are raised?"

Cassandra's gaze passed to Emma. "Is that so? One should hope your uncle has no need of such basic and essential skills in his impending housekeeper."

To this, Emma could only nod and wish she hadn't made the excuse of immobility so she might run right out of the Lower Rooms that moment and fling herself into the Avon.

Beside her, Miss Meyrick smoothed her dress and proceeded slowly. "I am sure Miss Woods has many skills besides and what she knows not, she could certainly learn. But if you will allow me, Mr. Baynes, I . . . erm, actually quite enjoy the caretaking of our small flock of hens. So if Miss Woods does not protest, I shall do my best to share what little knowledge I've gained."

Mr. Baynes nodded and, as a boon to Emma, repositioned himself so Miss Meyrick now had to calculate the risks of neck vs. crotch. Cassandra was asked to dance by Lieutenant Listle. Mr. Baynes listened raptly as Miss Meyrick explained how she cared for her brood, where she kept the chicks during cold seasons, the various strategies to prevent the infiltration of vermin, and finally, the most satisfactory method for boiling an egg. While those two seemed wholly engrossed in the topic, Emma had to admit it was the most boring conversation she had ever had the pleasure of trying to ignore.

A short time later, Mark came to solicit Emma's hand for another dance, but was once again intercepted by Jane's commitment to her office.

"Quite a pretty little method for securing partners," Jane threw over a shoulder as she followed Mark to the set.

With Miss Meyrick's farmyard knowledge exhausted and her hand once more solicited by another acquaintance, Mr. Baynes made it his duty to fetch Emma as much punch as she could possibly drink. Emma had to satisfy herself with watching Mark alternate between dancing with the Misses Brooksides and Miss Meyrick, trying not to notice how he animated he became when standing opposite the otherwise quiet Miss Meyrick, and Emma could not blame him. She was an amiable person and completely without guile. Nonetheless, Emma wouldn't have minded seeing *her* trip down the stairs by the end of the evening.

CHAPTER 19

The next morning, Emma followed demurely behind Jane, Cassandra, and their parents as they marched off to Sunday service.

Earlier that morning, Cassandra let out a huff of reproach at the breakfast table when Jane laid a prayer book down and Emma lifted the cover, then asked what it was. Jane placed one hand on Emma's arm and another on Cassandra's, sandwiched as she was between them. "We must not be small-minded, Cass," she said. "Perhaps Emma is Baptist? Or some other American version of Protestantism?"

Emma nodded and blinked her surprise. "Baptist. Yes," Emma said. "Yes, actually we were raised in the Baptist church." This was true: she had been raised as a Baptist. And she had also staunchly refused to attend services in her grandmother's church as soon as she was old enough to stand her ground in the face of Granny's guilt-laden comments that it would be awfully sad not to see one another in the Great Hereafter. The only other times she'd set foot in a religious house was when the local Episcopal church provided art space for the yearly art walk or the occasional concert in the cathedral downtown. Even then, she couldn't help feeling that the benign Jesus looking down from various windows and paintings might at any moment wrinkle his nose or waggle a stained-glass finger in her direction.

The family crossed back over the bridge toward the city center, then turned up Walcot Street, which soon became Cornwall Street at a slight bend in the road. Emma had learned long ago that street names often changed at these barely noticeable shifts in direction, sometimes with no shift at all, just bam – new name. When you have a history as rich as this, Harold would joke, the number of historical people deserving (or not!) of road appellation far outnumbered the actual amount of roads. Thinking of dear Carl swelled her chest, and Emma sent a quick prayer to whomever might be listening to watch over her friends on the other side of time.

The church stood out brightly. The spire could be seen from some distance, and up close, the building gleamed in the morning sun. The great wooden doors stood open, a not inconsiderable crowd milling on the steps.

Emma had been in St. Swithin's many times before, most recently hiding in that pew just over there, trying to ignore the taste of vomit in her mouth, failing to eradicate thoughts of Mark and Wanda in a tangled embrace. But there were happy memories too. Her eyes counted up the pews until she found the one where she and Mark had sat at last year's string quartet recital. She drifted back to that evening, how Mark had turned to speak to Lorna and Deb in the pew behind, slinging his arm casually over the back of their bench. But when the music started and he turned forward, his arm remained, his fingers occasionally sliding across her shoulder, tapping out a beat in time to the music. In time to her heart. What she wouldn't give to be back there now, a year ago, the possibilities seemingly endless. Could Time forgive her that much? If she wished or prayed or chanted enough between now and then, could they be dropped off one year earlier instead?

Everything that stood between her and Mark would be gone – the unanswered email and trial engagement, Quinn and Wanda. Her fingers reached for her shoulder, almost surprised that Mark's weren't there waiting.

Then her gaze landed on Miss Meyrick's figure sitting in the exact spot Emma had occupied last year – or, rather, all those years in the future. Miss

Meyrick's father sat beside, and many gentlemen stopped to tip their hat and issue the pleasantries a fine Sunday morning requires.

Up at the altar, Mr. Baynes perched in the large rector's chair, a pointy throne-like object which would have made any who sat in it puny between its commanding armrests and elongated back. Not that the large black cassock and white stole were doing him any favors, either. He looked rather like a baby penguin. A smaller wooden chair sat empty beside him and more than once, he glanced around, looking for Mark who appeared only after Mr. Baynes rose to begin the service, slinking from a door behind the organ and into that seat.

"Holy – " shit. Emma nearly dropped her prayer book as her brain focused on the work of closing her mouth. Mark was as pale as the white stole round Mr. Baynes' shoulders. Even from here, Emma could see him trembling, the pages of his sermon shuddering like leaves in a stiff wind.

Jane stuck an elbow in Emma's side and nodded meaningfully at the little red book before her, which might as well have been written in Latin for all the good it was doing her. Jane repeatedly took it, turned to the appropriate page, and jabbed her finger at the correct section. Emma affected her "I'm a dolt" smile, but found that Jane was not amused. Clearly, if there was one place where humor was not part of the repertoire, it was during service.

"Almighty God," Mr. Baynes intoned from the corner of the altar table. "unto whom all hearts be open, all desires known, and from whom no secrets are hid: Cleanse the thoughts of our hearts by the inspiration of thy Holy Spirit, that we may perfectly love thee and worthily magnify thy holy name, to the honor and glory of thy name."

"Amen," said the congregation, Emma adding her own so belatedly, her voice dangled into the edge of silence. Hearts be open? All desires known? No secrets are hid? Emma glanced from her book to Mark, slumped in his chair and tugging at his collar, as Mr. Baynes read from the Old Testament at the lectern. Had she worn a collar of her own, she would have been tugging at it too, jutting her head forward to swallow like a cartoon copy of herself. Could the desires of her own heart be willed back down to settle somewhere in the trenches of her core? As Harold had made clear, the desires of her own and Mark's heart had never been hidden or secret. But the words breaking a sweat under her arms and along her back was the first line of that call to prayer: open hearts. If anything, her own heart thumped somewhere beneath all the excuses she had piled on like dirty laundry accumulating in the corner.

Mr. Baynes left the lectern to read the gospel, standing before the altar, both hands raised toward heaven while the adolescent altar boy heaved the great book as high as his skinny arms would allow. The gospel over, Emma made to sit, only to find that no one else was and thus rose from what would have passed for a very good chair yoga pose – against the exclamations of her dance-fatigued thighs – and followed along with the Creed being intoned by the congregation. She kept her eyes forward so as to avoid the frequent glances of Jane the white moon of her face probably pinched in pious annoyance.

The Creed completed, Mr. Baynes then bowed and walked backwards, one hand extended toward Mark, now slightly rocking forward and back in his chair. He remained in that position a good long while as he glanced from the door behind the organ to the lectern, apparently debating which would be his final destination. Finally, Mr. Baynes rose halfway from his bent posture and glanced from Mark to the pulpit and back again. With one last tug, Mark stood, and Mr. Baynes allowed himself to rise. He stopped Mark on his way to the lectern to embrace and kiss each cheek, gestures which seemed to only heighten the congregation's anticipation of what was to come, as well as Mark's unease.

The first words from Mark's mouth were bleated out too soft and high-pitched for human ears. He cleared his throat and in a firmer tone, said, "excuse me." Shuffling his papers, he placed both hands on the lectern.

"Our readings this week come from the book of Mark. As I studied this text for the first time – which is to say that I have studied it many times in the past – but as I have, you know, read them again and it *felt* like the first time, I'm most struck by just how many life lessons Jesus includes here. About giving. About helping. About caring not for the things of this world but turning our eyes to those of the next. Because I believe that the ultimate measure of a man is not where he stands in moments of comfort and convenience, but where he stands at times of challenge and controversy."

He paused and pulled at his collar once again, flapping the sides of his long heavy cassock as though trying to coerce a breeze to its underparts. Emma's mind swirled over Mark's words, how good they were . . . and also how familiar. Then it hit her. Dr. Martin Luther King, Jr. It was the quote from a poster another faculty member hung in her office!

A chuckle threatened to ruin the solemn head-nodding going on around her, so Emma coughed into her hand and raised her eyes to find Mark seeking her eyes. His shoulders rose a bit, furrowed brow expressing his uncertainty, and she gave a bolstering nod.

Mark cleared his throat. "That is, we must not be so focused on the material gains of this world because they don't matter a bean when it comes to the important things in life. Being honest and truthful. Doing what is right, not what is easy. It doesn't matter how much money you have or how big your house is or how much – ". The pause drew out long, but finally he spoke. " – how much jewelry you own."

Emma felt the blood rush into her cheeks. Mark's eyes remained planted to his pages. Her finger traced over the white band of empty skin where Quinn's ring had already left a sun-deprived tattoo.

The pause gave Emma time to calm the quickening of her pulse and turn her face back to Mark, to his eyes seeking hers. He tapped a finger to his heart. "Jesus reminds us that what matters is what we hold in here."

"And Mark is also where Jesus taught us to pray. It's a simple prayer, but it reminds us that," once more his voice softened and wavered, then grew strong again, "forgiveness is not an occasional act; it is a constant attitude."

Silence fell over the sanctuary, not heavy and dour, but the silence of the contented. The silence of those savoring and digesting. A silence that, for Emma, held all the promise of reconciliation tempered with the truth of the past that waited for them in the future.

"Erm, thus sayeth the Lord. Amen," he said and retreated to his seat.

The service continued with a long series of prayers and then the communion, to which Emma remained sitting as the Austen family filed to the altar to kneel and receive. After another hymn and a final blessing by Mr. Baynes, they were released with a resounding "thanks be to God."

Out on the steps, many of the parishioners milled about, shaking hands and discussing Mark's sermon.

"Bit short," said one of the men.

"Length does not matter, my friend," said another. "It's the truth of the words."

"But why did he not preach on the readings? Mark wasn't on today."

"Perhaps he's one of these new London preachers. They just preach on whatever comes into their minds."

"Well," said the first speaker, "if the length of his sermon is a reflection of the breadth of his intellect- ", he shrugged and made a doubtful face, earning a playful cuff from his wife.

Emma could not say she had enjoyed Mark's sermon, exactly. Perhaps he had not meant to pierce quite so deeply, but he had. And regardless of whether he stole from King, Churchill, or any other tacky study hall poster, what he said rang true, and judging by the smiling faces emerging from the church, it resonated for those around her.

However, as much as she wanted to muse over his words, she found herself remembering his pallor.

She was about to run back inside and track him down, make Mr. Baynes send for an apothecary, when she saw him standing at the doorway, shaking hands with parishioners, their faces open and grateful, offering thanks. Mr. Baynes shuffled nearby, a step back and behind, on his face a tumult of emotions: respect for a fellow clergyman giving way to an undercurrent of doubt and anxiety. Poor man – based on the outpouring of thanks from those leaving the church, he would be hard-pressed to best Mark's performance, and his face showed he knew it.

Emma would have liked to shake his hand and offer appreciation for his sermon, a pretense that was as much about checking on his condition as discerning any changes in his own heart since they last met. However, Jane strode up to where she and Cassandra stood near the sidewalk and took each by an arm. She led them across The Paragon to a park on the other side. All of Bath, it seemed, had emptied on this fine morning, and the grounds of the park were overrun as attendees of St. Swithin's took a turn under the bright sun, as well as various maids, footmen, and others of the working classes, here to enjoy their half-day in the sun.

"A good sermon, I think," Cassandra said.

"A sermon not without merit," Jane started. Her tone was contemplative and marked her regard. "But I don't know that I've ever heard as short a one in my life."

"Brevity is the soul of wit, is it not, dear sister?"

"Of wit it may be, but brevity certainly does not feed the soul."

"Perhaps not," Cassandra conceded. "But I shall always prefer a short sermon from a tall preacher. He did look rather fetching in those robes." Cassandra blushed and turned away. "Oh what? I can't notice a fine-looking man when I see one?"

Jane held her hands up, conceding the point, but nudged Emma with her elbow and shot a ribald look her way.

Emma had to admit the truth of Cassandra's words. She had, in fact, found her eyes frequently gazing at Mark – when she hadn't been trying to find her place and flip back and forth through the prayer book – and not all her thoughts had been fears for his health. In their years together at the festival, he had always dressed as a clergyman, but an off-duty one – in the traditional garb of black breeches, black coat, and round hat, which, as a standing joke in their group, made him look a hybrid of chicken and scarecrow. But she had never seen him in the robes. Those – rather pricey, he told her, if you wanted authentic – he only wore for the weddings he performed, and of the photos she'd seen, Emma found it infuriating how the bride and groom had the gall to be the center of every one.

A ball rolled over to them, kicked by a little boy in short pants across a small grassy field. Cassandra lifted her skirts and kicked it back. "Now, let us enjoy this beautiful day, for who knows but it shall thunderstorm any moment!" With that Cassandra strode ahead, swinging her arms in the sunlight.

Emma looked from Cassandra to Jane and back again. Jane's face shifted from a stern frown to chastened smile. "Ahh well, Miss Woods, reverence is for Sunday mornings and joy for the rest of the time."

"Hear, hear," Emma said, closing her mouth before she risked bringing on the thunderstorms Cassandra had joked of. She broke into a little trot, not caring that ladies in this era did not run. It felt good to stretch her legs and within a moment, Jane outpaced her and the two ran the length of the park, laughing and panting as Cassandra caught up, shaking her head with a rueful grin.

Back at home, they ate lunch with Jane's parents, during which Emma received a note from a splotchy-faced Sarah.

"It's from my uncle," Emma said, avoiding Cassandra's quick eyes. "It appears he has left a message for me at the Pump Room." When the meal concluded, Emma excused herself and set off toward the abbey.

She found Mark by the potted tree in the Pump Room, just where his note directed her. Rather than standing nearby, one arm resting casually against his lower back, one foot forward and turned slightly – the consummate Regency posture – Mark sat hunched on a bench, legs crossed and foot wiggling, biting at a fingernail. A couple wandered near, an older man and woman Emma had seen at church that morning. When they noticed his fingers in his mouth, the occasional spitting of a hunk of nail and skin, their expressions of gratitude turned to disgust. Once more, the pale sallowness of his skin startled her and she stopped short, causing a woman and her daughter to spill their water. Seeing Emma, Mark jumped to his feet and pulled her back outside. Even here, all these years in the past, the sounds of street traffic and conversations of passing pedestrians gave them a kind of privacy.

"We may have a problem," he said.

She took in his face, his skin so pale. And were those bruises under his eyes or just the symbols of a sleepless soul? "Oh god, is it the plague? Or consumption?" She lifted a hand to touch his face, but he flicked it away.

"What? The plague . . .? No. Though I might have better luck with that." He moved them to a quiet corner away from the mingling throng. "I think it has to do with the timeline. Maybe I've been . . . I don't know . . . changing it?"

"You mean the storms? Yes, I wanted to tell you. Because I've also been borrowing a bit and quoting some lines . . . and I think . . . well, with these storms and all . . . it sounds crazy, but . . ."

Mark's face spiraled through confusion and into sheepishness. "I mean, yes, I borrowed a bit from . . . oh nevermind. Look, I don't need a lecture on plagiarism, Professor Woods. And no, I'm not talking about the weather. What we're dealing with is worse than a few thundershowers."

Mark strode ahead, then remembering his etiquette, returned and offered Emma his arm. She took it and the two strolled at a pace she couldn't quite classify as leisurely since his arm constantly jerked her forward. The only thing keeping Mark from breaking into a run was to place a hand atop his arm and apply firm pressure whenever he tried to move faster. He led them toward the Gravel Walk, a place they could disappear in the crowds. As they walked, he jiggled his arm, increasing the waggling until he elbowed her in the ribs.

"Jesus! What the . . . ?"

"Don't you feel that?" he said.

"You ribbing me? Yeah, I got that."

"No, this." Mark took her hand and placed it on his.

Emma shrugged. It felt like . . . a hand. She looked down and noticed it was pale, if not due to illness, then perhaps the many hours spent indoors and the frequent rain showers occluding the sun. Then she touched it again, gripping his palm as though shaking hands. She watched her own hand grasp his, and yet where her hand should have stopped at the edge of his skin, it . . . sank in. She jerked back and nearly screamed. Then she looked at his face and saw that it too bore a quality she could compare only to the strange consistency of skim milk, that translucent layer at the top, as if the real milk wafted below the surface. She raised her fingers to his face and this time he did not swat it away. These too sank in just slightly, and though she wanted to jerk her hand away, she let it rest.

A couple turned to stare and Emma let her hand fall. Mark drew it back through his arm and trudged forward.

"What's happening?" Emma said.

"I can't be sure, but I think it has something to do with me being at the Meyrick's. That maybe our intrusion into this world could be changing things."

Emma swallowed. Amidst all the other things she had wanted to say to Mark the night before and couldn't, this had been one of them. She'd managed to keep the storms at bay so far, but the thought that she might have been changing Jane's books, and not in good ways, could not help but intrude in every thought that wasn't already claimed by Mark.

But his next sentence took her by surprise.

"You remember my ancestors?"

It was a story she had come to know – and love – as well as any of her own family chronicles. How Mark's great-great-great grandparents met at a school run by a clergyman and his wife, a curate of St. Swithin's who later moved on to being rector of a smaller parish just outside of Bath. He had himself given a lecture last year on his own personal connection to Jane Austen, whose family could be given the credit of bringing the two together with their intimate evening parties. "But what has that got to do with now?"

"This past year," Mark continued, "I've been fine-tuning my research. The name of the curate who founded the school was Baynes." He paused to let this information sink in.

Emma halted as she processed. "So Mr. Baynes, that mousy little curate, founded the school? I don't see him as much of a teacher. So then, he must have married . . ." Emma's eyes widened. "Miss Meyrick?"

"Yes." Mark drew them forward into a little cove in the hedge. "The records show that he lived in Mr. Meyrick's household while subbing for Mr. Sibley during a protracted illness. And though I couldn't find his wife's maiden name, it only follows that . . ."

"He wooed Miss Meyrick."

"Exactly."

"But, Mark, I still don't understand. The two could end up together. Or perhaps he'll start the school himself."

Mark shook his head. "I don't think so. I think she's gotten . . . attached." Even Emma's ironic sense of humor could not conjure a smile at this, though she had to dip her head in agreement. "You see, she's been telling me how she has this dream of opening a school one day. And I've heard her father teasing her about being a governess, though of course that's not really an option."

"Yes, I could see her being good with children. So," Emma said, the truth breaking through, "it's her idea. This school. And if they don't marry."

"No school."

"And if there's no school."

"There's no . . ." He held his hand up before his face again, flexing his fingers. "Me."

Before she even realized what was happening, Emma was weeping. "I've killed you," she sputtered between fits of sobbing. "I was so angry and so stupid, and now I've killed you." She pulled away and strode forward. She found a bench and sank onto it. Mark caught up and stood before her.

"It's not," he started, but let the words float away on the breeze. They both knew he was going to tell her it wasn't her fault, and yet whose fault could it possibly have been? Who had fallen off that bridge and drug him with her? Who had been in a futile, hypocritical rage and turned to melodrama rather than forgiveness and honesty?

"So not only have I been rewriting Austen and making it storm, but I've also written you out of history as well?" She threw her hands in the air. She would have screamed but for a passing officer and young lady whom she seemed to have interrupted at a critical moment. "Oh, shove off," she told them as the young lady shot Emma a scowl and the officer removed his hands from the lady's shoulders and put his puckered lips away.

"Hold on," Mark said, taking a seat beside her. "You've been rewriting . . . what?"

Emma shook her head. She could not lay more burdens upon him. Not now, with his whole existence as firm as fog.

Once more, her fingers found his face. Once more, tears streamed in thin rivulets over her cheeks.

"I'm not hopeless," he said. "Mr. Baynes was formally installed as the permanent substitute. Thank god." He shook his head, likely remembering his sermon that morning, a hint of pink appearing below the milkiness of his skin. "Of course, he doesn't realize I'm in competition for his future wife, but we can get over that hurdle."

"How?" Emma said. But saying that word delivered the answer, and she knew at the exact moment precisely what it was they needed to do.

"Well, I haven't figured that out quite yet . . ." he was already saying, but Emma cut him off.

"Nevermind. There are only two things to do."

"Oh?" he said, his eyebrows rising and a smile curling the corner of his mouth, amused by the transformation from weeping mess to decisive take-charge. "And what are those."

"To get Miss Meyrick back with Mr. Baynes." She took a deep breath. "And get the hell out of here before we fuck anything else up."

"But you wanted to . . . stay."

"I did. Past tense. Now, I want you – all of you – safe and sound and . . . whatever else happens . . . back home, I mean . . . well, I just need you to be there."

Emma stood. She took Mark's hand and pulled him up. How heavy he felt. He was leaning on her, she knew. For her support. And she would give it. She would give anything.

To fix this. To fix him.

They continued along the walk together in silence. She held his hand in her own, squeezing it as though she could infuse him with her own life.

As she parted company with Mark at the bridge, she still had no idea how they were to fix it, but it would come. She knew it would. It had to.

CHAPTER 20

Emma excused herself after breakfast on the pretext of business for her uncle. Cassandra observed her closely as she departed, and Emma closed the door before the hint of an eye roll might falter her steps.

She set off in the direction of the Meyrick's residence at Russell Street. They could not sit by and allow Miss Meyrick's fancy to run away with her, nor risk Mr. Baynes finding a more suitable partner in the meantime, and the Miss Brooksides had certainly been casting about for any beau who would stand still long enough. Though she hoped they had not grown so desperate yet, being married to a dowdy clergyman was still far above the ignominy of their eldest sister's state, regardless what he might read them before bedtime.

Emma would have to invoke the prowess of her namesake and fix what she had broken.

As she strode across the bridge, she wondered whether the portal or whatever they had fallen through would open to them now. What would happen if it did? She stopped at the windows of the shop where she and Mark had fallen. Now, it was a stationer's and a long counter ran along the row of windows overlooking the river, barring customers from crossing to the other side. Even if they could get to those windows, a sickening lump in Emma's core said Mark would very likely not appear beside her when they came out the other end.

Not until they had fixed this.

So it was across the bridge and past the Guildhall, a building she would hardly recognize in its current form if she weren't so familiar with these streets. From within, she could hear the voices of stall owners and customers negotiating prices. Then up through the center of town, past Milsom Street, and finally to the smart row of tan stone buildings that looked nearly identical now as they did when Emma had wandered this lane searching for her friends only a few days before.

She waited in the foyer as the Meyrick's housemaid announced her in the drawing room above. When the footman appeared, Emma stopped him to ascertain the location of each of the gentlemen in the home.

"Could you deliver this to Mark . . . uh, Mr. Landen," she asked. "It's regarding my uncle," she included, when his expression hinted as to the propriety of her request.

With a nod, he took it, and Emma's heart flutterbumped. Her plan was underway.

A moment later, the maid returned and led Emma up to the drawing room. As she entered, Miss Meyrick stepped forward, both hands out to clasp Emma's in her own.

"Miss Woods! What a delightful surprise. I had no idea you would come calling this morning." Miss Meyrick drew Emma toward the fire, trying to hide a novel lying open on the arm of her chair.

"The delight is all mine, though I fear I've disrupted your morning. What have you got there?"

Miss Meyrick held it sheepishly behind her back. "Oh, just a novel. Some rubbish I'm sure you'd never know of."

In the hallways beyond, Mark passed by the open door, pausing to greet both ladies. In his hands, he held Emma's letter.

Emma drew the book from her hands. "Oh, *The Italian*. Have you read this?" she called out the door as he was about to move on.

Mark stepped forward. "Oh, well I've heard a lot about it," he began amiably. Then, seeing Emma's quick nod to the paper in his hand, his features gave way to a sneer. "Me? No, I never read novels. I've always something better to do." With that, he made a curt bow and left, bumping into the doorframe in his haste to exit.

Miss Meyrick was deflated. Emma took her hand and led her to the window. "Do not concern yourself with what such men as Mr. Landen think," she said. "A man who hasn't the time for novels is a stodgy man indeed."

"Oh, no, not Mr. Landen. He's so . . ." She blushed again and fell silent. "Which is only to say that he is a pleasant man and if he does not approve of novels, then perhaps I ought not . . ."

"Do not even say it! Do not ever let another person's opinion sway you from what you know to be true." She blushed at her hypocrisy. "And we both know novels are most delightful things, are they not?"

Miss Meyrick gave an unwilling assent. Emma nodded and patted the young woman's hand. The groundwork was laid. Mark had disagreed with Miss Meyrick, had made her feel chastised and small, and Emma would now use this game of romantic pong to volley Mark to the sidelines and Mr. Baynes over the net. Convincing Miss Meyrick they ought not lose such a fine morning, Emma and Miss Meyrick set out for a walk, though not without Miss Meyrick's first suggesting perhaps Mr. Landen might also wish to join them. Before such ideas could gain ground, Emma had pulled her onto the street and set them off in the direction of St. Swithin's.

Miss Meyrick drew up as they came before the church. "Oh," she said, "we can have no business there."

"We certainly do." Emma pushed open the heavy doors. "Did I forget to tell you? I promised Mr. Baynes to assist him with decorating the chancel this morning. And of course I immediately thought of you to help with such a task."

Miss Meyrick, ever too obliging to put up much of a fight – a fact Emma had relied heavily upon when stealing the idea for this escapade – followed meekly behind.

Mr. Baynes stood at the lectern, one hand raised imploringly in what he must have intended to be a very tender moment in his sermon. The other hand gripped a pencil with which to jot more notes on the pile of papers before him as his lips moved silently. "Miss Woods! Miss Meyrick!" He lowered his hands and descended.

Emma quickly moved up the aisle. "Do not tell me you have forgotten likewise, Mr. Baynes. Oh dear, I believe the early fogs of autumn may be sweeping our brains right out through our ears. We're here to assist you with decorating? The chancel? As we spoke of at the Lower Rooms?"

Mr. Baynes continued in his dumbfounded state, and seemed about to dismiss them, so Emma plowed forward.

"And here we are, interrupting you as you develop your next sermon. Is this not a good sign, Miss Meyrick, for this period of Mr. Sibley's absence, to have such a conscientious and prepared interim rector at the helm?" She leaned over toward Miss Meyrick and dropped her voice conspiratorially low. "Quite lucky for anyone whether parish or lady to gain such a thoughtful person, eh?"

Miss Meyrick nodded good-naturedly, and Emma couldn't help but suppress a smile in realizing the poor girl was likely noticing just how many papers lay stacked there, all filled front and back with what was going to be a monstrously long sermon. If Mark had confused the congregation with curtness, Mr. Baynes appeared ready to weary them with superfluity.

But Mr. Baynes took the compliment, his face lighting up at the praise. He seemed glad of company, and rather alarmingly partial to Emma's own presence. He moved to her side, standing so close, she could smell the sausage he'd had for breakfast. "Preparations are important, as you, Miss Meyrick well know when you lead our little ones in classes." He turned to the altar and seemed to ponder what he saw. "Well, I seem to have forgotten any such plans. But yes, yes I do believe we could brighten the place up."

"Marvelous," Emma said, disengaging Miss Meyrick's arm from her own. "I shall just pop back down to the florist's and purchase some wreaths, perhaps some vines." She hastily retreated down the aisle, though both Miss Meyrick and Mr. Baynes attempted to follow her. "No, no, dear," she said.

"You and Mr. Baynes shall put your heads together and come up with a design. I shall be no more than a jot."

"But Miss Woods," said Mr. Baynes. "You should not oblige yourself. The cost of..."

"Nevermind that," Emma said, striding away. "I shall be economical in my choices!" And she nearly ran the last few paces until she was back outside, the great wooden door firmly closed behind her.

Out on the street, Emma glanced first one way, then the other. Where in the hell, she wondered, would a florist's be? Shrugging, she gathered her skirts in a hand and set out. She had plenty of time to find one and the further afield it may be, the better.

Emma meandered toward the town center. She couldn't help but skip a bit as she walked, reflecting that her plan to foist Miss Meyrick onto Mr. Baynes could not have gone more swimmingly. She imagined returning to find them making out on the altar, then shuddered at the thought. That was, perhaps, too much to hope for, but extended time alone in a charming church must surely accomplish something.

At this time of day, Bath was all a bustle. That is, the visible members of Bath were all a bustle. Emma imagined that if she could wipe off the blackened sooty windows lining the sidewalk, she would peer in to find the cooks and kitchen maids finally getting a moment to put their feet up and enjoy a cup of tea. Still invisible, but hopefully enjoying a well-earned rest.

As she neared the cathedral and Pump Room, she could barely take a step without running into another person. Nurses pushed prams full of babies of indeterminate gender, dressed as they all were in white flounces, lace, and frills. Governesses shepherded their young charges down the streets, careful to harry them past any idle young men. And young ladies freshly graduated from their own governess' watchful glares slowed their steps in equal measure, glancing over their shoulders at said idle young men, who often had something impertinent to toss back to them.

Emma compared the many varieties of young men wandering the streets. There were swaggering coxcombs lolling about, all hair pomade and cravats to their ear lobes. Soldiers in red and blue strode by, debating politics and the outcomes of what, in another 200 years, would be near-forgotten battles, little hashmarks on the timelines of textbooks students would use less for information and more for concealing their smartphones. And of course, there were sensible men as well, simply clothed, voices moderated, giving Emma a pleasant nod and tip of their hats as they passed.

Pleasant men. Sensible men. This was what Emma had been in search of all along, men like the heroes of Austen's novels, men quite opposite to the anti-heroes she had always been drawn to. And the man she'd ended up with – well, he was sensible. He was smart – brilliant, even. Top of his class in med school, chief resident during his surgery training. But more than that, he was a sensible choice. Emma cringed remembering the time she'd gone home to pack up her books. How her mother had shrilled when Emma hinted maybe Quinn wasn't the man for her. Not the man for you, her mother demanded. And just what does the man for you look like, eh? What does he do?

It wasn't just a sensible man she wanted, nor a sensible choice. It was something else – it was . . . it was a man who was both sensible and sensitive. And this was what she'd told her mother, though in a rather rambling, half-coherent manner – about a man who understood how she felt, who actually cared about how she felt. But her mother had cut her off. Get your head out of those books, she'd said, tossing a brittle, yellowed copy of *Northanger Abbey* at Emma's feet, not terribly dissimilar from the advice Mrs. Morland gave to a less naive Catherine on her return home. Picking it up and smoothing a bent cover, Emma had to admit her mother was right – Quinn *was* a good man, a kind man, who had his fair share of ill nature, but not more than anyone else – certainly not more than herself. And yet, regarding sensitivity, whatever romance he had was by rote – flowers on Valentine's day (the few they'd ever actually shared), a sweater at Christmas (chosen by his sister), and an evening out for her birthday. She nodded and shrugged, and her mother had huffed away. But still, Emma couldn't help wondering whether Quinn, rather than being the Mr. Darcy everyone seemed to think he was, was more of a Mr. Collins to her scared, safety-seeking Charlotte's heart.

A pigeon darted down to the street to peck at a pile of crumbs fallen from a passing pram, and in that moment, an essay idea sprung to Emma's mind. Searching through her reticule and tiny pockets, she found her little diary, the black thick-papered cover starting to bend and pill, and she filled nearly two full pages with ideas for a comparison of men in Austen's age and how they paralleled modern tropes of masculinity. Words and phrases rushed through her and she absorbed as much as she could, eyes alternating between her pages and the pile of crumbs, now dwindling as more and more pigeons landed on the pavement. A group of young men strode past and the birds took to flight, pulsating the air with the beat of their wings. Holding this bit of inspiration in her hand, Emma watched them rise and disappear over the spire of the cathedral.

All her observations that day had been poignant, and almost – though not quite – painful. She was leaving. These would be the last days she would stand on this street and see a milliner's and not a souvenir shop, to smell the wafting aromas from a nearby bakery and not the greasetrap from a ubiquitous Bill's franchise. But the loss of this was nothing to the loss of Mark. In fact, she couldn't wait to get the hell out . . . well, almost. And thumbing through her notebook, the pages half full already, she had 6 months, maybe even a year's worth of writing here.

Emma reached Milsom Street. She wandered along, but knew from her previous foray to this part of town that she was not likely to come upon a florist's shop here. In fact, she wasn't even sure there were such things as florist's shops, but the day was warm and pleasant, and the longer she absented herself from St. Swithin's, the longer Mr. Baynes had to work his magic on Miss Meyrick.

She took the opportunity of ducking into a small shop at the end of the street, one Jane and Cassandra had deplored as a bedraggled flea stall which no respectable person would patronize. It was just the sort of place Emma hoped she would avoid any run-ins with acquaintance. Indeed, the inside was damp and musty, scents of mold and overripe bodies clinging to the air. Even from across the room, Emma could discern the cheapness of the goods within. She found herself implored by a woman to give an opinion on a bolt of muslin, and Emma returned with the only passable advice she had: "I do not think it will wash well, madam. I am afraid it will fray." At this, the woman nodded and thanked her, returning the bolt to the counter.

The shop was manned by two young, hungover and bedraggled-looking clerks. The few other customers in line reminded Emma of Fanny Price's slatternly mother, women with patched gowns and frazzled, greasy hair, one with an infant on her hip who wailed until the mother stuck a dirty finger in his mouth to silence him.

One of the clerks waved her forward. "Can I help you, miss," he said, in an accent so thick, Emma had to ask him to repeat his question three times.

"A compact?" she asked the clerk.

"Excuse me?"

"I need powder? And rouge."

The clerk looked at her askance as he bent to dig in the recesses of the counter. The few other shoppers observed her closely, whispering behind their hands, imagining, most likely, that Emma was some lady of the night, come to stock up on her wares with which to wile the men. Emma put her coin on the table and tucked the small parcel into her pocket as quick as she could. It had become almost painless to part with the money Mark had given her, a fact that was more painful perhaps than the parting itself. But this was a necessary cost and she was grateful to have thought of it.

Back on Milsom Street, Emma looked first one way, then the other, scanning the storefronts for bright displays of blooms. But she could discern no flowers in the stores, and none of the sidewalks were littered with flower vases arrayed display shelves as they would have been in present day Bath. She turned west toward Queen Square.

Ahead, Emma caught sight of the same man from the riverbank when she and Mark had first emerged, pushing a cart laden with roses and bright blooms. He was exiting the doorway of a shop down a narrow little street just across from her. Paying no attention to what passed around, Emma made to step off the curb to follow him. There was a shout of exclamation and a hand was at her elbow, jerking her back from the street. Another arm went round her waist, holding her fast to the body behind her. A pair of highly-fed and barely-controlled horses raced by at a pace that would have left Emma a trampled pile of pulp in another instant. The man holding the reins of the barouche turned to tip his foppish hat, then smirked and whipped his horses even faster.

"Holy Jesus, Mary, and Joseph!" she said, after which followed a few choice words for the driver now turning back onto the main thoroughfare. Emma's hand rose to her chest, covering the white-gloved hand of her savior who gripped a cane with a carved ivory cat's head. She spun to face him, his name already on her lips. "Dr. Lethbridge?"

"Miss Woods." He released her and straightened his own hat, which had been knocked rakishly askew. His own color had risen, though whether it was from saving her from or the resultant string of expletives remained unclear. "All my hard work was almost for naught." He handed back her reticule, fallen in the tumble. "You are unhurt?"

Emma could barely catch her breath. The warmth of his body remained on her back, the pressure of his arm across her chest. "Oh sure, I'm ok. That is, I'm quite well."

He held his arm out. Emma took it and did her best not to notice how strong it was, how well-muscled. "You seem quite intent upon crossing here," he said and stepped to the curb, carefully looking both ways, then leading them swiftly across.

"Flowers," she said. "I need flowers for the church. Miss Meyrick and Mr. Baynes are waiting for me."

"Flowers?" He let out a bark of laughter. When he smiled, his whole face lit up and his eyes crinkled at the corners. "You almost flattened yourself for flowers!"

"Your alliterative abilities do you credit, sir," she said, laughing alongside. "I am not used to . . ." Carriages, horses . . . any of it. "I wasn't paying attention," she ended lamely.

They reached the doorway and found it was indeed a flower shop, though the man behind the counter gave a hoot of surprise to learn they wished to purchase some. Apparently, he only sold flowers by order, which were usually picked up by footmen, maids, and the like. He seemed rather undone to have a gentleman and lady on his premises and frequently apologized for the disorder of the room, which to Emma appeared a cozy jumble of flowers, cut stems, and twine, every counter and corner a testament to this humble man's love for his work. The air was heavy with fragrant blooms, and for the first time, Emma breathed as deeply as she could.

Explaining her need, Emma and the shopkeeper began choosing an array of flowers whose blooms would last through the week's services and past Sunday.

Emma was surprised to find that Dr. Lethbridge was himself a keen naturalist and, more than once, suggested a flower to the shopkeeper, who admitted it a better choice than his own.

The shopkeeper's wife came out to assist them, a friendly woman who laughed at their messy shop and set to work cutting large swaths of brown paper with which to wrap Emma's wares. "Flowers for a church! My favorite kind." On seeing Dr. Lethbridge's alacrity in discussing various flora, she sidled up to Emma. "Any man knows his flowers, now that's a good man." And she turned a loving gaze on her husband.

Emma reddened and demurred. "Oh, no, we're not . . ."

But the shopkeeper's wife waved her off with her shears and began tying the flowers with brown twine. "Just saying, my dear. Just saying."

Exiting the shop, Emma and Dr. Lethbridge found themselves being hallooed by Captain Richards and Lieutenant Listle from the other side of the narrow street.

"Halloo, Miss Woods!" said Captain Richards. "What a great pleasure. And you as well, Dr. Lethbridge. Off to save the masses?"

Dr. Lethbridge tipped his hat. "One at a time, sirs. One at a time."

Lieutenant Listle quietly moved to Emma's side and eased the paperbound arrangements from her arms into his. He sniffed the blooms appreciatively and raised a hand, about to launch into a poem. The clanging of the cathedral bells called them all to attention and left Lieutenant Listle's mouth hanging open.

"Thank heavens for that," Captain Richards said. "Anything to end the incessant poetry!"

Dr. Lethbridge jerked to attention. "Oh, is that the time?" He handed his own parcels over to Captain Richards. "I promised to be at Dr. Bowen's by this hour." With a bow, he gave Emma a warm glance and set off before Emma had time to curtsey her farewell.

Captain Richards pulled out a rose and brandished a slew of parries as they walked, drawing quite a bit of attention from passersby – especially

those of the female kind – which only encouraged him into more extrav-
agant strikes and dodges, interspersed with bows and tippings of his hat.

Seeing the whispers and head shakings of those who observed them, Emma began to doubt the propriety of being alone with two soldiers. Though Lydia Bennet might wail at her good luck, Emma could not feel so fortunate when Captain Richards used herself as a prop in his mock battle with his friend, who stalwartly strode ahead, disregarding the rose being brandished in his face and thwacked across his back. At the end of the block, Captain Richards dealt Lieutenant Listle a killing blow, at which point the rose gave up its feeble attempt to keep its petals and the bloom fell off with a plump thud onto the pavement.

"Are you opening a shop, Miss Woods," Captain Richards said. "Or perhaps you are on a mission to save the flowers from the fate of a lady's forlorn nosegay? A gentleman's ill-used boutonnière?"

"These flowers will have a better home than either," Emma replied. "They shall decorate the altar of the church."

Captain Richards' face instantly drew serious. He beheld the flowers in his custody with a grave expression. "Oh, my poor dear friends. You shall be Amen'ed and Thanks-be-to-Godded unto death."

Once more, a laugh fell from Emma before she could help herself, though a glance at Lt. Listle's somber face immediately sobered her.

"This is the time, when most divine to hear. The voice of Adoration rouses me," he said.

Just as Emma was about to pick up the next line of Coleridge's poem, Captain Richards leaned over conspiratorially. "Listle really wishes the voice of poetry might rouse Miss Meyrick."

"Miss Meyrick?" said Emma. Captain Richards shot a meaningful glance across to Lieutenant Listle who began to blush. As he looked away, Emma detected the unmistakable signs of a crush – after all, Miss Meyrick herself showed plenty of the symptoms whenever Mark was mentioned.

"Aha!" Captain Richards stabbed a finger in the air. "I see Miss Woods has guessed it. Yes, indeed, Miss Woods, our dear lieutenant here has spoken of little else."

"Richards," Lieutenant Listle began in a tone that would have silenced even a minutely conscientious man, but was silenced himself as his friend persisted.

"A pleasant young lady, no mistake," said Captain Richards. "It was quite a stroke of luck that we should have sought out the famed lady of the river. For by meeting *you*, he has met *her*."

Luck, indeed! Emma could not have considered anything less lucky than to discover that not only did she have to rearrange Miss Meyrick's feelings toward Mr. Baynes, but she would also be running interference for the other young men who had come into her small circle because of Emma and Mark's arrival.

Captain Richards tapped a cadence on his leg with his flower as he walked. "She is rather a delightful young thing. Just the perfect sort of wife for a soldier." He glanced at Emma and winked. "Do you know, Listle, I think I shall throw my hat in the ring as well. You'd be better off showering poetry on Miss Woods here. After all, her uncle may have some interest in the Navy with which to dredge you up from that poor lieutenant's state."

"Richards, if we were not in the presence of a lady, I would set you down a peg or two."

Richards once more grabbed a new floral victim. "On guard!" He waggled the bloom at Listle's nose until the shorter man could not help but to laugh.

The cathedral bells chimed the half hour and Emma realized she had better hasten back to St. Swithin's. Despite her hopes of walking in on them in a romantic embrace, it was just as likely that Mr. Baynes would have bored poor Miss Meyrick into a coma. She eased the parcels from the hands of the other two men, rejecting their offers of assistance, and left them with a flower each to settle the duel.

As she trotted back the length of Broad Street, Emma shook her head and worried herself almost to tears. Not only had Lieutenant Listle, a pleasant young man in his own right, fallen for the girl, but Emma could not satisfy herself that Captain Richards might not try to win her merely for the fun of it and the added pleasure of teasing a good friend.

As Broad Street turned into The Paragon, Emma came to a conclusion: it would do them no good for Miss Meyrick to find her attentions drawn off by either of the soldiers. Mr. Baynes she was to have married, and Mr. Baynes it was going to be. But as she considered the how of it all, she grasped the unwelcome truth: the only way to fend off new suitors would be to catch those advances with her own net first.

Trudging back up the steps and heaving open the massive door, Emma was glad to come upon the church's caretaker sweeping the porch and discharged her purchases into his arms. She had not meant to buy so many really, and yet she'd found herself enjoying the process of choosing them with Dr. Lethbridge, imagining the running garland she might make across the length of the altar, full of blooms she recognized from Adelaide Garden's pristine flower beds. And while it appeared she might have spent a small fortune, Dr. Lethbridge had supplanted her efforts to pay the shopkeeper, and his wife had thrown in some extra bouquets, moved perhaps by the budding romance she insisted on seeing.

"Them's through that door yonder, miss," the caretaker said.

Emma returned up the aisle of the church, admiring its massive white columns and the overall spaciousness of it, which she could appreciate better now that it was empty.

She pushed through the door indicated by the caretaker and followed the sound of laughter. She stopped short of entering and tried to step backwards, realizing that perhaps her own time might be better spent back in the sanctuary where she could complete this task and leave the other two to what appeared to be good progress toward their – that is, Emma and Mark's – objective. But, as seemed to be her curse, she stepped on a creaky board and had no sooner muttered, "well, son of a bitch," than the door opened and into the hall stepped Mr. Baynes.

"Miss Woods," he said, and drew her into the cozy sitting room. "We had begun to fear for you." He poured a cup of tea and passed it to Emma, who took it gratefully, the smell of the tea raising the volume on the cacophony that was her stomach's pleas for food.

On the floor of the parlor, two little children played, both of them boys, both in short pants, and both rather scummy looking at their hairlines, as though their mother passed a rag over their faces, but did not bother with much else.

Miss Meyrick sat on the floor with them, munching happily on a lady-finger, and drawing out words on two little squares of chalkboard. She handed these back to the boys to copy, praising and patting them along, with exclamations of genius at each letter they finished.

"John and James," Mr. Baynes said. "Nephews of Mr. Meyrick's house-keeper. Her niece is in her confinement and so I offered to bring these two to church with me." At this, the older of the boys shot a look that said this offer of assistance was as much hell as helpful, but he seemed grateful for Miss Meyrick's attention and quickly finished his word so he could enjoy a biscuit off her plate.

"They are such dears," Miss Meyrick said, helping the younger boy cross his "t." "It has been a delight to spend some time with them."

Emma nodded pleasantly, but had to look away as a line of green snot oozed from the younger boy's nose, dealt with quickly and good-naturedly by Miss Meyrick.

Mr. Baynes clapped his hands. "All right, lads. Go see if Mr. Doring needs help sweeping out the sanctuary."

Miss Meyrick tucked a handful of cookies into the pockets of each boy's jacket and gave them a hug as they left.

The three enjoyed a companionable tea, and when Miss Meyrick or Mr. Baynes sought to include her in conversation, Emma did her best to deliver as taciturn a response as she could manage. More than once, she stepped over the border into discourtesy, at which point, she smiled warmly at Mr. Baynes, thus undoing whatever good her hostile tone had done.

Tea over, Emma began to make her farewells. Her hand tapped at a pocket, checking whether she had enough change to take a sedan chair home and give her aching feet a break, balancing that against whether she was willing to part with any more of Mark than what had already been taken from her.

"But the decorations," Mr. Baynes said, his face passing from confusion to excitement. "Now we can begin!"

Emma plodded behind the other two, glad to see that both seemed content to walk ahead without her. Her legs throbbed, her arms were sore, and she was fairly certain the cut on her palm from a rose thorn was going to fester.

CHAPTER 21

Back at 4 Sydney Place, Emma fell onto the sofa. She had missed Jane and Cassandra, Sarah told her, who had gone out, as had Mr. and Mrs. Austen, though their morning walk was often only a stroll through Sydney Gardens. On their return, Emma quickly gave up her sofa to Mr. Austen.

"How are you feeling, sir?" Emma asked, helping with a pillow he struggled to position comfortably behind his back.

"I am well, child. Thank you, thank you." He drew a long, shaky breath. "I cannot tell whether I'm more done in from the wet or the thunder. Damned unseasonable weather!"

Despite the guilt his statement drew, she could not help but smile.

He saw and made a deprecating one of his own. "Can you excuse an old man his occasional curses?"

Emma patted his shoulder. "I've an uncle in the navy, sir," she said, glancing away as the lie passed her lips. "I've heard a curse now and again." Uncle or not, she herself could have bested any of the Austen men in a swearing match.

"It's just these storms! I thought my heart would beat through my chest."

She searched for another playful speech with which to ease him, but her contrite heart left her tongue dumb. The wet and the noise – all were her fault, all the result of her fevered passion for the words his daughter would write, books he would never see in print though he must surely have known they would be, eventually. Emma could not undo the damage he had suffered, but she could ease his afternoon, a meagre return on the great many treasures she had gained. She picked up a book he'd left open on the mantel and turned to the marked page. She read to him until he dozed to sleep, then Emma too arranged three of the upright chairs in a row and lay down upon them.

This was how Jane and Cassandra found them.

"What a strange arrangement, Miss Woods," said Cassandra. "Why did you not lay upon the other sofa?"

"Oh," Emma said, pushing back a strand of loose hair as she rose. "I do apologize. I did not wish to prevent your mother's laying down." Emma returned the chairs to the table brought out for card games.

Jane tossed her bonnet on the table and sank into one of them. "She is happily chatting away with our neighbor's housekeeper. I believe they are entirely engrossed in the restorative properties of rhubarb." She gave a little roll to her eyes. "Now, my dear, where did you sneak away to this morning? There was a bit of gossip in the Pump Room about a young woman seen with Mr. Landen on the Gravel Walk yesterday afternoon and she did not match Miss Meyrick's description. Perhaps you found another rendezvous out of the public gaze for today?"

Cassandra cuffed Jane's shoulder. "Really, Jane. One should not tease about such things."

Emma cranked the cogs of her mind, trying to dispel her naptime fog. "Indeed, we took a walk along the Gravel Walk. Though why that should excite much interest is curious. That note, if you remember." At this, Emma avoided Cassandra's glare. Though she had agreed not to call Emma out on them, she likely did not enjoy hearing lies added onto lies. "But for this morning, I was at the church with Miss Meyrick. We decorated the altar. With Mr. Baynes."

"Did you indeed? What an interesting trio you must have made." Jane worked at a scuff on the table, then glanced sidelong at Emma. "And did

Mr. Baynes create a charming image of the life of a rector? . . . Or a rector's wife?"

Emma blustered a response that made little sense. Cassandra rose and excused herself, parting with a final warning to Jane to "be good."

"I certainly shall," she began, ending with "not," as soon as Cassandra was beyond the door, a twinkle brightening her eye. "But tell me Miss Woods, were Mr. Baynes' eyes turned toward you or Miss Meyrick? Perhaps a bit of both? Poor man, he'll need someone to make his mind up for him, I dare say."

Emma blanched and moved restlessly from chair to sofa and back again. She cocked an ear toward the window, wondering if that was distant thunder she heard. She'd stolen the idea from Emma and now Jane Austen herself was teasing her for the very same unexpected outcome a future heroine would encounter whilst about the very same escapade herself. "Well," she said, hearing nothing on the horizon, "whatever intrigues I may be guilty of now will hopefully yield results that are their own acquittal. I shall be gone soon enough anyway."

Saying it aloud was not nearly as painful as she thought it would be. Not when Mark's milky face swam before her eyes.

At Jane's look of alarm, Emma added, "which is to say, you know . . . uh . . . gone to be with my uncle." If anything, lying to Jane was most painful of all.

Jane sighed. "I must say, Miss Woods, that I have greatly enjoyed your impromptu visit, and I shall be much saddened to see you safely amongst your family. How very selfish I am."

Despite the joking tone, Jane's eyes remained lowered, and she picked at a bit of lint on her dress. Emma's heart surged with love for this woman, this idol, and for feeling that however small her role had been, Emma had brought some morsel of happiness into this otherwise shadowed time in Jane's life.

Jane rose and pushed aside the curtains, letting bright sun shine down into the room. "Ugh," she said. "I love the sunshine and yet – "

Emma went to her and looked out. It was indeed a beautiful day. The sun shone warmly on the glass pane. But the reflection off the white buildings was nearly blinding, and both women held hands to their brow to fend it off. "Perhaps it is a bit much. All the white glare of Bath in September," she murmured, not even realizing what she'd said until the words had left her lips.

Jane turned to her. "Yes," she said, "just exactly so." With that, Jane swept from the room, with the quickest of "be right backs!" before the door slammed and Mr. Austen awoke.

The sun they had been deploring made a hasty exit behind the thunderclouds Emma had known would appear. Just as Mr. Austen pushed up from the couch, thunder struck.

"Mercy," he exclaimed and clutched his chest. "Another one?"

Cassandra returned to the room and had time to cast Emma just one grateful look before her attentions were fully taken up with her father. Mrs. Austen appeared, followed by their houseman balancing a silver tray with a small glass goblet, a crystal decanter of dark liquid, and a smaller dropper of laudanum. Emma likewise excused herself and stole up to her room.

She sat on her bed. There was so much she still had to puzzle and parse. Captain Richards and Lieutenant Listle. How to throw Mr. Baynes and Miss Meyrick together once more. And of course, Mark. Always Mark. Perhaps her biggest fear about going home had been the question she could not answer – what would Mark do when they returned. What would she?

Emma lay back on the coverlet and drew a pillow under her head. She would just lay here a moment. Just lay here and think. It would all come if she could only rest, only give her mind a break. And that moment of rest quickly gave way to sleep as Emma sank beneath the waves of slumber.

Emma woke to Jane's knock on her door. "I thought you must be sleeping." She sat at Emma's dressing table and primped a few loose curls. "Careful, dear, or you'll get a reputation as a hypochondriac. Lord knows, one house only has room for so many."

Stretching, Emma caught a whiff of her own body and tried to remember when she'd last had a bath. Heavens! It must have been when they'd bathed in the Queens Bath and since then, all the hither-and-thithering, not to mention another evening spent twirling the ballroom, had encouraged a rather impressive stink.

Without a word, but with a smirky look saying Jane had diagnosed the trouble, she pulled the cord near the bed. In a moment, Sarah's quick steps pattered down the hall just beyond the door. She entered and curtseyed.

"Sarah, could you draw Miss Woods a bath?"

Sarah bobbed and exited.

"Only if it's no trouble," Emma called out. To Jane, she offered a simple, "thanks," trying to hide her blush.

Jane flapped a hand. "No prob," she said, laughing as she tried out a phrase Emma had let slip a few times. "Now, you'd better start undressing, and I'll stoke up the fire."

Emma slipped behind the screen and stripped down to her petticoat. "I hope we're not taking her away from something else."

"Who?" Jane knelt at the fireplace, blowing the embers back to crackling life and adding a few stout pieces of wood to the infant flames. "Sarah? Oh heavens, whyever for? It's her job."

"Yes, but," Emma's voice trailed away. There was no point trying to bring her modern perspective into this matter. As her pits and greasy hair could attest to, she needed a bath and she certainly had no idea how to draw one for herself. In fact, she wasn't even sure where the water came from! It was simply there, in a pitcher on the washstand when she woke. Austen had received plenty of criticism for her failure to address the issue of servants in her novels, and Emma began to see that for Jane and her family, for all the people who occupied this particular station of gentility and ease, servants were simply there, a bit of equipment occupying the background. How that all would change when Jane and Cassandra found their own time as much occupied in caring for Chawton cottage as any servant to a master or mistress.

Jane left at the sound of Sarah's heavy footsteps. Sarah entered, carrying a large metal tub, which she set before the fire. She stoked the embers and added more wood from the morning's bundle to it. She left again and returned, lugging two large kettles of water, one steaming, the other cold. She poured the water in, tempering the hot with dashes of cold, then moved the screen to block the door and was gone. Emma pulled on the bathing gown hanging over the bath and sank into the water. It was only six inches deep and Emma sighed. There would be no immersing up to her shoulders, at least not until they revisited the baths. She began to frantically wash before the water grew tepid.

Emma startled as the door opened again, but it was only Sarah, bringing another two buckets of steaming water. "Oh Sarah," Emma said as the girl poured the water in, covering Emma to the waist. The sore muscles of her feet and legs began to ease in the near scalding water. "Thank you, thank you. You have no idea how good this feels."

The blush on Sarah's cheeks said she was not used to being thanked. Or perhaps not used to being thanked by a naked woman in a tub. Plus, Emma realized, she probably had no idea how good it actually felt. Bathing for Sarah was likely an even starker experience than this one. Was it possible she might go her whole life never being fully immersed in a hot bath? It was enough to bring tears to Emma's eyes, tears of relief that for all she had wanted to stay, in another few days, she would – fingers crossed – be able to bathe in a proper porcelain tub, water as hot as she liked it right up to her earlobes.

Sarah moved to the door.

"And how are you doing, Sarah?"

"Who? Me, miss? Oh, I'm doing just fine. We got word from an aunt what lives up north that Mary can have a job in the factory after the . . . after she has the . . . you know."

"And the child?"

"Me aunt says she'll raise it as her own. Lord knows she's had enough already to have all the clothes and things." Still facing the door, Sarah handed a small metal pitcher to Emma for rinsing. Emma just caught the movement of a tear being flicked away.

"But this plan doesn't quite suit you?"

"No'm, not quite. You see, it's just my sister and me in this world, and if she goes up north, who've I got? No one. Just meself. And Mary don't like it much neither, but what can she do? We're both of us . . ." Her words trailed off as shuddering sobs replaced her voice.

"Trapped." Emma reached back to place her hand atop Sarah's. "There, there," she said. "It will turn out all right. Somehow."

Sarah dried her tears on her apron. "No, miss. If you don't mind my saying, I don't reckon it will. But I guess most people in this world live a life what hasn't turned out all right, don't they, miss? But with the good Lord's help, I reckon we'll get on with it and meet in heaven. Isn't that what the preachers be saying of a Sunday?"

Sarah bobbed a curtsey and left before Emma could offer any more empty gestures or even emptier condolences. Of course Sarah was right. Who did she know whose life had turned out all peaches and butterflies? Life, she had come to accept, was a series of negotiations one made with a younger self, trading dreams for realities. And yet, despite that acceptance, despite the ring tucked into the windowsill, a beacon shining out this exact truth, her heart still yearned to believe in a world where this bottom-line didn't sit, silently waiting, at the conclusion of every calculation.

What particularly touched Emma was the very deep love Sarah displayed for her sister, for the sense that radiated from her that losing Mary in her life would be like turning off the sun. And yet how differently were the lives of these two sisters who lived below stairs from the lives of the two who lived above. Sarah and Mary would always be navigating the stormy seas of a life dependent on others, on their whims and fortunes, on the uncertainty of their employer's health and wealth, each year's security determined on Michaelmas. Life lived by the twelvemonth and no more.

Jane and Cassandra would be dependent on another set of limitations: those of "polite" society and of a family whose brothers were ashamed of the accomplishments of their sisters, ashamed of their desire to make their own way in the world, to leave a mark for those who came after. And yet, at least they would be permitted to live their lives together – that is, when not playing midwife to one of their brothers' confined wives and nursemaid to an array of nieces and nephews– but to know they would come back together again – that had to be worth so much more than anything else.

And in that flash, an inspiration sprang upon her. Balancing on one foot, Emma reached over to the dressing table and eased open the drawer. She retrieved her little black-bound journal and pencil and jotted notes for an essay – or series of them, if she could lasso this muse before it darted away – about the lives of Jane and Cassandra and how their experience contrasted with other sisterly siblings from history, or in comparison to the lives of women in the laboring classes. She wrote and wrote until her fingers ached around the small pencil, until the water grew tepid, then cool. Between these notes and what she'd completed the previous days, she had more writing than she could lay claim to in longer than she cared to remember, enough ideas to complete her essay collection and then some.

These were not wasted words. They were flashes and revelations; any regret Emma felt about leaving was much tempered with the wealth of inspiration in her hands. On returning home, these words may be all she had to build a life upon and build it she would, however stark and empty it might be.

Shivering and chilled, Emma rushed through the rest of her ablutions, worried as much about the cold as the extra work she'd tacked on to Sarah's duties. But she came away feeling as squeaky clean as one can washing in so little water, which was a great deal squeakier than she'd been half an hour before. Best of all, her body smelled distinctly soapy. She dabbed a bit of perfume under her arms and along her neck. Out of the tub and shivering before the fire, Emma pulled the cord, wary of jerking it too hard and breaking it, but also fearful she had not jerked it hard enough. What a mesmerizing system – these wires running through the walls of the house to the little panel of bells in the servants' rooms below. It was more mystifying than electricity.

Moments later, Sarah arrived. Bucketful-by-bucketful, the girl carried her load downstairs, returning out of breath and sweating to drag the tub to its mysterious origins. Of course, Emma's offers to help were met by a scandalized look, and Emma quickly shut up and sat down to the dressing table to comb out her hair and continue jotting notes as they came to her.

CHAPTER 22

Inconveniences of a Crowded Drawing Room

The hours after the bath were once more taken up with needlework and letter-writing. Emma would have happily wiled away the time with more of Grandison, which had grown on her despite its poor comparison, but then she remembered the little package of powder and rouge waiting at the back of a drawer in her dressing table. Casting a little half-sentence about writing to her uncle, Emma sat at the round table reserved for correspondence and filled the entire front page and half the back of the stationary she'd also purchased at the ignominious little shop. A few times, she glanced up to find Mrs. Austen nodding her approval at her lengthy letter.

"Sign of a good niece," she crooned. "You must tell him all about your comings and goings. He will not think your time misspent, I should think, when you tell him of all the pleasant young men you've met."

At this, Jane rolled her eyes and smirked behind her mother's back. Cassandra observed Emma with what might have been wry irony . . . or perhaps unadorned dislike. Though Cassandra may have surmised Emma was not writing to her uncle, neither she nor her mother could have guessed the real contents of her letter: minute instructions on the application of powder and rouge, warning Mark not to powder just his face, but his neck and hands as well, to ensure that he dab the poof a good inch below the line of his collar to prevent the telling stripe so common along the jawlines of young women new to the use of foundation. When she was finished, Mrs. Austen was about to ring the bell, but Emma demurred having Sarah post it for her. After all, if this went into the actual post, it would find its way back to 4 Sydney Place and likely accompanied by a stamp indicating that the recipient did not exist.

"I shall just pop out for a moment," Emma said, gathering her bonnet. "The fresh air will do me good."

"Oh no," Jane said, "we'll be late for the Brooksides. Keep it for the morning and we'll post it together then."

"The Brooksides? Then we're not . . . that is, we are not staying at home?"

"At home?" Jane laughed. "And bore one another to tears? You must resign yourself, Miss Woods. In Bath, evenings during the season are spent at an assembly, a play, a recital, or in the constant exchange of invitations to evening parties." Jane pretended to gag, slumping over the end of her sofa, popping back to attention just as Mrs. Austen turned round to see what all the giggling was about.

"Time to change, girls," she said and clapped her hands.

"Yes, Mama," Jane replied, rising and taking Emma's hand. The two nearly fell over the banister cackling as they returned upstairs. Emma tucked the powder and rouge into her reticule, frowning over its obvious bulge, but it was better to be prepared. Back downstairs, she found Mr. and Mrs. Austen in dinner attire, and the five set forth the short walk to Bathwick Street where the Brooksides had their own permanent abode.

The town was alive with gentlemen and ladies. Chairs passed, the trotting chairmen dodging into the street on occasion, sometimes not even noticing that a carriage or barouche passed within inches of themselves. A man on stilts ambled from lamppost to lamppost, pulling open a little glass door and dipping his lighted wick inside. Flame burst forth and the friendly glow of firelight cast a corona of gold over the deepening shadows.

Once more, Emma's head swiveled as she strove to take in every possible detail she could. Despite her groans over another evening out, she was quickly softened in remembering that these would be her last evenings out. She had already done so much and yet it seemed to her she had not seen nearly enough. And time continued to slip away.

The Brookside's home sat at the upper end of Bathwick Street, which itself hosted large homes on one side and smaller townhomes like the Austen's on the other. It was to a large tan-colored stone home that Mr. Austen directed their steps. The door was opened by a footman, and once inside, another maid stepped forward to gather their light cloaks. Emma pegged her easily as Sarah's sister Mary. Arms laden with cloaks, she led them up the stairs to the second level, where they turned into a door at the top and were admitted to the drawing room.

Mary announced them and as she spun to leave, Emma tipped her head. "Thank you," she said by rote as she passed through the door.

Mary gave a double-take and Jane shook her head, then led Emma round the room. They stopped at each small coterie and curtseyed their helloes, Jane introducing her to the few who had not yet made their own introductions elsewhere. Emma's thighs burned by the time they finished.

"One might call it a perk that servants are allowed to remain nearly invisible," Jane said as she drew Emma to a couch, sinking with a sigh onto it. "But us, on the other hand. Well, you see that you remain anything but invisible." She nodded at a group of young ladies Emma recognized from both assemblies. Their faces remained hidden behind their fans, but their gaze darted between Emma and Jane.

Emma rolled her eyes, an act which did not go unnoticed by Jane, who tapped Emma's hand playfully with her own fan. "In a small party such as this, did you think you could be anything other than the topic of conversation? Did I not predict a satisfying level of mischief?"

Emma was about to scoff both at Jane's classification of this teeming drawing room as a small party – small only if compared with the crush of the assembly rooms – as well as beg off any claim to this supposed mischief, but the door opened and this time a footman appeared. "Mr. Meyrick. Miss Meyrick. Mr. Baynes. And Mr. Landen," he announced.

"Ahh," Jane said, "speaking of which. Two interesting – and interested – gentlemen. As well as your protégé."

Emma blushed. "Poor girl. I'm no suitable model for any young woman." And again, she was struck by the truth of what she'd said. Or perhaps struck once more that there were so few truths in any of what she'd said of late, that any veracity which sprang to her lips felt as fresh and new as the lies had become old and stale.

Miss Meyrick sought Emma out. Mark, true to their agreement, gave Emma a nod, but then moved away. What his own desires might be, Emma could not discern from his averted face, but they had agreed that wherever Miss Meyrick went, Mark would not. And poor Mr. Baynes seemed uncertain which direction to go at all.

With Miss Meyrick now in tow, they kept their position at the far end of the room. Emma kept expecting the younger woman to speak, but instead, her expression remained cloudy and concerned.

When Emma asked if she were feeling well, Miss Meyrick shook her head. "Oh no, I'm well, thank you. It's just . . ." Her gaze drifted across the room. "Does not Mr. Landen seem ill? I have thought so since his sermon. He is so pale, and yet he denies anything is the matter."

Jane followed Miss Meyrick's gaze to where Mark stood near a window. "Indeed," she said. "He looks quite ill."

"Oh," said Emma, striving for the most offhand tone she could manage. "He looks fine to me."

At this, both women looked at her as though she must be blind.

"Ok," she said with a flap of acknowledgement. "Maybe he looks a little peaked, but I assure you, this is not uncommon. My uncle has often commented that Mr. Landen goes from hale to pale by the hour."

Snagging a passing footman, Emma insisted everyone grab a glass of wine. "Now, Miss Austen and Miss Meyrick. I insist you tell me all the necessary events one must accomplish before one leaves Bath."

Both looked surprised. "Surely your uncle is not contemplating a move?" said one, while the other put a hand on Emma's arm and said, "but you cannot be intending to leave anytime soon!"

Emma finished her wine with a long swallow. "Well, no, of course not . . . which is to say, that while I have no intention . . . you know, of leaving, I mean . . . but that my uncle's responsibilities are of such a changeable nature . . . that I . . . cannot know for certain . . ." She ended by snagging another glass of wine from a footman who had clearly not intended to offer her one.

"For heaven's sake, Miss Woods," Jane said, "certainly we understand you. Tending house for your uncle may take you all over the country. While you may miss some delights this season, you can surely make them up the next."

While Emma sipped her wine and tried to concentrate through the ferment-fuzz taking over, Miss Meyrick and Jane began to list their favorite activities. Two in particular caught Emma's mind.

"Oh, could we? Tomorrow, that is? Could we go to Molland's and then take a country walk?" She was nearly as giddy at the prospect as Catherine Morland herself on receiving the invitation from Henry Tilney.

Jane put a hand once more on her arm. "Of course, Miss Woods. But I do hope you don't intend to run away from us quite so soon. For there are so many delights to be had, one of which is unfolding right here." And she gestured round the room. "Now, whom should we converse with next. It is not done to hole ourselves away in a corner like dormice."

Emma forced herself to nod and follow Jane and Miss Meyrick back into the throng of the party. If delightful was surrounding yourself with people you did not like and who did not like you, all while trying to make pleasant conversation and avoid any number of social pitfalls along the way, then sure, it was absolutely flipping delightful. True delight at this moment would have been flannel pajamas, her favorite Austen adaptation playing on the DVR, and a tub of Ben & Jerry's cradled in her lap. Emma shook her head and willed herself to stop salivating.

"Although I imagine Miss Woods might prefer to be flitting about a ballroom than sitting demurely by the fire," said Miss Brookside, as they moved toward her. She gestured with her fan and a footman Emma hadn't even noticed moved from his station at the wall and passed round small goblets of sweet wine.

"You have filled your rooms admirably," Jane said. "But, I do not see the officers of our acquaintance."

"Was Miss Woods expecting them?" Miss Brookside gave a little half-smile. Though she took in the room like an empress, her own face expressed a certain dissatisfaction. "Indeed, they would have been a delightful addition. Captain Richards is himself particularly agreeable. But I'm afraid Miss Woods will have to excuse our simpler tastes. Mama prefers smaller parties of good friends. She shall have to save her charms to distribute to the men at some future gathering."

Emma shook her head. "No indeed. I much prefer the comfort of a warm fire and good company." She glanced round the room searching for any topic of conversation. "What a lovely room you have here, Miss Brookside."

"Yes," Jane said, barely concealing a laugh. "Though surely, Miss Woods, it must seem to you to be very delightful. How did you describe our dining room? Oh yes, delightful."

Emma shot a withering look behind Miss Brookside's back, who merely sniffed and said, "it is sufficient, though if you truly wished to see an exceptionally well-appointed room, you ought to see the drawing rooms of my old schoolfellow, Mrs. Marches. I say rooms because there are many. They have an estate just outside Bristol and the size and grandeur of the rooms, I assure you, has not an equal in all of Somerset."

She turned to Miss Meyrick. "In fact, Miss Meyrick, I wished to speak to you of them. Mrs. Marches is looking for a governess for her daughters. They are sweet children, and knowing how you love to instruct, you came instantly to mind as someone who would fill the position admirably."

Miss Meyrick looked down, her face pink. "Oh indeed, I do love teaching young children, but I had not considered a post as a governess. I do not believe my father would . . ."

Miss Brookside flapped her fan. "Oh, fathers are all very well, but then they are not always so practical, are they?"

Across the room, Mrs. Brookside was in conversation with Mr. Werthing. She waved her hand and Miss Brookside rose. "Excuse me, it appears Mama needs some assistance."

"The only thing her mother needs assistance with is getting her eldest daughter off her own hands!" Jane opened her fan and flapped it briskly. "What impertinence. Leave it to her to find everyone a place. Whether they need one or not!" She patted Miss Meyrick's hand. "Do not mind her, Miss

Meyrick. If she can fill the post with someone else, she won't risk being offered it herself."

Miss Meyrick, still embarrassed, kept her eyes cast down. "She may be correct, Miss Austen. I may indeed need to seek my own living, but I had hoped that marriage would be my calling . . ." As her voice trailed off, her eyes flickered up just once, and a quick glance following their direction told Emma they had landed upon Mark's milky face.

Emma took her other hand. "And indeed, I believe it shall. Let us not consider such things this evening, my dear, but enjoy ourselves." She rose and beckoned Mr. Baynes, standing on the periphery of another group, to join them.

He gladly approached, practically bouncing in his haste to take her outstretched hand. "Miss Woods, how kind of you to invite me to join you. What thoughtfulness! What . . ."

"Nonsense," she said, before he could utter the word "condescension." Though the man was not quite so ridiculous as the Mr. Collins who would plague Lizzy Bennet, she could not be entirely sure those words weren't perched on his lips. "I do not wish to see a sensible man standing idle. Tell us, how go the preparations for your sermon? I trust the decorations Miss Meyrick installed are still as flowering as ever?"

Mr. Baynes began a discourse. It was to be the sermon on the Good Samaritan. He went over the main points in minute details, clarifying just which message he hoped to impart. He paused. "What do you think, Miss Woods? Do you believe you should garner spiritual fulfillment on hearing such a sermon?" And his eyes searched her own in a way that made her feel all too acutely how closely both Jane and Miss Meyrick observed them.

How wrong this all was going! She was trying her damnedest to make him appear interesting, and he seemed only interested in engaging her interest!

"Miss Jane, I believe Miss Austen is beckoning us over?"

"No, indeed," Jane said, picking up on the ruse. "I don't believe so. Mr. Baynes, please continue your . . ."

Emma took a step, pulling Jane up behind her. "No, I am sure of it. You just missed her wave." With a bob, Emma led Jane away.

Jane burst into laughter as soon as her voice could be swallowed amidst the general buzz of the room. "You delight and confuse me, Miss Woods. For the life of me, I cannot determine if you are trying to engage Mr. Baynes' interest or deflect it."

"Both," Emma said as they took up a position behind Cassandra. "Do not you think Miss Meyrick and Mr. Baynes would make a lovely couple?"

Jane watched them. Miss Meyrick appeared content sitting there, and Mr. Baynes seemed to be maintaining the conversation well enough on his own. Emma sighed.

Jane shook her head. "I think people ought best be left to form their own attachments. Matchmaking is a dangerous business, Miss Woods, and it seems to me that those who try to direct cupid's arrow often find themselves the unintended target. We should not wish the girl to make a commitment she may find odious later on."

At this, Emma felt the blood drain from her face. She could not determine which disconcerted her more: Quinn's hapless face springing to mind, or the name Bigg-Wither. She hid her discomposure in examining a filigree basket on a table nearby. Jane could not know how soon her own advice would be put to the test. An image flashed in her mind once again of Jane and Cassandra together, this time on a large opulent bed as the fire dwindled low, speaking furtively through night and into morning, weighing out all the options before arriving at one foregone and painful conclusion, Jane steeling herself before the mirror; Cassandra dashing out the note to James to hasten his carriage to them.

Emma made herself glance round the room, see the world she had delivered herself into, and feel the fabric of Jane's gown brushing her arm. How many days did she have left? How many hours? However many there might be, they would not be enough – never enough – but they were all she had. Glancing to Mark's lonely self still holding vigil in the corner, she only wished she could have spent more of them with him.

"I heartily agree, Miss Jane," Emma said and then excused herself when her bladder began to protest.

After leaving the drawing room, she turned opposite from the stairwell that led to the front door. Within a few steps, this hallway met a longer corridor and down each end, a series of closed doors. She began trying them one by one, worried as to what she may encounter. She was not likely to come upon a lone Mr. Darcy playing at billiards, but she would be quite grateful if she might just find the water closet!

She was about to open a door at the end of the hall, when the door itself popped open. Emma put her hands up to avoid running into the person emerging from the stairs and found her palms resting on the chest of Dr. Lethbridge.

"Miss Woods!" He made as good a bow as he could from his perch at the top of the stairs with Emma standing mere inches away, her hands still affixed to his coat.

Emma leapt back, rubbing her palms together. "Dr. Lethbridge? What are you doing here?" The brazenness of her tone stunned them both to silence. "That is . . . what I meant was . . . It's pleasant to see you. I had not realized you would be part of our evening party."

True to his good-nature, Dr. Lethbridge smiled warmly and bowed his agreement. "I had not thought so myself. I've come to attend Mr. Brookside's maid."

"Right," Emma said. "Mary. She's . . ." Realizing she was giving away what no polite woman ought to speak of, she lamely finished, "the sister of a maid in the Austen's household."

With that, Mary herself appeared at the top of the stairs. Startled to find both the doctor and a young lady on the landing, the girl bobbed quickly and looked as if she might spin on her heel and run right back through the way she'd come.

"Mary," Emma said, "I imagine you are to show Dr. Lethbridge to the drawing room?"

Mary nodded and strode forward. Dr. Lethbridge followed behind and Emma watched them go. Just before he turned the corner, he glanced back once and Emma averted her gaze, but not before their eyes met and he smiled.

A moment later, Mary returned, once more alarmed to find Emma still at the doorway to the servant's hall. Did the girl make an expression other than bugged eyes and a gaping mouth?

"Mary, thank heavens. I must find a place to . . . that is to say, I need to
. . ." Emma couldn't help but hop a bit from foot to foot, and Mary, catching on, flapped a hand.

She led Emma back down to the entrance level and opened the door.
Inside, it was unmistakably a grand dining room, twice as large or more
than the Austen's, with a long-running table that could seat at least twenty.
The remnants of the men's after-dinner drinks and the haze from their
cigars still lingered.

"In here?"

"Yes, mum." Mary led Emma to a screen in the corner, behind which
Emma expected to find another door, possibly to the outhouse or the servants' quarters. Instead, there was only a lidded chamber pot on the floor
and a shelf with half a dozen porcelain gravy boats arranged on top. Mary
picked up one of these, handed it to Emma, curtseyed and moved to the
other side of the screen.

Emma took it in both hands. "Uhhh, Mary?"

"Yes, mum?"

"What is this?"

"Beggin' your pardon?" After another beat, Mary's head appeared
around the side of the screen, eyes averted.

"Perhaps I didn't make my needs quite clear enough. I need, um, the
outhouse?"

"My apologies, mum, but the nightsoil men have just arrived. You'll
have to use the bourdaloe." She gestured at the gravy boat still cradled in
Emma's hands.

When no recognition dawned on Emma's face, Mary took it back and
mimed lifting her skirts, holding it between her legs, and then lifted her
eyebrows as though to say, now have you got it? She resumed her position
on the other side of the screen, impatiently tapping her boot.

"Ahhhh," Emma said, better informed but now completely at a loss as to
how she was expected to pee standing up while the maid stood arm's reach
away. As she debated whether she could hold it until they were back at the
Austen's, Emma's bladder screamed that a choice had to be made – pee on
her skirts or pee in the gravy boat.

Lifting her skirt, Emma reasoned it couldn't be that hard; men relieved themselves standing up all the time! And one of the other faculty members, Diana of music festival road-trip fame, showed Emma one of her festival must-haves – a little funnel-looking device one could insert under a skirt or the fly of jeans to pee standing up in porta potties. Or bushes. Or wherever else.

Convenient or not, it didn't change the fact that Emma was expected to perform this function standing and in public, two things she had never needed – or wanted – to do in her life.

"Umm, Mary?"

"Yes, mum?"

"Are you planning on standing there the whole time?"

"Of course, mum! It is my duty to carry the contents outside."

Emma put her mind to the task, but there was nothing doing. Worse, Mary's boot tapping increased in tempo until Emma thought she'd sprain it from the effort.

"Do you think you could sing something? You know, to cover the . . . uh . . . sound?"

Though Emma couldn't see the maid's face, the snort of amusement broke the tension. Emma laughed, Mary chuckled, and finally, she launched into a tune, humming rather than singing, but loud enough to provide the cover Emma needed.

Finally finished, she cleared her throat and Mary came round the screen, holding out her hands for the bourdaloe. She gave a curtsey and moved back into the hall, turning toward the servant's stairwell at the end.

"Mary," Emma called, jogging to catch up with her. "Are you . . . that is, your sister has told me of your . . . Are you ok?"

Mary sighed. She glanced down at where the little mound of her belly was just starting to strain the waistline of her uniform. "Sarah shouldn't have done that, miss, but everyone will know when I'm let go." Mary trailed off, blushing at her indiscretion. "I's all right, miss, but they've caught him. My beau." Her head dropped. "Only he ain't my beau, is he. Says he don't care two figs what happens to me. He's here in town but I can't see as how I'll ever cross the gulf between us."

At this, she burst fully into tears. Emma might have hugged her and wept her own commiseration if the girl wasn't still holding a gravy boat full of her own urine. Instead, she placed one hand on Mary's shoulder and rubbed her back with the other. For a moment, Mary allowed this, but then broke away and retreated through the door, a deeply shadowed staircase leading down into the bowels of the house.

And hopefully also a drain.

CHAPTER 23

Back in the drawing room, Miss Brookside was attempting to hold the room captive with the elegance of her vibrato. Emma's eyes first found Dr. Lethbridge, who sat beside Mr. Werthing near the piano. On seeing her enter, his face brightened and he stood, gesturing she could take his seat. The motion did not go unnoticed by Mark, who swiveled his face from Emma to Dr. Lethbridge and back again. Emma glanced away, this time her gaze falling on Mr. Baynes and Miss Meyrick, sitting contentedly quiet near the fireplace, drinking tea.

Emma sidled up to Jane and Cassandra and indicated they should follow her. Despite their questioning looks, she led them through the door to the stairwell and down into the cool dark basement.

They followed the sounds of clattering pans and found the kitchen. It reminded Emma of a dungeon more than a room for cooking one's meals. A string of windows ran along one wall, up high near the ceiling. In the daytime, it must have been sufficiently bright. At night, though, the fire cast odd shadows against the deep cracks of the walls. Mary stood at the table, kneading dough, while a younger girl washed dishes at a sink with a pump handle, and an older woman leaned over a book, tallying marks. Emma noticed the bourdaloe, still full, near a stack of unwashed pots.

"Mary," Emma began, "The Miss Austens are both aware of your . . . situation. And we all want to help."

Mary nodded and bobbed. "Sarah's told me you've been ever so kind." At a nod from the housekeeper, she led them to a small parlor close to the servant's stairwell. Mary paced in front of the small grate. She worried the corner of her apron in her calloused hands, her face showing her hesitation over just what she ought to say.

"Just tell them what you told me," Emma said with an encouraging nod.

It took another moment, a deep breath and a gulp, and then she began. "Caught him, they have," she said. "My Tom. Came for his wages at the blacksmith's just as I said he'd do, and the constable caught him." Mary paused to hiccup and wipe at her cheeks. "But he says he won't marry me nohow and there's no one as can make him. He says 'tis my own fault I got . . . you know . . . and who's to say it was him in the first place!"

A round of indignant huffs passed all.

"Constable says he'll try to hold him until the morning, but after that . . ." Mary shrugged. "And if he leaves, I'll be ruined." Mary's words dissolved in a fresh cascade of tears.

Emma, Jane, and Cassandra began to deliberate. They considered asking Mr. Brookside for his help but Mary was adamant he should not be drawn further in, fearing her position might terminate even sooner were he to realize how far her ignominy had spread. To that end, Mary refused to let them call for Mr. Austen, anxious her own shame might seep onto her sister.

"Mr. Baynes," Cassandra suggested. "After all, he'll have to do the service."

Jane considered this, then frowned. "I'm afraid I have an unsure opinion of Mr. Baynes' charitable mind as regards this situation." She turned to Emma with a bit of a smile. "What do you say, Miss Woods. You have perhaps spent the most time with him of us all."

"Funny," Emma returned. She did not herself have any qualms on that score, believing him to be charitable at heart, a trait the future Mr. Collins would be denied, but more importantly, she needed him to remain right where he was.

"What about Mark? That is, I mean, Mr. Landen. He is generous of mind and spirit. He will not judge either of them. And besides, he will be leaving soon and can safeguard the secret. While Mr. Baynes must perform the service, he need not know why it must happen so soon. It is the safest option."

Mark, Emma knew, would be Mary's staunchest ally, himself the product of a single-parent household with a mother who scraped by until cancer took what little of life she had left. There was a father he'd only met once, a man, Mark said, who made George Wickham look like a saint.

"I don't know," Cassandra said. "He's been looking quite pale, you may have noticed. Scurrying about the streets after dark surely could not be good for his health. I believe Mr. Baynes would be the better choice for all."

"Mark's fine," Emma said, too quickly, too loudly, as though the force of her words could make them true. "Excuse me. Mark . . . er, Mr. Landen said he's had some digestive ailments, but otherwise feels as healthy as ever. I am certain he would wish to be of help."

They sent Mary upstairs to fetch Mark.

Emma excused herself and waited for him in the hall. When they arrived downstairs, she sidelined Mark. "On business about my uncle," she told Mary, who bobbed and returned to the parlor.

She pulled out the powder and rouge along with the note and handed all to Mark.

"What's this for?" He turned the items over in his hands, recoiling when he recognized them as make-up.

"So you don't look as though you're about to keel over. People are starting to notice." She opened the powder and quickly dabbed it over his face. She had been uncertain as to its effectiveness – would it just sink in as well? Somehow mix with his liquifying skin to create a paste? But no, it remained on the surface and formed a kind of mask. Satisfied that he looked a few steps further from death than a moment before, Emma led him into the kitchen.

Ducking under the doorframe, Mark held his hands out, palms up, the way Emma imagined he might speak to a worried student during office hours. "Now, tell me what all this hubbub is about."

"Hubub, sir?" Mary said, "I don't under-."

"Nevermind," Emma interrupted. "Mr. Landen, this is Mary, Sarah's sister, who works at the Austen's. She has found herself in an . . . interesting condition." She raised her eyebrows for effect, waiting until Mark's face showed comprehension. "The young man who put her there has just been found and is being held by . . .?"

"Constable Morrow," Mary supplied. "A parish warden too." Emma pulled out a chair for Mary to sit on, then led Mark a little apart so as to speak more freely.

"Now," Emma continued, "the young man says he'll not marry her, but if he does not, Mary will be ruined. Mr. Brookside is keeping her on until Michaelmas, which is but days away. After that, Mary will have to move to a factory town, give up her child to a relative, and do God only knows what else to make ends meet."

Mark's face darkened. "And so you want me to . . .?"

"We're in need of a smock wedding," Jane said, stealing up behind them. "Have you the stomach for it?"

Mark paced the floor a bit. Finally, he said, "take me to the lad."

They made a strange procession onto the darkened streets of Bath. Mary led them first back to 4 Sydney Place. They all scurried round the back to knock at the servants' entrance. Baxter was all in a fit at what to do with three upstairs ladies and a gentleman in her kitchen, but had only just enough time to get a pot boiling before Mary collected Sarah and the group once more took to the streets.

The night was starlit, not a cloud in sight. Carriages passed, the horses clip-clopping along the cobblestones. Occasionally, they passed a group of gentlemen trying to walk as though they were not as drunk as they so clearly were. Less frequently, a troop of young ladies passed by, shepherded along by a matronly mother or aunt. More than one group of late night revelers turned to look at the odd convoy of two maids, three ladies, and a gentleman.

They arrived at the blacksmith's and were led through to a modest parlor off the kitchen. The blacksmith's wife offered tea, but Mark politely refused and asked to speak to the young man in question.

The constable, who had entered just behind their party and introduced himself as Mr. Morrow, stepped forward to shake Mark's hand. "It was fortunate I saw you pass by my house up the road. I see you are here to argue the maid's claim. Good, good. A young man what takes advantage of an ignorant girl ought to feel the sting of his actions. Isn't that right, you?"

Mary's Tom sat dejectedly at a table. He was nothing like Emma had imagined. She thought they'd encounter some burly young blacksmith's apprentice, well-muscled arms and dark eyes, with a smirk on his face and the look of a rake.

But what she saw before her was nothing like. He was rather scrawny, actually, all bone and sinew, his head thrust forward on his neck like a baby bird, and his face covered in pimples. This "man" was barely more than a boy. He was perhaps seventeen, maybe eighteen, and the red rims of his eyes said he'd done a fair bit of weeping himself. When he saw Mary, he hung his head and twisted his handkerchief in his hands.

The constable shoved Tom's shoulder. "Stand up, will you. You're in the presence of ladies." Tom rose to his feet and doffed his cap, then sank back into the chair again.

"I see," said Mark. "Gentlemen, ladies. If you don't mind, I should like to speak to Mr. . . . ?"

"Heald," Tom supplied.

"To Mr. Heald in private."

The constable nodded and excused himself back to his own home. The blacksmith opened the door into the kitchen. They all filed through and the blacksmith's wife blushed to be caught washing dishes.

Emma cut off her fumbling apology and took up a rag. "It's the least we can do after intruding into your home."

Taking the cue, Jane began gathering dishes from the table and Cassandra found a broom in the corner. They were not quite as adept at their tasks as Emma, for whom cleaning had always been a refuge, but this would be good practice for their future life in the cottage.

When Mary appeared about to help, Emma pointed a soapy finger. "You sit," she said. "If anyone deserves a break, it's you and your sister." Mary's stunned expression transformed into a grateful nod. She dropped into a chair, her hands laced over the small mound of her belly and Sarah pulled over the stool to sit beside her sister and pat her arm.

When they'd gotten the kitchen into spit-spot shape and the black-smith's wife had pleaded them into a cup of tea, Mark entered. "Mary? Tom would like a word with you."

He sank into Mary's empty seat and gladly took the cup offered him. Meeting the gazes of three expectant ladies, he sighed and recounted their conversation. "The boy started off intransigent, but I brought him round. Turns out, Tom had in fact promised Mary he'd marry her should she find herself... you know." He blushed and drained his cup. "And so I convinced him he was in fact already married in God's eyes and that to abandon her would be to abandon his wife and child. No future marriage would be possible, unless he wished to become a bigamist." He drew his hand down over his eyes and held his chin. "We'll have the ceremony in the morning in the side chapel."

With that, Mark opened the door into the small yard at the back of the home. Emma, Jane, and Cassandra followed, while Sarah was allowed to remain and see her sister safely back to the Brookside's.

Jane took Cassandra's arm and drew her ahead.

Mark offered his to Emma, who took it, feeling a little rush of elation as Jane and Cassandra moved further on. "What is it?" Emma said. "You look so ... downcast."

"I hated doing that," Mark said. He walked even more stooped than usual. "That boy was such a ... such a ... a bloody twerp! I mean, he's a child basically. He wants freedom, to live his life, to do what young men do. And now she's got to marry him. Saddle her life to his. It will not be a happy marriage, Emma. I think I told you once about my ..."

In the darkness, Emma took his hand and pressed it between both of hers. "Yes, you did. But maybe he's not like your ..." She didn't need to say the word; his nod was enough. "I'm sorry for them," she said. "But they ... they have to. Life for him would be hunky-dory. But for her?" She tried to imagine the life of a fallen woman and all that came to her were haunting photos she had once seen in the London Museum of factory workers, poorhouse residents, and women who had come upon the town, breasts tumbling from their unbuttoned shifts as they called from upper-story windows to potential customers passing below.

Mark drew Emma's hand back through his arm, placing his on top of hers. She lay her other over his, her thumb tracing the ridges of his knuckles, the thin lines of tendons.

Here in the darkness, she could not see her hand sink below the threshold of where his skin should be and was glad, for it turned her stomach when she thought of it. He felt full to her, real, perfectly himself. But she knew that a new day would reveal his deathly pallor, and that however real he might feel as she gripped his hand now, they were both of them running against the clock, against circumstances that felt so terribly out of anyone's control.

From the top of a lamppost, a bird cried into the darkness, repeating its call over and over, a long phrase of trills and chirps, ending on a heavy low note before rising back to the cadence of chirps and trills once more. Both of them turned to look at it, then at one another, smiling perhaps for the first time in days, glancing away again just as quickly.

"I never said thank you," Mark said.

"Thank you?" Emma repeated. "What for?" Her mind had whisper-skipped back to all the moments they had shared since he had led her into the street reel, but there was nothing she could lay a claim to gratitude for. Thanks for lying? For obfuscating? For gazing into his eyes and making him think it might all pass off the way he wanted – dreamed – it might?

Thanks for her jealousy and rage? For fleeing from him rather than owning up to her own mistakes? For denying him the chance to own up to his? For the melodrama that launched them out of that window and into here?

She shook her head. "Don't thank me," she said softly. "The scales are so horribly tipped. I don't think they'll ever balance out."

"We all have our own scales," he said. "And perhaps they never do balance. Not for any of us. But still, thank you." His grip on her hand tightened. "For going back, I mean. That's what I wanted to say thank you for."

As they walked, the bird overhead flew from lamppost to lamppost as though following them, continuing its song, pausing to listen to await a song in return.

"It's just," he said, his voice trailing as he stopped. "You did it without a second thought. Without hesitation. I know you don't want to go back. But you're doing it anyway." In the darkness, he sought her eyes. "For me."

Why was it so hard to stand here and feel his gaze? His hands had found both of hers, his eyes had not wavered. A hand came to her face, his fingers at her neck, his thumb sliding down the curve of her jaw.

It was almost that same feeling she'd had before, how he had drunk her in and she poured herself into him like wine ribboning from its bottle. But that was then, this was now. And so much had transpired between the two that she felt rather like wine which had turned to vinegar. She couldn't stand the thought of him drinking her in now, of the sour look that would surely pass his face. Because all the illusions necessary to maintain the ruse of this place, her own illusions – the ones she had hoped Mark would never see dismantled – were as brittle as an old cork, falling to pieces at every touch.

Ahead, Jane and Cassandra paused at the corner, turning back to wait for them. Emma took a step back, blushing that they had nearly caught such an intimate moment. She waved a hand and they turned down the street.

Emma took a step, then another, and pulled Mark with her, walking away from the moment she did not have the courage to embrace.

"So thank you," he repeated.

"Of course, Mark," she said, finding his hand again and clutching it tighter than ever. Even still, the weight of the moment was too much to bear. "What would the festival be without you?"

"The festival," he repeated. "Of course. The lovely, lovely festival."

His step quickened. Though he offered Emma his arm once more, it was done out of habit, manners. His other hand did not lay upon hers, nor could she muster herself to slide her own into his palm.

The bird darted to the lamppost across the street and with a final lonely cry, took to the air, flying back toward the bridge and the river and whatever awaited it in its forlorn, empty home.

CHAPTER 24

A heavy heart slowed Emma's steps as she followed Jane and Cassandra to the city center. She had awoken to the bells clanging the call to matins and knew the ceremony was complete. Mary and Tom were married. Sarah had been given the morning to prepare a wedding breakfast at the blacksmith's house, where Tom was to resume his apprenticeship. Emma's dreams from the night continued to muddle her mind: Mary beaming and proud on her new husband's arm. Tom smiling in spite of himself, animated by the power of a love Mary had offered freely, to an unwilling and undeserving recipient.

She tried to keep up with Jane and Cassandra, but she found her footsteps slowing, as if her body dragged all the weight of last night's realizations on an invisible pallet behind her. More than once Cassandra glanced back, her brows furrowed in what may have passed for concern, though Emma speculated any distress she felt was reserved solely for her sister. Had the muse gone silent?

She couldn't remember the last bit of "inspiration" she had let slip. Would her jumbling, fumbling presence be enough to sustain Cassandra's reluctant tolerance?

When Emma pondered how to drop lines as discretely as possible, images of the frothing, fuming river rushed in. Years ago, she and Quinn had once hiked to a waterfall where, they read on a sun-faded sign, the force of the falls churned so much oxygen into the water that anything which fell into it sank instantly to the bottom. More than one haphazard teen had jumped in on a dare, never to surface, so the beautiful falls had been cordoned off with 10-foot hurricane fencing.

Thinking of the river reminded her of Mark's pale face, of his skin that felt like the permeable membrane of bathwater, his surface tension barely holding it all together. And that brought her back to Miss Meyrick. If Emma didn't get the girl's eyes shifted soon, there would be no Mark at all.

It was all too much! Emma shook her head to clear the fog. Jane and Cassandra had stopped to wait for her, hasty words passing between. Jane stepped forward, hand extended.

"Miss Woods," she said, "we couldn't help but notice you don't seem yourself this morning. Ought we send for Dr. Lethbridge?"

Emma looked away. Overhead, two doves circled and played in the morning sun. They landed on a church spire and nuzzled. Then, one of them tipped forward into a dive and just before it crashed into a gargoyle, its wings extended and it rose, soaring over the rooftops and out of sight.

Send for Dr. Lethbridge? Frankly, the idea sent shivers up her spine. He had begun to hold a place of solace and refuge in her mind, a sense of familiarity and shelter. He bore all of Quinn's best traits – kind and generous, unexpectedly thoughtful – and something more, too: the model of a Regency gentlemen.

Still, she shook her head. "No, I thank you. I'm quite well."

"Well," Jane said, her expression betraying her uncertainty. "Though you had expressed such a keen interest in Molland's and our country walk, I am uncertain as to whether it is wise." She glanced at the sky, a bright clear blue, strung with lazy streamers of clouds. "Though it is a fine morning, perhaps a day spent at home would suit you better." She turned to lead them back the way they'd come.

"No!" Emma said. "That is, forgive me. I would not give up Molland's or the walk for anything. I have so been looking forward to them. And I don't know when I should ever get to see them again."

At this, Jane laughed while Cassandra's expression darkened further.

"Whyever not?" Cassandra said. "For once your uncle arrives, surely you will have every opportunity to see either at your leisure." The air quotes around 'uncle' were palpable.

"Oh, of course," Emma said, as sweat pricked her neck, rising on her upper lip and temples. "It's only that I should very much like to visit them with you. With the both of you."

Jane drew Emma's arm through her own and gave her fingers a squeeze. "And so we shall, Miss Woods. It is the best time now, before Bath becomes all a bustle. But surely, we shall find time throughout the season to enjoy these delights."

"Yes," Emma said, "surely." And she took a wavering breath, steeling herself against regret and sadness. She matched Jane's stride, determined to give no reason for further alarm or an insistence that she spend what little time she had left cloistered in the Austen's home.

Jane drew Emma on toward Milsom Street, turning in at the door with a wooden sign overhead reading "Molland's." Two bow windows extended into the street. On the shelves within, an army of carafes and glass jars held every sort of candy and jellied fruit imaginable. To one side was the shop where customers could make purchases and depart. On the other were tables and stools. It was to one of these tables Jane led them, settling just where Emma would have chosen for herself – a table near the back where one could sit unobserved while having a full view of the shop and the street beyond.

"Delightful," Emma breathed. "It's just as I imagined it would be."

"You've heard of Molland's then?" Cassandra said. "To know the confectioners's of London – the Pot and Pineapple or Gunter's, perhaps – is no surprise. But I had not realized our dear little Molland's had earned transcontinental renown."

Emma bent over, working at the lace of her half-boot. "Oh, well, it was that friend of mine I told you about. She recommended I visit here with my, um, uncle."

Thankfully, the waiter arrived to take their order.

"Shot in the dark," she said by rote.

He glanced from Jane to Cassandra, apparently asking them to translate the strange American's order.

"Coffee? With espresso?" Already, Emma was fighting off the pinch of her daily caffeine-withdrawal headache. For all the tea these people drank, any hope of flavor or a meaningful boost of caffeine was sacrificed to economy.

The waiter cocked his head in confusion.

"Nevermind. Whatever you have."

Within moments, the younger Miss Brooksides arrived with Miss Meyrick in tow. They took the table next to theirs, chattering happily about a new bonnet one of them had just purchased nearby.

"And Miss Brookside?" said Jane.

"Oh, she said she had some business to attend to," said Miss Margaret.

Miss Lucy leant forward, a sly smile playing at the corners of her mouth. "Though if you saw how much time she spent at her toilette, you'd imagine she had a very specific appointment to keep." She paused to wait for signs of comprehension from her listeners. "And I don't think it's for the sake of Mr. Werthing."

Miss Margaret, quick to ensure she was also understood to be in the know, gave an impish chuckle. "Oh no, our dear sister has quite another target in mind these days. I think if Mama wants Mr. Werthing, she may have to go after him herself."

The two girls continued to bandy cryptic statements meant to imply both their superior knowledge of the secret suitor while simultaneously capture the curiosity of their listeners. For their parts, the Austen sisters, Emma, and Miss Meyrick glanced out the window and commented on the fineness of the weather.

Giving up, Miss Margaret brought out her newest purchase. "Now, see here, Ann," she said to Miss Meyrick, "This bit of ribbon will be pulled off, and then I think I may try to weave in something wider, with a scalloped design and then I can lace the stems of flowers through it."

"Sounds atrocious, Meg," said Miss Lucy, laughing at her sister's plan. "You'll look like some forest maiden late for May Day."

Miss Margaret dropped the bonnet back in its box and kicked it under the table.

"Did you enjoy the party last evening," Emma asked, leaning toward Miss Meyrick.

"Oh yes," she said. "It was delightful all around. Though I couldn't help . . ." She broke off with a blush.

Miss Lucy jabbed her with an elbow. "Oh don't be so shy now, Ann. All the way here, Miss Woods, it was 'I hope Mr. Landen's not coming down with a cold' and 'Poor Mr. Landen, how he seems out of spirits.'" Lucy broke off with a laugh. Margaret looked as if she would have joined in but her mouth was stuffed with a petit four off the tiered cake stand just delivered by the waiter.

Miss Meyrick blushed even deeper. "I did not mean . . . I only meant to . . ."

Emma threw a rescue line. "It is kind of you to be concerned for others."

"Others?" Margaret scoffed. "What others? It's only Mr. Landen-this and Mr. Landen-that all day long!"

Jane and Cassandra rolled their eyes. Five or six years ago, Jane might have participated quite as equally in the ribbing and teasing, or perhaps might have been the object of it herself. But time, it seemed, had taught her the subtler arts of female ribaldry. Apparently, the man-crazy, husband-hunting butterfly had folded its wings and had little patience for the wild flutterings of the young who followed after.

Emma rose from the table. "Miss Meyrick. We were about to take a country walk this morning. Should you like to join us?"

Miss Meyrick nodded. "Very much." She turned to the Miss Brooksides. "Miss Lucy, Miss Margaret? A country walk?"

"And get our shoes muddy?" said one.

"This is a new petticoat!" said the other. And both young ladies shoved another pastry in their mouths.

In another minute, they were back on Milsom Street, the air ringing with clattering horse hooves and chaise wheels. Miss Meyrick had to run back inside, remembering the reticule she'd left at the table.

Jane sniffed at Emma. "What did you invite her for? Now *we'll* be Mr. Landened to death."

Cassandra tsked.

It was Emma's turn to pat the hand and placate the mind of her friend. "And leave her at the mercy of those two? I imagine Miss Meyrick has been shamed out of any additional Mr. Landening today."

But just as Miss Meyrick joined them, none other than Mark and Mr. Baynes should appear coming round the corner, the two absorbed in a text held open by Mr. Baynes. Jane groaned as Mark stopped short, rearranged the surprise on his face, and bowed. They all dropped a curtsey.

"Good morning," he said. His face was indeed grave, but he'd made use of the powder and rouge and at least had the look of a man who wasn't about to step into his own.

The greetings exchanged, Emma was about to curtsey a farewell, but Jane intercepted her with the briefest of winks.

"We're off on a country walk," she said, tucking her hand through Mark's arm. "How fortuitous to meet with two such able gentlemen who may assist us over fallen logs and down steep ravines."

Tossing a backward glance to Emma, a smirk playing at the edges of her mouth, Jane led the group onward. Mark looked as though he wished to protest. After all, the plan had been to spend as little time with Miss Meyrick as possible. But Emma gave a nod, and he allowed Jane to direct their steps further along the street, which would eventually lead to the gentle wilderness waiting beyond the city limit.

Mr. Baynes stepped forward to offer Emma his arm. "Oh heavens," she said, dropping to one knee. "Something happened to my lace. You and Miss Meyrick go ahead. I shall catch up."

With a bow, Mr. Baynes offered his arm to Miss Meyrick.

Cassandra stayed behind. When Emma finally stood, having spent as much time as she could reasonably manage unlacing and relacing her boot, Cassandra's face had taken on a wry irony very similar to the expression frequently found on Jane's. "Those laces appeared in good order to me."

"Things just needed . . . re-adjusting," Emma replied.

They caught up to the other four at the edge of town. The sound of hooves and carriage wheels gave way to the faint tinkle of a brook in a small valley below them and happy chirps from the forest canopy above.

Through the forest, Emma could just discern a rolling range of foothills and copses adorning the landscape beyond.

Mr. Baynes had stationed himself at the bottom of the ravine and Mark at the top, both helping the women down the steep, narrow trail. Emma maneuvered herself to be last, an awkward attempt that again did not pass unnoticed by Cassandra. A moment alone with Mark. It was worth any amount of eyerolling or brow furrowing.

Holding her hand all the way down the slope, a touch that once more brought the sparkle of sweat to her brow, Mark whispered, "what the . . .? I'm supposed to be avoiding her. And also, just FYI, Jane seems to think it hilarious to compel Miss Meyrick to talk to me. The whole way here, it was 'Mr. Landen, do tell us more about such-and-such.' And 'Miss Meyrick was wondering about so-and-so.' It's as if she's purposely trying to get in our way. Does she know –," his voiced dipped lower, "about the plan?"

A smile, half rueful, half amused, tugged Emma's mouth. Yes, she could imagine Jane might try to thwart Emma's matchmaking attempts between Miss Meyrick and Mr. Baynes just for the fun of it. "Avoid her as much as possible, yes," Emma said. "But when together, you've got to make yourself as unpleasant as possible too. That'll do the trick just as well. Maybe better." Continuing in silence, Emma reflected on her part of that task: run interference with Jane, which also meant outsmarting one of the cleverest satirists in written language.

Having reached the bottom of the slope, they strolled along the pine-needled floor, stopping when there was a break in the trees to gaze at the soft green blanket of hills spreading before them.

"How beautiful," Miss Meyrick sighed. "Just like the south of France. Or Italy maybe." She faltered. "That is, as I assume it must be from the books I've read."

"England has many beauties," Jane said. "What do you think, Mr. Landen? Is this not one of the more beautiful parts of our country?"

"Oh yes," Miss Meyrick continued. "I'm sure it is the most beautiful of all counties. The garden of England, or so our travel books tell us."

"Yes," Emma mused, "but many counties are called that." From a distance, the low rumble of thunder caught her attention. None of the others seemed to have heard it, but Emma quailed at the sound, the universe warning her like a mother scolding a child – "you're cruisin' for a bruisin'" her own mother used to say. Emma bit her lip until she tasted copper.

"Oh, yes, to be sure," Miss Meyrick said, "but I do believe Somerset is the beautifullest, erm, most beautiful . . . of them all. Which is to say, that if I were ever to travel outside of Somerset, I doubt I would encounter anything so beautiful." She sidled a little closer to Mark. "You, Mr. Landen, I should think you would be happy to settle in Somerset. Or Wiltshire, perhaps. Both are . . . near."

"To be sure, Miss Meyrick, beautiful country all round Bath, and I should imagine myself very happy . . ." He faltered as Emma shot daggers with her eyes. "That is to say, no, not at all. I prefer cities. London, York, Birmingham, Liverpool. I detest the country." With that, he strode forward, taking up a stick to whallop any poor fern so unlucky as to have made its home near the trail.

"He does seem out of humor," Jane said, her eyes passing from Emma to Mark and back again.

Emma slowed her own steps and Mr. Baynes held back with her. "Mr. Baynes," Emma began, grasping for any topic she could think of. "Did not you say you grew up by the seaside? Miss Meyrick, I believe that novel you were reading is set on an island, is it not?"

Miss Meyrick, shamed into silence, nodded. "Off Italy," she finally said.

Mr. Baynes held out his arm for Miss Meyrick. "Well, my home was not so beautiful as the shorelines of Italy, but it was a pleasant home for a young boy." Once more Emma feigned a problem with her boot and allowed the other two to walk on.

As they neared a stand of rocks, the pleasant silence of the forest was broken into by the halloes of a young man. It was Captain Richards, standing on a rocky outcrop, yelling for their group to join his. Lieutenant Listle was halfway up himself, climbing with an agility Emma had not expected from his stocky build. On seeing their approaching group, he dropped to the ground and tugged his blue coat back on.

Both Mark and Jane turned back to look at Emma, on Jane's face another look of mirth. On Mark's, something darker flashed. She had not been able to tell him about the officers's dual attraction to Miss Meyrick, or that Emma had decided to put herself firmly in the middle of the strange love triangle she'd found herself in, a triangle that threatened at any moment to become a polygon of unknown points and connections. Emma sighed and trudged forward. At the sight of the young men, Miss Meyrick's pace had quickened, leaving Mr. Baynes behind so she could look at some creature Captain Richards held captive in his palms.

Emma strode forward. "Captain Richards! Lieutenant Listle! How glad I am to see you. I am *absolutely* fatigued by the walk. I simply *cannot* take another step." Emma put the back of her hand to her forehead and started to swoon. Behind her closed lids, she rolled her eyes at the insipidness of what she was doing, how much she resembled Isabella Thorpe, a true mercenary husband-hunter if ever there had been one. Which was also the last thing she needed Mark to think – continue thinking – she was.

"Steady on." Captain Richards put a hand to her elbow.

"My dear Miss Woods," said Lieutenant Listle.

And from that moment on, she kept the two men at her side, one arm linked through theirs. Even when the path narrowed, Emma did her best to keep them attached to her, though she knew her face had gone crimson. But the young men accounted for it by her exertion, and she very nearly had to push Captain Richards away when he took it into his head to carry her back up the steep hill down which they'd originally come.

Looking back, she saw Mark happily situated between Jane and Cassandra, conversing easily. Further behind came Miss Meyrick and Mr. Baynes, their conversation having stalled for the moment. His gaze swung like a pendulum between Miss Meyrick's face and the ground, his mouth occasionally opening as though prepared to speak, then closing mutely again. For her part, Miss Meyrick appeared happy enough, occasionally pointing out a bird in the trees above or asking Mr. Baynes if he knew the genus of a flower along the trailside.

By the time they reached the start of the trail, Emma's neck was sore from swiveling to check on each of them, often finding Jane's laughing eyes meeting her own.

At the edge of town, the group parted company. Emma found her hand warmly pressed first by Captain Richards and then by his friend. Whatever distinction she felt was soon washed away when both officers gave similar farewells to Miss Meyrick. So Lieutenant Listle's admiration remained constant, and Captain Richards' attempts to wiggle his way between them was equally reliable. Emma felt a pang of regret at having to thwart the poor lieutenant's hopes, and yet one look at Mark's face, at how the sweat from their walk had drawn lines through the powder revealing the pale permeableness of the skin below, reset her convictions.

Following Jane and Cassandra back toward the bridge, Emma looped an arm through Miss Meyrick's and pulled her along with them. After all, she had to reduce the threat of an invitation from one of the officers. And to avoid any chance the girl might see Mark's stripey face, which had a rather otherworldly look to it. No ghost in clanking chains such as the one that would swarm Catherine Morland's agitated visions, but Miss Meyrick was not so far beyond her own girlhood that Mark wouldn't make a rather charming little dormouse in need of nursing back to health.

CHAPTER 25

In the hours before bed, Emma sat before the mirror of the dressing table, pulling a comb through her hair, watching the shadows from candlelight dance across her features. She could only ever see half her face at a time, the other half in dark emptiness. While the flicker of the candle cast a warm orange corona across the dressing table and a small semi-circle of floor, the opposite wall was obscured, hidden by shadows made darker relative to the candle's bright glow. Something was always in shadow.

They had passed the night at the theatre, an outing Emma had been looking forward to as an excursion of simple quietude, an opportunity to sit silently in the dark and watch someone other than herself fall into and pull themselves out of calamity in a 3-hour run-time.

"I cannot see why you should crowd so much into a few days," Jane had commented earlier, watching Emma pull briars from the hem of her dress after their walk. "Should we not delay until your uncle's arrival?" she queried, but saw Emma's look and held her palms up. "Fine then. The play is one I've been longing to see and it will likely be replaced by something more popular and coarse by the end of next month."

Cassandra, sitting across and tending to her own spikey stow-aways, began a line of questioning that hours later still brought a sheen of perspiration to Emma's brow. "But why are you so certain you shall not be in Bath much longer, Miss Woods? One might imagine you are preparing for a hasty getaway yourself, mightn't they?"

Over the last few days, Cassandra's suspicious glances had increased, her questions grew more pointed. However much she might couch her words under the tone of teasing, she was leery. Her last foray had been the simplest and worst of all: "does it not rather remind you of someone plotting an elopement, Jane?"

At this, both women turned their gaze on Emma, one sister discerning, quick, and shrewd; the other, interested, amused, and perhaps a bit alarmed. "Alas," said Jane finally, exchanging her concern for amusement, "for there to be an elopement, Miss Woods would have had to decide on just one gentleman, and I rather guess she has not quite managed that yet."

Whether this was meant to relieve Emma of her sister's fierce gaze or heighten it, Emma could not tell. It seemed to do neither. Or both. Whether Cassandra suspected her of making off with family heirlooms in the near future or casting their household in disgrace with her wanton ways, she perceived something was coming soon and she began to rip the briars off her own gown as though they were tiny little Emmas she could summarily eject into the smoking grate.

Finally, Emma had to excuse herself to make more meaningful preparations for the theatre, and once in her room, she rang the bell and asked Sarah to exchange the soupy grey water remaining in her bowl for a fresh pitcher and flannel towel. Aside from anything else, Cassandra's intense glares necessitated another swipe or two under her arms.

Going to the washstand now, in the dark, Emma dipped both hands into the black maw of the pitcher and drew fresh(ish) water into her cupped palms and splashed her face. In this dark, empty hour, she felt slimey and slick, and while water may wash away what had accumulated on the outside, there was nothing to squeegee the grime within. She rubbed her wet hands on her arms to release the film of soot that seemed to stick to her every time she took a step outside.

Grabbing her journal, she climbed into bed, determined to use the last few pages to sort the evening out. And if not sort it, at least own it.

The walk to the theatre had been lovely. The evening was warm and clear, the sky adorned like a courtesan, silk riffs and gamboling clouds cascading from a backdrop that bled from yellows to oranges to pinks and purples. As they turned a corner, Emma stumbled on a familiar curb. They were walking past the very building where Harold and her dear friends had applauded and praised her over their svelte dinner, where Wanda had blown the lid off Emma's secret, and where Emma could have, but didn't, own up to her mistakes. Turning round, she saw the familiar outlines of the street where she and Mark had trudged home –her betrayal writ plain across his face.

That evening felt like a lifetime ago.

And in those days, what had transpired on the other side? Was Quinn pacing the halls of the hospital awaiting news of her? Was he biding time in a sea of unwelcoming airport chairs, stuck in layover hell? Were searchers dragging the river for bodies, Harold, Lorna, and Deb holding vigil in the common room of Adelaide Garden? She gave a snort imagining the spectacle Wanda must be making or how she might, even now, be exulting in her new position as lover of the departed.

Or could it be that time stood still all those years in the distance? That this rip in the seam of time had brought everything to a sparkling halt – the café owner extending her hands as the bickering pair toppled out of sight, Wanda's spiked heel raised above the cobblestone as she stalked up and down the bridge in pursuit, the froth on the river resting still as a mountain, a bubble capturing the inverted image of the cathedral spire, holding it there unpoppable and pristine. And a waiter in that very bistro pouring a stream of merlot into an eternally upheld glass.

A light flared at the corner as the door to what was then (now?) a tobacconist's shop opened and closed again, a bell tinkling out a weak insistence into the falling dusk.

Here too, just as that morning, Jane had tugged Emma's arm, looked keenly into her face, and asked whether she were well, whether they oughtn't order a chair to return her home, whether she was, in fact, as "all right" as she claimed to be.

What a question. Was she all right? Was anyone? In that moment, she had no other words to offer, no answer that was nothing less than an absolute lie. But now, she was intent on capturing it in this book, a silent, waiting testimony to both her inspirations and her spinelessness.

At the corner, they turned onto Orchard Street and saw the squat stone building that, in her day, had long since transformed from the Theatre Royal to the Masonic Hall. Orchard Street itself teemed with chairs, and the streets beyond were quickly becoming impassable for all the carriages and carts delivering theatre-goers to its doors. However small the theatre may appear to be, a great many people intended to get inside.

Stepping from her chair, Emma followed Jane and Cassandra through a green door marked "Boxes" etched in the stone above, then up to the mezzanine level, and into a private box. Inside, the theatre was large and spacious, much more so than Emma had expected from her first impression. Over the stage, a great burgundy curtain cascaded in deep dips and gathers across the ceiling. Each side of the stage was lined with tall columns through which Emma could just see the passing of actors and scene setters preparing for the performance. Below, the orchestra sat on the floor-level, protected by a low arching wall from the penny audience scraping chairs as they took their seats.

The trills of flutes and oboes, the honks of bassoons and French horns drifted up to them, their notes moving in and out of harmony as the players tuned and warmed their instruments. And along the walls of the theater ran three levels of boxes, each minimally adorned on the outside, leaving one's gaze drifting over the faces and gowns and headdresses of the beautifully dressed sitting within them.

Shortly after they took their seats, Miss Brookside, her mother, and Mr. Werthing arrived. The younger Miss Brooksides, they were told, would be arriving soon. Emma had settled into a chair behind Jane, glad for the opportunity to sit and be silent. While Emma was correct in one assumption about the evening, she was sorely mistaken in the other.

No sooner had the first act begun than Captain Richards and Lieutenant Listle flung back the curtain and clattered into their box. For his part, Lieutenant Listle seemed to feel the intrusion and made gallant bows in apology. Captain Richards, however, took a position just behind Emma.

He spoke loudly through most of the first act and laughed at the wrong times through the rest. He claimed to be able to spot a quiz at twenty paces and proceeded to point them out, often drawing the attention of the recipient of his musings and making Emma cringe at her complicity.

Just in front of her, Emma observed Jane stealthily remove a square of paper and begin scribbling notes on it. Cassandra turned once to give Emma a look that combined pity and gratitude.

After that, Richards had exclaimed over the impertinent looks of someone across the theatre and following his boorishly pointed finger, Emma found herself gazing first into Mark's sour face, then Dr. Lethbridge's kind one, the two men occupying separate boxes on the other side of the theatre.

Mark's look was unmistakable. He held her to blame for Captain Richards' attentions. What she wouldn't give for some silent gesture that could say "don't be pissed at *me*. I'm trying to divert their attentions from Miss Meyrick who seems to only have eyes for *you*." But try as she might, she could not determine which combination of eyebrow waggles, frowns, and head shakes might accomplish it.

Dr. Lethbridge acknowledged Emma with a pleasanter bow, but his own face held something Emma could not discern: disappointment perhaps. There was something similar to Mark's jealous glances, a thought that made her pulse quicken. Surely not, she convinced herself, as confused by his face as by her own response to it.

Finally, Captain Richards turned to Lieutenant Listle and entangled him in a plan to wander about the boxes, searching for quizzes and "impressionable young ladies." To this, both men's gazes returned to Mark's box, at Miss Meyrick situated between her father and Mr. Baynes, but who, to Emma's great frustration turned around more often to speak with Mark than the other two. When Mark caught her looking sternly at him, he had looked pointedly at Captain Richards and, with a glance tossed over his shoulder, at Dr. Lethbridge. He returned a look that said two could play at this game and then gave Miss Meyrick his undivided attention.

At the close of the first half of the play, Jane and Cassandra rose.

"Well, Miss Woods," said Jane. "You have had a most encouraging evening thus far, I should think." Jane looked from Mark's box, to Dr.

Lethbridge's, to Captain Richards. "Am I mistaken or was Mr. Landen and Dr. Lethbridge rather more interested in our box than on the play?"

"Oh Jane, hush," Cassandra said.

Jane leaned forward and in a more intimate tone, continued, "Oh dear sister, we ought not be jealous, you know. Though I do think Miss Woods is being rather greedy in captivating three young men at once." Her eyes flickered to Lieutenant Listle and Mr. Werthing. "You must cast a stronger spell if you are to capture the rest." With that, she flapped her fan open and gazed at Emma mischievously over the top.

Emma let out a harrumph. "You cannot be ignorant what a harmless flirtation looks like, Miss Jane. One is often drawn on to give more encouragement than one wishes to stand by."

Jane laughed. "Oh, we are well aware of the high spirits of youth. What one says one day, one may not mean the next."

"And that's an excuse for deceiving well-meaning young men?" Cassandra asked, scandalized.

"Yes . . . I mean, no. That is, I don't . . ." Emma slumped back into her chair, just as she caught the booms of thunder in the night beyond. Jane laughed at Emma's discomfort and Cassandra shook her head. The general hum and buzz of the theater drowned out the sounds, but Emma could not mistake the broadcast of her blunder.

Next to her, Jane was feverishly composing on a scrap of paper from her reticule. Cassandra tapped Emma's knee with her fan and tilted her head imperceptibly in Jane's direction. She had perhaps just secured another night's stay under Cassandra's protection, but it had come at the price of knocking herself even further into the moral gutter Cassandra believed she'd crawled out of.

But what Emma hoped to capture with her pencil in the dying light of a candle burnt nearly to the little copper stand in which it sat, was what had happened at the play's end. Perhaps it was Jane's observation that Emma seemed to be the most enthralling occupant of the theatre. Or her sister's comment that Miss Woods' true skills would be lost as a housekeeper and that a career on the stage may suit her best. Or worst of all, when she found Mark as people meandered toward the doors and playfully reminded him to check his powder, joking that they weren't out of the woods yet, Mark had replied, "I rather suspect there are a few men here who would prefer to be *in* the woods." And he gave her a knowing look and a smirk, and gave her hand one hard squeeze before slipping out the doors to walk home with the Meyricks and Mr. Baynes.

And somewhere in between, the rush of activity, the crush of the crowd. Miss Meyrick sharing the invitation for an outing on the morrow and then dashing for the door after her father. And Dr. Lethbridge suddenly at her side as she waited in the foyer with Jane and Cassandra for a trio of chairs. Dr. Lethbridge asking if she would be of the party driving out into the country for the next day's excursion. Dr. Lethbridge putting a hand on her back as he took her other and guided her out to the chairs waiting in the dark.

The air pulsed between them, as if she could feel the swell of his body as he breathed, that same feeling she used to get when she would ask her bio professor some fabricated question just so she could feel the nearness of Quinn as he gathered papers and notes, cleaned the whiteboard with broad efficient strokes.

Quinn. Did he have any sense of the distance Emma had travelled, not just in miles, but in time? Could he feel the expanse laying between her heart and his, their love – or whatever it was – stretched across a tightrope of time into the black oblivion she'd fallen through? Did he wake at night and feel her absence or did he dream on, peaceful and warm below the film of safety he had offered her, secure in his belief of her promise when she returned?

Her hand cramped around the pencil, and she shook her fingers out. It did not take much of a stir in the air to extinguish the candle, but it was gone, and Emma was left alone in the quiet and dark, her mind at the point of the matter, her heart risen to her throat. And the look on Mark's face as he spun away from her. The touch of Dr. Lethbridge's gloved hand upon her back.

CHAPTER 26

Emma descended in the morning to find the family round the breakfast table.

"You have kept late hours this morning, Miss Woods," said Mrs. Austen as she passed a plate of bunns down to Emma. "You and Mr. Austen both keep abed longer than is good for you."

"Mama," Cassandra said. "Papa is very unwell. Dr. Bowen will be arriving soon and I fear the diagnosis will not be encouraging."

"My apologies, madam," Emma said. She turned to Cassandra. "I hope your father feels better soon, Miss Austen. I am so very sorry about these storms. That is, you know, the toll they've taken." Emma's eyes began to tear. She was indeed terribly sorry, but what could she say against the truth of their father's poor health which would cast all the Austen women into the fate of their male relatives? Cassandra nodded in reply, her eyes flickering up to Emma's face once and then back down to the plate before her.

Sarah started to bring Emma a cup of tea, then stopped. Returning to the sideboard, she returned with a small steaming cup of black coffee and set it before Emma, shifting from foot to foot as she waited for Emma's hands to take it. "I hope I made it right, miss. Me first time."

"Thank you, Sarah." Emma breathed in the heavy, sweet aroma and closed her eyes. She could almost imagine herself back at the Caffè Nero, that kid with his irritating skateboard, thoughts of Mark and Wanda broadcasting behind her closed lids – but herself safe – and more than that, Jane Austen safe as well – each on their own side of time.

Mrs. Austen watched Sarah with surprise. "I did not know we even had coffee in this house."

Jane leaned toward her sister but spoke in a voice Emma could hear. "Oh no, no coffee for Mama. Coffee invites too much reflection on the ills of society. Coffee is for the thinkers, the witty, the erudite . . ." she broke off as Cassandra interrupted with, "the unsavory."

"I wouldn't go that far," Jane laughed. "But it's certainly not for the Austens."

"Tell me, Sarah," Mrs. Austen broke in. "Has Baxter been adding it to our grocer's list?"

Sarah worried a corner of apron in her hands. "Umm, no'm," she said. "I just knew Miss Woods liked coffee so I went out early to get some. 'Twas me own savings."

"Oh Sarah," Emma said, taking another deep, appreciative sniff. "How very kind of . . ." Before she could finish, Sarah bobbed and darted out the door, scurrying away like a mouse, happiest unobserved, unnoticed, and unthanked.

Jane leaned toward Emma. "Sarah has not forgotten your service to her sister. Both sweet girls, Sarah and Mary."

Yes, Emma wanted to reply. But her kind thoughts toward Mary were twinged with sadness. Sweet and shackled to a man who may yet make her regret her youthful indiscretion all the days of her life. But she nodded. They had heard no more about Mary and Tom, other than that they were settled in a little house near the blacksmith's, he resumed at his apprenticeship on the charity of his master, and she working steadily on a stack of nappies and bonnets. "Very sweet, and hopefully a bit wiser for the pickle her sister just got out of."

"Pickle!" Jane laughed. "Pickle indeed. You Americans have the most interesting expressions, Miss Woods." With a wink, Jane took the last bunn from the plate. "And are you prepared for your outing, Miss Woods? I dare say all the beauty of the Americas cannot compete with the countryside of Somerset on a fine September morning."

"I imagine you are right," Emma said, wondering if Jane would say the same could Emma find the words to describe the beauty of the sun setting over the Grand Canyon or the fog rolling under the Golden Gate Bridge. Nonetheless, she did indeed love the fresh air and had woken excited for another foray into nature. But as she'd dressed she remembered the list of gentlemen attending, poking at the tranquility of her thoughts like the pins she jabbed into her scalp to hold her coiffure in place.

At ten, the carriages arrived, all in a pretty row out front. Captain Richards drove a gig pulled by a rather ornery-looking bay. Mr. Werthing arrived in a barouche drawn by a team of sedate chestnuts, a liveried coachman at the reins. Dr. Lethbridge drove a simpler curricle, his horse a dappled gray. One more carriage pulled up at the end, a great behemoth hired out from the livery stable further down Bathwick Street, pulled by a team of four horses.

Jane and Cassandra shared a look as the coachman lurched from his seat, tripping at the curb as he opened the carriage's door. He returned to hold the lead horse's head, swaying where he stood.

Cassandra lay a hand on Jane's arm. In response, Jane laughed and climbed in. "He's a trifle disguised, dear sister. Nothing more."

Brows knit so tight they might have spiraled into one curl in the middle of her forehead, Cassandra huffed and followed Jane. "Disguised? You can smell the Old Tom from here."

Emma turned to join them, hiding a grin behind her open fan. She was not more than a few steps, when both Dr. Lethbridge and Captain Richards leapt from their seats and extended hands toward Emma.

"Miss Woods, would you do me the pleasure . . ." began Dr. Lethbridge.

And "Miss Woods, I'm sure you'd prefer my . . ." said Captain Richards.

Both men laughed and bowed affably to one another. Emma shared a chuckle and curtseyed. She pretended to be deeply contemplating which to choose, and the men were quick to take up the joke. Dr. Lethbridge smoothed the lapels of his coat and dusted the top of his hat with his gloves. Captain Richards snapped to attention, clacking his heels together.

"Well, Miss Woods," came Mark's voice from behind her. "And so the triumphs of the theatre continue into the morning? Will fortune ever cease smiling on you?"

Emma spun to find Mark just pulling up in a carriage of his own, a pleasant little cart, with Mr. Baynes and Miss Meyrick situated in back. He clucked his horse up and continued down the road. Miss Meyrick waved happily at them, then returned to her conversation with Mr. Baynes. At the corner they turned, the cart wheel catching on the curb and jostling Miss Meyrick into Mr. Baynes' arms, the one laughing and blushing, the other stammering out as many polite apologies as he could make regarding someone else's driving. She hadn't even been able to catch a glimpse of Mark's face, so low was his hat pulled over his brow.

Emma sighed. Well, Miss Meyrick was safely out of reach of either Captain Richards or Lieutenant Listle, and seemed happy enough where she was. Before Emma had to make a decision, the Miss Brooksides arrived with their mother. Mrs. Brookside stopped at the larger carriage and climbed inside, spreading her skirts out over the seat opposite the one taken by Jane and Cassandra. Miss Margaret and Miss Lucy darted forward, examining the carriages and horses.

"Too sedate for me, I thank ye," cried Miss Lucy as she passed Mr. Werthing's barouche. He only smiled genially and shook his head.

"And I," said Miss Margaret with a flip of her chin to prove her disdain for something so unseemly like a calm horse.

Miss Brookside appeared as though she too would pass Mr. Werthing's barouche, though he made a bow and held his hand out, his face expressing little doubt she would take it and climb inside. Margaret and Lucy both nearly ran to reach Captain Richards, startling his horse in the process.

"Oh look at this," Margaret said, reaching out a hand. Captain Richards' horse snorted and his eyes rolled, thick lips curling back to reveal large snapping teeth. "This is all the crack."

"Indeed. Now here is a smart-looking gig!" said Lucy and the girls devolved into an argument over who should ride in it. Poor Captain Richards looked from the two girls to Emma, pleading with his eyes. In another minute, he might have placed his palms together in earnest.

But Emma did not like the look of that horse. While Mrs. Croft may not have minded being turned into the ditch by the Admiral, Emma was still queasy from Sarah's heady coffee, and calamity or not, she didn't have the stomach to be jostled or galloped away with.

Emma took a step toward Dr. Lethbridge. "A calmer steed will do me better. And I shall benefit from Dr. Lethbridge's medical advice on the drive."

As Captain Richards began to protest, Emma took Dr. Lethbridge's hand and was soon situated comfortably on the bench.

"Well," said Lucy, "we oughtn't make the others wait." Before a word could be uttered against, she climbed into Captain Richards' gig and arranged her skirts, careful to tuck the fabric in such a way that best showed off the slimness of her ankles.

Margaret slumped back to Mr. Werthing's barouche and climbed in the back. Fearful she should be the last in, Miss Brookside allowed Mr. Werthing to help her inside as though it were the thing she had been planning to do all along, as though she were just admiring the other carriages and that was all.

Lieutenant Listle came running up, finishing the last buttons of his blue coat. "You are welcome to ride with us," Dr. Lethbridge said.

From further back, Jane also called out. "Lieutenant Listle, we shall enjoy a discussion of poetry, if you please, sir."

Emma debated whether she herself wished Lieutenant Listle to join them or not. The idea of private conversation with Dr. Lethbridge unsettled her. And allured her. Worse still – or perhaps, better yet – the closeness of his gig meant they would be hip-to-hip, arm-to-arm the whole of the ride, thoughts which left her breathless and clammy. All this considered, she felt she would prefer Lieutenant Listle's company as a shield against the intimacy her choice had instigated.

However, the call of poetry overtook any attractions Emma offered, and she watched as Lieutenant Listle climbed in next to Mrs. Brookside. Jane shot Emma a wink and raised her eyebrows as though to say, "there you go, my dear. Enjoy."

And she did, actually. Emma found their conversation easy, once she reminded herself that not only had she approached the "years of danger," she had slid on by them without a second thought. She was not a chit of eighteen, but a woman who had travelled the world, read the masters, taught students of varying ages and professions, and been published in The New York Times, for heaven's sake. (Albeit her only publication worth noting so far.) But it did not help that the first 10 minutes of their drive had been spent in convincing him the shortness of her breath was but a trifling cold caught in a recent downpour, and to give her a few minutes to collect herself.

As the clattering streets of Bath surrendered to the peaceful fresh air of the countryside, Emma fell into easy conversation with Dr. Lethbridge. She learned that he had grown up beyond London, in Kew. Though Emma nearly exclaimed over how lovely it was to reach Kew and its gardens easily by train; she had to remember that for him, it was still at some remove from "Town," and an easy journey only for the elite few. His father, he said, had been a shopkeeper. He spoke of it apologetically, with a quick sideways glance at Emma. She smiled warmly and told him her own father had been regional manager of an office supplies store.

"A what of a what?"

"Oh, I mean, he was also a shopkeeper. Very much like what you've described."

"Aha," Dr. Lethbridge said. "Well, it is rather amazing then that we move in such circles, is it not? My own father was quite happy at his work and we were a happy family. Never wanted for music masters for my sisters or tutors for me. But he desired more for us. I think he'd have liked me to be a private gentleman, but I admit, I cannot be idle."

"No," Emma agreed. "Nor I. And yet I find it so difficult here. We – women, that is – cannot earn our living or we scandalize our families. There is but one profession open to us."

"Not so terribly different from your former home across the sea, surely? Our cultures cannot be quite so dissimilar as all that. And yet, you do not like the … erm … prospect of it? Running a household? And the other … accompanying roles?"

Emma found Dr. Lethbridge's eyes on her, kind but penetrating. She did not know what to say. Marriage in her time did not have to conflict with any of the other pursuits of her life – her academia, her writing. She did not have high ambitions, but she did have them. And she held onto the hope that she would someday achieve them. In this world, though, in this time, she would be relegated to a life such as Jane would live – solitary but for the support of a sister and friends. Scrambling to hide her work at the creak of a door. Having to bear in silence the reviews and condemnations of her novels and never be able to stand up and say, "look here! This is mine. I created this. Give me some credit, will you?"

Ahead, Mark's cart at the head of their caravan turned onto a dirt track leading to the top of a hill.

"Oh," Emma said. "We are here."

The carriages and carts all pulled to a stop. All alighted, expressing in a hundred worn-out ways how delightful the drive had been. The men carried baskets of food as the women strode toward the top of the green slope. Emma sought out Jane, hoping for a reprieve for her pounding heart.

"And did you enjoy your drive?" Jane asked. "Is the doctor's conversation as handsome as he?"

Cassandra jabbed her with an elbow. "Oh, let her be, Jane." Was it some tendency to defend the demoralized that made Cassandra stick up for Emma? Or merely a desire to avoid whatever sleazy, sordid thing she was certain Emma was about to say?

Jane only laughed. "Yes, I see Miss Woods prefers to be the matchmaker, rather than the matchmakee."

Emma tried to lighten up. Jane's words were but a mosquito bite to the wasp sting they could be. And yet, she could admit with a tip of her shoulders that while her intentions toward Miss Meyrick were all honorable, it was not, perhaps, the most pleasant experience to find your life being pulled this way and that like a marionette at the end of a tangle of strings.

Speaking of, Emma found Miss Meyrick trotting toward her with her hands out. Emma took them and gave a squeeze.

She drew Emma on to the top of the hill. They looked out over the expanse of countryside. Below them, the Avon snaked through meadows dotted with the white fluff of grazing sheep, houses and cottages and barns marking points of human habitation and industry. The blue ribbon of the river crawled across the landscape until it disappeared behind a bend. The spires of the cathedral and grey columns of smoke rising from Bath's innumerable chimneys marked the city. The sky was a blue made nearly white by the passage of thin wispy clouds, which allowed enough of the sun's warmth through without blinding them.

"And you had a pleasant drive?" Emma asked.

"Oh yes, very lovely," Miss Meyrick said. Her face darkened. "Though Mr. Landen did not seem at all in a good humor. He was rather pleasant this morning, but after seeing everyone off at the Austen's, he just – " Miss Meyrick's words faded away.

Overhead, a lone hawk circled high and small against the thin blue-white of the sky.

"But," continued the girl. "Mr. Baynes and I had a lovely discussion. He leant me this book." She handed over a small volume. As Emma opened it – a book on the local flora and fauna of Somerset – a pressed flower fell to the grass. Miss Meyrick quickly recovered it and blushed. "Oh, Mr. Baynes found this for me. A rather rare flower he said."

Emma held the book open so Miss Meyrick could return the flower to its page. "Leant or given?" she asked with a wink. "Perhaps he hopes it will not long be absent from his library." At Miss Meyrick's deepening blush, Emma offered her the book. "A very kind, thoughtful gesture."

Behind them, the men had finished unpacking the baskets. Blankets were spread upon the ground and Mrs. Brookside was already happily munching away. Emma took a seat near Mark. He handed her a glass of small ale but did not speak, his face shrouded below the low brim of his hat.

"You had a nice drive?" Emma held out her cup for another fill. She had borne his aloof silence as long as she could.

"Pleasant enough," he said. After a moment stretched to forever, he asked, "and you?"

Emma blushed and nodded. Mark watched her, then rolled his eyes. He stood. "I shall pick flowers," he said to the group in general. "Anyone care to join?"

Emma watched Miss Meyrick. She saw a flash of interest alight on her face, but then it passed. She remained seated where she was, with Mr. Baynes explaining something to her from her book of flowers.

"Gather flowers?" said Captain Richards, getting to his feet. "We must have more activity than that, surely." With a wink at Lieutenant Listle, Captain Richards addressed Miss Meyrick. "Perhaps you young ladies are not aware you have circus performers in your midst."

At this, Lieutenant Listle shook his head. "Richards, no one wants to see . . ."

"Of course they do!" Captain Richards took a seat next to Miss Meyrick and pushed the book out of his way. "Did you know that Lieutenant Listle, apart from being a repository for poetry, is also quite the gymnast?"

Miss Meyrick, along with the rest of the group, turned her attention to Lieutenant Listle, her face aglow with expectation and excitement. Captain Richards pulled Lieutenant Listle to his feet and began to unbutton his own red coat.

"Now, now, Listle. We cannot disappoint the young ladies."

Rather than resist, undertakings Emma thought the poor man must have to dole out and save up for quite carefully, Lieutenant Listle complied and shed his blue coat with a shrug of his wide shoulders. Lieutenant Listle held out a hand and bent his leg. In a moment, Captain Richards used Listle's leg as a boost and was on the man's shoulders. Lieutenant Listle reached up, clasping Richards' hands as the other man slowly raised his legs and made a handstand atop his friend's arms, both their arms quivering with the effort. Lowering down to stand on Listle's shoulders once more, he counted off and at three leapt into the air, turned a somersault and landed on the grass.

The women, Miss Meyrick especially, clapped heartily. Miss Lucy and Miss Margaret called out their Bravos! and Encores! Even Cassandra's face broke into an expression of unbridled delight.

"Now, show the ladies what you can do," Captain Richards said, stepping away from Lieutenant Listle.

"Richards, I – "

"Come, come, man. Show your tricks!"

"Oh yes," said Miss Meyrick. "Do!"

Lieutenant Listle gazed at Miss Meyrick a moment. Then he bent his knees, leapt into the air and turned a back flip, stumbling a bit on the landing.

Again, everyone applauded. Captain Richards grabbed his friend's hands and made them bow. "Now," he said, "you may believe his talents wasted, but there is among you, one such gentleman who, despite his blue coat, makes a better fencer than a sailor."

"No," Lieutenant Listle said. "No, Richards. I have done. You will have to display your fencing prowess on that tree." Pulling on his blue coat, he found a ready welcome from Miss Meyrick and both the Miss Brooksides, who made room for him on their blanket and then proceeded to question him relentlessly about where he had learned such tricks, did it take a lot of practice, was he really a good fencer, and more.

As best he could, Lieutenant Listle answered their questions with as much poetry as prose. Whereas the younger Miss Brooksides were more annoyed than satisfied, his eloquence had an alarmingly opposite effect on Miss Meyrick.

She smoothed out her skirt. "You do seem to recall so much poetry, sir," she said softly. "I'm amazed at the breadth of your knowledge. And all from memory. I struggle to remember anything I've read from one day to the next."

"Perhaps, Miss Meyrick," said Lieutenant Listle, matching her intimate tone. "You only have need of the proper instructor."

The Miss Brooksides burst into flippant cackles. "Oh yes," said one, "you must give her ever so much instruction."

"She is an apt pupil," said the other, "and will, I wager, learn the Romantics as quickly as anyone."

Alone on his own blanket, Mr. Baynes' finger tailed over a drawing he had been discussing with Miss Meyrick. Red began to seep from under his collar. The two long white rectangles of his clergyman's cravat flapped in the wind, slapping his cheeks as he struggled to hold them down.

Before the raillery could raise the blush on poor Miss Meyrick's cheeks any higher, Emma stood. "Lieutenant Listle, I believe I would rather enjoy picking flowers after all. Perhaps we may make a game of it and look for blossoms from your favorite poems."

Lieutenant Listle, his face expressing both his regret at leaving Miss Meyrick's side as well as his relief to be away from the silly jests of the younger women, rose and offered Emma his arm. As they stepped away, Captain Richards moved to take Lieutenant Listle's place at Miss Meyrick's side, but Emma deftly wove her other hand round his elbow.

"Captain Richards, how kind of you to offer your support."

Captain Richards needed but a moment to compose himself and bow gallantly.

"Jane?" Emma asked. "Cassandra? Will you join us?"

Jane drew a hand to her mouth, feigning a yawn. "Oh, my dear Miss Woods, we are but too tired and you see, the men have not arms enough for all of us."

Emma glanced round the group, desperate not to be left alone with the two men. "Miss Brookside, then. Surely you wish to get some air and join us?"

Captain Richards held out his hand.

Miss Brookside seemed ready to oblige and began to gather her parasol when her mother spoke. "We thank you, Miss Woods. But Augusta prefers to remain with our group. She and Mr. Werthing were just discussing a book they have both been reading. Flowers are pretty enough, I grant you, but there are other things worth staying put for."

This last was directed at Miss Brookside. She sat back down and attempted to make it seem as though she were just readjusting her position. But a cloud passed over Mr. Werthing's face, one that did not go unnoticed by Mrs. Brookside.

Dr. Lethbridge too wore the shadows of confusion and wounded feelings. He was seated between Cassandra and Mrs. Brookside and had been volleying questions on one side as to any remedies he could recommend for her father and queries on the other as to the business of his practice, whether he had a country house, who his family was, and all the impertinent inquiries a woman with three unmarried daughters feels compelled to make.

Emma and the two officers moved away from the group, toward a small copse of trees, which Emma hoped was the opposite direction from Mark. She missed him, an ache in her chest almost as strong as the first days when she would return home, still floating on the blissful cloud of their time together. And yet, she did not wish him near her, quailed at the thoughts of what he might see or hear, flinching from the explanation she still had not managed to provide, dodging answers she did not have to the question she wasn't sure he still wanted to ask.

Captain Richards energetically picked flowers and handed them to Emma, not noticing that in his haste to yank the flowers from their stems, he mangled the poor plants out of beauty. Emma took a seat on the hillside, begging fatigue and telling the men they should go on ahead and she would arrange the blooms as they brought them to her.

"I cannot determine, Miss Woods," came a voice from behind, "whether you are trying to nab the officers' attentions for yourself or simply away from anyone else."

Jane took a seat next to Emma and began helping her sort flowers.

"I hardly know myself," Emma replied.

"When you first arrived, I would have guessed Mr. Landen had only to make an offer, and you would have gladly accepted. Now, I am torn as to whether you prefer Mr. Landen or Dr. Lethbridge!" Jane picked up two daisies and plucked the petals off, showering them on Emma's lap. "I may be wrong, but I imagine you may receive some requests for portraits very soon. How fortunate Mr. William Hamlet is recently in town. Dr. Lethbridge will surely want the best, but his fees may be out of a poor unparished clergyman's means."

Emma shook her head. "Mark . . . that is, I mean Mr. Landen . . . and I are only friends." She found her lap filling with the little oval petals Jane dropped into it. "And Dr. Lethbridge is super nice . . . I mean, he is quite agreeable."

"And Captain Richards and Lieutenant Listle?" Jane glanced at Emma sidelong, her eyes twinkling. She picked up another two daisies and added them to her bouquet of disrobed flowers. "Four portraits at once? Perhaps he will give you a discount."

Emma groaned and fell back onto the grass. "Or a punch card." She heard the two men nearby. It sounded as if Captain Richards was once more goading Lieutenant Listle into a floriated duel. "No contest," Emma said.

"Beg your pardon?" Jane's forehead furrowed.

"Oh, I mean, I would not consider either of the soldiers at all."

"And yet you draw their attention away from anyone else." Jane sprinkled the last of her petals onto Emma's lap and brushed the naked stems from her own. "Is this common amongst American ladies? To flirt with as many men as possible, even at the risk of losing the one who suits you best?" Jane began gathering daisies within arm's reach. "Seems a better strategy for losing suitors than retaining them."

The shadow of a hawk passed over Emma's face. He let out a screech that set her ears ringing, but it was the accuracy of Jane's indictment which rang like a bell. The thing that brought tears to Emma's eyes, which forced her to her feet and down toward the riverside was that she had lost sight of who exactly suited her best. Mark? Quinn? Dr. Lethbridge? She had romanticized them all, flubbing over their flaws and limitations, until each sparkled and shone like a cubic zirconium in a strip mall's forlorn display case.

Standing on the riverside, Emma watched the clear waters swirl in gentle eddies. She leaped onto a boulder, and observed how the waters made a small tidepool on the downstream side, where it was shady and dark. A tree further down spread its low branches out over the water, almost making a bridge to the other side. Emma wondered what might happen if, just perhaps, she should walk out on that low branch, stand between the two shores, and jump.

"Emma?"

She knew the voice calling her name, had fabricated it from memory so many times in that hazy space that exists between waking and sleep, the last thing she heard before drifting off with Quinn's heavy arm across her back.

"I was thinking of the river, Mr. Landen," she said. She stopped, lips pursing together. It was the first time she had not called him by his Christian name, stumbling afterward to keep to the formal surname-only dictums of this era. "Mark. Mark. Mark. Mark." She continued saying it until it felt unnatural to do so, until the word on her mouth lost its meaning and gained novelty solely as a sound, soft to begin with, harsh at the end. Mark.

"Emma, those rocks can be slick."

From the hillside above came the boarish halloos of Captain Richards. Emma turned round, as did Mark, and they saw the hillside dotted with the figures of Captain Richards in red, Lieutenant Listle in blue, and Dr. Lethbridge in his fawn breeches and black coat. They all watched her, all waved their hands, beckoning her back to them.

"Miss Woods," said Jane. "Miss Woods, Mr. Landen is correct. The river is deeper than you think."

"Yes, Miss Jane," said Emma, turning back to stare into the wide, dark waters. "I believe it is. If I fall in, I shall be wet through. Perhaps I may catch a cold. You will have to sit by my bedside and will be obliged to give up your party tonight. Then again, people do not die of little trifling colds, do they? And if I did, Miss Jane, would you say it was all in pursuit of some gentleman? Would that be a good enough excuse?" She seemed unable to stop herself. As more lines came to mind, she began to bat them away as if they were gnats swarming about her. She tipped back and nearly lost her balance. Her carefully curated Austen treasure spilled out before her, the lid of her own Pandora's box flung open, Jane's words teeming and surging as they overflowed.

Thunder boomed in the distance. The sky darkened, great roiling clouds rolling in from the south, obliterating the sun and any trace of blue.

"Oh for heavens' sake, not again" said Jane, turning her face up to the sky. She held out a hand to Emma. "We'll have to run for it."

Emma picked her way back to the riverbank. "Go ahead, Miss Jane. I will follow directly."

Jane took off up the hill, darting from one copse of trees to the next as rain pelted them.

On the hillside above, the men had turned to run up to the group, all of whom were on their feet, gathering the blankets and baskets as fast as they could. What had started as an angry burst of raindrops quickly turned into an all-out downpour, the sky a threatening shade of grey. In moments,

Emma and Mark were drenched. He took her hand and began to pull her up the hillside, but Emma stopped.

"We should try," she said.

"What?" Mark had to yell over the booms of thunder, the clatter of rain on the river.

"Let's jump!" Emma said, and before he could speak again, she had turned back toward the river and was wading in. The current was faster than she'd realized, the river deeper. Within a few steps, she was up to her waist. With each step, she felt her feet might be lifted out from under her, and if that happened, she was sure to be carried far downstream before she could find them again. Her skirts gathered wet and heavy at her ankles. Still, she pushed on.

"Emma!" Mark yelled, close behind her.

Here in the water, the power of the current confirmed how helpless she was, just as helpless as in the current of her own life. She was a boat without a rudder, a skiff without a sail, whatever course she took was one set out for her, dictated by others. Here too, the water would do with her as it would and she would have to oblige. Mark continued to call her name and she could feel the water pulse as he splashed toward her. Did she wish Mark to reach her or not?

Before she could decide, a stiff eddy spun her around and her feet left the rocks. She was underwater in an instant. Her hands – empty – splashed at the surface. Mark, following behind as best he could, had not took hold of her in time. And her skirts were dragging her down, the current pushing her toward the deepest part of the river. Just as Emma began to understand she would not be able to get herself out, just as that urge to fight against the closing darkness rose within her, and just as Emma once again wondered whether she ought to just let it slip away through the bars of her soul's confinement, a hand closed around her wrist and pulled.

She broke the surface, gasping for air, her other hand grabbing onto her savior. Mark was belly-flat on that limb stretching over the water. Her two hands held in his, he pulled her onto the branches and held her tight to his chest as she coughed water and breathed, relieved after all when the air did not forsake her.

Together, they balanced on the slippery branch and inched back to the bankside.

"Here!" called a voice, and they turned to find Dr. Lethbridge approaching, his curricle clattering behind his galloping horse.

Mark heaved Emma in and jumped onto the seat next to Dr. Lethbridge. Emma lay quiet and shivering, her eyes drawn first to Dr. Lethbridge's wide strong back, then to Mark's thin height sitting on the seat next to him. Over and over, her eyes cast back and forth, sometimes seeing Dr. Lethbridge and sometimes seeing Quinn. But always, there was Mark, his hand draped over the back of the bench, her own too weak to reach up and take it.

At the Austens' home, Jane and Cassandra escorted Emma upstairs where a warm bath awaited her. Sinking into the waters, Emma could hear Jane and Cassandra just beyond the door.

Though the words themselves were lost below the roar of the storm outside and the rush of sound still whooshing in her head, Emma could feel the meaning of them – the pressure of Cassandra's speech, the imploring tone of Jane's in response. Heavy footsteps strode away, and a moment later, Emma's door opened and Jane entered, dressed for an evening engagement.

Though the water nearly scalded her skin, Emma continued to shiver. Jane busied herself in stoking up the fire with as much wood as she could fit in.

"There is a recital this evening," Jane began. "Dr. Lethbridge expressed his hope of seeing you there. Seeing you well."

Emma closed her eyes and sank as deeply into the water as she could manage. "I am well enough, but I shall not attend. I think we need –" space. From whom? Dr. Lethbridge or Jane? Both, she realized.

Jane picked at a cuticle, then dropped her hands back to her lap. "I cannot help but feel some responsibility for your . . . accident. I have been perhaps too teasing, too harsh." She stood and began straightening the covers of Emma's bed. "Cassandra tells me I am at my sharpest when unhappy. She tells me I am like a child, sometimes, only happy when others are as miserable as I. Fortunate to have a sister who speaks such harsh truths, am I not?" Jane's mischievous expression gave way to humble assent.

"Fortunate indeed," Emma said. "Such a sister, a friend, is to be greatly valued. I have no sister on which to rely. Only myself." And look where *that* comrade had led her.

They held one another's gaze. Jane's age suddenly hit Emma, a fact she had known on a scholarly level, but whose implications plummeted around her. 26 – such a young age in Emma's own world. But already, Jane's life had been marred by the losses of a much older woman: the losses of love, the displacement from home, and the confining truths that her society valued her only for how many other people her body might bring into it, male ones preferably. Jane stood with one toe at the line of the dreaded age of 27, the doom of the single woman, from whom only Anne Elliot managed to escape with any sort of self-respect. Though Emma was nearly ten years Jane's senior, their life experiences and the expectations of their times made them equals. Between them, this knowledge – or at least some semblance of understanding – passed back and forth, gently held by each in turn.

Jane tightened the sheets round the corners of Emma's mattress, pulled the coverlet smooth and folded it back, just as Emma's mother used to do for her when she was sick, giving her the comfort of a freshly made bed. Jane helped Emma rise from the tub and dry herself, then pulled the thin sleeping gown over her head, and eased her into bed.

"I will convey your regrets at the recital," Jane said at the door. "Tomorrow is a new day, Miss Woods. Let us start it fresh."

CHAPTER 27

At breakfast, Emma was regaled with stories of the recital: who wore what, who spoke to whom during intermission, the quality of the singing and accompaniment, and more. Jane had affected a flippant tone as she spoke, belied by the concerned glances she cast Emma's direction, the placating ones for Cassandra. Mrs. Austen was so intent on describing every detail, Emma felt she could have repeated the information to her imaginary uncle as if she'd been present herself, which, she rather suspected, was Mrs. Austen's aim, perhaps hoping to prevent any misgivings by a well-connected relation to consider his niece left-out and ill-used.

"Well," Mrs. Austen said with a final dab of her napkin to the edges of her mouth. "We shall have to recount all our activities to Charles." She turned toward Emma. "He arrives in a few days' time, and we shall be quite happy to introduce you. He and your uncle will have a great deal to discuss, I am sure, being both Naval men."

Emma nodded, coughing as the last of her porridge went down the wrong way. If Charles were arriving soon, then Jane and Cassandra would be off for their visit to Manydown. Emma and Mark were no nearer discovering a path back home, and Emma was not even sure it was possible for him to make the trip being still as milky-pale as ever.

Breakfast concluded and Mr. Austen snugly settled before the fire, Emma followed Jane and Cassandra into the city. They had both been generously quiet regarding Emma's mishap the day before, a silence for which she was profoundly grateful. Her actions did not bear up well under scrutiny, and her heart, had she dared rummage amidst its contents, even less so.

Their first stop was at the baths where Emma maintained her silence, more easily done as the soaking pool was more crowded than it had been on their last visit, the cavernous space filled with the rumblings of conversation, the shrill titters of giggles. They then revisited the tea shop where Emma claimed to be full, but still devoured one lard-riddled cake after another, her mother's voice popping unhelpfully to mind: tsk, tsk, sweetie. Is that a twinkie you're eating, or your stress? Next, they meandered past the shops along Milsom Street, overhearing rumors that a circus was due in town that day, and then returned to the Pump Room to take a turn and meet acquaintance to prattle away idly with little exchange of meaningful ideas.

"Miss Woods?" came Captain Richards' voice, pulling her out of the mist she'd been unable to clear since she woke.

She gazed at him with a look of wordless inquiry.

"Did you not hear me? I inquired as to your morning. Have you been occupied in pleasant pursuits?" He had drawn rather close since his arrival with Lieutenant Listle, and though Miss Brookside had made a foray into drawing his conversation, she had seen little success.

Emma stifled a yawn. "I do apologize. My mind is elsewhere. What can I say. Life seems but a quick succession of busy nothings."

As Captain Richards burst out laughing and Emma realized what she'd said, she clamped a hand over her mouth and ran from the room. She almost plowed over Jane and Cassandra in the vestibule, having just finished walking another acquaintance to the door. At least Emma could rest assured Jane had not heard, but she would not be stopped from her departure, not even by Jane's concerned calls following her out the door.

She ran back to the bridge and stood at the embankment, hands clasped around the wrought iron railing, drawing long, shaky breaths. Below, the water reflected her own rippling stippled image, the white of her muslin dress blending with her skin and hair, leaving a ghost gazing back up at her. Her image was broken by the sharp ker-plunk of a rock, the surface reforming as circles marked the point of entry. Behind her, a nurse scolded a little girl, smacking her hands and saying, "well-bred little girls do not throw rocks" before dragging the child, crying more for show than pain, over the bridge and into a little bakeshop where, presumably, the nurse would attempt to purchase an hour's worth of good behavior.

"Emma," Mark said, coming up beside her. "Emma, are you all right?"

"No!" she said. It wasn't the scream she thought it would be, her voice, when loosed from her body, barely more than a whisper, a hoarse exclamation that nothing at all was right. Not with her. Not with him. Not with this. She looked up and down the riverside. The sidewalk on which they stood was surprisingly empty. From far off, Emma heard the jangling music of a parade and remembered the circus. The crowd around them had been drawn toward it, leaving them alone on the embankment.

She grabbed Mark's hand. "Now," she said, starting to climb the railing. "Let's do it now."

Mark pulled away, but seeing how empty it was, he nodded. Emma felt how his hand mushed under her own, how the powder and rouge on his face barely concealed the filmy surface of skin. Together, they climbed over the fence, their feet stuck over the ledge, their hands gripping the railing behind them.

The last thing to flash across Emma's mind as they jumped was a fear Mark might simply melt away into the waters below them. His face, his hands, all of him, looked like they could simply wash right off, as though his body were slowly turning to a heavy, wet fog, corporeal only so long as the sun remained obscured, only until a stiff wind blew him to nothing.

But within moments, they had both emerged, struggling against the steep current. Mark's feet found bottom first and he hauled Emma to hers. She touched his face.

"Damnit." There was no change. He hadn't melted, but he wasn't better, and they were still right where they'd been a moment before, only *in* the river rather than standing on the embankment above. With the same frantic energy which had possessed her on the Gravel Walk, Emma grabbed the lapels of Mark's jacket and drove him down, herself on top of him. They surfaced again. Emma shoved him back in the water and jumped in likewise.

Mark struggled to his feet. "Emma, what the bloody – !"

But Emma was grabbing at his shoulders. "Why isn't this working?" she screamed into his face.

A crowd had started to gather. "Oi," called a rough voice. "She's trying to drowned him, she is!"

Emma turned toward the voices, Mark's coat still bunched in her hands. "Wait – what? No, I'm not!" And she let go of his jacket. Mark fell back into the water and thrashed a bit before finding his feet again.

The man jabbed a finger at her. "See!" He waved back into the crowd. "Get the constable. There'll be no missies drowning misters today."

Constable Morrow pushed his way through the crowd. "Miss Woods?" he said, surprise clear on his face. He helped both Emma and Mark onto the embankment and kept a hand on Emma's arm.

"There's no trouble here, constable," Mark said, still coughing river water. "Just a slip."

Slowly, the crowd began to disperse, but Emma caught a familiar bonnet near the back, and sure enough, Jane and Cassandra appeared, likely having heard a lady had fallen into the river, losing no time in confirming which person they already knew it to be.

"Perhaps we ought to have you see Dr. Lethbridge," Constable Morrow said to Emma, and began to lead her away.

"No wait," Emma said, "I don't need Dr. Lethbridge. I'm not crazy. I'm not . . ." Emma spun as best she could with her arm in Morrow's chunky fist. The crowd was moving off, observers shaking their heads at the poor daft woman and her evident destiny as the asylum's newest inmate.

Worse still, when Emma sought out Jane and Cassandra, she saw the latter speaking earnestly with Jane, starting to pull her away, her head shaking as she looked from Emma to Mark and back again. Her hands were open, palms down, and as she spoke, she punctuated her demands. There was no doubt to the meaning of those sharp fingers. Enough is enough.

The constable now had his hands on both Emma's arms and was pulling her the opposite direction. And Mark, his voice weak, made a limp protest.

She had no choice. Emma jerked out of the constable's hands, ran forward a few steps, balled her hands into fists at her sides, and yelled, "It is a truth universally acknowledged that a single man in possession of a large fortune must be in want of a wife!"

The wind roared down the shallow valley of the river. It lifted men's hats and rolled them along the green. A slew of gusts loosed pins from women's hair, sending tendrils whipping about their faces. The sky lowered over them, a ceiling of menacing clouds descending so low, Emma thought she could reach out and touch them.

Then the sky split open and white flooded Emma's eyes as a lightning bolt struck the tree where Jane and Cassandra had run for cover. Constable Morrow released his grip on Emma's hands and ran toward the cathedral. Another lightning bolt struck ground just in front of Emma, throwing her into the air. She landed some yards back, unconscious and seemingly dead, as the river began to swell with the torrential shower pouring from the sky, as though the heavenly beings had kicked their mighty bucket right on top of them.

CHAPTER 28

Emma woke in bed. Her eyelids resisted, dragging down, seeking to keep her below the film of wakefulness, but she struggled to open them against the immeasurable weight of the aching in her head. Eyes open a slit, she could almost convince herself she was in her small room under the eaves at Adelaide Garden.

But if the past week in 4 Sydney Place had taught her anything, it was that nothing would come easily to her, including – perhaps especially – returning to a world that had long been as perplexing and pitfall-laden as this one she had fallen into. She sat up, shielding her eyes against the bright. Yes, it was day, and rain continued to stream down the pane. An inexorable weight pulled her back down. She felt it like a slow-moving lava flow, each day dragging her further from the world she'd left behind. Dragging her and being dragged itself. The invisible rope of time tied to the burden of her life back home had become weighted with the mass of her choices in this one.

A fire burned in the grate and a kettle waited on the white-washed hearth. On the bedside table, she found a plate of bunns, which she greedily devoured, caring not about trans fats or cholesterol levels. Next to the plate sat a small bottle full of laudanum. She stared long at that bottle. Her hand reached for it. She imagined passing off into a blissful doze. Could there be a dose that would plummet her into sleep and out the other side of time?

Just as she began to untwist the lid, the door opened and Dr. Lethbridge entered.

"Miss Woods," he said, "glad to see you are awake." Then he noticed what she clutched in her hands. "We must be careful, Miss Woods. These drugs are more powerful than a shopkeeper would have you know." He held out his hand and when she delayed returning the bottle, he waggled his fingers at her, much the same as Quinn when he caught her with the occasional pack of cigarettes.

She handed it over and settled back onto the pillows, too exhausted by the pounding of her head to be more than miffed. Dr. Lethbridge took the little stool from the dressing table and set it next to her bed.

"You gave us quite a scare," he said. "I saw what happened from the top of the embankment. I've never seen anyone struck so close with lightning and live to speak of it." He shuddered with the memory, and Emma held her hand out to him, which he took with a gratefulness that made her heart thud.

"I'm ok," she began, "that is, I am perfectly well, sir. Perhaps a bit of the headache, but nothing that will not fade."

In the hall outside the open door, Emma saw Mrs. Austen stride past, Dr. Bowen waddling behind, and just caught the words, "will she live, do you think, doctor?"

Emma jerked upright and would have climbed from the bed but for Dr. Lethbridge's hands at her shoulders. "Who?" Emma demanded. "Not Jane? Please God, not Jane."

"Hush now," he said, easing her back. He shook his head. "Miss Jane and Miss Austen will both recover. 'Twas a scare, that's all. But Jane does seem to be quite shaken by it."

Of course, Emma realized. If it was to be Addison's that would kill her, then any sort of stressor – and standing so near two lightning strikes could certainly be called that – would send her system into high alert. A cold sweat broke out across Emma's shoulders and down her back. Her heart galloped within her chest and one thought pounded over and over: I've killed Jane Austen.

Dr. Lethbridge went to the fire. He bent to stoke the embers and add more wood. He set the kettle on the little hook and pushed it over the flames. He stood, but did not turn round. Picking up this tchotchke and that from the mantle, he turned them over in his hands and set them down again. "Miss Woods, you are, perhaps, not aware that I have begun to develop feelings for," he stopped and shook his head. "No, I think you cannot have mistaken my attentions . . . to you, that is. And the truth is that seeing what happened yesterday . . . Well, my resolution was formed shortly after." He turned back to face Emma. Though she knew what was coming, the pounding of her head slowed her mind and before she could raise a hand to stop him, he had said the words. "Miss Woods, I am asking you to do me the honor of becoming my wife."

He moved back to his position on the stool, and when he took her hand again, Emma could not feel it.

"But surely you must think I'm crazy. Everyone does. Why would you want to marry Bath's infamous crazy woman?"

Dr. Lethbridge laughed, once, and then saw she was serious. "I assume you mean insane or deranged. Crazy?" He shook his head thoughtfully. "No, Miss Woods, it's not insanity I would diagnose you with. But something else." He ducked his head, drawing a finger over the back of her hand. "If you will permit me, you're not crazy. I think you're confused." He drew a breath and hurried on. "And it is my belief that life is an eternal source of confusion, and the best any of us can do is to find someone to help us make sense of it. That's all I'm offering, really. A partner. You hand your confusions to me, and I'll hand mine to you, and onward we will go."

It was the nicest marriage proposal she had received yet. And spoken like this, by him, with his face all open and earnest, she very nearly believed in it. There was Quinn and his ring and the park at sunset. Had he even said the words or had his gestures and a Hollywood patina of meaning done the work for him? There was Mark and his ellipses at the end of his email, another unspoken offer of a nebulous life that even now she couldn't imagine. And now Dr. Lethbridge, glancing at her sideways like a schoolboy, wondering if he had calculated the equation correctly.

Just as he prepared to speak again, offer more persuasions, there was a knock at the door jamb and Emma, mouth agape, eyes beginning to tear up, found Mark there, worrying his hat between his hands.

Dr. Lethbridge made a hasty bow. "I see others are concerned as well." His face reddened from embarrassment, but as he moved toward the door, ceding his stool to Mark, something else flashed across his face: jealousy. The combination of the two made his otherwise unnoticeable freckles stand out like little points of red light burning below his skin. "I shall return this evening to check on you. Now I must assist Dr. Bowen." Closing the door, he was gone but the weight of his intention hung heavy across her shoulders.

Mark moved the stool closer to the bed. He took Emma's hand and before either of them could speak, he brought it to his lips and placed a kiss on her knuckles, the first he had ever given, a touch so soft and delicate, she placed her other hand on top to catch and hold it there.

Seeming to only just realize what he'd done, Mark blushed. "Emma," he said. "I'm sorry. Perhaps I shouldn't have."

He made to put her hand down, but Emma clung to his fingers. They felt different. Firmer. She looked at his hand. It was tanner than before. She spit on her thumb and rubbed his skin, but no powder came off.

"Thanks, mom."

Emma smiled. "Did it work? Can we be sure?"

Mark held his fingers out before him and flexed them open and closed. "Mr. Baynes came to me last evening saying he had determined on asking Miss Meyrick to marry him. He wanted to ask my . . . permission, I guess you'd called it. Said he thought there might have been a former attachment and didn't want to overstep." Mark chuckled. "Poor Miss Meyrick, we certainly set her right, didn't we."

Emma murmured her assent. "But we don't know if she's accepted him?"

Mark shook his head. "There's to be a small gathering here this evening," he said. He rolled his eyes. "Mrs. Austen wouldn't dare lose the opportunity of showing off her three invalids."

The kettle at the fire began to whistle. Mark drew it off with the poker. He searched around and found a towel with which to lift it, still managing to burn his hand in the process. As he put a finger in his mouth, he waggled his eyebrows at Emma. "I can burn myself. That must be a good sign." He brought Emma a cup of tea. "So what did Dr. Lethbridge want?"

Emma made drinking her tea an excuse to put off his question. What did Dr. Lethbridge want? That is, what could it mean to her, to Emma? Was it possible she could stay here and live her days as the wife of a respected Bath physician? Her years would unfold before her in an endless series of assemblies and plays, evening parties, and the Pump Room. It was the very thing she had been trying to get Mark to commit to. In fact, when Quinn would get jealous over how much time she spent reading Austen, she'd tease that his only real rival was time travel, that if she had the opportunity to go back to this very era, to this very place, she'd jump at it in a heartbeat. And now . . . that joke had become her reality. She could, now, if she chose, stay right where she was, perhaps remain lifelong friends with Jane Austen and when her novels appeared, mischievously query the identity of "the lady" who had written them.

Yes, it was possible. And what had her mother said that time? If you leave Quinn, you damn well better have something better lined up. Was Dr. Lethbridge better? He was perhaps just the same, the only difference being that he was here, in this era, in this world.

Sarah entered. She brought a tray of fresh bunns and took the teapot from Mark to pour a cup for him too. Mark made small talk, asking how Mary got on, how she liked her new home. Sarah moved about the room as she answered with more 'thank you, sir's' and 'oh, god bless you's' than actual information, tidying the dressing table and placing freshly-laundered petticoats behind the screen. Doling out as many 'your welcomes' as he could reasonably manage without becoming too ridiculous, he turned back to Emma, the question still perched in his eyes.

Emma resolved not to tell Mark what had happened. Not yet. "Oh, nothing." Emma began. "He just wanted . . ." But before she could finish with something lame and half-true, Mrs. Austen bustled in the door.

"I wish you joy, my dear. Great joy." She clasped Emma's hand and tipped Mark's tea into his lap. "My apologies, Mr. Landen. I could not wait another instant, Miss Woods, after Dr. Bowen told me the news. Married to a doctor? Almost as good as a clergyman," she laughed, "if I do say so myself. And are you to have a long or short engagement? You must wait of course for your uncle. How surprised he shall be! What good friends he will think you have."

Mark was trying to mop his lap with a towel Sarah provided, but his head shot up and his cup once more tumbled off his saucer, this time falling to the floor and shattering. "Engagement?"

Emma sat up. "Mark . . . er, Mr. Landen, I . . . wait . . . it's not . . ."

"Oh heavens," said Mrs. Austen, "I have preempted you. My apologies. I was simply so delighted. Well," she said at the doorway. "I shall leave you two to discuss it. Perhaps Mr. Landen would like to perform the ceremony before he moves on?" She leaned in and spoke softly, though in a voice still too loud for Emma's aching head. "I understand from Dr. Bowen the young man has such a fortune that a special license is not out of the question." She straightened and flapped her hands. "Well, well, you may settle it all together tonight." With that, she was gone and Emma's heart felt like the remnants of that tea cup crunching under Mark's boot as he stood.

"Engaged," Mark said. "Again." In two steps, he was at the door. He stopped and turned back toward Emma, his mouth opening to speak. Instead, a tear rolled down his cheek and with an angry swipe of his hand, he brushed it away and was gone.

Emma cried herself back to sleep. When she woke, dusk had fallen. She rose and pulled the cord for Sarah, who appeared a few moments later. She helped Emma change into an evening gown, then assisted her in pulling back her hair. When Sarah went to add some curls and ribbons, Emma stayed her hand.

"No," she said, "I do not wish for any of that." She looked in the mirror. Her skin was pale and splotched, her eyes sunken and shrouded. Haggard, a word that described her inside and out. The headache persisted, though it had dulled, and she could not seem to pull her shoulders from their defeated position.

Emma went down the hall to Jane and Cassandra's room, where she found Cassandra assisting her sister with the last of their toilette. Cassandra appeared no worse for the experience, but Jane was paler even than Emma, her own eyes darker, more bruised-looking. She seemed to have aged a decade, her face exposing every line that marked the harshness of this life, the tarnishes of her disappointments and regrets.

"Miss Woods," Jane exclaimed weakly. She held out a hand and Emma took it.

"Oh, Jane," Emma said, not caring to have forgotten the 'Miss.' "I am so very sorry. Are you feeling better?"

Jane laughed. "Sorry? Whatever for? If we're going to take credit for the weather, then please oblige me and take credit for something pleasanter, like the sunshine or a fresh breeze off the ocean." Her eyes went somber as she touched a place at her neck, just below her ear. "The breeze at Devon. The pleasantest I've felt." Jane turned her face one way, then the other, and sighed at her reflection.

Cassandra stepped to Emma's elbow. "Miss Woods, may I speak with you?"

Out in the hall, Cassandra pulled the door closed. "I am resolved, Miss Woods, that since your "uncle" is due in Bath any day and our brother Charles returns tomorrow, it shall be best if we consider this your last night in our home. I have asked Sarah to begin packing your things."

Emma's eyes shot open. "Tomorrow? But Cassandra . . . Miss Austen, perhaps my uncle will be delayed again. God knows when . . ."

Cassandra held up a hand. "I beg you would not importune me with more unlikely tales. Your uncle may as well be a mythical jackrabbit as an Admiral. I understand you have made an advantageous match, Miss Woods. Between Dr. Lethbridge, yourself, and Mr. Landen," here, Cassandra's eyes flashed in what could have been jealousy or judgement – both? – "I have every confidence you will not be long without a home." With that, Cassandra spun and descended the stairs.

Emma returned and found Jane in the worn wingback next to her fire, a shawl around her shoulders. Emma perched on the little footstool at her feet. Before she realized what she was doing, she'd laid her head on Jane's lap. She felt Jane stiffen for a moment, but she did not care. Frankly, she needed a hug.

After a moment, Jane's hand was at Emma's forehead, smoothing back the frizz at her hairline, petting her like a cat. "I understand I am to wish you joy."

Emma buried her face and groaned. "Why does everyone assume I'm going to marry Dr. Lethbridge?"

There was a pause, then Jane said, "well, aren't you?"

"No!" Emma said into the folds of Jane's skirt. "I don't . . . – " –know.

Jane continued to stroke Emma's hair. "I felt sure Mr. Landen was your choice, but that only shows how much I know. Most women would be quite content with such a proposal. Dr. Lethbridge is already a rich man and will have a good practice. He will provide an amply comfortable home. And handsome children, though the red hair is a shame."

Emma smiled. "But what if I want more than keeping house?" Emma turned to look at the flames. She stared at the point where flame met wood, where it burned hottest, leaving a white after-image when she looked away. "More than raising children."

"Hmmm," Jane said. "More. Yes, it does seem . . . I don't know – unfortunate – that our lives have but one track to them. I almost envy whatever poor creature goes off to be the governess for Miss Brookside's friend. At least she has ownership of her life, may do as she pleases. Well, somewhat anyway." A moment passed. "But there is comfort in marriage, in children. Especially if there's love."

"But you," Emma began before putting a fist to her mouth. Will become one of the greatest authors of the English language, she nearly said. Will be familiar to every half-educated person across the globe, even to those who haven't read a single word you've written. People will quote you for hundreds of years, will spend their lives studying your own, will adore you through the distance of time and culture, and will revel in pretending to be part of your world, if only for 10 days a year.

"But I what?" Jane asked. Her eyes sparkled in the firelight. She swallowed and looked up at the ceiling. "I have not lost hope. Not entirely. Marriage may yet find me."

Emma watched her friend, saw the memories of Lefroy and the clergyman pass behind her eyes, ghosts in a forest. Marriage certainly would find Jane, at least the offer of it would. And Jane would have to make her decision as to whether to be the flame dancing white-blue or the log being consumed by it. The fire reached a pocket of air and popped, sending embers and sparks flying up into the chimney, carried away on the smoke and draft, turning to black ash and soot.

Emma sat up. She looked in Jane's tired eyes. "You have been a very great friend to me, Miss Jane. And I shall never forget this time with you."

At this, Emma's eyes began to overflow, her tears laced with love and adoration, regret and shame.

Jane rose and pulled Emma to her feet. "Forget me? I should hope not. We shall be friends for a great many years, I hope. Even if you do not marry the handsome Dr. Lethbridge, and choose instead to end an old maid." She whisked a handkerchief from her pocket and snapped it open. She dabbed Emma's eyes, then kissed both her cheeks. "Now," she said, "I imagine we are to be put on display as the two ladies almost struck dead by lightning. And I believe you have an answer to deliver."

They entered the drawing room with the party well in progress. Mr. Austen sat wrapped in a blanket near the fire, his glass of port half-empty, enjoying conversation with Mr. Brookside and Mr. Meyrick. The Misses Brookside played at lottery with Miss Meyrick and Mr. Baynes, the two sitting cozily close, as well as Captain Richards and Lieutenant Listle. Mr. Werthing stood scowling over the game, behind Miss Brookside's chair, though he seemed to be shifting his weight from foot to foot, ready to stay, ready to walk away. Dr. Lethbridge sat between Mrs. Austen and Mrs. Brookside, once more fielding an array of medical questions. And then there was Mark. It took Emma some minutes to find him, concealed as he was in a shadowy corner, sipping what appeared to be a second, or even third, glass of wine.

The gentlemen rose on their entrance and the necessary curtseys were made. Mark started forward, a little wobbly, but Captain Richards' booming voice halted his steps.

"My dear Miss Woods!" he exclaimed, rising and offering both Jane and Emma his arm. He led them to the corner with the smaller table, the one where Emma had written her letter to Mark some days ago, a stupid thing about make-up and concealer. What she wouldn't give now for another pen and paper, a note written under the pretense of some other correspondence, a little folded thing she could leave upon a table like a furtive Captain Wentworth, a letter to confess . . . what? She did not know what, only that by writing down all the things flooding through her, she might find the truth like a bubble of mercury slipping away across a mirror surface.

Captain Richards applied all his gallantry to ensure they were situated comfortably. He took his chair from the card table and set it down, rather pointedly close to Emma. "Are you well, Miss Woods? And you, Miss Jane? We've heard all about it. The town is practically buzzing."

Miss Brookside put on an arch expression. "Indeed. Miss Woods once again finds herself the talk of the town. Tell us, Miss Woods, can you settle into anything like a quiet life now you've been the rage of Bath for a whole week together?"

Emma did her best to smile. "Most happily," she responded. She looked at Mark. "I would be very happy for my life to go back to normal as soon as possible." Mark looked away. What comfort did the idea of normal offer *him*? Normal was a half-furnished flat on the edge of campus, a table set for one. Normal was waving goodbye from the stoop of Adelaide Garden as she drove to Heathrow, flew home to Quinn.

Captain Richards took Emma's hand. She attempted to draw it back but found it held fast. "I am so glad to hear you are well. The news was so very distressing to me." He paused, then seemed to realize his forwardness. "And Lieutenant Listle, of course." He looked to Jane. "Both of your illnesses. They were *both* very distressing."

Jane rose. "Excuse me, but I believe my sister needs some assistance with my father." With an arch look and ironical brow, Jane smiled, if rather weakly, at Emma and left. Emma tried to reach for her hand, but was intercepted by Captain Richards, who took the opportunity to hold both Emma's hands tightly in his own.

He surveyed the room, then in a low conspiratorial voice, began. "Well, she can take a hint," he said with a laugh. "Now, Miss Woods, let me get down to it. I know I've been a bit of a flirt." He cast meaningful glances at Miss Meyrick and Miss Brookside, the latter of whom, Emma noticed, watched their conversation rather keenly. "But you must realize that it's you all along who's caught my attention. What do you say, Miss Woods? Could the most celebrated lady of Bath settle on a (rather dashing, I wager) soldier?"

He pulled his chair closer, placing one hand across the back of Emma's chair over-familiarly, possessively. "You see, you're just the type of woman who can give a soldier the establishment and position he deserves. My own circumstances are a bit, how should I say – straightened? In fact, I had thought perhaps your uncle might assist me, perhaps with connections in the Army." His fingers traced his chin in contemplation. "Or I might give up my commission and become a naval man. With your uncle's connections, such a transition may be possible. But of course, we need not worry over those things, not with your fortune to ease our way."

Emma felt like she might fall over dead. Or perhaps just faint, but either way, her body was about to give out. She jerked her hands away and leant forward, saying as quietly and with as much composure as she could summon, "Captain Richards, I do not understand why you address me thus. You have confused and misconstrued the situation abominably. I cannot decide which offends me more – your vanity or your poor attempt to conceal your mercenary motives!" She drew breath, rather pleased at her refusal; it would have done Lizzy Bennet proud.

He sat back, the features of his face realigning with the heat of her words. "Come off it," he said. "You've been flirting shamelessly with me! Don't tell me you're actually going to marry that quiz of a doctor. Not when you can have a dashing officer."

Emma sat back. "Captain Richards, you have utterly mistaken me." Emma stood and was about to push in her chair when she ran into Miss Brookside, hastening over.

"Captain Richards," she said, darting glances between Emma and the deflated Captain Richards. "Please rejoin our table. I am quite lost without you to guide my wagers."

But Captain Richards would have none of it. He stood, the legs of his chair juddering across the floor. "Perhaps you ought to take guidance from Miss Woods. Here is a lady who knows how to hedge her bets, I dare say." He made them a stiff bow, turned, and walked out of the drawing room. Miss Brookside looked once more from Emma to the door, then turned back to her table, trying to walk as though she had not just been so publicly rejected herself. Mr. Werthing likewise made a formal bow and moved to the door, but not before Miss Brookside could put herself in his path.

"Mr. Werthing, you are not also going. Do not you see that a space has opened at our table?"

He held Miss Brookside's gaze for a moment. "I find, madam," said he, "that I no longer wish for a space at your table." With that, he began to make the rounds, bowing his adieus to the remaining guests. Miss Brookside followed behind, presenting every argument in favor of his staying.

Mrs. Brookside lumbered to her feet. "Mr. Werthing! Please do not go. Do not you see how Augusta wishes for you to stay?"

But Mr. Werthing would not be deterred. "I thank you, madam, but no. I leave for the country in the morning."

"But dear John," cried Mrs. Brookside, "the season is just beginning!"

At the door, Mr. Werthing turned for a final bow. "Indeed, mum, but it appears my season has drawn to its close." With one last look at Miss Brookside, he turned and was out the door.

Emma sank back into her seat, her addled brain trying to muddle through everything she'd witnessed. She found Jane taking the seat vacated by Captain Richards and Cassandra joined them not long after.

"So," Jane said, with a smirk toward the deflated Miss Brookside now sitting beside her mother, getting what appeared to be a rather severe tongue-lashing. "She has lost him. I believe Miss Brookside may have just found the perfect governess for her friend."

Cassandra nodded, a look of pity on her face. "Indeed. Mama said that Mrs. Brookside has been threatening that if she do not marry soon, she will have to make her own way."

Both Jane and Cassandra shuddered.

"Well," said Jane, "let us hope Mr. Marches will find himself the sole caretaker of his children. Perhaps Miss Brookside will have her estate after all, if perhaps it comes on the train of a mourning gown."

Cassandra huffed. "Really, Jane. And dying in childbed is a joke?"

Jane shook her head, her face grown somber. "No, Cass, dear. There is never anything funny about a woman's life cut short in the course of *doing her duty*." At these last, Jane's words dripped with a biting iciness, laced with seeds of rage, seeds planted by a woman about to embark on a life of her own choosing. Seeds that would blossom into an eternal garden of delights for generations to come, though the gardener herself would find her own life yanked like a weed amongst the columbine.

Mark swayed over to them, well on his way into more wine than was good for him. He could make a rather fitting rival for John Thorpe and his six pints a day at this rate. "Well, Miss Woods, it appears you continue to conquer the room. Do I guess that Captain Richards made you an offer?" He slumped down into a chair beside them. "And you have refused him, poor man? Well, you can, you know, only be engaged to one man." He threw back the last of his wine. "At one time, that is."

"I believe our mother is in need of us," Jane said. She rose and pulled Cassandra behind her.

Emma vacillated between relief that Jane would not hear what was coming and dread that her desertion had created the opening for it. "Mark," she said, "please. Not tonight. Let's talk tomorrow."

"And do you fear so much what I might say?" His voice was slippery, drunk with wine and rage. He assumed a position of informal ease, as though they were just passing a few moments in polite conversation, but his tone belied his posture. "You know, I used to think we had something. Something special. Oh, I know it sounds ridiculous. Oh so PG-13, right? But God help me, I did." He paused long enough to swipe another glass from Isaac as he passed with a tray. "Now, I realize I was just the closest warm body in the room. Harold was out, eliminated both by age and predilection. But what if there'd been another man in our little group, Em? Huh? Any other man than me. Perhaps that's all this has ever been. A chance of a seat in a crowded cafeteria."

Emma's mind flooded with memories of their first meeting. Harold, Lorna, and Deb at a large table in the corner, friends for a decade or more by then. And Emma, balancing her tray as she scanned for a seat, asking tentatively if she could join them and Harold's booming voice welcoming her to the table. And then Mark appeared. She watched him from across the room, recognizing him as the man she'd seen following his girlfriend outside the cathedral, his own face rotating as he looked for any open spot. He'd been approaching another table, she suddenly remembered, but just before he got there, a woman with a baby plopped into the only open chair. And so he had continued to snake through the busy refectory to them instead.

What a chance all of life was! That she had taken the 7 am anatomy lecture and stared for the next two hours at the hunky pre-med TA – simply because the 10 am slot she'd really wanted was full. That Mark chose their table only because an over-tired mother who needed to nurse elbowed her way into the seat he'd been moving toward.

"You know," Mark said, leaning forward, his breath vinegary with wine, "I used to think about how lucky I was to choose that table, that you were sitting at it. I used to thank whatever God I don't even believe in for the fortuitous coincidence of that moment. That woman and her brat. Now I see it was all ever so arbitrary. I could have been anyone, couldn't I? And you, you'd have strung me – or him – along either way."

With that, Mark rose. He bowed formally, his eyes watery and red. "I take my leave of you, madam." He turned on a heel and walked to the card table, pretending to be interested in the game progressing there.

Emma rose to her feet, jaw clenched. She curtseyed and exited the drawing room. Halfway up the stairs, she burst into sobs. She held onto the railing and sank onto a step. The door to the drawing room opened, and fearful Mark would stagger out and continue his barrage, Emma began to run up the steps.

"Miss Woods," called a voice.

Emma turned, but she did not descend. "Dr. Lethbridge, I. . ."

He held up a hand. "No," he said, his eyes all kindness and care. "We shall not speak of it now. Let us await your uncle's arrival. I was myself too much in haste. But just know that I shall be thinking of you and holding you close in my . . ." He flushed, once more bringing out his freckles like little spots of starlight on his cheeks. "Thoughts," he finished lamely. He made a gallant bow.

Emma finished her trek upstairs, down the long hall to her room, and fell onto her bed, fully clothed, wishing she might wake up anywhere – anywhere at all, in any time – but there.

CHAPTER 30

Of course, dreams such as those were not to be answered. Emma woke early once again, put on one of Jane's gowns, a pale yellow muslin, and gazed at the packet of her belongings, folded and wrapped in brown paper. Emma stood at the window, gazing out on the street below, the blue dawn fighting against the smoke and ash rising from the chimneys. Something large and dark circled overhead, eventually turning north and disappearing into the haze, a crow or possibly a vulture. Emma eased the ring out from its hiding spot and lay it on the sash. She put it in her pocket, then on her finger, then back in the folds of her gown. The pocket felt like a decision she wasn't sure she'd made; her finger a promise she wasn't confident she could keep.

On the edge of the dressing table lay the pink ribbon Jane had chosen for her that first day, when she had danced with Mark at the Upper Rooms, felt the icy interest of society, and been saved by, as well as come to, her hero's rescue. She tied the ring to the ribbon and slipped it in her pocket.

Downstairs, she once more listened for the tinkle of the piano keys, but hearing none, she pushed into an empty drawing room. The dishes had all been cleared away, but the tables remained in their arrangement from the previous night, chairs askew, the remnants of the lottery game sprawled across the card table. On the floor near a window, she found a feather fallen from Miss Brookside's hair. She twirled it in her fingers. Beyond the window, a breeze blew the tops of trees. Emma heaved the sash up and dropped the feather into the wind. It floated away from her, twirling up and around, flipping end over end, drifting down until the wind caught it once more and repeated the dance. She watched as far as she could see it until the feather fell out of sight, likely into some midden heap hidden behind a house.

Emma took her place at the breakfast table. Mrs. Austen passed a porcelain dish on which lay an apple custard tart.

"We are gladdened to hear of your uncle's arrival," Mrs. Austen began, in a voice that betrayed how un-glad she was. "Though we had hoped to introduce you to our dear son Charles. He is due in Bath this very afternoon if I am not mistaken."

"I thank you, ma'am," Emma began, but was preempted by Cassandra.

"Dear Mama, Miss Woods is very anxious to be reunited with her uncle. It must be very difficult to rely on the charity of strangers for so long a time together." Cassandra took the dish from Emma, her lips curled in a smile more smug than charitable.

"Strangers?" Mr. Austen said, extending a hand toward her from his place at the top of the table. "Why, Miss Woods is quite a part of the family now. It is as though we have known you an age, Miss Woods, if I could be forgiven for saying so."

Emma lay a hand atop his and squeezed. "I feel quite the same, sir." And it was her turn to deliver a smug glance. Just as Cassandra opened her mouth, Emma continued, "but alas, my uncle *is* come and I must depart. I hope you will wish Mr. Charles Austen my compliments and the hope we may meet in future."

"Well, well," Mrs. Austen said, something disappointed, even resentful, in her tone. "It is perhaps all for the good. You've the dear doctor to think of, haven't you?"

Before Emma could reply – with words that threatened to refuse to form – a creak in the hallway and an exaggerated yawn in Jane's tones halted her words.

Cassandra rapped the table quickly with her spoon. "We shall say no more of this at present," she said to the table. "Jane has not yet been apprised of your departure."

Jane's face remained wan, her eyes dark as though the night had been equally unrestful. "Forgive my lateness," she said, taking her chair. "Of what are we speaking?"

Glances were exchanged, but it was Cassandra who was quick to bridge the awkward silence. "Of dear Charles' arrival, of course." And she produced a letter for Jane to peruse as Sarah brought in fresh tea and a plate of bunns.

After breakfast, Emma, Jane, and Cassandra walked to the Pump Room. There, they met with Mr. Baynes, Miss Meyrick, and her father, who was sharing tidings of his daughter's engagement to every person who joined the party. Miss Meyrick clutched the book of flowers Mr. Baynes had given her as though a talisman of her future happiness. And Mr. Baynes was charmingly flushed with pride, his eyes brimful as he gazed on his betrothed. Emma's fingers tapped at the ring dangling in her pocket, then drew away.

"There, Miss Woods," said Jane, leaning in conspiratorially. "You pulled it off in the end."

Emma did her best to smile. Whatever good she had done for Miss Meyrick had come at a very dear cost to herself.

"I knew it all along," said Miss Lucy, with a knowing smile.

"You never!" said Miss Margaret. "You always thought she preferred . . ."

"Hush," said Lucy. "Here come the officers."

Emma turned to find Captain Richards and Lieutenant Listle just beginning their circuit round the Pump Room. Catching sight of Emma, Captain Richards stopped, spun on his spurred heel and joined another pair of officers surrounded by a group of young ladies.

"Come on," Lucy said, pulling Margaret behind her. "I shall tease Richards about his losses at lottery." And the two girls went off to join the other group, there to flirt and be flirted with, a prospect which held absolutely no appeal to Emma.

They soon left the Pump Room and wandered up to Milsom Street. Jane stopped at the corner and fumbled at her sides.

"Oh heavens," she said. "I seem to have left my pin money at home. Cassandra, dear, do you mind if we run back and then return for our shopping. I dare not venture back alone."

Though Jane's spirits had rallied after breakfast, Emma had observed with concern how Jane leant on Cassandra's arm and sat on the bench in the Pump Room, seeming always just a bit short of breath, always a beat behind the conversation.

They turned back toward the churchyard. The town bustled and it seemed everywhere she looked, Emma saw fresh faces. All around town, church bells clanged, announcing new arrivals.

"And the season begins," Cassandra said, at which she and Jane shared an annoyed look.

Ahead, Emma caught sight of Mark, heads taller than anyone near, gazing at the spire of the cathedral. He turned and began walking as though to cross over the bridge. Clutching her skirts, Emma dashed after him.

"Mark," she yelled. "Mark, wait!"

Everyone nearby stopped to stare, and she could only imagine what a sight she made, half-running, skirts gathered almost to her knees, the pins in her greasy hair not doing their job. She lost sight of Mark over and over as he wove through the crowd. She stopped, put two fingers in her mouth, and let out the loudest, shrillest whistle she could manage.

Mark waited for her to catch up. "I . . . wasn't sure I'd see you. I stopped at the Austen's and they said you were leaving today. I thought maybe you were leaving with . . ."

Emma took in his face. It was slightly pale, but the milkiness had fully gone. She smiled and placed a palm on his cheek. "You're . . . you."

"Me," he said, pulling her hand away. The word seemed foreign on his lips, two letters containing a collection of indefinable meanings.

They stood near the embankment once again. The water roiled from the two days of lashing rain.

Mark looked into the river below. "I came to say goodbye."

Emma shook her head. "Mark, I'm going to say no. I'm not marrying him." A question passed over his face. "Dr. Lethbridge, I mean."

"You're not?" He took her hands. Relief showed until his eyes narrowed. "But you thought about it, didn't you."

In an instant, Emma knew affirmation had passed across her face. Mark pulled away, his mouth curling in disgust. "You did, didn't you?"

And in this moment, the gravity of all the mistakes Emma'd made – had been making – for so many years flooded over her. Mark had read the flash of a look as it passed across her face – the flare of eyelids, the parting of her lips – and discerned the questions of her heart. He knew her, she realized, better than Quinn ever had or ever could. For if Quinn knew Emma, then he would have recognized the flicker of fear and dismay when he'd dropped to his knees, would have stopped before the words were out of his mouth. Instead of that self-assurance and an upraised velvet box, he would have stood and realized, "you don't really want this do you?" But Emma had hastily covered it over, laughed right along too when he told his friends how surprised she'd been, as if her heart hadn't continued to beat out against the wrong she was doing to it. In the days that followed, the change in Quinn, the reassurance she felt at having just been asked, it all combined to dampen and mute the clanging in her chest.

Looking now at the man beside her, his own face turned away, eyes fixed on a point she could not see, an awakening rolled up through Emma, bursting open behind her eyes: it was Mark who was the beacon upon the sunny hilltop, out of the valley of fog, the point her heart's map had been directing her toward all along and which she, stubbornly at the wheel, circled again and again, finding all sorts of excuses for avoiding the turn up the untraveled path toward him.

Mark looked at her, then turned, staring off upstream. "It doesn't matter. My goodbye is because I'm not going back with you. I'm not the same man I was before. Something has shifted inside me. Turned off." He placed his hands on the railing and leaned over. "And it's not your fault, either. It started before we came. Wanda was just another symptom of it."

Emma reached for his hands, tried to ease them off the wrought iron.

He shook his head, fingers curling even more tightly away from her. "I don't know, but I have this feeling that maybe if I stay here, something about the simplicity of this place, the decency of it. . ." He shrugged. "Maybe I can turn it back on."

She grabbed his arm and spun him to face her. "After all this time, now you're saying this? Now that I want to go back, you want to stay?" It was all too ridiculous! In the flash of realization that Mark was her "it," she had also realized that she had to return. Had to give Quinn her answer, had to take all the notes she'd compiled and make something of them. If not for herself, then for Jane, for the many inspirations and gifts Jane had given her. And not least to make sure Jane Austen was still Jane Austen.

"I'll shelter you as best I can, tell you when to jump. But I have a chance at happiness here. Now that I haven't written myself out of history. Maybe find a little bookstore of my own. Be a little Cratchety clerk somewhere. And there's nobody back then to miss me."

The cathedral bells began to ring the noon cadence.

"Mark, you can't do this. What if I can't get back without you? What if we're a . . . a package deal?"

"Your package deal waits for you back home." He began scanning up and down the bridge, looking for the best opening for her to leap. "Something tells me things are ready now. What is it they say in baptism – wash and be free?"

The bells continued to chime and an insanity seemed to be taking her over little by little. By God, she needed it to stop, all of it. Go back without him? Impossible! It was too much to contemplate, and with each clang of the bell, time slipped away from her. From them.

Jane waved from the other side of Great Pulteney Street. "Miss Woods!" she called, "Miss Woods, we really must. . ." But her voice was lost to the cacophony of the bridge at noon, to the passing traffic of so many chaises, phaetons, and carriages.

"Now, Emma," Mark said. "Go! You must do it now!"

"I can't, I can't!" Emma stepped away from the railing, away from Mark. She tried to call for Jane, to ask her to wait. The resolution had come in an instant: if Mark was staying, so was she. And if it took years, if it required every degradation of poverty, even the loss of Jane's friendship as she sank into penury, she would win him back. A split second of pause broke into her thoughts. What about Jane? She had perhaps already ruined Austen for the rest of humanity with her compulsive quoting. How else might she alter things if she remained? But it did not matter. There was only Mark's sad face staring into the froth.

She raised both hands over head, arms waving toward her friend, a weak attempt to call all the things she was losing back to her. "Miss Austen, I'm coming!" But Emma was not loud enough. She watched as Cassandra began to pull Jane away, saying something that drew a confused and hurt expression across Jane's face.

Emma staggered forward just as a barouche driven far too fast for the crowds drew abreast.

"Emma!" came the screams of Jane, Cassandra, and Mark.

Emma leapt back just as Mark took hold of her arm to yank her, and the compounded momentum sent her right over the embankment railing and into the swirling brown water below.

Once more, time expanded around Emma. The blue of the sky stretched out into an infinity that warped and flexed, then folded over her, a soft blanket of suffocating nothingness. All she could perceive was that this moment of falling would follow her the rest of her life. That through the years with Quinn, perhaps even as mother to his children, into their old age, and after he'd died, long past the hope of any second attachment, she would eternally feel herself tumbling into an abyss, would find no sanctuary, but only this endless free fall into a space that had been carved out for someone else, someone who would live out his own life hundreds of years divided from her own.

And then a hand reached through and found hers, fingers interlocking with her own, and they hit the water.

CHAPTER 31

Something took Emma by the arm and dragged her from the water. She lay on her back, clenched her eyelids, and just breathed. Opening her eyes, a black line divided the blue sky and swayed in the breeze. Then a pigeon landed upon it, then a second, then more until the wire dipped under their weight. She blinked, shook her head, and pushed up on her elbows.

"Oi!" a man's voice boomed. "Shove off. Give her room." The birds took to the sky, their wings pulsating the air, and a feather drifted down to land near Emma's outstretched fingers. Harold's face loomed into Emma's vision. "Em, love, thank God."

Emma heaved to her feet, wobbling like she'd just come off a week-long bender.

"Mr. Landen!" she yelled, "Mr. Lan . . . Mark!"

"Find this lady a Mark," someone in the crowd called out.

Lorna and Deb pushed through, followed by Wanda, picking her way across the green in the same stilettos she'd been wearing the night before.

"Don't be a bloody idiot," Wanda returned. "Call an ambulance, you tosspots."

Emma spun back toward the river and thwack! – bumped right into Mark, knocking them both back into the muck.

Mark lifted a hand and flung a glob of river slime from his fingers. It soared up and landed right in Wanda's cleavage. She gave a little squeal and dashed away as best she could in high heels on a grassy slope, followed by Lorna trying to give her a handkerchief.

Harold offered Mark and Emma a hand and pulled them to their feet. "You idiots. Gave us all a scare. This is not a bloody swimming festival."

Emma coughed and spat on the ground. "I am well aware, sir. It shall be quite a relief never to jump into that river again," she started.

Debra put a hand to Emma's forehead.

Harold's face darkened. "'*Well aware*'? And since when am I 'sir'?"

Emma held out a muddy hand. "Might I have the borrowing of your cell phone?"

Harold and Deb shared a look, then Harold dug his phone out from an inside pocket of his waistcoat and passed it over. Emma opened his library and found what she was seeking – The Collected Works of Jane Austen. Thumbs frantically sliding over the screen, Harold's face descending into doom as he watched his phone become a muddy mess, Emma's grin grew.

"Mark, it's all still there. All of Jane. Nothing's changed."

"Changed?" Harold took his phone back, holding it like a dead fish between forefinger and thumb, dropping it into a handkerchief. "Em, let's get you to an urgent care."

Off to the side, Mark was brushing off his own pants. Emma tried to get him to look at her, but he refused. Was he angry she had brought him back with her? He couldn't have been serious about staying. Could he? Her heart pounded itself to a pulp, about to ooze out of her ears, and yet there was all this clamor of horns, the ringing of cell phones, sirens blaring in the distance, and the voices of her friends, welcoming her back to a world they had not realized she'd left.

Mark took off toward the street.

"Hey, stop!" a voice called. "You stole my flowers!" The café owner from the bridge shop approached, followed by two Bath policemen. "It was these two, officers. He took a bouquet of my glass flowers. And she . . . she just smacked 'em into the river. Not five minutes ago." She pointed back at the open window over the river, a halo of faces watching them from the inside.

Mark patted his pockets, as did Harold. They held their palms up. "Sorry," Harold said, "if you'll give us your address, we'll run a couple quid over this evening."

"A couple quid? Those were hand-blown glass flowers. We're talking eighty pounds, plus tax."

One of the officers stepped forward and began to pull Mark's hands behind his back. Harold, Deb and Emma all protested.

Emma placed a hand on the nearest officer's arm. "I beg you would not importune us in this way. Mr. Landen has as unobjectionable a character as you will ever meet. 'Tis a misunderstanding only."

Harold leaned toward Deb. "Did she just use 'unobjectionable' in a sentence?"

Deb's face drew down, furrowed and confused. "And since when did Mark become Mr. Landen?"

Emma looked from the officers to her friends, unsure who needed the first round of explanations.

"Look folks," the officer said. "Theft of goods under a hundred pounds is minor, but compounded with your attempted escape out the window, and we're going to let the barristers decide about prosecution. You can gather him at the courthouse tomorrow. Wear something that *doesn't* make you look delusional and the judge may be lenient."

They began leading Mark away, and he followed as meekly as a lamb. Emma thought she saw perverse pleasure pass over his face. Perhaps he even relished the thought of a night in the clink. And, she had to admit, perhaps he savored the idea of getting to a place Emma couldn't reach.

But he wasn't getting away from her, not this easily. If she wouldn't let him live on the other side of time, she certainly wasn't going to let him sleep on the other side of steel bars. She untied the ring from her pocket and tossed it at the vendor. "Here. Our debt is settled."

The owner looked at the garish diamond in her palm and was about to return it. "Miss, I can't take your engagement ring. It's too much."

And in the moment of passing the ring from her hand to the vendor's, something loosed its hold on her. It dripped from her shoulders like a trickle of mud, a slick release and sudden weightlessness. A breeze blew a tress of dirty hair across her face and sent a chill down her spine. She shuddered and cursed, laughing as the expletives fell awkwardly from her mouth, and yet what a relief to be back home where she could say and do anything she wanted.

"No, seriously. I don't need that anymore. I don't want it." With a second thought, she reached over and slid the ribbon through the band and tucked it back in her gown pocket. She took Mark's elbow and held onto it while the officer released the cuffs. "I take full custody of this clergyman."

The officers looked from Mark, Emma, and Harold to the vendor. The vendor tucked the ring down into her pocket and waved the officers off. "No theft here." She turned toward the path up to the bridge, whistling a tune that reminded Emma partly of a song she had danced to in the Lower Rooms and partly of a pop ballad she'd heard on the drive in from Radstock.

Harold flagged down a cab. "We'd better get you changed for your lecture." He looked her up and down. "Hey, that's not the same dress you were wearing earlier . . ." But before he got further, Emma pulled Mark's arm away from the waiting taxi.

She dropped to her knees. Lorna and Harold shared the same expletive and Deb sighed a willowy, "finally."

"Marry me."

Mark looked down at her, somber and dazed. "What? Emma, I – ."

"I mean it. Marry me. Right now. You have registry offices here, right? City halls? Let's go."

Mark shook his head. "This isn't the way . . ."

"Mark Landen," she said, still on her knees. "In the past twenty-four hours, I've been engaged to one man – ."

"Still are," he interrupted.

"Shush. Engaged to one man and proposed to by two others. I finally pulled my head out of my ass, so don't go sticking your's up your own. You're going to marry me, and that's it."

A smile nearly broke through, but clouds descended over his features once more, his face darkened by shadows and doubt. If only he could let the light of her love shine on him, could come to her as radiantly as he had that first day when he took her hand on the street and drew her body to his.

"Fine." She jumped in the cab, pulling Mark behind her. Through the open window, she waved Harold closer. "Go back to my room and get my ballgown. I'll meet you at the theatre in an hour." To the cabbie, "to Radstock."

The cabbie groaned. "Not 'less you promise the return fare, miss."

Emma waved her hand. "Fine, fine," she said, knowing she had nothing to pay him with but what she could get from the generosity of friends, but if this week had taught her anything, it was that true friends could be relied on.

The car stopped before the inn, the patio overflowing with Harold's harem of rugby players getting drunk at noon. To a one, they turned and watched the be-gowned woman pull the skinny-breeched man to the streamside.

"Here," she said. "Do you remember this place? Every year we've come here. We walk this path."

She pointed out the bench. "That's where you told me about your dad. You said maybe disappearing was the most fatherly thing he could have done for you." She pulled him farther along. "That's where I told you about mine. How he wore his regret like a shroud. How I knew he wanted out. How neither of them . . ."

"Had the courage," Mark finished.

They reached the stone arch. "This is where you told me about your mother. About the nights with her in the hospital. How at the end, you started to pray, never really sure which outcome you were praying for most." She put her hands on his cheeks and forced him to look at her. "Do you remember what else you said?"

He nodded. "Things I'd never told Nora. Never felt safe enough to."

She nodded in return. "And I told you about high school. About Martha Hardwicke. I never told anyone what happened in that bathroom."

He pulled her hands off his face. "So what, Emma. You think all this can make up for everything else?"

Emma looked down and shook her head. "No, but I told you things I've never told Quinn. And you told me things you never told Nora. Why did we do that, Mark?"

He shrugged. "Because in a few days' time we'd go back to our regular lives and nothing we'd said would matter?"

"No, damnit. We said them because all of it mattered. Because this, right here!" She stamped her foot. "This was the regular lives we wanted. We just didn't know how. We weren't," she paused and swallowed, took a deep breath. "*I* wasn't brave enough to figure out how."

"But Emma." Mark drew his hand down his face, fingers gripping his chin. "Don't you think too much has happened? Maybe we've seen too much. Of each another."

But before he could speak another word, Emma grabbed his face and drew it to her own. He resisted, but she held him fast. That flash of electricity bloomed across her hips, the spark that always existed between them from the first moment she'd seen him scrambling across the churchyard in Nora's wake, when they shared a look, and he'd smiled and waggled his eyebrows, and she'd laughed to herself and watched them pass.

And then he yielded. His arms folded round her, pulled her to him, and she knew she had come home.

Back in Bath, Emma and Mark ran, hands clasped toward the Theatre Royale. They met Harold in the foyer, who quickly ushered them both to the long hallway backstage, where a beaming Debra and Lorna waited. Debra held a little bouquet of crisp white flowers and Lorna flapped a veil at her.

"Just in case," they cried.

Emma and Mark laughed. They hastened to the bathrooms to change. In the hotel lobby, a woman in a chic suit strode back and forth, tapping a rolled-up paper against her arm, which Emma recognized as the Times edition with her article in it. The woman turned at the sound of their group on the stairs.

Mark stopped short. "Dean Haverforth." He straightened his coat and held out a hand.

"Ahh, Professor Landen." She shook his hand once and let it drop. "Finally." Turning to Emma, she smiled and extended The Times. "And you must be Ms. Woods. How glad I am to meet you. Have you told her?"

"No, I," Mark faltered. "I'm afraid the last week's been rather . . ."

"Hectic," Emma finished.

"A week? You were at the department meeting two days ago. No matter. Well, Ms. Woods, the English Department would be greatly honored to have you as our writer-in-residence and Austen lecturer for the next academic year."

Emma's knees nearly went out from under her and she found the hands of all her friends – her family – there to hold her up.

"Writer-in-residence?" Debra repeated.

"Austen lecturer?" Lorna said breathily, not so very unlike Lydia Bennet's swoons over a whole camp full of soldiers.

"I don't . . . that is, I'll have to . . ." Emma began, but Harold rapped her knuckles with his festival program.

"She accepts."

"Marvelous," Dean Haverforth said, pulling open the door to the auditorium. "I'll see you both inside for what I'm sure," – she tapped the newspaper to Mark's chest, – "will be an inspiring discussion."

The door closed, Emma turned to her friends. They gripped hands and danced in a circle, letting out as much of a scream as they dared with a cranky, delayed audience on the other side of the wall.

Deb was first to pull it together. She took a deep breath and put her hands on Emma's shoulders. "Ok, now focus."

The door opened and a festival concierge emerged. "Finally," he said, and spoke into a headset attached to his crackling radio. "Yeah, we got her. Theatre Royale's a go."

Emma entered the hall to find a roomful of attendees observing her. She walked up the aisle, offering apologies to both sides, until she reached the stage and the podium. "Very sorry, folks. Lost track of time. Now, before I begin, is anyone here a clergyman?"

Around the room, a dozen men rose, all garbed in the traditional attire of black short breeches, black coat, and round hat. Emma laughed. "No, I mean, a real one."

All but one of the costumed clergymen sat, the gentleman who had fallen asleep on Emma's shoulder during the morning session – a few hours for him, and what felt like a whole lifetime to Emma.

"Great," Emma said. "You, up here." As he trundled forward and the room broke into confused, excited titters, Lorna tried to fit Emma's veil.

"Good heavens," she said, digging pins from Emma's hair to secure the veil. "Wherever did you get these old things? I've never seen bobby pins like this before!"

"I'm 100% authentic today," Emma said.

The clergyman had taken the stage and introduced himself as Charles Edge. "I'm afraid I don't have the necessary things," he said, patting his pockets. "A prayerbook at least."

"I can help." Mark pulled a small volume from the inside of his coat jacket.

Charles opened it, his face cringing at the mud-stained, wet, and floppy pages. "Hold on. Is this genuine?"

Mark shrugged. "I guess so."

Charles leaned forward. "Let's talk after this lecture. I know some museum curators who'd want to see this." His eyes widened and he looked back at the waiting crowd, leaning in to whisper. "A wedding in a hurry, eh? Smock wedding, is it?" He winked. "Just a joke. A joke."

He turned to the crowd and waved his hands to silence them. "Dearly beloved, we are gathered together here in the sight of God, and in the face of this congregation, to join together this Man and this Woman in holy Matrimony; which is an honourable estate, instituted of God in the time of man's innocency ..."

Emma offered her hand and Mark took it. Their fingers interlaced, and as their palms met, a bit of river mud squelched between their fingers, drying as the clergyman spoke the words that bound them together now, forever, always. The ceremony over, they looked at the dried grains of mud and sand on their palms. No words needed to pass between them. With one mind and one heart, they raised their hands and blew the dust out over the crowd.

IMAGE CREDITS

ABOUT THE AUTHOR

Amy Foster Myer earned her MFA from Queens University of Charlotte. She currently lives in Swarthmore, PA with her wife, daughters Jane and Evalyn, a geriatric dog and cat, and three rescued guinea pigs. She is a life-time member of the Jane Austen Society of North America. She has published short fiction widely. Her collection of flash fiction titled Where we are going to next is available at Finishing Line Press. More about Amy can be found at amyfostermyer.com. Additional Austen antics from Amy's life can be found at Alifeinausten.com.

ACKNOWLEDGEMENTS

There are so many people to thank in the development and creation of this book that to try to put them in any kind of order would be an exercise in insanity. Chronological credit is tidiest, and therefore, the first acknowledgement must go to Jane Austen. Next would be my High School Honors English teacher, Dorie Maxwell, for introducing me to one of the loves of my life. Some twenty-odd years later, the Literary Arts organization in Portland, Oregon, particularly Emily Chenoweth for the workshop which created the structure and support to draft this novel in nine weeks. Next, to Amber Keller, Chad Lykins, Evan Morgan Williams, Quinn Read and Stephanie Argy, (aka The Keanu Reeves Debate Society), for their ongoing support and readership of this novel in its many forms and iterations over the many years since we met in that workshop. Next to Elaine Schumacher for her lovely design of the cover and interior of this book. Then, to you, dear reader, who must love Jane and her era as much as I do. And last, but certainly never the least, to my wife Sarah who has not only supported every endeavor I have undertaken (and talked me out of the spectacularly mad ones), but who has endured endless hours of Austen adaptations, documentaries, podcasts, and random trivia thrown at her at all hours of the day and night. You, Sarah, have given me the life I wish Jane could have had – endless love and happiness with a partner, children, and abundant support for our writing. Which leads, of course, to my two daughters, Jane and Evalyn, the brightest beings in my orbit.

Before I go, I must offer a final note to Jane Austen, who may, through some space-time continuum/multiverse/time-travel phenomenon be capable of hearing me: Thank You. Over and over again, thank you.

9 798989 361809